AND OTHER EARLY HORRORS FROM THE MUNSEY PULPS

THE PEOPLE OF THE PIT

AND OTHER EARLY HORRORS FROM THE MUNSEY PULPS

Edited and with an introduction by Gene Christie

With a foreword by Robert Weinberg

2010
Normal, IL

PUBLICATION HISTORY AND COPYRIGHT

"The People of the Pit" Copyright 1917 The Frank A. Munsey Company, from ALL-STORY WEEKLY, January 5, 1918.

"Behind the Curtain" Copyright 1918 The Frank A. Munsey Company, from ALL-STORY WEEKLY, September 21, 1918.

"Number Thirteen" Copyright 1913 The Frank A. Munsey Company, from THE ALL-STORY, November 1913, under the title "A Man Without a Soul."

"The Orchid Horror" Copyright 1911 The Frank A. Munsey Company, from THE ARGOSY, September 1911.

"The Tenth Question" Copyright 1915 The Frank A. Munsey Company, from ALL-STORY WEEKLY, December 18, 1915.

"Disappointment" Copyright 1917 The Frank A. Munsey Company, from ALL-STORY WEEKLY, May 19, 1917.

"The Pretty Woman" Copyright 1917 The Frank A. Munsey Company, from ALL-STORY WEEKLY, March 24, 1917.

"The Living Portrait" Copyright 1919 The Frank A. Munsey Company, from ALL-STORY WEEKLY, April 5, 1919.

"An Offer of Two to One" Copyright 1911 The Frank A. Munsey Company, from THE SCRAP BOOK, November 1911.

"Beyond the Violet" Copyright 1920 The Frank A. Munsey Company, from ARGOSY WEEKLY, November 27, 1920.

"The Elixir of Life" Copyright 1903 The Frank A. Munsey Company, from THE ARGOSY, December 1903.

"The Mystery of the Shriveled Hand" Copyright 1922 The Frank A. Munsey Company, from MUNSEY'S MAGAZINE, February 1922.

"Fear" Copyright 1908 The Frank A. Munsey Company, from THE ALL-STORY, November 1908.

"Monsieur de Guise" Copyright 1911 The Frank A. Munsey Company, from THE SCRAP BOOK, January 1911.

"The Ship of Silent Men" Copyright 1922 The Frank A. Munsey Company, from ALL-STORY WEEKLY, January 3, 1920.

ISBN 13 978-1-928619-96-3
Foreword © 2010 Robert Weinberg
Introduction © 2010 Gene Christie

Cover art by Harry T. Fisk.

Project acquisition, editing and proofreading: Gene Christie.
Book layout and design: Tom Roberts.

Black Dog Books, 1115 Pine Meadows Ct., Normal, IL 61761-5432.
www.blackdogbooks.com / info@blackdogbooks.com

CONTENTS

FOREWORD

Reading through this fine collection of horror and dark fantasy stories from the early days of the Munsey pulps, I'm struck by two things. These stories are quite different than their modern counterparts in a pair of very distinct ways. Whether these traits make the stories better or worse than what's being published today is entirely a matter of opinion. As a lifelong fan and devotee of the pulp magazines, I think my preference is fairly easy to guess. Is yours? Read further before deciding.

The first difference between the tales in this volume and modern horror stories is a matter of taste. I mean exactly what those words imply. The horror stories of the pulps were told with a modicum of good taste. While there often was violence in the adventure, blood and gore was kept to a minimum. Long, detailed descriptions of the wounds suffered by the hero, the heroine, or the villain rarely, if ever, appeared. The pages of the story weren't soaked in blood.

Contrast that with today's horror fiction. There's a trend called "splatterpunk" that's still quite popular. The name pretty much defines the type of story it embraces. Splatterpunk fiction is horror taken to its extreme; with blood and guts and brains and gore splattered everywhere in sight. Plots are kept simple, so as not to crowd out the grisly details of every murder, every mutilation and every torture possible. Splatterpunk loves taboos. It loves trampling on them. Old horror told stories with a nod to good taste. Splatterpunk murders good taste.

The second difference between old horror and modern horror requires intelligence. Most likely you can guess where I am going with this notion. The pulp horror stories require that the reader possesses some smatterings of intelligence. The tale assumes that you can follow a plot and don't need to be force fed every clue or every twist and turn of the story. Take, for example, "The Tenth Question" by George Allan England, in this book. When the hero asks the final question in the story, there's not five pages of explanation on how he came to his conclusion. The reader is expected to be able to follow the man's reasoning and understand how he knew what to ask. Imagine that being the case today. Can you imagine that happening? Can you? Read the story and then answer the question.

Somehow, the notion of an intelligent readership has fallen by the wayside. Books and short stories are written for the lowest common denominator, which means they have very little intelligence at all. While our best and our brightest are just that, our average is terribly low. And it shows.

Take a look at horror films, a genre that grew up with the pulp magazines. Remember when a horror movie meant you would actually be scared when leaving the theater, not merely disgusted. There were pulp pleasures, to be sure. No one took Bela Lugosi's *Dracula* very seriously or felt sorry for Lon Chaney, Jr.'s *Wolf Man*. But Karloff in *The Devil Commands* was creepy and Deborah Kerr in *The Innocents* turned my hair white. Neither with a drop of blood being shed.

Compare those films with the joys of today's market. Horror has become the cinema of blood and gore, mass murder, and cannibalism. Flesh-eating zombies have become the favorite villains, with vampires a close second. The dead hate the living and seemingly need to bathe in warm human blood to feel alive. It's a sickening credo, lacking both intelligence and good taste. But, somehow it sells. Such movies are a sad commentary on today's movie-going public.

Taste and intelligence. The pulps had them both. Which are two of the reasons I love them so.

Robert Weinberg
Oak Forest, Illinois

In a career spanning more than forty years, Robert Weinberg has worked as a freelance newspaper journalist, college instructor, and freelance writer, contributed hundreds of articles for books and magazines on topics ranging from mathematics to collecting art. Along the way he has written sixteen novels, sixteen non-fiction books, and edited over a hundred anthologies. His work has been published in hardcover and softcover all over the world.

An authority on genre fiction, Bob Weinberg has edited over a hundred and fifty books in the science fiction, fantasy, horror, mystery, young adult, and western fields. He has written columns on all these branches of fiction and is a well-known lecturer at conventions and seminars. He has acted as consultant on genre fiction for a number of paperback publishers and is widely regarded as one of the leading experts on horror and dark fantasy fiction in the world.

Bob is a two-time recipient of the World Fantasy Award. In 2007, Bob won the Lifetime Achievement Award from the Horror Writers Association.

You may learn more about Bob at www.robertweinberg.net. He can be contacted at robert@robertweinberg.net.

INTRODUCTION

"In general . . . the Munsey publications did more to publish weird
fiction than any other magazine enterprise of the early 20th century."

H.P. Lovecraft to Richard F. Seawright, March 31, 1932

With his creation of the first "pulp magazine" in 1896, Frank A. Munsey ushered
in a new era of modestly-priced reading material well within the reach of the
average wage-earning American.

Within the hundreds of millions of copies of Munsey magazines produced
over the ensuing decades, authors who would become some of the biggest names
in American popular literature tried their fledgling writing wings in thousands
of adventures, romances, westerns, mysteries, fantasies, even early science fiction
stories—and tales of horror: Edgar Rice Burroughs, Talbot Mundy, Sinclair
Lewis, Erle Stanley Gardner, Mary Roberts Rinehart, Sax Rohmer, Raymond
Chandler, Edna Ferber, Theodore Dreiser, Max Brand, Robert E. Howard,
Damon Runyon, Cornell Woolrich, Dashiell Hammett, Albert Payson Terhune
and literally hundreds more.

Not only horror in the tradition of Edgar Allan Poe, Robert Louis Stevenson
and Ambrose Bierce, but horror of the mysterious East, the everyday-gone-
wrong, fantastic inventions and discoveries, and unexplained phenomena
graced the pages of *The Argosy, All Story, The Cavalier, Munsey's Magazine* and
The Scrap Book under Frank Munsey and his successors.

Although he never appeared outside the letters to the editor columns,
Howard Phillips Lovecraft was a voracious consumer of Munsey pulps, boasting
in 1911 that he had been a "Reader since 1905" of *The Argosy,* and volunteering
the quote that heads this piece decades afterward in private correspondence.

The Munsey magazines showcased many excellent fantasy and horror tales
far too long to be included here, but these fifteen stories—many never reprinted
since their initial magazine publication a century and more ago—will reward
both the longtime connoisseur of horror fiction and the casual reader who may
be largely unfamiliar with these authors and their works.

Gene Christie
Springfield, Virginia

THE PEOPLE OF THE PIT

A. MERRITT

North of us a shaft of light shot halfway to the zenith. It came from behind the ragged mountain toward which we had been pushing all day. The beam drove up through a column of blue haze whose edges were marked as sharply as the rain that streams from the edges of a thundercloud. It was like the flash of a searchlight through an azure mist and it cast no shadows.

As it struck upward, the five summits were outlined hard and black, and we saw that the whole mountain was shaped like a hand. As the light silhouetted it, the gigantic fingers of the peaks seemed to stretch the bulk that was the plain of the hand to push. It was exactly as though it moved to thrust something back. The shining beam held steady for a moment, then broke into myriads of tiny luminous globes that swung to and fro and dropped gently. They seemed to be searching.

The forest had become very still. Every wood noise held its breath. I felt the dogs pressing against my legs. They, too, were silent; but every muscle in their bodies trembled, their hair was stiff along their backs, and their eyes, fixed on the falling phosphorescent sparks, were filmed with the terror-glaze.

I looked at Starr Anderson. He was staring at the North, where once more, the beam had pulsed upward.

"'The mountain shaped like a hand!'" I spoke without moving my lips. My mouth was as dry as though Lao T'zai had poured his fear-dust down my throat.

"It's the mountain we've been looking for," he answered in the same tone.

"But that light—what is it? Not the aurora, surely," I said.

"Whoever heard of an aurora at this time of the year?"

He voiced the thought that was in my own mind.

"It makes me think something is being hunted up there," he said. "That the lights are seeking—an unholy sort of hunt—it's well for us to be out of range."

"The mountain seems to move each time the shaft shoots up," I said. "What's it keeping back, Starr? It makes me think of the frozen hand of cloud that Shan Nadour set before the Gate of Ghouls to keep them in the lairs that Eblis cut for them."

He raised a hand, listening.

From the north and high overhead there came a whispering. It was not the rustling of the aurora, that rushing, crackling sound like the ghosts of winds that blew at Creation racing through the skeleton leaves of ancient trees that sheltered Lilith. This whispering held in it a demand. It was eager. It called us to come up where the beam was flashing. It—drew!

There was in it a note of inexorable insistence. It touched my heart with a thousand tiny fear-tipped fingers and it filled me with a vast longing to race on and merge myself in the light. It must have been so that Ulysses felt when he strained at the mast and strove to obey the crystal sweet singing of the sirens.

The whispering grew louder.

"What the hell's the matter with those dogs?" cried Starr Anderson savagely. "Look at them!"

The malamutes, whining, were racing away toward the light. We saw them disappear among the trees. There came back to us a mournful howling. Then that too died away and left nothing but the insistent murmuring overhead.

The glade we had camped in looked straight to the north. We had reached, I suppose, three hundred miles above the first great bend of the Kuskokwim toward the Yukon. Certainly we were in an untrodden part of the wilderness. We had pushed through from Dawson at the breaking of the spring, on a fair lead to a lost mountain between the five peaks of which, so the Athabascan medicine man had told us, the gold streams out like putty from a clinched fist.

Not an Indian were we able to hire to go with us. The land of the Hand Mountain was accursed, they said.

We had sighted a mountain the night before, its ragged top faintly outlined against a pulsing glow. And now by the light that had led us, we saw that it was the very place we had sought.

Anderson stiffened. Through the whispering had broken a curious *pad-pad* and a rustling. It sounded as though a small bear were moving toward us.

I threw a pile of wood on the fire, and as it blazed up, saw something break through the bushes. It walked on all fours, but it did not walk like a bear. All at once it flashed upon me—it was like a baby crawling upstairs. The forepaws lifted themselves in grotesquely infantile fashion. It was grotesque, but it was—terrible. It drew closer. We reached for our guns—and dropped them. Suddenly, we knew that this crawling thing was a man!

It *was* a man. Still with that high climbing *pad-pad,* he swayed to the fire. He stopped.

"Safe," whispered the crawling man in a voice that was an echo of the whispering overhead. "Quite safe here. They can't get out of the blue, you know. They can't get you—unless you answer them—"

"He's mad," said Anderson, and then gently to this broken thing that had been a man: "You're all right—there's nothing after you."

"Don't answer them," repeated the crawling man. "The lights, I mean."

"The lights," I cried, startled even out of pity. "What are they?"

"The people of the pit!" he murmured.

He fell upon his side. We ran to him. Anderson knelt.

"God's love!" he said. "Frank, look at this!"

He pointed to the hands. The wrists were covered with torn rags of a heavy shirt. The hands themselves were—stumps! The fingers had been bent into the palms and the flesh had been worn to the bone. They looked like the feet of a little black elephant! My eyes traveled down the body. Around the waist was a heavy band of yellow metal. From it fell a ring and a dozen links of shining white chain!

"What is he? Where did he come from?" said Anderson. "Look, he's fast asleep—yet even in his sleep his arms try to climb and his feet draw themselves up one after the other! And his knees—how in God's name was he ever able to move on them?"

It was even as he said. In the deep sleep that had come upon the crawler, arms and legs kept raising in a deliberate, dreadful climbing motion. It was as though they had a life of their own—they kept their movement independently of the motionless body. They were semaphoric motions. If you have ever stood at the back of a train and watched the semaphores rise and fall, you will know exactly what I mean.

Abruptly, the overhead whispering ceased. The shaft of light dropped and did not rise again. The crawling man became still. A gentle glow began to grow around us. The short Alaskan summer night was over. Anderson rubbed his eyes and turned me a haggard face.

"Man!" he exclaimed. "You look as though you have been sick!"

"No more than you, Starr," I said. "That was sheer, stark horror! What do you make of it all?"

"I'm thinking our only answer lies there," he answered, pointing to the figure that lay so motionless under the blankets we had thrown over him. "Whatever they were—that's what they were after. There was no aurora about those lights, Frank. It was like the flaring up of some queer hell the preacher folk never frightened us with."

"We'll go no further today," I said. "I wouldn't wake him for all the gold that runs between the fingers of the five peaks—nor for all the devils that may lie behind them."

The crawling man lay in a sleep as deep as the Styx. We bathed and bandaged the pads that had been his hands. Arms and legs were as rigid as though they were crutches. He did not move while we worked over him. He lay as he had fallen, the arms a trifle raised, the knees bent.

I began filing the band that ringed the sleeper's waist. It was gold, but it was like no gold I had ever handled. Pure gold is soft. This was soft too—but it had an unclean, viscid life of its own.

It clung to the file and I could have sworn that it writhed like a live thing when I cut into it. I gashed through it, bent it away from the body and hurled it away. It was—loathsome!

All that day the crawler slept. Darkness came and still he slept. But that night there was no shaft of blue haze from behind the peaks, no questing globes of light, no whispering. Some spell of horror seemed withdrawn—but not far. Both Anderson and I felt that the menace was there, withdrawn perhaps, but waiting.

It was noon the next day when the crawling man awoke. I jumped as the pleasant drawling voice sounded.

"How long have I slept?" he said. His pale blue eyes grew quizzical as I stared at him.

"A night—and almost two days," I said.

"Were there any lights up there last night?" He nodded to the north eagerly. "Any whispering?"

"Neither," I answered. His head fell back and he stared up at the sky.

"They've given it up, then," he said at last.

"Who have given it up?" asked Anderson.

And once more—"The people of the pit!" the crawling man answered.

We stared at him and again faintly I, for one, felt that queer, maddening desire that the lights had brought with them.

"The people of the pit," he repeated. "Things some god of evil made before the Flood and that somehow have escaped the good God's vengeance. They were calling me!" he added simply.

Anderson and I looked at each other, the same thought in both our minds.

"No," said the crawling man, reading what it was, "I'm not insane. Give me a very little to drink. I'm going to die soon. Will you take me as far south as you can before I die? And afterwards will you build a big fire and burn me? I want to be in such shape that no hellish wile of theirs can drag my body back to them. You'll do it when I've told you about them," he said as we hesitated.

He drank the brandy and water we lifted to his lips.

"Arms and legs quite dead," he said. "Dead as I'll be soon. Well, they did well for me. Now I'll tell you what's up there behind that hand. Hell!"

"Listen. My name is Stanton—Sinclair Stanton. Class 1900, Yale. Explorer. I started away from Dawson last year to hunt for five peaks that rose like a hand in a haunted country and ran pure gold between them. Same thing you were after? I thought so. Late last fall my comrade sickened. I sent him back with some Indians. A little later, my Indians found out what I was after. They ran away from me. I decided I'd stick, built a cabin, stocked myself with food and lay down to winter it. Did it not badly—it was a pretty mild winter, you'll remember. In the spring I started off again. A little less than two weeks ago, I sighted the five peaks. Not from this side, though—the other. Give me some more brandy.

"I'd made too wide a detour," he went on. "I'd gotten too far north. I beat back. From this side you see nothing but forest straight up to the base of the hand. Over on the other side—"

He was silent for a moment.

"Over there is forest too. But it doesn't reach so far. No! I came out of it. Stretching for miles in front of me was a level plain. It was as worn and ancient looking as the desert around the broken shell of Babylon. At its end rose the peaks. Between me and them—far off—was what looked like a low dike of rocks. Then—I ran across the road!"

"The road!" cried Anderson incredulously.

"The road," said the crawling man. "A fine, smooth, stone road. It ran straight on to the mountain. Oh, it was a road all right—and worn as though millions and millions of feet had passed over it for thousands of years. On each side of it were sand and heaps of stones. After a while I began to notice these stones. They were cut, and the shape of the heaps somehow gave me the idea that a hundred thousand years ago they might have been the ruins of houses. They were as old looking as that. I sensed man about them and at the same time they smelled of immemorial antiquity.

"The peaks grew closer. The heaps of ruins thicker. Something inexpressibly desolate hovered over them, something sinister; something reached from them that struck my heart like the touch of ghosts so old that they could be only the ghosts of ghosts. I went on.

"And now I saw that what I had thought to be the low rock range at the base of the peaks was a thicker litter of ruins. The Hand Mountain was really much farther off. The road itself passed through these ruins and between two high rocks that raised themselves like a gateway."

The crawling man paused. His hands began that sickening *pad-pad* again. Little drops of bloody sweat showed on his forehead. But after a moment or two, he grew quiet. He smiled.

"They were a gateway," he said. "I reached them. I went between them. I sprawled flat, clutching the earth in awe and terror. For I was on a broad stone platform. Before me was—sheer space! Imagine the Grand Canon three times as wide, roughly circular and with the bottom dropped out. That would be something like what I was looking into.

"It was like peeping over the edge of a cleft world down into the infinity where the planets roll. On the far side stood the five peaks. They looked like a gigantic warning hand stretched up to the sky. The lips of the abyss curved away on each side of me.

"I could see down perhaps a thousand feet. Then a thick blue haze shut out the eye. It was like the blue you see gather on the high hills at dusk. But the pit—it was awesome! Awesome as the Maori's Gulf of Ranalak, that sinks between the living and the dead and that only the freshly released soul has strength to leap—but never strength again to leap back.

"I crept back from the verge and stood up, weak, shaking. My hand rested against one of the rocks of the gateway. There was carving upon it. There in sharp outlines, was the heroic figure of a man. His back was turned. His arms were stretched above his head and between them he carried something that looked like a sun disk with radiating lines of light. There were symbols on the disk that reminded me of Chinese. But they were not Chinese. No! They had been made by hands that were dust ages before the Chinese stirred in the womb of time.

"I looked at the opposite rock. It bore an exactly similar figure. There was an odd, peaked head-dress on both. The rocks themselves were triangular and the carvings were on the side closest the pit. The gesture of the men seemed to be that of holding something back—of barring. I looked closer. Behind the outstretched hands and the disks, I seemed to see a host of vague shapes and, plainly, a multitude of globes.

"I traced them out vaguely. Suddenly I felt unaccountably sick. There had come to me an impression—I can't call it sight—an impression of enormous, upright slugs. Their swollen bodies seemed to dissolve, then swim into sight, then dissolve again—all except the globes which were their heads, and that remained clear. They were—unutterably loathsome. Overcome by an inexplicable and overpowering nausea, I stretched myself upon the slab. And then—I saw the stairway that led down into the pit!"

"A stairway!" we cried.

"A stairway," repeated the crawling man as patiently as before. "It seemed not so much carved out of the rock as built into it. Each slab was perhaps twenty feet long and five feet wide. They ran down from the platform and vanished into the blue haze."

"A stairway," said Anderson incredulously, "built into the wall of a precipice and leading down into a bottomless pit—"

"Not bottomless," interrupted the crawling man. "There was a bottom. Yes. I reached it." He paused again. "I reached it," he went on dully. "Down the stairway—down the stairway."

He seemed to grip his mind.

"Yes," he went on firmly. "I went down the stairway. But not that day. I made my camp back of the gates. At dawn I filled my knapsack with food, my two canteens with water from a spring that wells up there by the gateway, walked between the carved monoliths and stepped over the edge of the pit.

"The steps run along the side of the pit at a forty-degree pitch. As I went down and down, I studied them. They were of a greenish rock quite different from the granitic porphyry that formed the wall of the pit. At first I thought that the builders had taken advantage of an outcropping stratum, and had carved the gigantic flight from it. But the regularity of the angle at which it fell made me doubtful of this theory.

"After I had gone down perhaps half a mile, I stepped out upon a landing. From this landing, the stairs made a V-shaped turn and again ran on downward, clinging to the cliff at the same angle as the first flight. After I had made three of these turns, I knew that the steps dropped straight down to wherever they went in a succession of such angles. No strata could be so regular as that. No, the stairway was built by hands! But whose? And why? The answer is in those ruins around the edge of the pit—never, I think, to be read.

"By noon I had lost sight of the lip of the abyss. Above me, below me, was nothing but the blue haze. Beside me, too, was nothingness, for the further breast of rock had long since vanished in the same haze. I felt no dizziness, and no fear; only a vast curiosity. What was I to discover? Some ancient and wonderful civilization that had ruled when the poles were tropical gardens? A new world? The key to the mystery of man himself? Nothing living, I felt sure—all was too old for life. Still, a work so wonderful must lead to something quite as wonderful I knew. What was it? I went on.

"At regular intervals I had passed the mouths of small caves. There would be three thousand steps and then an opening, three thousand more steps and an opening—and so on and on. Late that afternoon, I stopped before one of these clefts. I suppose I had gone then three miles down the pit, although the angles were such that I had walked in all fully ten miles. I examined the entrance. On each side was carved the same figures as on the great portals at the lip of the pit. But now they were standing face forward, the arms outstretched with their disks, as though holding something back from the shaft itself. Now, too, their faces were covered with veils and there were no hideous shapes behind them.

"I went inside the cave. It ran back for twenty yards like a burrow. It was dry and perfectly light. I could see, outside, the blue haze rising upward like a column. I felt an extraordinary sense of security, although I had not been conscious of any fear. I felt that the figures at the entrance were guardians—but against what? I felt so secure that even curiosity on this point was dulled.

"The blue haze thickened and grew faintly luminescent. I fancied that it was dusk above. I ate and drank a little and slept. When I awoke, the blue had lightened again, and I fancied it was dawn above. I went on. I forgot the gulf yawning at my side. I felt no fatigue and little hunger or thirst, although I had drunk and eaten sparingly. That night I spent within another of the caves. And at dawn, I descended again.

"It was late that day when I first saw the city—"

He was silent for a time.

"The city," he said at last, "The city of the pit! But not such a city as you have ever seen—nor any other man who has lived to tell of it. The pit, I think, must be shaped like a bottle; the opening before the five peaks is the neck. But how wide the bottom is, I do not know—thousands of miles, maybe. And what may lay behind the city—I do not know.

"I had begun to catch little glints of light far down in the blue. Then I saw the tops of—trees, I suppose they are. But not our kind of trees—unpleasant, reptilian trees. They reared themselves on high, thin trunks and their tops were nests of thick tendrils with ugly little leaves like narrow heads—or snake heads.

"The trees were red, a vivid, angry red. Here and there I began to glimpse spots of shining yellow. I knew these were water because I could see things breaking through their surface—or at least I could see the splash and ripple, but what it was that disturbed them, I never saw.

"Straight beneath me was the—city. Mile after mile of closely packed cylinders that lay upon their sides in pyramids of three, of five—of dozens—piled upon each other. It is so hard to make you see what that city is like—look, suppose you have water pipes of a certain length and first you lay three of them side by side and on top of them you place two and on these two one; or suppose you take five for a foundation and place on these four and then three; then two and then one. Do you see? That was the way they looked.

"And they were topped by towers, by minarets, by flares, by fans and twisted monstrosities. They gleamed as though coated with pale rose flame.

Beside them, the venomous red trees raised themselves like the heads of hydras guarding nests of gigantic jeweled and sleeping worms!

"A few feet beneath me, the stairway jutted out into a titanic arch, unearthly as the span that bridges Hell and leads to Asgard. It curved out and down, straight through the top of the highest pile of carven cylinders and then—it vanished through it. It was appalling—it was demonic—"

The crawling man stopped. His eyes rolled up into his head. He trembled and again his arms and legs began their horrible crawling movement. From his lips came a whispering. It was an echo of the high murmuring we had heard the night he came to us. I put my hands over his eyes. He quieted.

"The things accursed!" he said. "The people of the pit! Did I whisper? Yes—but they can't get me now—they can't!"

After a time he began as quietly as before.

"I crossed that span. I went down through the top of that—building. Blue darkness shrouded me for a moment and I felt the steps twist into a spiral. I wound down and then I was standing high up in—I can't tell you what. I'll have to call it a room. We have no images for what is in the pit. A hundred feet below me was the floor. The walls sloped down and out from where I stood in a series of widening crescents. The place was colossal—and it was filled with a curious mottled red light. It was like the light inside a green and gold flecked fire opal. The spiral stairs wound below me. I went down to the last step. Far in front of me rose a high columned altar. Its pillars were carved in monstrous scrolls—like mad octopuses with a thousand drunken tentacles; they rested on the backs of shapeless monstrosities carved in crimson stone. The altar front was a gigantic slab of purple, covered with carvings.

"I can't describe these carvings! No human being could—the human eye cannot grasp them any more than it can grasp shapes that haunt the fourth dimension. Only a subtle sense in the back of the brain grasped them vaguely. They were formless things that gave no conscious image, yet pressed into the mind like small hot seals—ideas of hate—of combat between unthinkable, monstrous things—victories, in a nebulous hell of steaming, obscene jungles— aspirations and ideals immeasurably loathsome—

"And as I stood, I grew aware of something that lay behind the lip of the altar fifty feet above me. I *knew* it was there—I felt it with every hair and every tiny bit of my skin. Something infinitely malignant, infinitely horrible, infinitely ancient. It lurked, it brooded, it saw me, it threatened and it—was invisible!

"Behind me was a circle of blue light. Something urged me to turn back, to climb the stairs and make away. It was impossible. Terror of that unseen, watching thing behind the altar raced me onward like a whirlwind. I passed through the circle. I was in a way that stretched on into dim distance between the rows of carven cylinders.

"Here and there the red trees arose. Between them rolled the stone bur- rows. And now I could take in the amazing ornamentation that clothed them. They were like the trunks of smooth-skinned trees that had fallen and had been clothed with high reaching, fantastic orchids. Yes—those cylinders were like that—and more. They should have gone out with the dinosaurs. They were—monstrous! They struck the eyes like a blow and they passed across the nerves like a rasp. And nowhere was there sight or sound of living thing.

"There were circular openings in the cylinders, like the opening in the temple of the stairway through which I had run. I passed through one of them. I was in a long, bare, vaulted room whose curving sides half closed twenty feet over my head, leaving a wide slit that opened into another vaulted chamber above. I saw nothing in the room save the same mottled reddish light of the temple.

"I stumbled. Still I could see nothing, but—my skin prickled and my heart stopped! There *was* something on the floor over which I had tripped!

"I reached down—and my hand touched a—thing—cold and smooth—that moved under it— I turned and ran out of that place. I was filled with a sick loathing that had in it something of madness— I ran on and on—blindly—wringing my hands—weeping with horror—

"When I came to myself, I was still among the stone cylinders and red trees. I tried to retrace my steps, to find the temple; for now I was more than afraid. I was like a new soul panic-stricken with the first terrors of hell. But I could not find the temple! And the haze began to thicken and glow; the cylinders to shine more brightly.

Suddenly I knew that it was dusk in my own world above and that the thickening of the haze was the signal for the awakening of whatever things lived in the pit.

"I scrambled up the sides of one of the burrows. I hid behind a twisted nightmare of stone. Perhaps, I thought, there was a chance of remaining hidden until the blue lightened, the peril passed, and I could escape. There began to grow around me a murmur. It was everywhere—and it grew and grew into a great whispering. I peeped from the side of the stone down into the street.

"I saw lights passing and repassing. More and more lights—they swam out of the circular doorways and they thronged the street. The highest were eight feet above the pave; the lowest, perhaps two. They hurried, they sauntered, they bowed, they stopped and whispered—and there was *nothing* under them!"

"Nothing under them!" breathed Anderson.

"No," he went on, "that was the terrible part of it—there was nothing under them. Yet certainly the lights were living things. They had consciousness, volition—what else I did not know. They were nearly two feet across, the largest. Their center was a bright nucleus—red, blue, green. This nucleus faded off gradually into a misty glow that did not end abruptly. It, too, seemed to fade off into nothingness—but a nothingness that had under it a—somethingness.

"I strained my eyes, trying to grasp this body into which the lights merged and which one could only *feel* was there, but could not *see*.

"And all at once I grew rigid. Something cold, and thin, like a whip, had touched my face. I turned my head. Close behind were three of the lights. They were a pale blue. They looked at me—if you can imagine lights that are eyes.

"Another whiplash gripped my shoulder. Under the closest light came a shrill whispering. I shrieked. Abruptly the murmuring in the street ceased.

"I dragged my eyes from the pale-blue globe that held them and looked out; the lights in the streets were rising by myriads to the level of where I stood! There they stopped and peered at me. They crowded and jostled as though they were a crowd of curious people on Broadway.

"That was the horrible part of it. I felt a score of the lashes touch me—I shrieked again. Then—darkness and a sensation of falling through vast depths.

"When I awoke to consciousness, I was again in the great place of the stairway, lying at the foot of the altar. All was silent. There were no lights—only the mottled red glow.

"I jumped to my feet and ran toward the steps. Something jerked me back to my knees. And then I saw that around my waist had been fastened a yellow ring of metal. From it hung a chain, and this chain passed up over the lip of the high ledge.

"I reached into my pockets for my knife to cut through the ring. It was not there! I had been stripped of everything except one of the canteens that I had hung around my neck, and which I suppose they had thought was part of me.

"I tried to break the ring. It seemed alive. It writhed in my hands and drew itself closer around me!

"I pulled at the chain. It was immovable. There came over me in a flood consciousness of the unseen thing above the altar, and I groveled at the foot of the slab. Think—alone in that place of strange light, with the brooding, ancient horror above me—a monstrous thing, a thing unthinkable—an unseen thing that poured forth horror—

"After a while I gripped myself. Then I saw, beside one of the pillars, a yellow bowl filled with a thick, white liquid. I drank it. If it killed, I did not care. But its taste was pleasant, and as I drank, strength came back to me with a rush. Clearly I was not to be starved. The people of the pit, whatever they were, had a conception of human needs.

"And now, once more the reddish, mottled gleam began to deepen. Again outside arose the humming, and through the circle that was the entrance to the temple came streaming the globes. They ranged themselves in ranks until they filled the temple. Their whispering grew into a chant, a cadenced whispering chant that rose and fell, rose and fell, while to its rhythm the globes lifted and sank, lifted and sank.

"All the night the lights came and went; and all that night the chant sounded as they rose and fell. At the last I felt myself only an atom of consciousness in the sea of that whispering; an atom that rose and fell with the bowing globes.

"I tell you that even my heart pulsed in unison with them! And the red glow faded, the lights streamed out; the whispering died. I was again alone, and I knew that again day had begun in my own world.

"I slept. When I awoke, I found beside the pillar another bowl of the white liquid. I scrutinized the chain that held me to the altar. I began to rub two of the links together. I did this for hours. When the red began to thicken, there was a ridge worn in the links. Hope rushed up within me. There was, then, a chance to escape.

"With the thickening, the lights came again. All through that night the whispering chant sounded, and the globes rose and fell. The chant seized me. It pulsed through me until every nerve and muscle quivered to it. My lips began to quiver. They strove like a man trying to cry out in a nightmare. And at last they, too, were whispering—whispering the evil chant of the people of the pit. My body bowed in unison with the lights.

"I was—God forgive me—in movement and sound, one with these nameless things, while my soul sank back sick with horror, but powerless. And as I whispered, I—saw *them!*

"Saw the things under the lights. Great transparent, snail-like bodies—dozens of waving tentacles stretching from them; little round, gating mouths under the luminous, seeing globes. They were like specters of inconceivably monstrous slugs! And as I stared, still bowing and whispering, the dawn came, and they streamed to and through the entrance. They did not crawl or walk—they floated! They floated and were—gone!

"I did not sleep. I worked all that day at my chain. By the thickening of the red, I had worn it a sixth through. And all that night, under their spell, I whispered and bowed with the pit people, joining in their chant to the thing that brooded above me!

"Twice again the red thickened and lessened and the chant held me. And then, on the morning of the fifth day, I broke the worn links. I was free! I ran to the stairway. With eyes closed I rushed up and past the unseen horror behind the altar-ledge and was out upon the bridge. I crossed the span and began the ascent of the stairway.

"Can you think what it is to climb straight up the verge of a cleft-world—with hell behind you? Well—worse than hell was behind me, and terror rode me.

"The city of the pit had long been lost in the blue haze before I knew that I could climb no more. My heart beat upon my ears like a sledge. I fell before one of the little caves, feeling that here at last was sanctuary. I crept far back within it and waited for the haze to thicken. Almost at once it did so, and from far below me came a vast and angry murmur. Crouching at the back of the cave, I saw a swift light go shooting up through the blue haze, then die down and break, and as it dimmed and broke I saw myriads of the globes that are the eyes of the pit people swing downward into the abyss. Again and again the light pulsed, and the globes rose with it and fell.

"They are hunting me! They knew I must be somewhere still on the stairway, or, if hiding below, I must sometime take to the stairway to escape. The whispering grew louder, more insistent.

"There began to pulse though me a dreadful desire to join in the whispering as I had done in the temple. Something told me that if I did, the sculptured figures could no longer save me; that I would go out and down again into the temple forever! I bit my lips through and through to still them, and all that night the beam shot up through the abyss, the globes swung, and the whispering sounded—and I prayed to the power of the caves and the sculptured figures that still had power to guard them."

He paused—his strength was going.

Then almost in a whisper: "I thought, what were the people who had carved them? Why had they built their city around the verge, and why had they set that stairway in the pit? What had they been to the things that dwelt at the bottom, and what use had the things been to them that they should live beside their dwelling-place? That there had been some purpose was certain. No work so prodigious as the stairway would have been undertaken otherwise. But what was the purpose? And why was it that those who had dwelt about the abyss had passed away ages gone and the dwellers in the abyss still lived?"

He looked at us: "I could find no answer. I wonder if, even when I am dead, I shall know? I doubt it.

"Dawn came as I wondered, and with it—silence. I drank what was left of the liquid in my canteen, crept from the cave, and began to climb again. That afternoon my legs gave out. I tore off my shirt and made from it pads for my knees and coverings for my hands. I crawled upward. I crawled up and up. And again I crept into one of the caves and waited until again the blue thickened, the shaft of light shot through it, and the whispering came.

"But now there was a new note in the whispering. It was no longer threatening. It called and coaxed. It—drew.

"A terror gripped me. There had come upon me a mighty desire to leave the cave and go out where the lights swung; to let them do with me what they pleased, carry me where they wished. The desire grew. It gained fresh impulse with every rise of the beam, until at last, I vibrated with the desire as I had vibrated to the chant in the Temple.

"My body was a pendulum. Up would go the beam, and I would swing toward it! Only my soul kept steady. It held me fast to the floor of the cave, and it placed a hand over my lips to still them. And all that night I fought with my body and lips against the spell of the pit people.

"Dawn came. Again I crept from the cave and faced the stairway. I could not rise. My hands were torn and bleeding, my knees an agony. I forced myself upward step by step.

"After a while my hands became numb, the pain left my knees. They deadened. Step by step my will drove my body upward upon them. And, time after time, I would sink back within myself to oblivion—only to wake again and. find that all the time I had been steadily climbing upward.

"And then—only a dream of crawling up infinite stretches of steps— memories of dull horror while hidden within caves, with thousands of lights pulsing without, and whisperings that called and called me—memory of a time when I awoke to find that my body was obeying the call and had carried me halfway out between the guardians of the portals, while thousands of gleaming globes rested in the blue haze and watched me. Glimpses of bitter fights against sleep, and always—a climb up and up along infinite distances of steps that led from a lost Abaddon to a paradise of blue sky and open world!

"At last a consciousness of clear sky close above me, the lip of the pit before me. Memory of passing between the great portals of the pit and of steady withdrawal from it. Dreams of giant men with strange, peaked crowns and veiled faces who pushed me onward and onward, and held back pulsing globules of light that sought to draw me back to a gulf wherein planets swam between the branches of red trees that had snakes for crowns.

"And then a long, long sleep—how long God alone knows—in a cleft of rocks; an awakening to see, far in the north, the beam still rising and falling, the lights still hunting, the whispering high above me calling—and knowledge that no longer had they power to draw me.

"Again crawling on dead arms and legs that moved—that moved—like the Ancient Mariner's ship—without volition of mine. And then—your fire—and this—safety."

The crawling man smiled at us for a moment, then quickly fell asleep.

That afternoon we struck camp and, carrying the crawling man, started back south. For three days we carried him, and still he slept. And on the third day, still sleeping, he died. We built a great pile of wood and we burned his body, as he had asked. We scattered his ashes about the forest with the ashes of the trees that had consumed him.

It must be a great magic, indeed, that can disentangle those ashes and draw them back in a rushing cloud to the pit he called accursed. I do not think that even the people of the pit have such a spell. No.

But Anderson and I did not return to the five peaks to see. And if the gold does stream out between the five peaks of the Hand Mountain like putty from a clenched fist—there it may remain for all of us.

· · · · ·

BEHIND THE CURTAIN

FRANCIS STEVENS

It was after nine o'clock when the bell rang, and descending to the dimly lighted hall, I opened the front door, at first on the chain to be sure of my visitor. Seeing, as I had hoped, the face of our friend, Ralph Quentin, I took off the chain and he entered with a blast of sharp November air for company. I had to throw my weight upon the door to close it against the wind.

As he removed his hat and cloak, he laughed good-humoredly.

"You're very cautious, Santallos. I thought you were about to demand a password before admitting me."

"It is well to be cautious," I retorted. "This house stands somewhat alone, and thieves are everywhere."

"It would require a thief of considerable muscle to make off with some of your treasures. That stone tomb-thing, for instance; what do you call it?"

"The Beni Hassan sarcophagus. Yes. But what of the gilded inner case, and what of the woman it contains? A thief of judgment and intelligence might covet that. Don't you agree?"

He only laughed again, and counterfeited a shudder.

"The woman! Don't remind me that such a brown, shriveled mummy-horror was ever a woman!"

"But she was. Doubtless in her day my poor Princess of Naam was soft, appealing; a creature of red, moist lips and eyes like stars in the black Egyptian sky. 'The Songstress of the House,' she was called, ere she became Ta-Nezem the Osirian. But I keep you standing here in the cold hall. Come upstairs with me. Did I tell you that Beatrice is not here tonight?"

"No?" His intonation expressed surprise and frank disappointment. "Then I can't say goodbye to her? Didn't you receive my note? I'm to take Sanderson's place as manager of the sales department in Chicago, and I'm off tomorrow morning."

"Congratulations. Yes, we had your note, but Beatrice was given an opportunity to join some friends on a Southern trip. The notice was short, but of late she has not been so well and I urged her to go. This November air is cruelly damp and bitter."

"What was it—a yachting cruise?"

"A long cruise. She left this afternoon. I have been sitting in her boudoir, Quentin, thinking of her, and I'll tell you about it there—if you don't mind?"

"Wherever you like," he conceded, though in a tone of some surprise. I suppose he had not credited me with so much sentiment, or thought it odd that I should wish to share it with another, even so good a friend as he. "You must find it fearfully lonesome here without Bee," he continued.

"A trifle." We were ascending the dark stairs now. "After tonight, however, things will be quite different. Do you know that I have sold the house?"

"No! Why, you are full of astonishments, old chap. Found a better place with more space for your tear-jars and tombstones?"

He meant, I assumed, a witty reference to my collection of Coptic and Egyptian treasures, well and dearly bought, but so much trash to a man of Quentin's youth and temperament.

I opened the door of my wife's boudoir, and it was pleasant to pass into such rosy light and warmth out of the stern, dark cold of the hall. Yet it was an old house, full of unexpected drafts. Even here there was a draft so strong that a heavy velour curtain at the far side of the room continually rippled and billowed out, like a loose rose-colored sail. Never far enough, though, to show what was behind it.

My friend settled himself on the frail little chair that stood before my wife's dressing table. It was the kind of chair that women love and most men loathe, but Quentin, for all his weight and stature, had a touch of the feminine about him, or perhaps of the feline. Like a cat, he moved delicately. He was blond and tall, with fine, regular features, a ready laugh and the clean charm of youth about him—also its occasional blundering candor.

As I looked at him sitting there, graceful, at ease, I wished that his mind might have shared the litheness of his body. He could have understood me so much better.

"I have indeed found a place for my collections," I observed, seating myself nearby. "In fact, with a single exception—the Ta-Nazem sarcophagus—the entire lot is going to the dealers."

Seeing his expression of astonished disbelief, I continued: "The truth is, dear Quentin, that I have been guilty of gross injustice to our Beatrice. I have been too good a collector and too neglectful a husband. My 'tear-jars and tombstones,' in fact, have enjoyed an attention that might better have been elsewhere bestowed. Yes, Beatrice has left me alone, but the instant that some few last affairs are settled, I intend rejoining her. And you, yourself, are leaving. At least none of us three will be left to miss the others' friendship."

"You are quite surprising tonight, Santallos. But, by Jove, I'm not sorry to hear any of it! It was not my place to criticize, and Bee's not the sort to complain. But living here in this lonely old barn of a house, doing all her own work, practically deserted by her friends, must have been—"

"Hard, very hard," I interrupted him softly, "for one so young and lovely as our Beatrice. But if I had been blind, at least the awakening has come. You should have seen her face when she heard the news. It was wonderful. We were standing, just she and I, in the midst of my tear-jars and tombstones—my 'chamber of horrors,' she named it. You are so apt at amusing phrases, both of you. We stood beside the great stone sarcophagus from the Necropolis of Beni Hassan.

Across the trestles beneath it lay the gilded inner case wherein Ta-Nezem the Osirian had slept out so many centuries. You know its appearance—a thing of beautiful, gleaming lines, like the quaint, smiling image of a golden woman.

"Then I lifted the lid and showed Beatrice that the onetime songstress, the handmaiden of Amen, slept there no more, and the case was empty. You know, too, that Beatrice never liked my princess. For a jest she used to declare that she was jealous—jealous of a woman dead and ugly so many thousand years! Or—but that was only in anger—that I had bought Ta-Nezem with what would have given her, Beatrice, all the pleasure she lacked in life. Oh, she was not too patient to reproach me, Quentin, but only in anger and hot blood.

"So I showed her the empty case, and said, 'Beloved wife, never again need you be jealous of Ta-Nezem. All that is in this room save her and her belongings I have sold, but her, I could not bear to sell. That which I love, no man else shall share or own. So I have destroyed her. I have rent her body to brown, aromatic shreds. I have burned her; it is as if she had never been. And now, dearest of the dear, you shall take for your own all the care, all the keeping that heretofore I have lavished upon the Princess of Naam.'

"Beatrice turned from the empty case as if she could scarcely believe her hearing, but when she saw by the look in my eyes that I meant exactly what I said, neither more nor less, you should have seen her face, my dear Quentin—you should have seen her face!"

"I can imagine." He laughed rather shortly. For some reason my guest seemed increasingly ill at ease, and glanced continually about the little red-and-white room that was the one luxurious, thoroughly feminine corner—that and the cold, dark room behind the curtain—in what he had justly called my "barn of a house."

"Santallos," he continued abruptly, and I thought, rather rudely, "you should have a portrait done as you look tonight. You might have posed for one of those stern old *hidalgos* of—which painter was it who did so many Spanish *dons* and *donesses?*"

"You perhaps mean Velasquez," I answered with mild courtesy, though secretly and as always, his crude personalities displeased me. "My father, you may recall, was of Cordova, in southern Spain. But—must you go so soon? First drink one glass with me to our missing Beatrice. See how I was warming my blood against the wind that blows in, even here. The wine is Amontillado; some that was sent me by a friend of my father's from the very vineyards where the grapes were grown and pressed. And for many years it has ripened since it came here. Before she went, Beatrice drank of it from one of these same glasses. True wine of Montilla! See how it lives—like fire in amber, with a glimmer of blood behind it."

I held high the decanter, and the light gleamed through it upon his face.

"Amontillado! Isn't that a kind of sherry? I'm no connoisseur of wines, as you know. But—Amontillado."

For a moment he studied the wine I had given him, liquid flame in the crystal glass. Then his face cleared.

"I remember the association now. 'The Cask of Amontillado.' Ever read the story?"

"I seem to recall it dimly."

"Horrible, fascinating sort of a yarn. A fellow takes his trustful friend down into the cellars to sample some wine, traps him and walls him up in a niche—buries him alive, you understand. Read it when I was a youngster and it made a deep impression, partly, I think, because I couldn't for the life of me comprehend a nature—even an Italian nature—desiring so horrible a form of vengeance. You're half Latin yourself, Santallos. Can you elucidate?"

"I doubt if you would ever understand," I responded slowly, wondering how even Quentin could be so crude, so tactless. "Such a revenge might have its merits, since the offender would be a long time dying. But merely to kill seems to me so pitifully inadequate. Now I, if I were driven to revenge, should never be contented by killing. I should wish to follow."

"What—beyond the grave?"

I laughed. "Why not? Wouldn't that be the very apotheosis of hatred? I'm trying to interpret the Latin nature, as you asked me to do."

"Confound you; for an instant I thought you were serious. The way you said it made me actually shiver!"

"Yes," I observed, "or perhaps it was the draft. See, Quentin, how that curtain billows out."

His eyes followed my glance. Continually the heavy, rose-colored curtain that was hung before the door of my wife's bedroom bulged outward, shook and quivered like a bellying sail, as draperies will with a wind behind them.

His eyes strayed from the curtain, met mine and fell again to the wine in his glass. Suddenly he drained it, not as would a man who was a judge of wines, but hastily, indifferently, without thought for its flavor or bouquet. I raised my glass in the toast he had forgotten.

"To our Beatrice," I said, and drained mine also, though with more appreciation.

"To Beatrice—of course." He looked at the bottom of his empty glass; then, before I could offer to refill it, rose from his chair.

"I must go, old man. When you write to Bee, tell her I'm sorry to have missed her."

"Before she could receive a letter from me, I shall be with her—I hope. How cold the house is tonight, and the wind breathes everywhere. See how the curtain blows, Quentin."

"So it does." He set his glass on the tray beside the decanter. Upon first entering the room he had been smiling, but now his straight, fine brows were drawn in a perpetual, troubled frown, his eyes looked here and there, and would never meet mine—which were steady. "There's a wind," he added, "that blows along this wall—curious. One can't notice any draft there, either. But it must blow there, and of course, the curtain billows out."

"Yes," I said. "Of course it billows out."

"Or is there another door, behind that curtain?"

His careful ignorance of what any fool might infer from mere appearance brought an involuntary smile to my lips. Nevertheless, I answered him.

"Yes, of course there is a door—an open door."

His frown deepened. My true and simple replies appeared to cause him a certain irritation.

"As I feel now," I added, "even to cross this room would be an effort. I am tired and weak tonight. As Beatrice once said, my strength beside yours is as a child's to that of a grown man. Won't you close that door for me, dear friend?"

"Why—yes, I will. I didn't know you were ill. If that's the case, you shouldn't be alone in an empty house. Shall I stay with you for a while?"

As he spoke he walked across the room. His hand was on the curtain, but before it could be drawn aside, my voice checked him.

"Quentin," I said, "are even you quite strong enough to close that door?"

Looking back at me, chin on shoulder, his face appeared scarcely familiar, so drawn was it in lines of bewilderment and half-suspicion.

"What do you mean? You are very—odd tonight. Is the door so heavy, then? What door is it?"

I made no reply.

As if against their owner's will, his eyes fled from mine; he turned and hastily pushed aside the heavy drapery.

Behind it, my wife's bedroom lay dark and cold, with windows open to the invading winds.

And erect in the doorway, uncovered, stood an ancient gilded coffin-case. It was the golden casket of Ta-Nezem, but its occupant was more beautiful than the poor, shriveled Songstress of Naam.

Bound across her bosom were the strange, quaint jewels that had been found in the sarcophagus. Ta-Nezem's amulets—heads of Hathor and of Horus, the sacred eye, the *uræus,* even the heavy, dull-green scarab, the amulet for purity of heart—there they rested upon the bosom of her who had been mistress of my house, now Beatrice the Osirian. Beneath them her white, stiff body was enwrapped in the same crackling, dry, brown linen bands, impregnated with the gums and resins of embalmers dead these many thousand years, which had been about the body of Ta-Nezem.

Above the white translucence of her brow appeared the winged disk, emblem of Ra. The twining golden bodies of its supporting *uræii,* its cobras of Egypt, were lost in the dusk of her hair, whose soft fineness yet lived and would live so much longer than the flesh of any if us three.

Yes, I had kept my word and given Beatrice all that had been Ta-Nezem's, even to the sarcophagus itself, for in my will it was written that she be placed in it for final burial.

Like the fool he was, Quentin stood there, staring at the unclosed, frozen eyes of my Beatrice—and his. Stood till that which had been in the wine began to make itself be felt. He faced me then, but with so absurd and childish a look of surprise that, despite the courtesy due a guest, I laughed and laughed.

I, too, felt warning throes, but to me the pain was no more than a gauge—
a measure of his suffering—a stimulus to point the phrases in which I told
him all I knew and had guessed of him and Beatrice, and thus drove home
the jest.

But I had never thought that a man of Quentin's youth and strength could
die so easily. Beatrice, frail though she was, had taken longer to die.

He could not even cross the room to stop my laughter, but at the first step
stumbled, fell, and in a very little while lay still at the foot of the gilded case.

After all, he was not so strong as I. Beatrice had seen. Her still, cold eyes
saw all—how he lay there, his fine, lithe body contorted, worthless for any use
till its substance should have been cast again in the melting pot of dissolution,
while I, who had drunk of the same draft, suffered the same pangs, yet stood
and found breath for mockery.

So I poured myself another glass of that good Cordovan wine, and I raised
it to both of them and drained it, laughing.

"Quentin," I cried, "you asked *what door,* though you thought you had
passed that way before and feared that I guessed your knowledge. But there
are doors and doors, dear charming friend, and one that is heavier than any
other. Close it if you can—close it now in my face, who otherwise will follow
even whither you have gone—the heavy, heavy door of the Osiris, Keeper of
the House of Death!"

Thus I dreamed of doing and speaking.

It was so vivid, the dream, that awakening in the darkness of my room,
I could scarcely believe it had been other than reality. True, I loved, while in
my dream I had shared the avenging poison. Yet my veins were still hot with
the keen passion of triumph, and my eyes filled with the vision of Beatrice,
dead—*dead in Ta-Nezem's casket.*

Unreasonably frightened, I sprang from bed, flung on a dressing gown
and hurried out. Down the hallway I sped, swiftly and silently, at the end of it
unlocked heavy doors with a tremulous hand, switched on lights, lights and
more lights, till the great room of my collection was ablaze with them, and
as my treasures sprang into view, I sighed, like a man reaching home from a
perilous journey.

The dream was a lie.

There, fronting me, stood the heavy, empty sarcophagus; there on the
trestles before it lay the gilded case, a thing of beautiful, gleaming lines, like
the smiling image of a golden woman.

I stole across the room and softly, very softly, lifted the upper half of the
beautiful lid, peering within. The dream indeed was a lie.

Happy as a comforted child, I went to my room again. Across the hall, the
door of my wife's boudoir stood partly open. In the room beyond a faint light
was burning, and I could see the rose-colored curtain sway slightly to a draft
from some open window.

Yesterday she had come to me and asked for her freedom. I had refused, knowing to whom she would turn, and hating him for his youth and his crudeness and his secret scorn of me.

But had I done well? They were children, those two, and despite my dream, I was certain that their foolish, youthful ideals had kept them from actual sin against my honor. But what if, time passing, they might change? Or, Quentin gone, my lovely Beatrice might favor another, young as he and not so scrupulous?

Everyone, they say, has a streak of incipient madness. I recalled the frenzied act to which my dream jealousy had driven me. Perhaps it was a warning, the dream. What if my father's jealous blood should someday betray me, drive me to the insane destruction of her I held most dear and sacred?

I shuddered, then smiled at the swaying curtain. Beatrice was too beautiful for safety. She should have her freedom.

Let her mate with Ralph Quentin or whom she would, Ta-Nezem must rest secure in her gilded house of death. My brown, perfect, shriveled Princess of the Nile! Destroyed—rent to brown, aromatic shreds—burned—destroyed—and her beautiful coffin-case desecrated as I had seen it in my vision!

Again I shuddered, smiled and shook my head at the swaying, rosy curtain.

"You are too lovely, Beatrice," I said, "and my father was a Spaniard. You shall have your freedom!"

I entered my room and lay down to sleep again, at peace and content.

The dream, thank God, was a lie.

• • • • •

NUMBER THIRTEEN (EXCERPT)

EDGAR RICE BURROUGHS

Professor Maxon and Von Horn were standing over one of the six vats that were arranged in two rows down the center of the laboratory. The professor had been more communicative and agreeable that day than for some time past, and their conversation had assumed more of the familiarity that had marked it during the first month of their acquaintance at Singapore.

"And what of these first, who are so imperfect?" asked Von Horn. "You cannot take them into civilization, nor would it be right to leave them here upon this island. What will you do with them?"

Professor Maxon pondered the question for a moment.

"I have given this matter but little thought," he said at length. "They are but accidents of my great work. It is unfortunate that they are as they are, but without them, I could have never reached the perfection that I am sure we are to find here."

He tapped lovingly upon the heavy glass cover of the vat before which he stood.

"And this is but the beginning. There can be no more mistakes now, though I doubt if we can ever improve upon that which is so rapidly developing here."

Again he passed his long, slender hand caressingly over the coffinlike vat, at the head of which was a placard bearing the words:

NUMBER THIRTEEN

"But the others, professor!" insisted Von Horn. "We must decide. Already they have become a problem of no small dimensions. Yesterday, Number Five desired some plantains that I had given to Number Seven.

"I tried to reason with him, but, as you know, he is mentally defective, and for answer he rushed at Number Seven to tear the coveted morsel from him. The result was a battle royal that might have put to shame two Bengal tigers.

"Twelve is tractable and intelligent. With his assistance, and my bull-whip, I succeeded in separating them before either was killed.

"Your greatest error was in striving at first for such physical perfection. You have overdone it, with the result that the Court of Mystery is peopled by a dozen brutes of awful muscularity, and scarcely enough brain among the dozen to properly equip three."

"They are as they are," replied the professor. "I shall do for them what I can. When I am gone, they must look to themselves. I can see no way out of it."

"What you have given, you may take away," said Von Horn in a low tone. Professor Maxon shuddered.

Those three horrid days in the workshop at home flooded his memory with all the gruesome details he had tried for so many months to forget. The haunting ghosts of the anguish that had left him an altered man—so altered that there were times that he had feared for his sanity.

"No, no!" he almost shouted. "It would be murder. They are—"

"They are—things," interrupted Von Horn. "They are not human—they are not even beast. They are terrible, soulless creatures. You have no right to permit them to live longer than to substantiate your theory.

"None but us knows of their existence—no other need know of their passing. It must be done. They are a constant and growing menace to us all, but most of all to your daughter."

A cunning look came into the professor's eyes.

"I understand," he said. "The precedent once established, all must perish by its edict—even those which may not be grotesque or bestial—even this perfect one."

He touched the vat. "And thus you would rid yourself of rival suitors. But no!" he went on in a high, trembling voice. "I shall not be led to thus compromise myself and be thwarted in my cherished plan. Be this one what he may, he shall wed my daughter!"

The man had raised himself upon his toes as he reached his climax—his clenched hand was high above his head—his voice fairly thundered out the final sentence, and with the last word, he brought his fist down upon the vat before him. In his eyes blazed the light unchained madness.

Von Horn was a brave man, but he shuddered at the maniacal ferocity of the older man and shrank back. The futility of argument was apparent.

Sing Lee was late that night. In fact, he did not return from his fruitless quest for gulls until well after dark, nor would he vouchsafe any explanation of the consequent lateness of supper. Nor could he be found shortly after the evening meal, when Virginia sought him.

Not until the camp was wrapped in the quiet of slumber did Sing Lee return—stealthy and mysterious—to creep under cover of a moonless night to the door of the workshop.

How he gained entrance, only he knows, but a moment later there was a muffled crash of broken glass within the laboratory, and the Chinaman had slipped out, relocked the door, and scurried to his shack.

But there was no occasion for his haste—no other ear than his had heard the sound within the workshop.

It was almost nine the following morning before Professor Maxon and Von Horn entered the laboratory.

Scarcely had the older man passed the doorway when he threw up his hands in horrified consternation.

Vat Number 13 lay dashed to the floor—the glass cover was broken to a million pieces—a sticky, brownish substance covered the matting.

Professor Maxon hid his face in his hands.

"It is all ruined," he cried. "Three more days would have—"

"Look!" cried Von Horn. "It is not too soon."

Professor Maxon mustered courage to raise his eyes from his hands, and there he beheld, seated in a far corner of the room, a handsome giant, physically perfect.

The creature looked about him in a dazed, uncomprehending manner. A great question was writ large upon his intelligent countenance. Professor Maxon stepped forward and took him by the hand.

"Come," he said, and led him toward a smaller room off the main workshop. The giant followed docilely, his eyes roving about the room, the pitiful questioning still upon his handsome features.

Von Horn turned toward the *kampong*.

Virginia, deserted by all, even the faithful Sing—who, cheated of his sport on the preceding day, had again gone to the beach to snare gulls—became restless of the enforced idleness and solitude.

For a time she wandered about the little compound which had been reserved for the whites, but, tiring of this, she decided to extend her stroll beyond the palisade, a thing which she had never before done unless accompanied by Von Horn—a thing against which both he and her father had cautioned her.

What danger can there be? she thought. We know that the island is uninhabited by others than ourselves, and that there are no dangerous beasts. Anyway, there is no one now who seems to care what becomes of me, unless—unless—

I wonder if he does care. I wonder if I care whether or not he cares— and as she soliloquized, she wandered past the little clearing and into the jungle that lay behind the *kampong*.

As Von Horn and Professor Maxon talked together in the laboratory before the upset vat No. 13, a grotesque and horrible creature had slunk from the low shed at the opposite side of the *kampong* until it had crouched at the flimsy door of the building in which the two men conversed.

For a while it listened intently; but when Von Horn urged the necessity for dispatching certain "terrible, soulless creatures," an expression of intermingled fear and hatred convulsed the hideous features, and, like a great grizzly, it turned and lumbered awkwardly across the *kampong*, toward the easterly or back wall of the enclosure.

Here it leaped futilely a half dozen times for the top of the palisade; then, trembling and chattering in rage, it ran back and forth along the base of the obstacle, as a wild beast in captivity paces angrily before the bars of its cage.

Finally it paused to look once more at the senseless wood that barred its escape, as though measuring the distance to the top. Then the eyes roamed about the *kampong,* to rest at last upon the slanting roof of the thatched shed that was its shelter.

Presently a slow idea was born in the poor, malformed brain.

The creature approached the shed. He could just reach the saplings that formed the framework of the roof. Like a huge sloth, he drew himself to the roof of the structure.

From here he could see beyond the palisade, and the wild freedom of the jungle called to him. He did not know what it was, but in its leafy wall he perceived many breaks and openings that offered concealment from the creatures that were plotting to take his life.

Yet the wall was now fully six feet from him, and the top of it at least five feet above the top of the shed—those who had designed the *kampong* had been careful to set this structure sufficiently far from the palisade to prevent its forming too easy an avenue of escape.

The creature glanced fearfully toward the workshop.

He remembered the cruel bull-whip that always followed each new experiment on his part that did not coincide with the desires of his master; and as he thought of Von Horn, a nasty gleam shot his mismated eyes.

He tried to reach across the interval between the roof and the palisade, and in the attempt lost his balance and nearly precipitated himself to the ground below.

Cautiously, he drew back, still looking about for some means to cross the chasm. One of the saplings of the roof, protruding beyond the palm-leaf thatch, caught his attention.

With a single wrench he tore it from its fastenings. Extending it toward the palisade, he discovered that it just spanned the gap, but he dared not attempt to cross upon its single slender strand.

Quickly he ripped off a half-dozen other poles from the roof, and laying them side by side, formed a safe and easy path to freedom. A moment more and he sat astride the top of the wall.

Drawing the poles after him, he dropped them one by one to the ground outside the *kampong.*

Then he lowered himself to liberty.

Gathering the saplings under one huge arm, he ran lumberingly into the jungle; he would not leave evidence of the havoc he had wrought; the fear of the bull-whip was still strong upon him.

The green foliage closed about him, and the peaceful jungle gave no sign of the brute that roamed its shadowed mazes.

As Von Horn stepped into the *kampong,* his quick eye perceived the havoc that had been wrought with the roof at the east end of the shed. Quickly he crossed to the low structure. Within its compartments a number of deformed monsters squatted upon their haunches, or lay prone upon the native mats that covered the floor.

As the man entered they looked furtively at the bull-whip which trailed from his right hand, and then glanced fearfully at one another, as though questioning which was the malefactor on this occasion.

Von Horn ran his eyes over the hideous assemblage.

"Where is Number One?" he asked, directing his question toward a thing whose forehead gave greater promise of intelligence than any of his companions.

The one addressed shook his head.

Von Horn turned and made a circuit of the *kampong*. There was no sign of the missing one and no indication of any other irregularity than the demolished portion of the roof. With an expression of mild concern upon his face he entered the workshop.

"Number One has escaped into the jungle, professor," he said.

Professor Maxon looked up in surprise; but before he had an opportunity to reply, a woman's scream, shrill with horror, came to their startled ears.

Von Horn was the first to reach the *kampong* of the whites. Professor Maxon was close behind him, and the faces of both were white with apprehension.

The enclosure was deserted. Not even Sing was there.

Without a word, the two men sprang through the gateway and raced for the jungle in the direction from which that single, haunting cry had come.

Virginia Maxon, idling beneath the leafy shade of the tropical foliage, became presently aware that she had wandered farther from the *kampong* than she had intended. The day was sultry, and the heat, even in the dense shade of the jungle, oppressive.

Slowly she retraced her steps, her eyes upon the ground, her mind absorbed in sad consideration of her father's increasing moodiness and eccentricity.

Possibly it was this very abstraction that deadened her senses to the near approach of another.

At any rate, the girl's first intimation that she was not alone came when she raised her eyes to look full into the horrid countenance of a monster that blocked her path toward camp.

The sudden shock brought a single, involuntary scream from her lips.

The thing before her was hideous in the extreme. A mountain of deformed flesh clothed in dirty, white cotton pajamas. Its face was of the ashen hue of a fresh corpse, while the white hair and pink eyes denoted an Albinistic absence of pigment.

One eye was fully twice the diameter of the other, and an inch above the horizontal plane of its tiny mate. The nose was but a gaping orifice above a deformed and twisted mouth. The frightful thing was chinless, and its small, foreheadless head surrounded its colossal body like a cannon-ball on a hilltop.

One arm was at least twelve inches longer than its mate, which was itself long in proportion to the torso, while the legs, similarly mismated and terminating in huge, flat feet that protruded laterally, caused the thing to lurch fearfully from side to side as it lumbered toward the girl.

A grimace lighted the frightful face as the grotesque eyes fell upon this new creature.

Number One had never before seen a woman, but the sight of this one awoke in the unplumbed depths of his soulless breast a great desire to lay his hands upon her.

She was very beautiful. Number One wished to have her for his very own; nor would it be a difficult matter, so fragile was she, to gather her up in his great arms and carry her deep into the jungle, far out of hearing of the bull-whip man and the cold, frowning one who was continually measuring and weighing Number One and his companions, the while he scrutinized them with those strange, glittering eyes that frightened one even more than the cruel lash of the bull-whip.

Number One lurched forward, his arms outstretched toward the horror-stricken girl.

Virginia tried to cry out again; she tried to turn and run; but the horror of her impending fate and the terror that those awful features induced left her paralyzed and helpless.

The thing was almost upon her now. The mouth was wide in a hideous attempt to smile. The great hands would grasp her in another second; and then there was a sudden crashing of the underbrush behind her—a yellow, wrinkled face and a flying pigtail shot past her, and the brave old Sing Lee grappled with the mighty monster that threatened her.

The battle was short—short and terrible.

The Chinaman sought the ashen throat of his antagonist, but his muscles were as reeds beneath the inhuman power that opposed them.

Holding the girl at arm's length in one hand, Number One tore the Chinaman from him with the other, and, lifting him bodily above his head, hurled him, stunned and bleeding, against the bole of a giant buttress tree.

Then, lifting Virginia in his arms once more, he dived into the mazes of the jungle.

As Professor Maxon and Von Horn rushed from the workshop to their own *kampong,* they neglected, in their haste, to lock the door between, and for the first time since the camp was completed, it stood unlatched and ajar.

The professor had been engaged in taking careful measurements of the head of his latest experiment, and while he coached the young man in the first rudiments of spoken language, now the subject of his labors found himself suddenly deserted and alone.

He had not yet been without the four walls of the workshop, as the professor had wished to keep him from association with the grotesque results of his earlier experiments; and now a natural curiosity tempted him to approach the door through which his creator and the man with the bull-whip had so suddenly disappeared.

He saw before him a great walled enclosure roofed by a lofty azure dome, and beyond the walls, the tops of trees swaying in the soft breezes. His nostrils caught the incense of fresh earth and growing things. For the first time he felt the breath of nature, free and unconfined, upon his brow.

He drew his giant frame to its full height and drank in the freedom and the sweetness, filling his great lungs to their fullest; and with the first draft he learned to hate the close and stuffy confines of his prison.

His virgin mind was filled with wonder at the wealth of new impressions that surged to his brain through every sense. He longed for more, and the open gateway of the *kampong* was a scarce-needed invitation to pass to the wide world beyond.

With the free and easy tread of utter unconsciousness of self, he passed across the enclosure and stepped out into the clearing that lay between the palisade and the jungle.

Here was a still more beautiful world!

The green leaves nodded to him, and at their invitation he came, and the jungle reached out its million arms to embrace him. Now, before him, behind, on either side, there was naught but green beauty shot with splashes of gorgeous color that made him gasp in wonderment.

Brilliant birds rose from amidst it all, skimming hither and thither above his head. He thought that the flowers and the birds were the same, and when he reached out and plucked a blossom tenderly he wondered that it did not flutter in his hand.

On and on he walked, but slowly, for he must not miss a single sight in the strange and wonderful place.

Then, of a sudden, the quiet beauty of the scene was harshly broken by the crashing of a monster through the underbrush.

Number Thirteen was standing in a little open place in the jungle when the discordant note first fell upon his ears, and as he turned his head in the direction of the sound, he was startled at the hideous aspect of the thing which broke through the foliage before him.

What a creature!

But on the same instant, his eyes fell upon another borne in the arms of the terrible one.

This one was different—very different—soft and beautiful and white. He wondered what it all meant, for everything was strange and new to him; but when he saw the eyes of the lovely one upon him, and her arms outstretched toward him, though he did not understand the words upon her lips, he knew that she was in distress.

Something told him that it was the ugly thing that carried her that was the author of her suffering.

Virginia Maxon had been half unconscious from fright when she suddenly saw a white man, clothed in coarse, white, native pajamas, confronting her and the misshapen beast that was bearing her away to what frightful fate she could but conjecture.

At the sight of the man, her voice returned with returning hope, and she reached her arms toward him, calling upon him to save her.

Though he did not respond, she thought that he understood, for he sprang toward them before her appeal was scarce uttered.

As before, when Sing had threatened to filch his new possession from him, Number One held the girl with one hand while he met the attack of this new assailant with the other; but here was different metal than had given way to him before.

It is true that Number Thirteen knew nothing whatever of personal combat, but Number One had but little advantage of him in the matter of experience, while the former was equipped with great natural intelligence as well as steel muscles no whit less powerful than his deformed predecessor.

So it was that the awful giant found his single hand helpless to cope with the strength of his foeman, and in a brief instant felt powerful fingers clutching at this throat.

Still reluctant to surrender his hold upon his prize, he beat futilely at the face of his enemy, but at last the agony of choking compelled him to drop the girl and grapple madly with the man who choked him with one hand and rained mighty and merciless blows upon his face and head with the other.

His captive sank to the ground, too weak from the effects of nervous shock to escape, and with horror-filled eyes watched the two who battled over her.

She saw that her would-be rescuer was young and strong-featured—altogether a very fine specimen of manhood. To her great wonder, it was soon apparent that he was no unequal match for the mountain of muscle he fought.

Both tore and struck and clawed and bit in the frenzy of mad, untutored strife, rolling about on the soft carpet of the jungle almost noiselessly except for their heavy breathing and an occasional beast-like snarl from Number One.

For several minutes they fought thus, till the younger man succeeded in getting both hands upon the throat of his adversary, and then, choking relentlessly, he raised the brute with him from the ground and rushed him fiercely backward against the stem of a tree.

Again and again he hurled the monstrous thing upon the unyielding wood, until at last it hung helpless and inert in his clutches, then he cast it from him, and without another glance at it turned toward the girl.

Here was a problem indeed. Now that he had won her, what was he to do with her? He was but an adult child, with the brain and brawn of a man, and the ignorance and inexperience of the new-born.

So he acted as a child acts, in imitation of what it has seen others do. The brute had been carrying the lovely creature; therefore, that must be the thing for him to do, and so he stooped and gathered Virginia Maxon in his great arms.

She tried to tell him that she could walk after a moment's rest, but it was soon evident that he did not understand her, as a puzzled expression came to his face and he did not put her down as she asked.

Instead, he stood irresolute for a time, and then moved slowly through the jungle. By chance his direction was toward the camp, and this fact greatly relieved the girl's mind.

After a moment she gained courage to look up into his face. She thought that she never had seen so marvelously clean-cut features, or a more high and noble countenance, and she wondered how it was that this white man was upon the island and she not have known it.

Possibly he was a new arrival—his presence unguessed even by her father. That he was neither English nor American was evident from the fact that he could not understand her native tongue. Who could he be? What was he doing upon their island?

As she watched his face, he suddenly turned his eyes down upon her, and as she looked hurriedly away she was furious with herself as she felt a crimson flush mantle her cheek. The man only half sensed, in a vague sort of way, the meaning of the tell-tale color and the quickly averted eyes; but he became suddenly aware of the pressure of her delicate body against his, as he had not been before.

Now he kept his eyes upon her face as he walked, and a new emotion filled his breast. He did not understand it, but it was very pleasant, and he knew that it was because of the radiant thing that he carried in his arms.

The scream that had startled Von Horn and Professor Maxon led them along the trail toward the east coast of the island, and about half way of the distance they stumbled upon the dazed and bloody Sing just as he was on the point of regaining consciousness.

"For God's sake, Sing, what is the matter?" cried Von Horn. "Where is Miss Maxon?"

"Big blute, he catchem Linee. Tly kill Sing. Wakee up—all glone," moaned the Chinaman as he tried to gain his feet.

"Which way did he take her?" urged Von Horn.

Sing's quick eyes scanned the surrounding jungle, and in a moment, staggering to his feet, he cried: "Look, see klick! Footplint!" and ran, weak and reeling, along the broad trail made by the giant creature and its prey.

Von Horn and Professor Maxon followed closely in Sing's wake; the younger man, horrified by the terrible possibilities that obtruded themselves into his imagination despite his every effort to assure himself that no harm could come to Virginia Maxon before they reached her.

The girl's father had not spoken since they discovered that she was missing from the *kampong,* but his face was white and drawn; his eyes wide and glassy as those of one whose mind is on the verge of madness from a great nervous shock.

The trail of the creature was bewilderingly erratic. A dozen paces straight through the underbrush, then a sharp turn at right angles for no apparent reason, only to veer again suddenly in a new direction. Thus, turning and twisting, the tortuous way led them toward the south end of the island, until Sing, who was in advance, gave a sharp cry of surprise.

"Klick! Look see!" he cried excitedly. "Blig blute dead—vely muchee dead."

Von Horn rushed forward to where the Chinaman was leaning over the body of Number One. Sure enough, the great brute lay motionless, its horrid face even more hideous in death than in life, if it were possible. The face was black, the tongue protruded, the skin was bruised from the heavy fists of his assailant and the thick skull crushed and splintered from terrific impact with the tree.

Professor Maxon leaned over Von Horn's shoulder.

"Ah, poor Number One," he sighed, "that you should have come to such an untimely end—my child, my child."

Von Horn looked at him, a tinge of compassion in his rather hard face. It touched the man that his employer was at last shocked from the obsession of his work to a realization of the love and duty he owed his daughter—he thought that the professor's last words referred to Virginia.

"Though there are twelve more," continued Professor Maxon, "you were my first-born son and I loved you most, dear child."

The younger man was horrified.

"Are you mad, professor?" he cried. "Can you call this thing 'child' and mourn over it when you do not yet know the fate of your own daughter?"

Professor Maxon looked up sadly.

"You do not understand, Dr. von Horn," he replied coldly. "You will oblige me, in the future, by not again referring to the offspring of my labors as 'things.'"

With an ugly look, Von Horn turned his back upon the older man—what little feeling of loyalty and affection he had ever felt for him gone.

Sing was looking about for evidences of the cause of Number One's death and the probable direction in which Virginia Maxon had disappeared.

"What on earth could have killed this enormous brute, Sing? Have you any idea?" asked Von Horn.

The Chinaman shook his head.

"No savvy," he replied. "Blig flight. Look see!"

He pointed to the torn and trampled turf, the broken bushes, and to one or two small trees that had been snapped off by the impact of the two mighty bodies that had struggled about the little clearing.

"This way," cried Sing presently, and started off once more into the brush, but this time in a northwesterly direction, toward camp.

In silence the three men followed the new trail, all puzzled beyond measure to account for the death of Number One at the hands of what must have been a creature of superhuman strength.

What could it have been? It was impossible that any of the Malays or lascars could have done the thing, and there were no other creatures, brute or human, upon the island large enough to have coped even for an instant with the ferocious brutality of the dead monster, except—

Von Horn's brain came to a sudden halt at the thought. Could it be? There seemed no other explanation. Virginia Maxon had been rescued from one soulless monstrosity to fall into the hands of another equally irresponsible and terrifying.

Others, then, must have escaped from the *kampong*. Von Horn loosened his guns in their holsters, and took a fresh grip upon his bull-whip as he urged

Sing forward upon the trail. He wondered which one it might be, but not once did it occur to him that the latest result of Professor Maxon's experiments could be the rescuer of Virginia. In his mind he could see only the repulsive features of one of the others.

Quite unexpectedly, they came upon the two, and with a shout, Von Horn leaped forward, his bull-whip upraised.

Number Thirteen turned in surprise at the cry, and sensing a new danger for her who lay in his arms, he set her gently upon the ground and advanced to meet the German.

"Out of the way, you monstrosity!" cried Von Horn. "If you have harmed Miss Maxon, I'll put a bullet in your heart, so help me!"

Number Thirteen did not understand the words that the other addressed to him, but he interpreted the man's actions as menacing, not to himself, but to the creature he now considered his particular charge, and so he met the advancing man, more to keep him from the girl than to offer him bodily injury, for he recognized him as one of the two who had greeted his first dawning consciousness.

Von Horn, possibly intentionally, misinterpreted the other's motive, and raising his bull-whip, struck Number Thirteen a vicious cut across the face, at the same time leveling his revolver point blank at the broad breast. But before ever he could pull the trigger, an avalanche of muscle was upon him, and he went down with five fingers at his throat.

His revolver exploded harmlessly in the air, and then another hand wrenched it from him and hurled it far into the underbrush. Number Thirteen knew nothing of the danger of firearms, but the noise had startled him and his experience with the stinging cut of the bull-whip convinced him that this other was some sort of instrument of torture of which it would be as well to deprive his antagonist.

Virginia Maxon looked on in horror as she realized that her rescuer was quickly choking Dr. Von Horn to death. With a little cry she sprang to her feet and ran toward them just as her father emerged from the underbrush through which he had been struggling in the trail of the agile Chinaman and the young German.

Placing her hand upon the great wrist of the giant, she tried to drag his fingers from Von Horn's throat, pleading meanwhile with both voice and eyes for the life of the man she thought loved her.

Again Number Thirteen translated the intent without understanding the words, and releasing Von Horn, permitted him to rise. With a bound, the German was upon his feet and at the same instant brought his other gun from his side and leveled it upon the man who had released him; but as his finger tightened upon the trigger, Virginia Maxon sprang between them, and grasping Von Horn's wrist, deflected the muzzle of the gun just as the cartridge exploded.

Simultaneously Professor Maxon sprang upon his assistant like a madman, wrenching the revolver from his grasp and hurling him back with the superhuman strength of a maniac.

"Fool!" he cried. "What would you do? Kill—"

Then, of a sudden, he realized his daughter's presence and the necessity for keeping the origin of the young giant from her knowledge.

"I am surprised at you, Dr. von Horn," he continued in a more level voice. "You must indeed have forgotten yourself to thus attack a stranger upon our island until you know whether he be friend or foe. Come! Escort my daughter to the camp while I make the proper apologies to this gentleman." As he saw that both Virginia and Von Horn hesitated, he repeated his command, adding: "Quick, now; do as I bid you."

The moment had given Von Horn an opportunity to regain his self-control, and realizing as well as did his employer, but from another motive, the necessity of keeping the truth from the girl, he took her arm and led her gently from the scene.

Now, in Number Thirteen's brief career, he had known no other authority than Professor Maxon's, and so it was that, when his master laid a hand upon his wrist, he remained beside him while another walked away with the lovely creature he had thought his very own.

Until after dark, the professor kept the young man hidden in the jungle, and then, safe from detection, led him back to the laboratory.

On their return to camp after her rescue, Virginia talked a great deal to Von Horn about the young giant who had rescued her, until the German feared that she was more interested in him than seemed good for his own plans.

He had now cast from him the last vestige of his loyalty for his employer, and thus freed, had determined to use every means within his power to win Professor Maxon's daughter, and with her the heritage of wealth which he knew would be hers should her father, through some unforeseen mishap, meet death before he could return to civilization and alter his will, a contingency which Von Horn knew he might have to consider should he marry the girl against her father's wishes, and thus thwart the crazed man's mad, but no less dear, project.

He realized that first he must let the girl fully understand the grave peril in which she stood, and turn her hope of protection from her father to himself. He imagined that the initial step in undermining Virginia's confidence in her father would be to narrate every detail of the weird experiments which Professor Maxon had brought to such successful issues during their residence upon the island.

The girl's own questioning gave him the lead he needed.

"Where could that horrid creature have come from that set upon me in the jungle and nearly killed poor Sing?" she asked.

For a moment Von Horn was silent, in well-simulated hesitancy to reply to her query.

"I cannot tell you, Miss Maxon," he said sadly, "how much I should hate to be the one to ignore your father's commands and enlighten you upon this and other subjects which lie nearer to your personal welfare than you can possibly guess. I feel, however, that after the horrors of the day, duty demands that I must lay all before you. You must not again be exposed to the horrors from which you were rescued only by a miracle."

"I cannot imagine what you hint at, Dr. von Horn," said Virginia, "but if to explain to me will necessitate betraying my father's confidence, I prefer that you remain silent."

"You do not understand," broke in the man. "You cannot guess the horrors that I have seen upon this island, or the worse horrors that are to come. Could you dream of what lies in store for you, you would seek death rather than face the future.

"I have been loyal to your father, Virginia; but were you not blind or indifferent, you would long since have seen that your welfare means more to me than my loyalty to him—more to me than my life or my honor.

"You asked where the creature came from that attacked you today. I shall tell you. It is one of a dozen similarly hideous things that your father has created in his mad desire to solve the problem of life. He has solved it; but at what a price in misshapen, soulless, hideous monsters!"

The girl looked up at him, horror-stricken.

"Do you mean to say that my father in a mad attempt to usurp the functions of God, created that awful thing?" she asked in a low, faint voice. "That there are others like it upon the island?"

"In the *kampong* next to yours, there are a dozen others," replied Von Horn, "nor would it be easy to say which is the most hideous and repulsive. They are grotesque caricatures of humanity—without soul and almost without brain."

The girl buried her face in her hands. "He has gone mad—he has gone mad," she cried.

"I truly believe that he is mad," said Von Horn, "nor could you doubt it for a moment were I to tell you the worst."

"The worst!" exclaimed the girl. "What could be worse than that which you already have divulged?"

"There is much worse than I have told you, Virginia. So much worse that I can scarce force my lips to frame the words, but you must be told. I would be more criminally liable than your father were I to keep it from you, for my brain, at least, is not crazed.

"Virginia, you have in your mind a picture of the hideous thing that carried you off into the jungle today?" he continued.

"Yes," and as the girl replied, a convulsive shudder racked her frame.

Von Horn grasped her arm gently as he went on, as though to support and protect her during the shock that he was about to administer.

"Virginia," he said in a very low voice, "it is your father's intention to wed you to one of his creatures."

The girl broke from him with an angry cry of disbelief.

"It is not true!" she exclaimed. "It is not true. Oh, Dr. von Horn, how could you tell me such a cruel and terrible untruth."

"As God is my judge, Virginia," and the man reverently uncovered as he spoke, "it is the truth. Your father told me it in so many words when I asked his permission to pay court to you. You are to marry Number Thirteen, when his education is complete."

"I shall die first!" she cried.

"Why not accept me instead?" suggested the man.

For a moment Virginia looked straight into his eyes, as though to read his inmost soul.

"Let me have time to consider it, doctor," she replied. "I do not know that I care for you in that way at all."

"Think of Number Thirteen. It should not be difficult to decide."

"I could not marry you simply to escape a worse fate," replied the girl. "I am not as cowardly as that—but let me think it over. There can be no immediate danger, I am sure."

"One can never tell," replied Von Horn, "what strange vagaries may enter a crazed mind to dictate the actions of this moment or the next."

"Where could we wed?" asked Virginia.

"The Ithaca would take us to Singapore, and when we returned, you would be under my legal protection and safe from the sad mental disorder of your father."

"I shall think about it from every angle," she answered sadly. "And now, good night, my dear friend." With a smile, she entered her quarters.

• • • • •

THE ORCHID HORROR

JOHN BLUNT

So the four of us, Helen Chadwick, Dufresne, who was our host, Loring and I, went into the conservatory. The argument, begun at dinner, as to whether the sensitive plant is responsive to the breath as well as to the touch, had to be settled. Dufresne, laughing, promised that we should soon see how wrong we were—how little we really knew.

The warm damp of the place was a trifle disagreeable to me. I would much rather have kept my seat at table, where the port and cigarettes were, than to have made one of this pseudo-scientific investigating party. But, idly drawn into the discussion at first, nothing would do save that I come along and have my chance-expressed opinions beaten to earth under the demonstrated truth of Dufresne's assertions.

He and the girl had paused near the door of the hothouse to admire a rhododendron in full bloom; I was loitering a little way behind them on the brick-paved walk—when it happened. Nothing more thoroughly unexpected could have been imagined. Loring, who had wandered a bit farther along, suddenly turned and came hurtling toward us, his jaw hanging, eyes a-bulge, the light of stark madness on his face!

I took a step forward.

"What, in the name—"

And then he was upon the two beside the pink-blossomed bush. Dufresne, knocked clean off his feet, with a stifled cry and a wild upflinging of his arms, sank from view in a whirlpool of swishing leaves into the foliage beside the path. Miss Chadwick, sent spinning to the opposite edge of the walk by a glancing blow from Loring's shoulder, staggered a moment, strove ineffectually to regain her balance by clutching at the nearby shrubbery, then toppled ungracefully to her knees in the moist loam.

"Loring!" I cried out. "In pity's name, man—"

Sidestepping quickly, I reached out and tried to hold him. As well try to detain a runaway express-train. My grip on his shoulder was off in a twinkling, and on he plowed, with huge, swift strides toward the conservatory door.

Another moment and he had gone.

Dazed, I stared at the aperture through which he had fled. Behind me I heard fat Dufresne struggling to get out of the branches into which he had fallen, vaguely gathered that he had at last extricated himself and approached the girl, inquiring with wheezing solicitude as to her state.

Loring was sane when he came into the greenhouse. Sane up to thirty seconds ago. And then—mad.

"What in the world—"

Then I came to myself with a start. Loring was my friend. I had brought him to this house tonight. In a way, I was responsible for his actions. Curse the fellow! Yet he hadn't cut up as he had because he wanted to be eccentric. Something had happened to him. Something back there along the walk had given him a bad scare. Something terrifying enough to unbalance his reason.

Great Heaven, he was at large now in the crowded drawing rooms beyond! What might he not be up to? I was his friend, accountable to my host and hostess.

Swiftly I turned and went out of the door. No trace of him, or of any freakish action of which he might have been guilty appearing among the gay party in the ground-floor rooms, I mounted the stairs to the chamber set apart for the men's hats and coats, and there found Loring's things. Evidently he had not left the house.

"Beg pardon, sir!" the servant at the front door met me at the foot of the stairway. "The gentleman who came in with you this evening, sir. I thought I ought to say something to you. Left without a thing on his head, just the way you are now, Mr. Murdock, not ten minutes ago. First I thought he was going after something he'd left behind in the motor you came in. But he ain't come back. I thought—"

I had run upstairs, got into my overcoat and hat, and was descending the steps of the stoop in another two minutes. The fellow *was* mad! Whatever had upset him in the conservatory had driven him in a panic of fright from the very house itself, bare-headed, coatless.

I was frightfully worried. Unconsciously, my steps were taking me in the direction of our club, where, I suppose, I had an unformed idea he might have run. As I entered the place, the first man I saw was—Loring!

He sat at a table nearest the open door of the café. His dress-coat had been exchanged for a dinner-jacket; there was something liquid in a glass before him. I crossed to his side. He did not look up. To all outward appearance, he was as cool and collected as ever I had seen him.

"Well?"

I let a pent breath escape me and dropped into the opposite chair. I stared, speechless, at the man. And what a man he was! Six feet three, huge in proportion, with a bronze-skinned, smooth-shaven face. A man to look at with an involuntary straightening of the shoulders, inflation of the chest and general attempt at "bigening"—if I may coin the word—in instinctive imitation of his splendid physique. Indeed, a man!

And he had been thrown into a paroxysm of fear so great that heedlessly he had knocked down his host of the evening and a frail woman, then bolted from the house to flee through the streets without stopping for proper covering, temporarily a lunatic through excessive fright—*this* near-giant, as badly scared as that?

"Well?" I repeated eagerly after him. "What's it all about?"

He said nothing.

"Don't you mean to talk?" I blurted, amazed. "Am I entitled to an explanation—or not?"

His eyes had not yet met mine.

"Can't you see," he said through his set teeth, "that I've had a shock, and a bad one? I'm trying to hold myself together. It isn't easy. I'd be obliged to you if you wouldn't ask questions. Not just now, anyway."

I sat back, gnawing my mustache. Could any but a strong man have held himself even thus well in check after the way he had gone to pieces not a half-hour before? Yet, if he was strong-willed enough for that, what could have shaken him so completely at Dufresne's house? Curiosity such as mine could not be concealed under even the wettest blanket.

"Will you tell me this?" I said after a while. "What threw you into such a funk?"

In silence he tore the bar check between his fingers into tiny bits.

"You didn't see a reptile in the greenhouse?" I hazarded. "There wasn't a tarantula hidden on some transplanted bush? Nothing like that?"

He gave a scornfully negative gesture.

"Well, what the deuce was it?" I rapped out. "Dufresne, the girl and myself were the only living human beings besides yourself in the place. We didn't do anything to alarm you, surely. Did you go stark, staring mad on account of the silly flowers themselves?"

At last he looked full at me.

"What would you say," he almost whispered in his intensity, "if I told you it was the flowers? A little cluster of exotic plants that you didn't see in the far corner of the room, and that I didn't see either, but that I smelled? That those drove me clear out of my mind for a minute and more—eh?"

He leaned back.

"What would you say?" he went on. "You'd have nothing to say, because you don't understand. You don't know the past. It won't make pleasant telling, I promise you. But you must know. Very well. Listen to me.

"Nine years ago I sat in this very club. Thirty at the time, I had realized every ambition in life but one. I had money, plenty of it, all earned by myself. Thirty, you understand, and with a fortune means hard work. I had worked hard. Harder than most men ever do, I guess; but I was built for doing hard things.

"The one attainment I lacked was a wife. No woman so far had pleased me. If that sounds egotistical, remember that my financial success had convinced me that I was the sort of a man capable of entertaining for a woman that thing known as a 'grand passion'; that I must pick and choose the girl upon whom to lavish a powerful love with care. Hence I had been waiting all these years, waiting for the one woman.

"But I was tired of waiting. And that night a man came and sat in the next lounge chair to mine in the billiard room and gave me hope that perhaps my waiting was over. A queer-looking individual he was. A new member of the club, I believe. A corpse was what he would have reminded you of; his yellow skin was drawn tight over his cheekbones; there was far too little flesh on his limbs to make him an attractive figure to contemplate; and his eyes—I don't like to think of those burned holes in a sheepskin even now.

"His talk was full of a wonderful collection of exotic plants he had seen in a house near Washington Square. To my monosyllables of polite interest, he brought forth an invitation to visit the place and look at the collection. I protested myself ignorant in such matters. That made no difference, said he; I would enjoy seeing this botanical display, he was sure. Besides, the collector had a daughter. I would surely like to see *her*.

"And then, for a solid hour, the emaciated stranger poured into my ear a description of a woman such as no one ever listened to, I'll take oath upon, since the world began. Impassioned, inspired of his theme, he set my brain on fire with the picture of his friend, the daughter of the floramaniac.

"I jumped to my feet.

"'Take me there!' I exclaimed. 'I want to see—these wonderful plants.'

"We went straight to the house, a large brownstone dwelling of the old-fashioned type. The conservatory was in the rear of the building. My breath caught in my throat as I entered the heated room. Orchids, nothing but orchids, thousands, tens of thousands of the flowing, multi-shaded flowers, hung from the walls and ceiling of the place. Having seen nobody but the servant at the door, my corpse-like acquaintance told me that doubtless the collector was too busy at the moment to welcome me; however, he assured me that it was all right; I might stay as long as I chose; then he left me.

"As I stood gazing around the room, I felt my senses swaying within me in time to the languorous nodding of the rows upon rows of trailing blossoms everywhere in view. What was this feeling? I looked down at my outstretched hand. Steady as a rock. Yet all inside my arm, the nerves, the tissue, the blood, the muscle, were in motion, in swaying motion.

"How long I stood entranced, deliciously thrilled by that movement within me which the rhythmical moving of the flowers inspired, I cannot say. Perhaps it was five, ten minutes—perhaps an hour, two—that I stood spellbound, hypnotized, incapable of any other sensation but that one of inner motion. And then—

"Before my eyes the rows of orchids bent apart. Slowly, with exquisite grace, it was like the waving open of a lane in a wheat field caused by the wind. Yet there was no wind, not the faintest breeze, in the room. Wider became the opening of that aisle in the blossoms' close ranks. Suddenly, at its end, I saw— the collector's daughter!

"How the man who had brought me here had lied! She was a million times more perfect than he had pictured her. Beautiful—she transcended beauty. A tall woman, lithe, well-rounded as to figure, black-haired and with eyes and lips which were the only 'remembrable' feature of her face for me at the moment, I felt love at first sight—a stirring of my grand passion at last!—at my first glimpse of her, this goddess of the orchids.

"Slowly, with the languid grace of the swaying flowers, she advanced toward me through the lane they had made, as though by her royal command. She put out her hand. I took it in mine. The words I would have said to explain my presence there did not pass my lips. What use were words—between us? Eye to eye, hand clasped in hand, it was as if all the words in the world had already been spoken to perform our introduction.

"After a while we talked. What of is no matter. Hours later I left the house—alone. The next afternoon I returned. The day following found me there as well. The days sped into weeks, the weeks into a month, and we were engaged. I did not declare my love. I had no need to do so. It was plain without speech—as was her regard for me.

"'When will you marry me, my Goddess of the Orchids?' I whispered.

"At first she hesitated. She could not leave her father; he was very old; she was all he had, and he would be unhappy without her. I remarked that his unhappiness could not be of long standing, surely, if she came with me, since he had never manifested enough interest in her welfare even to see me from the first time I came into the house.

"'You do not understand,' she told me gently. 'My father's way is strange, perhaps, but he loves me. Next to his flowers, I come only second in his heart. If he lost me, he would grieve. I cannot cause him pain. There is only one way—'

"She stopped.

"'What is the one way?' I asked.

"'There's an orchid,' said she, 'that he would give his life to possess if he could. So rare is it that not one has ever been seen by a white man; only rumors of its existence have come through the natives in the region of its growth. If my father could own one of that rare species, a single specimen—well, don't you see that he would be so happy, so completely absorbed in its possession, that he would not mind the shock of giving me up—not till long after you had brought the *Cattleya Trixsemptia* back and we were married, at all events.'

"'I am to bring him this orchid, am I?' I smiled.

"'You love me?' she asked, anxiously.

"We were sitting on the ledge of a splashing fountain in the center of the conservatory. I rose and took her hands.

"'You shall see,' I said. 'Tell me where this flower grows. I will get it. Not till I have proved my love for you will I look into your eyes again.'

"We parted. That night I made one at a dinner given in honor of a celebrated Englishman who was a professional orchid-hunter. Bound for South America next day, to the section of the country, indeed, near which I had been told the plant I sought was to be found, I decided that I would be in luck if I could persuade this experienced traveler to let me accompany him into that strange land. Of course, after we arrived in Venezuela, our ways would part; he was after a type of orchid different from the species I desired, and, in hunting his quarry, he would go along one route inland, I another.

"He was sincerely glad of my offer to join him. I explained that I wanted to go on an orchid hunt 'just for the adventure.' Next morning we took a steamer together; in a week had reached South America, and then—a queer thing fell out.

"An Indian came to the Englishman with word of an orchid field that lay behind the Orinoco. It was the same spot toward which I had been directed to go. According to the native's story, it was perilous work getting to the place, and would take at least a month of the hardest kind of journeying. But the orchids there were very fine, very rare. If the professional cared to make the attempt—

"'Look here,' said he to me, 'I'm going to have a try for some of those flowers.'

"Here was a second stroke of luck. Since there was an entire field of these plants, I could come out with the truth at last, that this, I felt certain, was the species of orchid I was hunting on my own hook. There was no longer any danger that the Englishman would hunt the same flower that I wanted if he knew my purpose, and perhaps be lucky enough to 'nose me out' in the search. Plainly, there were enough orchids of this description for all. So, together with this expert huntsman, I could journey to the spot with much less difficulty than alone.

"'But I won't take you with me,' he went on. 'You heard what his nibs, the native chief, said just now. The trip's mighty dangerous. You couldn't stand it. Sorry, old man, but you've got to be left out of this.'

"'Just the same,' I informed him, 'I'm coming.' And I told him the business that had brought me from home. 'That's all—I'm coming,' I added.

"'No, you aren't,' said he firmly. 'That's all right about your hunting this kind of an orchid. Don't know where you ever heard of it, or what put the notion of finding one into your head. But you've got to give it up. You don't know what you're about. A green hand at the business, and take a journey like this—man, you'd die!'

"'Will you?' I asked.

"'That I can't say,' and he shrugged his shoulders. 'I'll stand a better chance of getting to the place than you, though. I'm inured, rather, to this sort of thing. Though I don't mind saying that I'd rather not go on this particular journey. From maps and hearsay of the trail it's going to be a little bit of a crosscut through Hades.'

"'Then why go?' I pursued.

"'There's an incentive in my case. A group of collectors is behind me, money coffers open to pay a prize for whatever I get. My reason's clear. But, blame me if I can see yours in wanting to come along with me so headstrong and keen.'

"This time I shrugged.

"'Oh,' said he, 'so it's a girl? Been thrown over by some woman, have you, and want to go into danger to forget?'

"'On the contrary,' and I smiled. 'I'm doing it to please the girl I've won.'

"'Good Lord!' he blurted out, gaping at me. 'Good Lord—you mean to tell me a girl, a girl who cares about you, has let you come down here to hunt a trophy in the spot you want to go? Does she know anything about the way orchids are found? Oh, her father's a collector? Then she does know.'

"He continued to stare at me.

"'Look here, Loring,' he said suddenly. 'Don't mind if I ask you a question. But weren't you introduced to the lady of your choice by a rack-boned skeleton of a man with a yellow skin, deep-burning eyes—sort of an upheaval-from-the-crypt sort of chap?'

"'Yes,' I exclaimed, my eyes widening.

"'I thought so,' he said. And after a moment: 'I see,' he added. 'The same old game. I know the woman who sent you down here. Everybody in the orchid-collecting business knows her, more or less. She's a plant fiend. Same sort of mania as attacks people by way of drugs, the drink, and so on, you know. Seen her collection? It's the finest in the world; pretty nearly every orchid known is there. Shall I tell you how she got them?' He leaned toward me. 'Through just such fools as you, Loring.'

"I stumbled to my feet, furious.

"'Steady on!' he cried. 'Hear me out! I want to do you a friendly turn, old fellow; upon my soul, I do. Listen. That woman, I tell you, is a fiend. We all know her well. See if this isn't the way she's hoodwinked you. Told you, didn't she, that her father would never be happy if she married and left him; that just one thing might be counted on to take his mind off losing her—a certain rare orchid? Anyway, that's what she's told other men time and again. All of them have started out to bring her the plant, too. Some succeeded. And the reward? She laughs at them, and then tells the truth. There is no doting father. The orchid she wanted for herself. It's all she cares for—orchids. Men are nothing. Orchids—they cost men—she wants orchids.

"'That's the fate of the men who succeed. But those who fail? Loring, the bones of a dozen, a score of the men who have tried to perform her mission lie bleaching now in the swamps and along the roots of jungle-trees the world over. Only one man failed to bring back the orchid for which he was sent and still lives. Do you know who he is? The man who brought you and the orchid queen together!

"'You remember his looks. She put that brand on him down this very way three years ago. Since then he's been trying to win her in the only way that seems possible—through her passion for the flowers. Men like you, big and strong, he seeks out, brings to her so that she can send them forth to complete her collection. When she has a specimen of every orchid ever known, he hopes that she will marry him. That's the living, disgusting truth, old man, as I breathe here before you.

"'Believe me, you're designed for a victim like all the rest. I'm telling you the truth. And I'm warning you to turn back before it's too late. Will you take my word—will you go home?'

"'No!' I roared. 'You lying hound—'

"I think I meant to kill him then with my own two hands. But suddenly, reason came to my aid. Evidently it was going to be no easy matter for an untoughened white man to penetrate alone to the spot where the orchids I was after were to be found; I must bring what I had vowed I would back to my affianced. With this man's aid, I might better be able to do so. What if he had dared to traduce the woman who was to be my wife? I could gloss even that over for the time, for the sake of getting what I sought. Afterward, the lies he had told me—the lies built up on some rumor of the girl's existence which he had come upon, and retailed to me for the purpose of causing me to abandon the field, with the glory of being first to find a new plant to him—I could cram these down his throat with my fists.

"'I beg your pardon,' I said, appearing to be cool. 'You'll have to overlook what I've just said. I'm a good deal upset over what you've told me. I—I've no doubt you mean to be decent to me.'

"'And you'll quit this idea of hunting the orchid?' he asked eagerly.

"'No,' I replied, and the sneer with which I glanced him over must have been plain. 'I'm going with you.'

"His face reddened.

"'As you like,' he said curtly.

"Followed a week of busiest activity. Our outfit was purchased, porters hired, guides engaged. At length, when everything was in readiness, we assembled, a small army with enough supplies for quite that body to start the march into the solitude. One month it took us to reach the head of the Orinoco. Then began the real hardships of the journey into the unbroken jungle.

"No such strain could be imagined as was put upon our party in the next fortnight. A bare chronicle of the events that befell us would not convey a tithe of what the suffering really meant. Menaced by reptiles, crawling creatures of every revolting description; attacked by the wild men of that forest region with their deadly blowguns; racked by swamp fevers, and always pressing on—on into the unknown—in a silence that daily grew more and more oppressive—the memory of that trip will be with me always in its harrowing details.

"And now our chief guide died. Before him had dropped off a third of our original number of porters and choppers. Without the leadership of the native, who knew the general direction in which lay the orchids, we were helpless. A party of Indians were encountered three days later, and, in response to our questions, they waved their hands toward the sun as the course we must follow before the 'poison plants' were in reach.

"And in another week a perceptible odor was in the air; an odor which the Englishman said meant that we were nearing the orchids. Each day, as we progressed, this odor became more clearly defined. Finally it was distinctly unpleasant, then disagreeable, lastly uncomfortable. Another day and the scent grew positively menacing. Each breath one drew into the lungs seemed charged with fumes of a poisonous, sickish-sweet drug. Five porters fell senseless on the fifth day as we drew nearer to the source of the noxious aroma.

"And yet, the orchids were not yet in sight, seemingly no nearer than when we started. Another day, and the odor in the air was insupportable. The natives refused to go farther. My white companion, the professional hunter, lay senseless in his tracks. I was near swooning myself. With the wind in our faces, blowing that poison off the orchid field somewhere in advance of us, it was useless to think of keeping on any further.

"Then, and then only, did I believe the truth of what I had heard of the woman who had sent me on this wild-goose chase. Indeed, she must have known something of the perils into which I had gone at her bidding. And she had let me go. I was to have been another victim.

"I cursed her to high heaven, there in the middle of that black, silent forest, with the spirals of the invisible poison odor coiling around me in the air. And I swore that I would have revenge—the revenge of bringing her what she had driven me out to get!

"Alone, I essayed one final dash forward in the endeavor to reach the flowers which seemed so near, yet were ever so far from my touch. Surely, we could not have halted many miles distant from the field. Perhaps by running, with body bent close to the ground—but it was useless. The wind brought the deadly fumes full in my face, cramming them down throat and nostrils. Reeling, half dead, I returned to the others.

"At once we began the homeward march. More than half our corps were dead by the time we had progressed a quarter way back along our trail. Halfway to the coast, and only a miserable handful of our original party remained. How those of us who survived managed to do so is a mystery. But at last, four shattered ghosts of human beings, two Indian porters, the Englishman, and myself, returned to the civilization of Venezuela.

"But I was not through. A month's rest, and I was trying to organize another party to start back toward our abandoned goal. Not in the same way we had gone before. I had worked out a plan. By approaching that unseen field of orchids from the opposite side, the wind blowing the other way, a chance might hold good that the flowers could be reached by circumventing the full effect of the poisoned perfume.

"No one would attempt the journey with me. The Englishman was finished—forever, he said, with all orchid-hunting. His motive was now not so strong as mine, I thought with a smile. Money could not tempt him to keep up the search for the *Cattleyea Trixsemptia*. My revenge, though, kept me in full enthusiasm for the hunt; it was all I thought of, waking or sleeping.

"When I was satisfied that nobody would accompany me, I set back toward the head of the Orinoco myself, alone. This time, traveling swiftly because lightly burdened and unaccompanied by any laggards, I made the edge of the jungle in a little over two weeks. The plunge through the forest, however, took longer alone than when I had expert choppers to clear a trail before me. But I made progress somehow.

"Often as I fought my way through the tangle of rank underbrush, waist-high and almost inextricable, I muttered aloud: 'So they picked you for a strong man, eh? A strong, robust man? A good one to send on a difficult mission, yes. Well, I'll show them yet—I'll bring back that flower!'

"And—how I do not know—I reached the orchid field at last! For two days previously, the same old noxious odor had been in the air, but not nearly so perceptibly as before, because I had figured well in keeping the wind in my back. Inside an hour, all the gathering force of the perfume which had turned our party back on the first attempt was compressed; dizzy, almost stupefied, drugged into partially insensibility, I parted the leaves in the foliage before me—and gazed upon the end of my journey!

"There were the flowers—blue, blue orchids! The only ones ever looked upon by white man's eyes. A thrill ran through me; almost I had the feeling then of the collector, the scientist in untrod fields, the primal discoverer of the miraculous.

"And then—drowsiness, languid heaviness, an overwhelming desire to cast myself down to sleep then and there, came to replace the momentary feeling of elation. I must pick my blossom, and be quick. The fumes of those waving, ultramarine flowers before my eyes were stealing over me more powerfully than ever before. Quick! I must be quick!

"I advanced. Step by step I drew near the largest cluster of the nodding, swaying, poisoned cups of light, dark, dappled blue. Another dozen paces forward. My sensations were those of the opium smoker yielding himself gradually to the influence of the drug, yet withholding full surrender to prolong the delicious agony of complete capitulation. Could I reach an orchid, pluck it, get away, before—before it was—too late—

"Heavens, I must fly! I could not hold out against that overpowering odor. I wheeled drunkenly. Blindly I lurched forward. Something swept my face. My eyes flew open—it was a cluster of orchids behind me that had been drawn across my cheek. With a scream of fright, I bounded sidewise, tripped over a vine, fell—

"And for that interval I knew no more.

"When I awoke it was to find that the breeze which blew over the tiny clearing where the poison plants were had shifted. Their perfume was no longer in the air. I staggered up. My head ached and my eyeballs burned. What had I been doing lying there on the ground?

"It came back to me. I had been overcome by the odor of the flowers. Only for the changing of the wind, preventing more of the fumes entering my lungs as I slept that drugged sleep—I shook myself together. Now was my chance to get away.

"Not for any price on earth would I have sought once again to pluck one of those blossoms so near to me. My plan of revenge against the woman who had sent me into this Gehenna was completely driven out of my head. Now—while I yet could—was my chance to get away. Facing about, I started running.

"On and on I sped. Gradually, though, my speed was diminishing. Not from weariness, not from fatigue. Something else. I slackened to a walk. I stopped short in my tracks. Turning about, I sniffed the air. No trace of that odor—no trace—

"Wildly I dashed back toward the clearing and its orchids. *I must have that scent in my nostrils again!* I must go to sleep under its spell once more. I could no more resist the impulse that brought me back toward the poisonous blossoms than I could voluntarily stop breathing. I burst into the clearing. On tiptoe, I reached up to the nearest cluster of the blue buds, drank deep of the awful, sickish odor—once—twice—

"In my tracks I fell, overcome, a smile on my lips.

"I ought never to have walked again, I know. Yet I did. How, long after it was, I have no means of telling. It was still daylight—or was it another day? I was heavy, sluggish, deeply depressed. I felt suddenly so frightened there alone in that clearing with those hideous, mocking plants swaying around me, that I hurled myself upon the ground, screaming, beating the moss with my hands and feet, frantic with fear of my loneliness, my dreadful plight.

"Then that feeling passed. I would get out of here. I would break and run now, and never stop running till I had put the length and breadth of the jungle between me and those ghastly plants. I sprang up. With a wild yell—a sort of farewell to the fearful spot—I leaped away into the neighboring forest.

"This time I did run until I was physically exhausted. I dropped down on a fallen, moss-hung log to gather breath. An hour or more I sat there. And when I rose—it was to hobble off in the direction of the *Cattleyea Trixsemptia* again, the lustful light in my eyes of the opium fiend returning to his den, the drunkard to his dive!

"I was caught. Useless to try to break away from the spell now. That poisonous perfume of the blue orchids had enchained me to the spot forever. I spent the next interval of time—three days, as near as I could judge—in the heart of the clearing, drugging myself with the scent of the flowers, waking, drugging myself again.

"Why didn't I die? I prayed for death, a release from my agonizing dilemma. Weak, now, to the point of prostration, yet I continued to live. I knew that I had wasted away to a mere skeleton of skin and bones—by no effort could I make my lips meet over my teeth—that I was emaciated by lack of food as well as the injurious effects of the poison I was inhaling, to the point almost of bloodlessness in all my veins—and yet I lived on.

"What was to be the end? I felt only a curiosity as to this, so it be soon. Another day went by. I was weaker now. Sixteen hours of the twenty-four, at a guess, had been spent in drugged sleep on my back in the middle of the clearing.

"With glazed eyes I looked around me. And looked again.

"Was I mad at last?

"There, before my eyes, stood my Goddess of the Orchids—she who had brought me to this plight!

"Slowly she approached across the noiseless moss. She stretched out her hand. I tottered to my feet. The claw at the end of my broomstick arm went out, encountered her fingers—*real flesh and blood!*

"'Drink this,' she whispered in my ear.

"A flask was held to my chattering teeth. Something scalding hot ran down my parched throat.

"'Now, lean on me,'—again her voice, wondrous soft.

"And slowly, carefully she began to lead me out of the clearing, through the jungle. A little way and we met her train of porters and guides. While a rough litter was being made for me, I sat upon the ground, leaning against her knees as she stood. Strangely, now that I was with this party, I felt no craving for the drugged breath of the blue orchid to which I had been the slave.

"The journey back to the coast I do not remember. Something of my days of convalescence in Venezuela, though, I can recall. There it was that I heard the story of her search for me from the woman who had saved my life.

"Her passion for orchids was really so powerful that she had served men very much as the Englishmen had told me for years. I was to have been treated no better nor worse than the rest. Only me—of all the others—she really loved. After she had sent me forth on her mission, she recalled the fate of so many of her suitors who had gone into the wildernesses before; she realized then that she could not let me die or suffer as she knew I would.

"That was the strange point. You see, she knew the dangers that would beset anyone upon that trail into the jungle. And, knowing the perils of such a journey, she took it upon herself to save me if she could. Much as she had always loved orchids, never once had she sought a rare plant herself. With me, though—she thought me worth seeking after, it seems."

"So, I suppose," I remarked, "you married her and lived happily ever after?"

He looked at me, wild-eyed. "*Married her?*" And he shuddered.

· · · · ·

THE TENTH QUESTION

GEORGE ALLAN ENGLAND

"Dr. Nasmyth?" inquired the voice over the wire.

"Yes."

"This is Mr. Varian speaking. No. 29-A West Eleventh Street. I should like to see you at once."

Nasmyth frowned. The prospect of abandoning slippers, pipe and book to face the slush and sleet of that February night by no means pleased him.

"You'll come, of course?" the voice persisted—the voice of an oldish man.

"Yes."

"Very well; thank you. Goodbye."

Nasmyth growled an imprecation under his breath as he hung up the receiver. His practice had long since passed the point where a new patient was greatly to be desired.

None-the-less, he kept his word. Fifteen minutes later, he presented himself at the door of 29-A West Eleventh—a three-story brick house, closely shuttered, against which the storm-drive blustered savagely.

Varian himself let the physician in. Nasmyth's appraising eye beheld a big-chested, thick-bearded man of sixty-five or seventy, with a God-bless-you expression and mild eyes that peered from behind thick-lensed glasses. The house, dark save for the front hall and the library, impressed him as being rather unusually well furnished; a scholar's house, thought the doctor.

Varian led Nasmyth into the library and produced liquor. He insisted on pouring the physician a stiff drink.

Nasmyth did not object. Warmth and green Chartreuse were grateful, after having breasted such a night.

When he had drunk it, Varian sat down and told him about some symptoms or other; Nasmyth never knew just what. The soporific in the Chartreuse struck him down as though he had been hit with a club.

It was morning when the doctor struggled back to consciousness. He discovered that he was lying on a padded quilt spread on a cement floor. His clothing was gone. In place of it he wore a Japanese quilted gown, with white cotton *tabi* or socks on his feet.

Astonished, he struggled up, and beheld Varian peering at him through metal bars.

The old man nodded and smiled when he saw that the doctor's eyes were open.

"Good morning," said he with perfect composure. "I hope you slept quite well. The little potion I administered ought to have made you, at any rate. I learned its secret in Nagasaki. Wonderfully efficient; marvelously so!"

The man's infernal nerve—for already Nasmyth realized that he had been trapped for some purpose or other—kept the doctor from speech. That, and his dazed condition, effectually muted him. He sat there on the quilt, stupidly enough.

Varian regarded him with a cynical expression. His smile grew bitter.

"Just as dull as all the rest, I see," he remarked acidly. "And these are the men to whom society trusts its lives and welfare!"

That stung Nasmyth to action. Mentally vague and confused as he still was, he managed to return the old man's look with compound interest. For a minute their eyes met, the doctor's in rage, Varian's eloquent of scorn.

Then Nasmyth articulated:

"What is the meaning—of this farce? What—"

"No farce, but stern reality!" Varian interrupted. "If all your judgments turn out as mistaken as this, my hidden service to humanity will soon be enriched by one more heroic act, and the world will soon be rid of one more charlatan!"

II

This brought Nasmyth up all standing, as the saying is. He catapulted off the quilt in spite of a dizzying headache, grabbed the bars like a gorilla, and snarled:

"Here, you! Let me out of this, or—"

"Or what?" Varian smiled calmly. "Really, I'm interested to know what you can possibly threaten."

Nasmyth could find no answer to such amazing effrontery. He stared in silence at the old man, who sat down on a chair close to the cage and regarded him with a mildly curious air of scientific speculation. Thus for a moment, captor and captive gazed upon each other in that strange place.

Strange, indeed, it was. The prison seemed a kind of basement, divided in the middle by a row of steel rods. Light entered through two windows at the far end, behind Varian; windows glazed with ground-glass, translucent, but preventing clear vision. Near these windows stood a table with books, papers, and writing material. At the left a metal-encased door with a combination-lock, formed the only exit from the den. Above the table hung a small clock.

The cage itself was provided with nothing but the simplest of Japanese furnishings, none of which could be converted into any weapon or any tool wherewith to break jail. Beside the quilt, a frail little table of lacquered cedar, with pencils and paper, and a wash-basin and pitcher of some heavily waxed, paperlike material completed the arrangements.

A single powerful incandescent hung from the ceiling, near enough the cage to furnish light for it at night, yet too far to be reached through the bars. Evidently Varian had no intention of entrusting even a piece of glass in the hands of his prospective victim.

By the subdued light from the windows, Nasmyth continued to stare dumbly at his captor. The physician was able to distinguish clearly the old man's expression of impersonal interest—just the same kind of impression that Nasmyth himself had more than once assumed when confronted with a new and interesting pathological condition.

The doctor needed only very brief observation to assure himself that Varian was entirely in earnest and terribly dangerous. No doubt existed in his mind, from the first minute of clear realization, that he was confronted by a case of dementia, with delusions and probably homicidal mania.

Blackmail, ransom, or anything of that kind was out of the question; and as for personal revenge, what motive could it have?

Nasmyth had never seen or heard of Varian till last night.

A real madman, he felt convinced, sat before him in that chair; a madman of the most sinister type, because highly educated and of extreme intelligence. Nasmyth felt that he could have outwitted a dull, brutish cretin, in one way or another. But this elderly, professorlike gentleman of scientific attainments—this man with the observant eyes and well modulated voice—evidently could not be circumvented by argument or stratagem,

Just what problem Nasmyth now faced he could not tell. But that it was fearfully urgent and freighted with extreme perils he was thoroughly convinced.

The doctor was terrified. Never in all his life had he felt so sickening, so instinctive a fear. Every medical man has to face death, legitimately, in his profession; and none dread it under those circumstances, if they are worthy of the name of doctor. But to be made a rat of, and murdered in a basement cage by a lunatic, is quite a different story.

Varian, regarding Nasmyth's blanched face and wild eyes, said nothing for a minute. But his smile was eloquent. It meant: "Coward!"

That smile revived the doctor; it galvanized him out of his terror. In a moment he managed to pull himself together. He grew rather unusually calm.

"You seem to have the advantage," said he. "You've caught me, right enough. I don't know why. Perhaps it's a case of mistaken identity. You may take me for somebody I'm not? Or your motive may be something else. Whatever it is, I have a right to know it!"

Varian, struck by this logic, nodded assent. The physician now, for the first time, remarked that the old man's face was perceptibly asymmetrical, his skull plagiocephalic, and his expression indicative of some mental unbalance, though not markedly so. His beard and glasses helped to conceal this appearance. Yet Nasmyth knew the diagnosis was correct.

"Well?" he demanded. "What are you imprisoning me for, and what do you want with me?"

Varian's manner denoted culture, and his words were perfectly coherent as he answered:

"I will tell you. In the first place, there has been no mistake in your identity. You are a practicing physician; that is enough for me. I chose your name at random, last night, from a physicians' directory. Any other one would have answered my purpose as well. My choice simply happened to fall on you, by fortune. My summoning you, as if for illness, was of course a mere deception. I am perfectly sound in mind and body. I—"

"For God's sake, then, what do you want of me?"

"You ask an explanation, and you shall have it. All the others have had one. Why not you?"

"*The others?*" demanded Nasmyth, horribly startled.

"The others," Varian repeated with satisfaction. He drew out a cigar case and offered his prisoner a smoke. Nasmyth shuddered. The old man, smiling, calmly chose and lighted a Londres.

"What others?" gulped the doctor.

"Those who have preceded you here, of course," Varian answered slowly, as he blew a feather of smoke. He crossed his legs, at ease, leaned back and observed his victim with attention. "You must know about the mysterious disappearance of several physicians and surgeons from New York during the past eighteen months. You must remember that they all seemed to have left suddenly for foreign parts, leaving their personal affairs and their practices unsettled, and that they all appeared to have been lost in various ways—by fire, flood, or what-not."

"What then?" Nasmyth snarled at him, still weak and dizzy as he clung to the bars.

"Every last man of them all," continued Varian, smiling, "at one time or another occupied this identical testing-cage of mine, now honored by your presence. Each one failed in the necessary trial. I was therefore compelled, much against my will—for really, doctor, I am the most humane and kind-hearted of men—to expedite their departure from a world certainly the better for their absence."

"Horrible! Impossible!" gasped Nasmyth, unable to believe his ears. The man, he felt, must be suffering from some megalomania, some obsession of power or the like.

"No, neither horrible nor impossible," Varian replied. "On the contrary, perfectly just, virtuous, and true. Some years ago, in 1908 to be exact, a surgeon did me a tremendous, irreparable wrong, not through malice, but through ignorance, stupidity and misjudgment. After long deliberation, I determined to devote my life to the testing of the intelligence of medical practitioners.

"Money was no object. I have enough, more than enough. I spent a good deal preparing this place, where my researches should be undisturbed, and much more, subsequently, in issuing reports about the unsuccessful men's disappearance. It has been a long, hard task; but results have justified it. So far, not one physician or surgeon has passed the required test. They have all been eliminated, therefore, from a society they could only have injured by having remained in it and—"

"This cannot be!" cried Nasmyth, horrified.

"Perfectly true, I assure you," smiled Varian, obviously with a clear conscience. "If you insist, I can furnish you complete data that will prove it. There was Henderson, for instance. He came here on the 11th of August 1912, insisted on hastening the test—claimed the full ten days would drive him mad—failed, and was eliminated on the 17th at 8:45p.m."

Varian drew a small, red-leather notebook from his pocket, thumbed the leaves, and continued:

"Then there was Maltby, October 21 to November 7. He really did go mad. I waited some time for him to recover his reason, but when I realized this was quite futile, I had to eliminate him in that unfortunate condition. His body-ash joined that of all the rest, in my electric volatilizer. I had reports sent in from Sao Pablo, in the Azores, establishing his drowning there, just as I had Henderson reported killed by aborigines near the Essequibo Rapids in British Guiana.

"Van Cleave's case was interesting," he continued, still consulting his notes. "On the fifth day of the test he broke his incandescent lamp—it hung inside the cage, then—and cut his radial arteries. I rescued him just in time.

"In a week he had convalesced sufficiently to resume the work; but after all," and Varian regretfully shook his head, "he failed, and I was forced to do my duty. I then removed the lamp from the cell, as you notice. I couldn't afford to take any more risks, you see."

"You inhuman monster!" cried Nasmyth, his prudence all swept away by horror and indignation. Calm judgment would have told him that it was worse than futile to accuse a madman, but in his weakened condition of nerve and body he could not keep calm.

He shook his clenched fist through the bars at the calm, smiling face of the old man. A sudden tremor almost overcame him. He had to grip the steel to keep his feet.

"Philanthropist, you mean," Varian asserted mildly, showing no slightest trace of anger or resentment. "My only idea is this: To try the intelligence of all the medical practitioners I can reach; and, if this proves too low to warrant their continuing in the profession, then mercifully and quickly to eliminate them from society. I have long been hoping to find a man of brains and wit enough someday to stand the test and emerge victorious.

"So far, however," he concluded, sighing with genuine regret, "I am very, very sorry to say that not one of my subjects has stood the experiment."

Keenly, he peered at Nasmyth with appraising interest.

"I wonder," he remarked musingly—"I wonder now if *you* are going to stand it?"

III

Nasmyth stared at him with horror-stricken eyes.

"What—what kind of a test?" he stammered thickly.

"Draw your quilt up here, near the bars," said Varian. "Sit down on it and calm yourself, and I'll explain."

Nasmyth shook his head in objection, but the old man insisted.

"You really mustn't stand any longer," said he. "It's tiresome to us both. Make yourself comfortable, by all means. And, by the way, how about a little breakfast? Rolls, coffee, cocoa? A bit of tobacco, maybe?"

"Nothing!" the captive declined. "All I want is the conditions of your infernal test!" Subconsciously, he knew he should accede to anything, fall in with the madman's plans, and seem to work with him; but for the present, at least, indignation and rage inhibited deception.

He suddenly felt very weak, and, yielding to Varian's command, hauled his quilt up close to the cage and squatted there, cross-legged, his whole body shuddering in a nervous chill, his teeth chattering violently.

Varian pulled at his cigar a moment, then began:

"Of course, I don't expect you to grasp the social significance of my reform work among physicians. From your point of view I'm a mere assassin—"

"The test!" interrupted Nasmyth. "For Heaven's sake, man, the test!"

"Very well, the test, which alone can set you free. You understand that your only chance for life is through it. Succeed, and this door swings wide to you. Fail, and a vial of hydrocyanic acid gas extinguishes you, painlessly, instantaneously, absolutely. That's quite understood?"

"Go on!"

"You are familiar, of course, with the old game of Twenty Questions? Yes? Of course. Almost everybody is. A most useful diversion. Nothing can so clearly index the intellectual capacity of a man as an analysis of the processes he uses, his inferences and deductions, in approaching the answer.

"Agreed, then. Through a series of *ten* questions, on the plan of the old game, I have gauged the powers of all my subjects and shall measure yours."

"Just how do you mean?" inquired Nasmyth, striving for self-control.

"This: I have in mind a certain thing, the identical thing that all the others have tried to guess, and failed. I will give you ten questions on ten consecutive days to discover that thing. Twenty questions is a child's game. Ten will be a man's.

"I will be honest with you, doctor. If you guess my thought, I will so inform you, and will certainly set you free. If you fail, you will have shown your mental unfitness to practice medicine, and I shall be under the painful necessity of administering the hydrocyanic-acid gas and of volatilizing your body. You will simply vanish from society.

"In due time reports will reach New York that you have been lost in Lake Victoria, Nyanza, or something of that sort. There will be some sort of investigation, of course; but it will all blow over presently, and you will be forgotten. Society will be freed of another incompetent. It is all quite simple."

Nasmyth gazed at him with despairing eyes.

"So I perceive," he answered. "And when is this ghastly play to begin?"

"Today, if you wish. The sooner, the better. Evening will be the best time. Shall we make it nine-thirty?"

"Eight will be better," said the captive.

"Very well; eight it is. So then, that's settled. Everything will be arranged most comfortably. You shall eat and drink of the best, smoke my finest cigars, and have plenty of reading matter. This push-button, here"—and he indicated one on the wall—"will summon me at any time. I am sure we shall get on admirably together."

He asked a few questions relative to Nasmyth's wishes about material comforts, peering in through the bars, meanwhile, with a benevolent expression on his asymmetrical features.

Then, presently, he withdrew, leaving the captive alone with thoughts such as never till then had he believed it possible to entertain.

IV

The horror of the situation at first quite overmastered the unfortunate physician. He sat there, shuddering, on the quilt which had been used by so many miserable members of his profession; seemingly obsessed by the presence of the dead men who had preceded him in the cell, all doomed—as he himself was doomed—to annihilation at the hands of this madman.

His thoughts dwelt on different phases of the tragedy and of the oft-repeated crime. Where, he wondered, was the volatilizing furnace for the disposal of the bodies, and how did it operate? How long had it been since the last victim had been made away with?

How could it be that in a great and civilized community, human beings could be lured to death and could drop out of the world without this monstrous den of murder being discovered?

He knew now only too well that Varian had told the truth about those disappearances. Insane though the old man might be, yet in the matter of his records of crime he was lucid enough.

Strange, was it not? thought Nasmyth, *that the murderer had never given any consideration to the inevitable results of letting a victim go in case of a successful guessing of the question. This contingency spelled certain arrest and confinement for Varian; but probably the insane man, with characteristic fatuity, had never even given this matter a thought.*

Or, in the event of success, would he still carry out his murderous desires and, breaking all promises, execute his captive?

At thought of this strong probability, black despair overcame the prisoner, and for a while he gave himself up as hopelessly lost. But gradually, as calmer reason asserted itself and his physical disturbance subsided, a reaction set in and he began to entertain more hopeful thoughts.

He got up and wandered about the cell—a space of some twelve by fifteen feet—narrowly examining it for any possible chance of escape; but against cement and steel, what could bare hands hope to accomplish?

There remained, Nasmyth clearly perceived, only one possibility of salvation—the chance of wresting from Varian the secret thought he harbored. Yet to do this in only ten questions—how horribly tenuous a hope!

Tired and very weak, the prisoner threw himself at length on the quilt, buried his head in both arms, and tried to think his way through the diabolical maze enmeshing him. He reflected on the disturbance his vanishment would cause and the ill effects it would surely have on two or three of his patients urgently needing his personal attention. This added to his despair.

Came, then, a comforting conviction that the old maniac was at least sincere in his testing of the intellect, and that he might fairly be depended on. Mad though he undoubtedly was, he still remained of a highly intellectual type, with every indication of honesty of purpose.

Nasmyth felt sure Varian was acting on moral grounds, with a strong psychic imperative. He would play a ruseful and intelligent, yet perfectly fair game. He would not change the subject of his thought during that game; and at its end, if Nasmyth should succeed, he would undoubtedly admit it and set him free. But if he failed, the captive knew that Varian would positively kill him with as little compunction as though stamping on an insect.

Nasmyth recognized the fact that on his own wits depended not only his own life, but also the lives of many others who—in the event of his failure—must still follow him in that abominable rat-pit. He perceived that he owed a profound duty to society to beat this madman, to regain his freedom, clear up the many mysteries and tragedies he now understood, and finally to have Varian incarcerated for life.

At these reflections every fiber of his being quivered with the intensity of his determination to succeed and to be free.

God grant—he thought with passionate eagerness as he lay there on the Japanese quilting—*that I may live to work out justice from his horrible calamity!*

His thought passed now to the test itself, the horrible mockery of a game that was to be played with him. He determined to meet the situation like a man of intelligence, determination and grit. In no event, even though he should see that all was lost, would he play the coward or utter vain pleas for mercy. His burning ambition was to meet Varian on his own ground and beat him.

He felt positive he would not ask to have the game hurried, would not go mad with the suspense, and would not allow himself to be driven to suicide. Carefully, thoughtfully, and with patience, he would apply the totality of his mind to the problem, would take the full allotted time, and would see the hideous gamble through to the bitter end.

He pondered then on the probable direction that old Varian's thought would take and the nature of the subject he had probably chosen. That it would be obscure and difficult, he did not doubt. The man's subtlety vouched for that, as well as the fact that all his predecessors had failed—among them men of more than usual attainments, witness Maltby and Van Cleave.

The thought of Van Cleave, in particular, filled him with despair. Where *he* had gone down to defeat, he, the logician, chess expert and skilled debater, how could Nasmyth hope for success?

All the disheartening factors of the case, however, he resolutely put aside, rallied his strength and began making active preparations for the battle royal of the intellect. Toward nine o'clock he rang for Varian, ordered some breakfast, and indulged in a cigar.

He now began to feel much more fit. Courage rose appreciably. He chatted a little with the old man; hoping to sound his thoughts and, if possible, discover in what direction his special interests lay. This, he hoped, might give him some faint clue to work on; but Varian was wary and let nothing slip which might in any way be interpreted by his adversary.

When Varian was gone, Nasmyth set to work with a will, logically classifying all the categories of things animate, inanimate and abstract. He based his work as nearly as possible on the arrangement of Roget's famous *Thesaurus*, a work with which, as a writer on medical topics, he had become familiar.

Using the writing materials at hand, he drew up headings and classifications, and before night had finished a fairly complete general outline of matters and things. This done, he found his confidence greatly restored, and began to face the ordeal with more than a little assurance.

At noon, and again at six o'clock, Varian made his appearance with excellent meals. A box of cigars, a pipe and half a pound of Perique—in a cloth bag, not a metal box, since even this metal might have served for an instrument of suicide—added to Nasmyth's comfort.

The captive noticed with a smile that dishes, knife, fork and spoon were all of boxwood. He felt minded to tell Varian that he had no intention whatever of putting himself out of the way, but thought better of it and held his peace.

"Will you be quite ready tonight at eight?" the old man asked him at the evening meal.

"Entirely so!" Nasmyth replied. Varian passed a few commonplaces with him, apparently well pleased with his latest victim; then turned on the electric light and withdrew.

Promptly at eight, he reappeared. He sat down close to the bars, with his features—sinister, now that Nasmyth understood them—strongly illuminated by the incandescent above.

For a moment the two men gazed at each other in silence. The physician's heart was pounding strongly, and an extreme nervousness strove to possess him; but he mastered his emotion and assumed a *sang-froid* he could not feel. At least he was determined that Varian should never have the satisfaction of seeing him disturbed.

"Ready?" asked the madman, smiling. "Think well of your question! Remember, there can be no discussion. My answers shall be yes or no—nothing but yes or no! Are you ready?"

"I am," the captive replied, as he stood there by the bars.

"First question, then."

"First question: This thing that you are thinking of, does it fall into the category of material things?"

"No!" answered Varian. "I wish you a very good night!"

He arose and departed, leaving Nasmyth much depressed. Since the object of Varian's thought was not material, it must lie in the realms more vague and uncertain, outside the material world. This confirmed the captive's suspicion that the old man would choose a subject of great subtlety, and assured him the task was to be fearfully severe.

Nasmyth spent the evening in profound thought, poring over the categories of the immaterial and the abstract—having rejected and destroyed all the others—until the light went out at ten-thirty. He then wrapped himself in the folds of his Japanese attire, admirably suited to such a confinement, and lay down on his quilts to sleep as best he might.

V

To detail each day's analyses and thoughts would unduly prolong this narrative. If it be kept within bounds, the progress of Nasmyth's investigation must now be handled somewhat in outline, as day by day it led Varian and his captive onward through the strange maze that tortured the unfortunate physician.

On the second day, in order to make positively certain of being on the right track, Nasmyth used a question that perhaps he might have spared, but did not dare to proceed without.

"Is this thing an abstract concept?"

"Yes," Varian replied.

The captive now felt himself headed in the right direction, with eight questions still remaining. True, he reflected, the realms of the abstract would prove far more difficult to penetrate than would those of the concrete, where some material object was to be discovered. But with eight questions to his credit, and with a strictly scientific system of eliminations, there might still be some chance of success.

Strange as it may seem, despite the desperate character of the game, and the stakes of life or death, Nasmyth could not help feeling a kind of savage pleasure in matching his wits against those of the old man in this cynical *danse macabre* of the intellect. Even in those despondent hours when he felt positive nothing but extinction awaited him, he lost nothing of his powerful determination to fight on and on, to the very end.

The third day, having carefully analyzed all the classes of abstractions, Nasmyth propounded the following query:

"Does this idea you have in mind fall into the categories of the esthetic or the moral?"

"No," Varian answered. Then, smiling, he added:

"Let me compliment you on your progress. You still have seven questions left, and you have already advanced further than any of the others, with the possible exception of Van Cleave. Several died, either by their own hand or mine, before they had even reached the knowledge that I was thinking of an abstraction, outside the limits of the moral and the esthetic."

"That is to say," put in Nasmyth, hoping to win some information gratis, "within the limits of the practical?"

"Yes. But you must count that as a question," said Varian with solemnity. "Remember, there are but six left. I pray you, do not waste them."

Nasmyth, sickened at realization of the intellectual keenness of the madman, made no further speech, but returned to his reflections. Obviously he could win nothing from Varian without paying the full price. He must not hurry matters or lose his head, but must day by day, with relentless precision and logic, prosecute his ghastly search for the practical abstraction which alone could save him from merciless annihilation.

The knowledge that now only six chances remained to him served both as a terrible depressant and a most active stimulus. Out of many thousands of things, one specific thing now had to be discovered; a task, surely, that would have baffled Sir Isaac Newton.

That night was spent in a careful study of the written categories of the useful abstractions, and—after the extinction of the light—in profound mental analyses. Nasmyth eventually fell asleep, toward morning, and awoke only at ten, with deep despondence assailing him.

He fought this off, however, and by night had formulated the fifth question, thus:

"Has this practical abstraction anything to do, primarily, with existence, time, change, or causation?"

"No," smiled Varian, obviously elated at his captive's failure; and departed.

The next day was a bad one for Nasmyth. Confinement—despite his attempts at calisthenics—loss of appetite, intense mental labor and anxiety, all had cumulated to bring on a severe nervous headache. He recognized the fact, moreover, that his body was losing weight and his strength declining.

His mind, however, felt supernormally keen. Its grasp and scope seemed quadrupled; yet in its intense application and dwelling on the problem, he felt lay perils of madness. The strain, he knew, must soon be over in one way or the other.

Were it to last another ten days—he shuddered to think of the result.

The sixth question, tediously formulated, he put this wise: "I shall now divide the remaining categories of the abstract, namely: relation, quality, order and number, into two halves, of two categories each. The first is relation and quality. Does your concept fall in that group?"

"No," said Varian. "Remember now, you have but four more questions. I warn you, be extremely careful!"

Nasmyth felt very ill that night. He had at last narrowed the thing down to one of the two categories of order and number, so that now he was within striking distance of the goal. But to attain the thing itself, ten or a dozen questions more would have been none too many, and he now had but four.

His physical condition was growing very bad. Nervous tremors assailed him; he perspired profusely at times, and again had chills, due to the long continued and intense mental excitement of this ordeal.

At times he was assailed by a mad rage against Varian, whom he had come to hate with desperate intensity; a rage that set him shivering and quaking whenever the madman appeared on necessary errands. He was assailed by mad ideas of guessing wildly and at random, quickly using up his last four chances and thus ending the horrible farce.

He now well understood how Henderson had insisted on hastening the test; how Maltby had gone mad, and how Van Cleave had tried to commit suicide.

Resolutely, however, he controlled his every untoward impulse, and with a savage kind of determination, whipped himself to obedience, to labor and to dogged patience.

Pacing the floor of his cell, head gripped in both hands, or lying on his quilts, he fought the fight with his own soul, and won. Came, thus, another day; and with it the seventh question, thus:

"A process of elimination reduces your idea to one of the two categories of order or number. Does it fall in either, or in both?"

"That is not a fair question," objected Varian. "It cannot logically be answered with yes or no. You interest me, however, so extremely by your extraordinary method, worthy of my own intellect, that I will strain a point and answer: It falls in both, but more particularly in the latter. Good night."

Nasmyth felt courage reviving. He now was close on the trail of the elusive abstraction. The thing had to do with order and number, but more particularly with number. That is, it must be some mathematical concept.

Carefully he analyzed. By midnight, he had thought his way to this conclusion: It might be either some branch of mathematics, like arithmetic, algebra, geometry or calculus; or it might be some component part of one of those sciences. Infinite possibilities opened out ahead of him in the realm of mathematics. Despite his anguish, he could not help admiring the astuteness of Varian in entering this field, where guessing the object was a practical impossibility.

And at thought of this, once more despair seized the unhappy victim of the maniac's delusion.

There remained, now, but three questions, each of vital importance. Nasmyth pondered long before propounding the eighth:

"Have you in mind some mathematical science as an entity?"

"No! Remember, now, you have but two more chances!"

Nasmyth felt his brain reel, but by a powerful effort controlled himself and went on with his analyses. Next day he had prepared the following:

"Since it is no special branch of mathematics, it must be something common to them all. The only common factor is the mathematical sequence known as numbers. Is it any number you are thinking of?"

Varian paused a moment before replying. Nasmyth felt himself irrevocably lost. Were it a number, what hope could be entertain of ever discovering it? From one to infinity, he might spend years in trying to guess a certain specific number. Thus it was with a feeling of enormous relief that he heard Varian reply:

"No."

"No number, you say?" the doctor asked.

"Do you mean that as the tenth question?" And Varian's eyes gleamed.

"Certainly not! It is merely a confirmation of your ninth answer."

"Very well. I repeat, it is no number, no number at all, that I am thinking of. Yet your inference that it is something common to all branches of mathematics is absolutely correct.

"You are now verging on the absolute edge of the correct answer. In all my experience, I have never met an intellect anything like yours. Not one of my experimental subjects has even approximated the answer. I congratulate you, doctor, on your marvelous keenness and insight.

"If you fail, as I confidently expect you yet will, my regret at having to eliminate you will be very sincere and deep-seated. I wish you good night, and beg you to think carefully, now; for tomorrow night I shall require you to speak the one, exact, identical word that shall free you. Otherwise—you understand—much as I regret the necessity—"

Varian, suddenly lapsing into incoherence, began gesticulating and muttering into his beard, with all the characteristics of madness. He shuffled up and down the open space outside the cage a few times, stared in at Nasmyth, laughed loudly, and all at once departed.

The unfortunate captive shuddered violently. Even though he should guess the secret, he now had begun to doubt his captor's ability to recognize his rights, or his willingness to release him. Dealing with a man *non compos mentis* opened up all kinds of horrible possibilities.

A vast sense of weariness oppressed him. Without further thought that night, he lay down on his quilts, shut out the light by burying his face in his arms, and so—quite exhausted—fell into a kind of torpid sleep.

The final day found him feverish and wan, unable to eat or to remain a minute in one place. Like the condemned man he now realized himself to be, he paced the floor of his cell. Only by a strong effort of the will could he restrain himself from dashing his head against the walls or beating his fists on the steel cage.

Ideas of suicide obsessed him. By stripping his robe into cords and twisting them he could make a rope and manage to hang himself from the bars.

This thought took a strong hold on him for some hours, but he fought it off and, by noon, had managed to calm himself sufficiently to force his mind once more to the loathed and execrated task of analysis.

Analysis now supremely vital; since on its accuracy, on the pronouncing of the one, specific word, his life inevitably depended.

All that afternoon and evening, up to seven o'clock, he labored on the problem of discovering a common factor to all mathematics, which should yet not be a number. By seven, his head was aching desperately and his nerves were raw.

A trembling weakness possessed his whole body. He could hardly remain upright, but sat or lay on his bed, his mind now fixed on the one, final idea which he had reached as the only possible solution of the ghastly problem.

This idea, voiced in a single word, rang and hummed in his fevered mind, now close to madness. Voices seemed shouting it at him. Fiends chanted it; hammers, glowing hot, pounded it upon his brain; wild visions swept it across his sight.

Again he lay down, groveling to escape it; and thus he lapsed at length into a kind of merciful oblivion.

A voice, calling him, roused his wandering mind to consciousness.

"Well, Nasmyth! Are you ready?"

Sitting up, he stared in horror at the strangest apparition he had ever yet beheld.

VI

The figure that stood there before him would have shaken stronger nerves than his. It was clad in a long linen gown, such as surgeons use for operations. The entire head and face were covered by a singular apparatus, a respirator, with round, glazed eye-holes, through which Nasmyth could see the gleam of the madman's eyes. In his right hand, Varian held a thin vial.

Nasmyth understood. He struggled to his feet, recoiling from the vision.

"Do not be alarmed," came a voice from the respirator. "Death is nothing but sleep and rest. He who has not earned the right to life should hold death as a blessing. Are you ready for the last, the deciding question?"

Unable for a moment to speak, the captive stared at his tormentor. Then he raised a trembling hand, pointing.

"You—you mean to murder me?" he gasped. "Murder me, and stand by, immune in that devilish apparatus?"

"I am not here to argue!" answered Varian sternly. "I am here to answer your last question, and either to free you or to work inexorable justice. Are you ready?"

Realizing the worse than futility of argument, Nasmyth, by a supreme effort, steadied himself to face the inevitable. Folding his arms, he faced the madman.

"Ready, yes," he said.

"Very well!" And the old man, vial of deadly gas in hand, advanced close to the bars. "What is your tenth and last question?"

Nasmyth kept a moment's silence, shuddering, then—unable to take his eyes from that venomous flash—began:

"According to your own answers, you are thinking of a useful, mathematical abstraction, not a branch of mathematics and not a number."

"Correct. Can you name it?"

"I can!"

"Do so—and on your own false reasoning be the responsibility of your death if you fail!"

"Is it—is—it—" Nasmyth stammered, but could not bring himself to speak the crucial word.

"Well, is it *what?*" cried Varian impatiently. He raised the vial, ready to hurl it to the concrete floor in case of failure.

"Is it—*zero?*"

The word burst from his parched and quivering throat in a supreme and anguished effort.

For a second, the madman stood there motionless and dumb. Then a gasping groan issued from the mask.

"Yes!" came a hoarse whisper. "I am beaten! You—have won!"

Nasmyth's consciousness lapsed a second. Before his eyes a kind of shimmering mist seemed to float and swim. A humming roar, as of a distant surf upon a rocky coast, filled his ears. He swayed forward, felt the contact of cold metal, and found that he was clutching the bars of his cage.

Reeking with sweat, shivering and utterly unnerved, he clung there a moment, while steadfastly upon him, the malevolent gaze of the masked Varian seemed burning through his soul.

"You have won!" he heard the madman's voice again. "For the first time, my intelligence has had to bow before another man's. The impossible has happened. In ten questions—it is incredible—monstrous—"

"Let me go!" panted the captive, utterly unstrung. "I have stood the test! Let me go free!"

Varian nodded, muttered to himself and approached the door of the cage. Mute and weak, Nasmyth watched him turning the combination.

The prisoner's eyes fastened themselves on that operation with a terrible intensity. Nothing mattered now but that. While the mood should last, would Varian really let him escape? Would he hold firm to that diabolical flash of death; would he open the door, let the captive pass from the cage and through the basement door?

Beyond that, Nasmyth had no thought. Once he could gain the exit, he felt that he could fight his way to liberty in spite of all that Varian might do. His weakness mattered nothing, now. New, latent strength welled up in him.

His costume made no difference. Given the chance, he would rush into the public street in that strange garb, shouting for help, for the police, for the arrest of Varian, the maniac and murderer!

All at once, he heard a sharp, decisive *click*. Varian stepped back from the door, which now was swinging wide.

Unable to believe his eyes, still fearing some treachery, some ruse, the wretched captive tremblingly advanced, his every sense keenly alert lest, in the very moment of liberation, his insane captor strike him down.

Now he was at the door, now through it, while Varian stood back, vial in hand, still peering at him through those round, death's-head goggles in the respirator. Nerving himself to a supreme self-control, forcing himself to walk instead of yielding to the mad impulse to run in stark panic toward the half-open basement door, Nasmyth passed in front of the madman.

In silence, Varian watched him go. Nasmyth made a yard toward the door, two yards, three. Already half the distance was traversed. Already he sensed liberty, and hope, and life—

Came a shrill cry, a rush behind him, a snarling scream of rage:

"If you go free, I am *lost!*" screamed Varian. "You will tell the police—you must not go—you shall *not!*"

Whirling, his flesh acrawl with horror, Nasmyth saw the maniac's arm toss up, as, with a beastlike howl of rage, he hurled the vial of liquid gas, the deadliest poison known to science.

A quivering faintness flashed upon him at that right. Instinctively he flung up both arms. His loose Japanese sleeves, outspread like a bat's wings, intercepted the spinning tube of death.

He heard its impact against the padded softness of his right sleeve. Something fell upon his right foot, upon the white cotton *tabi,* or sock, that shod it. Then, with a tiny clattering, the frail glass capsule of annihilation skittered across the rough concrete and came to rest.

Howling, Varian precipitated himself toward it. One stride more and his boot would have crushed it to powder.

But ere that stride fell, Nasmyth was upon him. Leaping, he smote the madman on the masked jaw with all the power of his being. Varian fell sprawling, with wild blasphemies. Upon him, as he scrabbled toward the flask, Nasmyth hurled himself.

A horrible struggle began. Weakened by confinement and the desperate nerve-strain of the past days, Nasmyth still for a moment was able to hold his adversary.

Over and over they rolled on the floor, grunting, striking, gouging, tearing. At every moment danger was acute that they might fall upon the vial and crush it. All Varian's surprising energy was now concentrated on just that ambition—to smash the vial; all Nasmyth's, to hold him back from it.

Off ripped the long kimono, in grotesque shreds and tatters. Off tore the respirator, stripped away by the physician's clutching desperation.

"You—die with me—if I *die!*" he panted, straining for a vital grip on the madman. He felt the old man's wiry hands grappling his throat. Furiously he flung his head from side to side, avoiding that clutch. Tearing like a wild beast, Nasmyth for a moment held his assailant off. Then, once, twice, full in the face, he struck the maniac.

Varian's grip loosened a second. With a heart-bursting effort, Nasmyth wrenched himself free.

Rip!

Long shreds and tatters of silk remained in the old man's clutch as the physician struggled up, away. Again he struck; and now, free for an instant, he staggered to the vial, caught it up and ran for the door.

With incredible agility and strength, the old man flung after him, howling like all the fiends of the pit. Just at the door, Varian caught him.

Whirling, Nasmyth let drive a blind right-hander to the eyes. The crash of that blow, going home, was music to his soul.

In a haze of wild confusion, he sensed that Varian was staggering backward. Fate hung on fractions of a second. Up he slung his left, holding the vial, and with all his last remaining strength hurled it smashing against the wall below the clock.

Even as the old man, rallying, clutched at him once more, he burst through the door and slammed it after him. With a clang of metal, a catch fell into place.

Muffled, a hideous scream echoed within—a scream choked off short in the middle—a scream that ended in a silence terribly eloquent.

Nasmyth stood there, pale as milk, bloodless to the lips, with staring eyes, his quivering body racked in spasmodic tremors. He turned, then, toward some stairs dimly seen ahead of him.

Three or four steps he made toward those stairs, along a kind of passageway. All at once, he burst into a jangling laugh that rose, rose, rose in horrible, mad mirth.

The laugh died suddenly.

"Free! Free!" gasped the doctor in a choking whisper.

He pressed both hands to his burning head, took one more step, and—all his vital forces drained to the uttermost dregs—plunged forward and fell, face downward, in a swoon.

· · · · ·

DISAPPOINTMENT

ACHMED ABDULLAH

It was Paul Mayol, the inimitable low comedian of the Scala, who started the ball rolling, as far as Paris was concerned.

Perhaps he had the original tip from the desk clerk of the Hotel Saint James, where Prince Pavel Narodkine had put up temporarily; perhaps he had it from his mistress, who had it from her sister, the laundress of the hotel, who, in her turn, had it from the prince's Austrian courier; perhaps, even, he had brought it back from the green-rooms of Moscow, where he had filled a triumphant engagement the season before, and whence Narodkine had recently arrived.

At all events, it was Paul Mayol who was the first to sense the tang of mystery which clung to the big, melancholy Russian, and who—since in Paris it is the stage, and not, as in New York, the yellow press which does the scavenger work for society—included him among the characters whom he impersonated and satirized in the new Scala Revue.

He came on in act two, in the comedy make-up of a Russian aristocrat, which was a farcical mingling of whiskers, sable furs, vodka bottles, icons and a *obligato knout,* did a Cossack dance with Argentine excrescences and Georgecohanesque frills, and introduced himself to the audience with a tense, cavernous "*Sh-sh!* I am Pavel Narodkine, the great Moscow enigma!" after which he peered right and left with all the time-hallowed stage business of a conspirator, caused his legs and whiskers to shiver violently, whipped the property calves of the chorus girls with his property *knout,* and then danced off to the *pizzicato* of a dozen *balalaikas* which were striving to syncopate the Russian national anthem.

Thus the beginning, and the boulevards caught the ball of rumor and mystery that Mayol had tossed in the air. They gilded and tinseled and embossed it. They flung it wide and caught it again.

The next morning, cut in below a screaming bit of editorial hysterics which accused the ministry of having sold the country to the Freemasons, the atheists and the stock exchange, the royalist *Gaulois* brought half a dozen lines about Prince Pavel Narodkine speaking with pontifical unction about his great ancestry which partook of Rurik Vikings and Tartar Khans of the Silver Horde, and congratulating the legitimist clique of the Faubourg on the arrival of such a thumping blue-blood—and tossed the gossip ball to its editorial neighbor, the *Vie Parisienne.*

The latter weekly acted up splendidly. It printed a rotogravure portrait of the prince in a border of cupids, chorus girls, three-horse *troikas,* sacks of gold and grisettes; mentioned that he was young, a bachelor, and immensely wealthy; and added that, as yet, he had not thrown his scented handkerchief at the feet of either *mondaine* or *demi-mondaine.*

"*Why?*"—demanded the final, tart, succinct word of the page in four-inch Gothic.

The next move was up to the *Revue Diplomatique.* In its personality column, entitled "Mustard and Cress," and signed, "Junior Attaché," it alluded to the fact that even in his native Russia the prince was considered an enigma. "The Sphinx" was the nickname by which he was known in the salons of Moscow and Petrograd.

And justly.

For he had no intimate friends; he had used all sorts of political influence until he was finally excused from military service; he never set foot in a dark place; he eschewed all sport; and he never went abroad without a bodyguard of five heavily armed peasants.

"*Sic semper tyrannis!*" screamed the socialistic daily, *La Patrie.*

It stated boldly that Prince Pavel Narodkine was a reactionary, a leading member of the Black Hundred, a blood-gorged oppressor of the masses, and that it was his fear of becoming the target of a patriot's bullet which caused him to shun the dark and to seek the protection of steel-girt retainers—a report promptly branded by the *Gaulois* as "a filthy and reeking falsehood sired and damned in the fetid gray matter of our socialistic colleague." The article added that the prince had no enemy, either among the revolutionists or the reactionaries; that he had, in fact, never occupied himself with politics.

Here the *Vie Parisienne* scored again with a snapshot of the prince walking down the Boulevard des Italiens surrounded by his armed bodyguard; *La Patrie* followed by demanding why "the titled bloodsucker" should thus be allowed to break the laws of the republic which enjoined the carrying of arms; the official *Mercure de France* explained that the prince had applied for a special permit, and had been granted it—and thus Paris discovered that it housed a deep, mysterious sensation, and began to wonder what it was all about.

From Montmartre to the Quartier Latin, from the Porte Saint Martin to the Ternes, the great macrocosm of Paris commenced to stir and buzz like a beehive. A string of would-be visitors besieged the desk of the Hotel Saint James—shirt-makers and boot-makers and English breeches-makers, perfumers and florists and jewelers, cranks and reporters and solicitors for charitable institutions, beggars, genteel and ungenteel—they came, they were met by the urbane Austrian courier, and were sent on their way without having gratified either their curiosity or their greed.

The great society ladies fared no better. They littered the prince's writing desk with invitations to balls and dinners and receptions and garden fetes and theater parties. Those with marriageable daughters made ready for a regular siege. They consulted with milliner and modiste, with Paquin and Virot and Doucet and Reboux; slim, clever fingers manipulated silk and lawn, satin and gauze, lace and embroidery, canvas and whalebone; the granite paving blocks of the Place Vendome echoed under the rapid feet of models and saleswomen and errand-runners; mothers, and daughters stuck their heads together—they consulted—they sought the advice of ancient dowagers versed in marital and premarital warfare—and still more invitations were heaped on the prince's breakfast table with every morning mail.

But the crested notes were acknowledged by the Russian's secretary, who read them, threw them away, and regretted "the inability of Monsieur Le Prince to accept *madame's* so charming hospitality"—and then the real-estate brokers came to the rescue of Mme. Gossip, though they only succeeded in deepening the mystery which enveloped the prince.

It became known that he had sent for MM. Dufour and Cazanet, a reputable and well-known firm of real-estate men who in the past had sold palaces and chateaux to Chicago pork kings, Westphalian coal barons and Oriental potentates. They called on Narodkine—flattered, delighted, expectant; and they left—sadder, but no wiser.

For the prince refused to buy the sort of showplace which befitted his rank and station in life. He asked, instead, MM. Dufour and Cazanet to get him a house somewhere in the most crowded quarter of Paris.

"No, no, no!" he exclaimed when Dufour spoke of an aristocratic old stone pile buried under the pink chestnut trees of the Rue de Varenne. "I want light, gentlemen. I want crowds around me." Here Dufour thought of the armed retainers who accompanied the prince everywhere, and he winked at his partner; but the Russian did not seem to see the incongruity of his remark.

"Yes," he continued, "I want to sense the stir and throb of life—life—right, left, everywhere!"

"But, Monsieur le Prince, I assure you this house in the Rue de Varenne is—"

"It is gray and dark and lonely," the prince cut in. "I know. And I want life"—he shivered a little—"life and the dear breath of life!" He bent over a map of Paris and pointed at a certain section. "Here, gentlemen," he went on in a tone which admitted of no further argument; "get me a house here—if not a house, then a flat, a hut, a hovel—anything, anything! But it must be here—where there are crowds and light and life!"

The two Frenchmen looked at the prince, who had dropped, trembling, into a chair. Then they looked at each other. Dufour shrugged his expressive shoulders and motioned to his partner.

"Very good, Monsieur le Prince."

And they bowed themselves out of his presence and set about to fulfill his wish; but, of course, they talked, and Paris listened and wondered—and laughed a little.

Society, still smarting under its recent defeat, tried to attribute Prince Narodkine's choice of residence to stinginess—a report quickly given the lie when it became known that he had been the anonymous donor of a lavish contribution to Paris's pet charity. The *Patrie* made sinister allusions to royalist intrigues; the *Vie Parisienne* to a tragic love affair back home; but nobody could explain the prince's choice.

For, as soon as the lease had been negotiated, he moved to a little house of the Cour de Rouen—the tortuous alley which branches off from the Passage du Commerce, and which, generations ago, had been the Paris home of the Archbishops of Rouen—a packed, crowded, noisy alley where mansions of the sixteenth and seventeenth centuries lean against each other for mutual support; where the windows are spotted with birdcages and linen hung out to dry and the frowzy heads of housewives; where there is no verdure except an occasional sickly fig tree straggling along a rusty, bent water pipe, and here and there a dusty bit of clematis and convulvulus stretching up—a neighborhood echoing to the shrill sounds and shouts of its motley population, news venders and fruiterers, bookbinders and cobblers, dealers in all kinds of second-hand odds and ends, locksmiths and knife-sharpeners—a neighborhood made yet more noisy with the screams and laughter and jests of a school for little girls who file through the alley twice a day, copybooks and satchels under their arms.

Indeed, an alley clanking and beating with life! And Prince Pavel Narodkine moved in, together with his armed peasant retainers—while Paris sat on its haunches and waited developments.

There were none.

Prince Pavel Narodkine lived in his little house of the Cour de Rouen as he had lived in the Hotel Saint James, and as formerly he had lived in Moscow, never leaving the house after dark, never setting foot in a lonely place nor where the shadows were blotched and deep, never moving an inch without his armed peasants—big, lumpish, brooding men, savagely silent and intensely loyal, who shook their heads and gave no reply when curious people addressed and questioned them about their master.

So, with the slow, pitiless swing of time and the familiarity which time breeds, Pavel Narodkine became part of the city's contemporary history—he became one more of Paris's unexplained and, in a way, accepted mysteries; like the tall, white-bearded Highland Scot who for years has walked every afternoon from the Porte Saint Martin to the Arc de Triomphe, dressed in kilts and plaid, horn-handled dagger in his stockings, sporran swinging rhythmically to the skirl of an imaginary war-pipe; like the blind American who twice a week, rain or shine, takes his seat on the pavement outside of the Café de Naples and distributes gold pieces to all passers-by; like the plum-colored, turbaned Senegalese who promptly, every morning at five, prays in front of the statue of Strasbourg, his hands spread out like the sticks of a fan, his huge, round head bobbing up and down with the fervor of his incantations.

Another year came and passed. Another sensation boomed along and stirred the boulevards and set the tongues of Paris a-wagging; the personality of the prince blended still more deeply into the shadow of accepted things—and when strangers saw him walk down the street, accompanied by his armed servants, with his big body slightly trembling, his great purple-black eyes shooting anxiously from right to left, as if expecting something or somebody to pop out at him from every corner and doorway, the people of Paris smiled—kindly and, too, tolerantly.

"Why, yes," they would say; "it's that Russian—Prince Pavel Narodkine—it's a habit of his, you know"—as if that were sufficient explanation.

Perhaps the whole mystery would have been forgotten for all time to come if it had not been for Dr. Marc Henri, who explained it, but only after the death of the prince, and even then very gently and apologetically—quite on the side of the prince, you understand! For the doctor, a short, stocky, ugly little man with a clever, narrow face which sloped wedge-shaped to a pointed, inquisitive chin, was a Frenchman, with the sane, sweet logic and the sane, sweet sympathy of the Frenchman; a man who endeavored to understand everything and everybody, and to condone according to his understanding.

He lived just around the corner from the prince, in an old house of the Passage du Commerce, next door to Durel's quaint bookshop—a stone's throw from the spot where, many years ago, famed M. Guillotine had made experiments on sheep with the blade of his newly invented "philanthropic machine for beheading."

He was a busy man. The bell of his little apartment was forever tinkling; he had no time to read more than the headlines of either *Gaulois* or *Patrie,* and he had never had sufficient leisure to speculate about Prince Pavel Narodkine's strange habits.

And then, late one warm spring evening, a lumpish Russian, in tall, oiled boots and silken blouse, burst into his office and implored him, in a terrible jargon and by half a dozen assorted Greek orthodox saints, to come at once to the bedside of his master. "He is sick, sick, very sick!" There was no time to lose, and so the doctor picked up his ever-ready black leather case and was out of the house on a run.

"I am suffering! I cannot sleep!" was Narodkine's thin, querulous greeting, and the physician smiled. "I don't wonder," he replied tartly, with a comprehensive gesture that took in the whole of the bedrooms.

For the windows were tightly closed, in spite of the warm spring air; every lamp—there were half a dozen of them—was lit; and the air was yet more hot and stuffy with the presence of the prince's peasants—big, hulking men who filled the atmosphere with a tang of tobacco and leather and raw spirits.

The doctor was astonished, and a little angry, too, when he had finished examining the patient. He was in the habit of being called away from his house at all hours; but the prince's messenger had led him to believe that his master was on the very point of death, and there was really nothing the matter with him except a slightly congested head and a corresponding rise in temperature—an ailment cured easily with a little aspirin, a sound night's sleep, and, of course, fresh air.

So it was with something like impatience that he threw open the window and ordered Narodkine's peasants to leave the bedroom, and he was more than ever astonished when the latter remained stolidly where they were and when the prince backed their dumb, passive refusal with eager, excited words.

"No, no!" he cried. "They will remain with me— I need them—"

"You tell 'em to clear out!" the doctor cut in impatiently. "You have to do as I tell you if you want me to treat you!" And it was only when he picked up his leather case and threatened to leave that Narodkine spoke to his servants in purring Russian, ordering them out of the room.

They left—and the doctor, keenly tuned to observations and impressions, was positive that they had only gone as far as the next room, ready to return at their master's slightest gesture or word. But he paid no further attention to them.

"You need sleep," he said to the prince, "and a cool, dark room."

But when he lifted his hand to turn out the great Venetian chandelier that swung from the center of the ceiling, a cry from the bed halted him. He turned—and he was aghast when he saw the prince's face. The man had suddenly turned a grayish yellow—"yellow as a dead man's bones," the doctor described it afterward—and his whole body was trembling with a terrible palsy.

"No, no!" he cried. "Leave the lamps burn—all of them!" And then, in a sort of whine which was both ridiculous and pathetic, given the size of the man:

"I will not have a dark room—by myself! The thing will come!"

"What thing?" asked the doctor, and he added jestingly: "You aren't afraid of the dark, are you?"

He was utterly amazed when he heard the prince's reply.

"Yes, doctor," in a hushed voice, but absolutely matter-of-fact, like stating a tiresome sort of truth, "I *am* afraid."

And when the doctor, who had no respect for titles, made a succinct allusion to "cowards," Narodkine told him.

Dr. Marc Henri never found out if it was because of a sudden liking Narodkine had taken to him, or because of a sudden, crushing feeling of loneliness that the other confided in him. But he *did* confide.

"It was terrible," the doctor said afterward, when speaking of the whole happening to some colleagues of his at the Café des Reines; "it was dramatic, and it was true what he told me! You see, in a few words he gave me the reason for those strange habits of his that so intrigued Paris at the time.

"His choice of residence, there, in that packed, pulsing quarter—on the other hand, his refusal to take his share in the amenities of society—sport, dancing—anything in fact which, in the slightest degree was connected with danger—yes, danger!—accidents, you see; his hatred of dark places and of the hours of night; his demand for bright lights; the armed servants who accompanied him everywhere—why, my friends, it was nothing but a huge and intricate stage-setting for his daily, continuous fight with death.

"Yes!—he feared death! Nor was it the everyday, shivering fear of the coward. It was something more terrible, more gigantic. It was something in a way primitive and sublime"—and Dr. Marc Henri continued in the prince's own words:

"Doctor," said the prince, "it is not that I love to live, nor that I am afraid to die. I fear *dying*—not *death*. I fear that fraction of a second when my body will step from life to death, don't you understand? I dread the—ah—the utter uselessness of it—and, too, the utter ignorance! What is it? What does it feel like? What does the whole mystery consist in? Why are we so helpless against it?

"I—I have felt this fear all my life—since I can remember—waking and sleeping, my life has been a continuous martyrdom—and I have always tried to fight death—to fight sickness and accidents—with light and life and even with steel. For I shun sport, I shun darkness and loneliness, and my servants never leave my side! But what is the use, doctor? What is the use?

"For death is a coward—death may be watching me even now—from the corner of the room—about to pounce on me and strangle me!"

"You see," the doctor went on as he told his colleagues across the marble-topped table of the Café des Reines, "the prince convinced me that there is a grain of truth in the Bible after all. His fear of death was not the result of his character, his temperament, his mode of life, his education, or his ancestry—as we reckon ancestry. It was an atavistic throwback to our first forefather—Adam, or perhaps Adam's son, Cain—when he realized first that there was such a thing as cessation of life, but before his racial memory and instinct allowed him to coin the word or to feel the meaning of death. That was the trouble with Prince Pavel Narodkine—"

"Was?" demanded Dr. Ruoz, and the other inclined his head. "Yes—he died just a moment after he finished telling me about his fear of death—"

"But—why—you said he had only a slight congestion—"

"Exactly! But you know how it is with these big, full-blooded people. His confession excited him terribly—a blood vessel burst in his brain."

"Did he realize that he was dying?"

"Yes," Dr. Marc Henri smiled gently, "and he—why—he was disappointed! You see—right on the moment of death, when he knew that he had lost his life-long battle, he whispered a few words—to himself really—'Death!' he breathed; and then, not with relief, but in an agony of disappointment, 'Is that all?'"

"Yes," added the doctor, rising and calling for his check, "and he repeated it, I should say, about a minute later—"

"When did he say it—just before he died, I suppose?" asked a young medical student who had joined the party. And the doctor replied rather wearily as he walked toward the door:

"No, no—he said it—just *after* he died, you know!"

· · · · ·

THE PRETTY WOMAN

OWEN OLIVER

Not mad? Hush! Hush! Sir, I throw myself upon your mercy. You have penetrated my secret. I am *not* mad, but for Heaven's sake, don't tell the superintendent. He is a narrow-minded man; and inquisitive; tryingly inquisitive. Sometimes I fancy he suspects me.

You don't think so? What did he say about me? As mad as a March hare? Good, good! If he asks what I said to you, tell him that I gibbered like an idiot. An idiot! *Ha, ha, ha!* No! If I have any mental failing, it is not lack of intelligence, but the reverse. I am too clever. Cleverness is a net that you catch yourself in!

There's another net that catches the cleverest man. The snare of a woman! That was what caught *me!* Damn her! I— I— I am not mad; but sometimes I feel as if I shall be, if I don't get out to her!

What was I talking about? Oh, yes! The superintendent. You mustn't let him guess that I'm sane. If you did, my last chance of escape would be gone. Better off here? Yes, yes! I know. I quite realize the position. If I escape and they find out that I am sane, they will send me to prison. I must take the risk. Foolish? Ah! It is not a question of expediency, but of right.

I have a duty to perform in the world; a plain duty. It's a painful duty, because she's a pretty woman; a very pretty woman. *Just to kill her!* I— I— Thank you. I will have a cigar. It soothes the nerves, as you say. Let's sit here in the sun and I'll explain the matter. We'll wait till the superintendent has passed.

I'm going to gibber for his benefit. *Ha, ha, ha! He, he, he!* That's how I take him in! He's just what you might expect from an army officer. If you laid his brain open, you'd find that one hemisphere was regulations and the other prejudices. I don't blame him for being a fool; but he needn't show it by wearing a single eyeglass! This is an excellent cigar.

Now, for the pretty woman. We won't have names. I'll call her just that. She had bright brown hair, and a bright little face, and a quick, bright smile, and a voice that seemed to laugh in words, and a saucy, red mouth, and mine burned for it! She was five and twenty and she had been married for three years, and she was visiting some friends without her husband. I was staying there, too. I was a clever man, as I've said, but I wasn't clever about women.

At first I took her for a pretty grown-up child. She prattled to me so innocently. "I always thought a professor was dry and horrid," she told me when I first took her in to dinner, "and I should be afraid of him! But you're not, and I'm not!" And then she smiled up in my face.

I'd never had a woman look at me like that before. She was *so* pretty. Oh, Heaven! She was so pretty! I fell in love with her, and she flirted with me.

I didn't know it was only flirting till I tried to kiss her. *She* knew. If she hadn't dreamed of such a thing, as she said, I should have had the kiss, but she knew exactly what was coming; sprang away like a little cat, and got her hand to the bell. Then she turned round to me, panting, and let the bell go.

"No, no!" she said. "I won't do that. I couldn't be unkind to you. You have made a dreadful mistake. I hadn't dreamed of such a thing. I— I love my husband, and I don't do things like that. I am very, very silly, but I am not wicked! Oh, don't look like that. Don't, don't! You are so much older, and I never dreamed of such a thing. How *could* you?"

I think I was nearly mad for the moment. I raved at her; told her that she had deliberately led me on, and made me love her. She cried. Crocodile tears! Some women can!

"Oh!" she sobbed. "I have hurt you! I have hurt you! I didn't mean to. I thought you understood. You seemed like a big-brother friend. I was nice to you because I liked you in that way. I do like you that way."

"And I," I said, "love you!"

"But it's absurd," she declared. "You're so much older, and—"

"Absurd?" I cried. "Absurd?"

I was very near taking her little white throat in my big hands then! I wish I had. If I hadn't been so clever, I should have. But I relied on my cleverness. I didn't want her dead; I wanted her alive.

If I *am* mad, I went mad then. No, you are quite right. I did not. If I had been mad, I could not have formed my clever plan in those few seconds. I did more than form the plan; I began to play my part, put my hands to my face and groaned, and she cried more crocodile tears.

"No, no!" she said. "Not absurd; not absurd at all absurd. It isn't because you're old. You're not *very* old." She said that like a coaxing baby. "If I weren't married, perhaps I shouldn't have thought you old at all, but I didn't ever think of it, and I mustn't, and I'm not going to. I do like you very, very much in a little-friend way. Will you be friends, please? I am so sorry, truly sorry. I am sure it was my fault too. I am a very thoughtless girl. My husband calls me 'little silly.' But I will be a very true friend."

She put her hand on my arm. I could show you exactly where. I seem to feel the touch ever since. I said we would be true friends. I asked for a kiss as "a consolation prize," and I got it. Don't tell me it was her innocence. She might be silly, but if she wasn't a thorough flirt, she wouldn't have put her hands on my shoulders and kissed me back. And she did. She did!

Flirt or no flirt, she liked me. That was the one word of truth in all her lies. If I could get her husband out of the way, I knew that she would come to me. I decided to remove him.

If I had been mad, I should just have gone to the place where he lived and shot him, but I wasn't mad. I saw quite clearly that if I killed him, I should be caught and sent to an asylum (I should have pretended to be mad, of course), and shouldn't get her, and besides, she would be ashamed to marry me if I killed her husband. I decided that the first step was to separate them.

I made a clever plan for that; a very clever plan; but it had a flaw! I'll tell you about it presently.

The first thing was to teach her to trust me. I behaved very discreetly for the rest of the visit, took the line of the fatherly friend. I knew it piqued her that I could be so "fatherly." She was always trying to draw me on. She would take my arm and smile at me, and run about to fetch things for me; "not because you're old, but because I'm so young," she would smile at me and say, "and because I love to do things for my friend!" Sometimes she'd look up at me and say, "You're not very unhappy now, are you?"

And I would struggle with myself till my muscles felt like steel. "I am quite happy, little friend," I always told her, and then she used to draw a long breath and dab her eyes quickly.

If I had been a fool, I might have been taken in, and have believed that she was just an innocent, grown-up child who had hurt me by inadvertence and wished to make amends. But I wasn't a fool, and I saw through her. She wanted to gratify her vanity by bringing me to my knees! I am not going to kill her merely for revenge. It is a duty. Women like her are cancers in society. They must be removed.

I am ashamed to own it; but you are a man of insight, and you will be merciful to human weakness. There were times when I shirked the duty. She was so—so lovable. If she had repented of her cruel coquetry, even at the eleventh hour, I would have snatched the excuse to forgive her. If she was not utterly heartless, I told myself, she must feel that tortured me sufficiently and dismiss me when her visit came to an end; but she wanted to play with me a little longer.

"Your friendship is much to me," she said on the last evening; "and I want to make mine much to you. If you will come and see me at home, I shall be so very glad. Will you come?"

She touched me with her hand. If I had not been a clever man, I must have thought it was sheer kindness and compassion. She looked so innocent and sweet; so very sweet. That was another time when I was tempted to strangle her.

"I will come," I said, "my dear." I called her that in a fatherly way. It made her eyes blink with anger; or perhaps it was disappointment. Sometimes I thought that if I took a kiss now, she would not run to the bell! But I would not risk it. I wanted to make sure of her; quite sure. I would wait till she ran away from her husband. Then she would run to me!

I thought too much of myself, and too little of my duty. This is my punishment. You would make some excuse for me, if you saw her. She looks so sweet and lovely.

Well, she went. I kissed her forehead, just where the bright brown hair stopped, at parting; and she squeezed my hand in both hers.

"God bless you," she whispered, "dear friend, and make you happy. I shall pray it in my prayers!"

Her *prayers!* That was when I condemned her finally. There is pardon, I often think, for all the sins that one sets out as sins; but none for the sins that are cloaked by hypocrisy. I did not cloak mine. I prayed to play with her heart as she played with this broken, broken heart of mine. Do you know, I sometimes think I *am* mad! Yet it was clever, my plan. It may seem far-fetched to you, but it would have succeeded, except for one trifling flaw. No, I won't tell you the plan yet. You will see it as I go along.

I went to the town where she lived about a month later. I was there for four days before I called. I had let her see me in the distance two or three times. That was part of the plan. I made a good many inquiries about her husband. He had what someone called "a sporting past," but people thought well of him now. He was a long, lean, strong-featured young man; "a hard-headed chap," they said, "except about his wife." He obviously worshiped her. I did not wonder that she had taken him in, for she had done it with me, and with most of the townsfolk.

"A thoughtless little person," they said, in effect, "but good and affectionate. She looks as if she flirted a bit, but she doesn't mean anything; and she can't help being such a little beauty."

On the fifth day I called. She was tearfully petulant at my neglectful delay.

"Now I don't believe I am your best friend," she said. "I mean, you don't think so!"

She pouted like a baby.

"My dear," I said, in my most fatherly way, "I could not like you so much, 'loved I not honor more.'"

"Oh!" she cried. "Oh! Don't talk of that. I thought you would forget those things, and—"

"Tut, tut," I interrupted. "I don't mean that, little goose!" I patted her hair—the bright brown hair—"I wasn't afraid to see my little friend, although— Never mind about that. I meant that duty had a prior call for the moment."

"You say 'duty!'" She tossed her pretty head. "I suppose you mean nasty business? Business! Ugh! If money is more than friendship—"

"It wasn't money, Bessie," I declared; "and it wasn't friendship. There is none to compete with yours. I will prove my trust in your friendship by telling you the story. I would not tell it to any other on earth."

"I won't tell a soul!" she volunteered eagerly; "not a soul! Not Jack, even!"

She was alight with curiosity, and her eyes sparkled.

"I trust you," I said. "You are transparently honest, my dear." I had a curious impulse to kill her when I said that. If only I had! "Let me make the story brief, because it hurts me to tell it. Years ago I had a sister. She married a man. Well, she thought so. The marriage was a sham."

"Oh!" she cried. "Oh-h-h!" She began dabbing at her eyes. The crocodile tears were always at her command.

"He took her away—never mind where. He defrauded his employers and had to fly. She fled with him; worked her poor fingers to the bone sewing for their bread. Sometimes he earned a little butter by cheating at cards and even theft. There's a long history of robbery; robbery of those who befriended him. She was ignorant of his doings for a time. Then she learned the truth about him. Then he killed her!"

"Oh!" she cried. "*Oh!*"

"Killed her as she lay by his side at night; fled away before the morning, and has remained undiscovered for six years. For six years I have been tracking him. I have reason to think that he is in this town of yours."

"Oh!" she said again. "Oh! You must not do anything violent, dear friend. The law will punish him. I don't want my friend to get into trouble."

She stroked my coat sleeve gently.

"Yes, dear," I said, "Yes; I will hand him over to the law when I find him."

"Won't the police do that," she suggested, "if you tell them?"

"I don't know the name that he goes under," I said. "A friend of mine saw him here, and told me. I have been hoping to see him, but I haven't met him yet. Perhaps you might know him. He would be a few years over thirty; very tall and thin; at least he used to be thin. He may have filled out. He has a big nose, and dark eyes and hair. He used to sway a little as he walked. He was slow-spoken, but he rather surprised you by the way he always went to the point. Do you know anyone here like that?"

She shook her head. The bright brown hair always seemed to glitter when she did so.

"I don't believe I should ever recognize anyone from a description," she apologized. "If you hadn't told me who the man was, I should have thought you meant my husband!"

"Ah!" I said. "You told me he was a fine big man! I must make his acquaintance when I've settled this business. If he's on the lines of this man externally, I congratulate him, and you! Burton—that was his real name, but he's gone by many others—was an attractive scoundrel in looks; in more than looks. He had a very fine voice; a light baritone. He was particularly good at oratorio music." I laughed bitterly.

"Oratorio music?" she repeated slowly. Her lips moved restlessly I noted, and there was a startled look in her eyes. I had seen in the local paper that her husband took the baritone solos for the town choral society.

"For the matter of that," I said, "he could sing anything. I believe he once traveled with a comic opera company."

"Indeed!" Her lips were trembling violently now. I had learned that her husband was in comic opera in his careless youth.

"He was a good French scholar, too," I remarked; and this also I had learned of him.

"A good French scholar," she murmured. "I— I—" She was evidently struggling with herself. "I am stupid at French," she said desperately.

"Ah!" I protested. "You aren't so stupid as you make out, my dear! You are quite a clever little lady. Well, to continue with my story, Burton got away six years ago; and ever since I have been trying to track him, without success. I was within twenty-four hours of him once. I had traced him to a mining camp.

They called it the Gray Hill Settlement. You don't look well today."

She swayed a little in her chair.

"I feel the heat,'" she said in a husky little voice. "I—feel—the—heat."

"I am afraid that my story worries you," I apologized. "You are too tender-hearted, my dear. Shall I stop?"

"No, no! Go on! I am all right. Go on!"

"He went by the name of Holbrook there, and— You are *not* well, my dear. I am sure you are not."

"But I am. It is just a passing faintness. It is gone now. Go on! I am so interested."

She pulled herself together and smiled. I was glad to see that she could smile, for I took it as a sign that she did not really love her husband. If she had, I reasoned, she must have fainted. For the mining camp was where he had spent two years was where he had spent two years of his "sporting past"; and the name he gave then was Holbrook. Oh, no! There was nothing against him, except a young man's wildness; nothing at all!

"I don't know if it was chance, or if the detective who was assisting me was in league with him and sent warning," I continued; "but he left the camp by the Tuesday train, as I arrived on the Wednesday. The reason they suggested for his hasty departure was that he feared they might lynch him on account of a curious run of luck at cards; but as a matter of fact, they meant to catch him in the act first, and they hadn't succeeded yet, though they felt 'morally sure' that he did cheat. They may have been in league with him, too, and have made up the story to deceive me. Anyhow, I missed him for six years.

"As you say, it's hard to identify a man by a description; but there's a good identification mark if I can catch him. He has a ship tattooed on his right forearm, a kind of Chinese junk, and a flowery circle round it. My sister— My dear, I am *sure* you are faint! You really must see a doctor. Shall I ring for some water?"

"I am not—very—faint," she denied. Her face was ashen. "It is—it is only my heart— I think."

"Oh, my *dear!*" I cried. "Don't say that!"

"There is nothing wrong really," she protested. "Don't—don't worry, my—my dear friend. Ring, will you? We will have some tea. That will set me right. Oh, you've brought the tea, Mary! Thank you. It's one lump of sugar and the tiniest drop of milk, isn't it? You see, I remember. It is such a sad story. So dreadful!"

"So dreadful!" I assented.

I said no more for some time; neither did she. She kept shivering; tried to keep still by holding the arms of her chair.

"I must come in and meet your husband," I proposed presently. "Do you expect him soon?"

"No, no!" she said quickly. "Not soon. I think he will be quite late. Are you sure that he murdered your sister? The man you are looking for?"

"Quite sure, my dear; but we won't talk of it any more. I didn't know that you weren't well, or I wouldn't have worried you."

"I—I am *not* well," he cried. Her voice was almost a wail. "I suppose there was a quarrel, and he struck a hasty blow, and didn't mean to—to—"

"My dear," I answered, "there was no quarrel and no haste. I often wonder whether she anticipated anything of the sort. I pray and pray that she did not; but sometimes I picture her lying beside him night after night, afraid to sleep, fearing every movement. No, no! She could not have done it. She must have run away and come to me if she had suspected that. She *must* have run away, don't you think?"

"Yes!" he cried. "Yes!"

Her voice was almost a scream, and I rose to go. My clever plan had succeeded, I told myself. She believed the story, and she would run away before her husband came home that night. One little hint where to run, and the mine was laid.

"If she had only come to *me!*" I remarked, as I held the pretty woman's hand for goodbye. "*I* should have guarded her from him. She was the dearest of all women to me, until— But we have forgotten all that. Forgive me. When I see you ill, it makes me want to—to comfort you. If ever you need help— But, of course, you would come to me. I shall be in town tomorrow afternoon, at my office; but I shall see you soon. Goodbye, my dear."

"Goodbye," she said. "Dear, dear friend, goodbye!"

She clung to my hand for some time. I think she was half inclined to ask me to take her away then; but presently, she released my fingers.

"I shall see you soon," she said, "very soon!"

"Very soon!" I echoed as I went. I smiled as I walked along. She would come to my office the very next afternoon, I predicted, and I should keep her! I smiled and smiled at the thought. She was such a pretty creature!

I had no doubt that she would come to me, or that she would let me take her away; but a day was long to wait, and it seemed surer to take her that night. If I could meet her on her flight, when she was wild with fear and saw her husband in every shadow—when she wanted a strong arm to protect her—she would fall readily into mine.

She would come with me more readily than tomorrow, when she had had time to think of other friends. She would not betray her husband to me, and she could not conceal her desire to escape from him. So she would probably say that she was flying from him because she loved me—and with my arm round her, she would—and I would offer to put the seas between them. Yes, I must meet her on her flight.

I made sure that she was going that night. I will not bore you with details of my inquiries. They really were made very cleverly. I found that she was packing trunks, and gave out that she was called away to a sick cousin. She was going by the seven twenty-two.

She went by it; so did I. I lurked at the far end of the platform till I saw her. Then I got into the train. Twenty minutes after we had started, I walked along the corridor.

I found her in a compartment, alone except for one man. He was her husband, and she was clinging to his hand! You may think I was mad to do what

I did. Perhaps I was. God in heaven! Hadn't I cause to be?

But I could not have been mad, for I reasoned the whole business out in three seconds; constructed what had happened, just as it was told at the trial. She had not told him of my accusation, but had declared that her nerves were upset, and she would be ill if he didn't take her away that very night; and he had humored her, as he always did.

She believed him a thief, a cheat, and a murderer; believed that her own life was in danger from him. She denied that at the trial, but she lied! And she cared only to save him from me. She did not love me at all; and she loved her husband. I did not think of that. It was the one flaw in a very clever plan!

There was an error in the charge that they made against me at the trial. I did not shoot at him, but at *her*. That was my second great mistake. She thought I should aim at him, and sprang in front of his great body. The bullet went exactly where the bright brown hair had been a moment before.

If I had wanted to shoot *him*, I could have done it before he was on me; but I tried to get round him to shoot her; and he had me down and twisted the revolver from my hand. My face was cut and bleeding, and he had dislocated my wrist; but she didn't think of me, only of him.

"He is mad," she cried to the people who gathered round. "He is mad! If he says things about my husband, don't believe them! Don't believe them!"

I jeered at her then.

"There is no one in the world who would be fool enough to believe such things of your husband, *except you!*"

"Oh," she cried. "Oh, thank God! *Thank God! It's not true!*"

Then she fainted, and he caught her in his arms. I often picture her like that. It is how she will look when I have killed her. Her hair had come loose. It looked so beautiful hanging down; her bright brown hair—when I have killed her, I shall take a piece of it.

Do you know, I wavered in my intention of killing her even then, until the trial. She loved her husband; she had flirted heartlessly with me. They were crimes, but I wondered if they were quite unforgivable crimes. Heaven, I think, forgives a great deal; and who was I to judge? Well, at the trial she committed the crime that is not to be forgiven here, or hereafter—the crime of hypocrisy. She pretended to plead for me.

"I was to blame," she said, with the tears running down her cheeks—she held them at call, as I have said. "I was so foolishly careless. I loved my husband, and I never dreamed of flirting; and I never thought that anyone could think it of me.

"But I ought to have seen how he felt about me, and afterward, I ought to have gone away. It was my thoughtlessness that led him to do this. He is a good man really—a kind, good man. He just went mad for a moment, I'm sure he wouldn't do it again. I do feel I am to blame; but I meant it for the best. I—I tried to be kind!"

"My dear lady," the judge said, as if he soothed a child, "I don't believe there is a person in the court who thinks badly of you!"

"Yes!" I shouted. "There is one!"

They regarded that as conclusive evidence of my insanity, I think. She deceived them all—all—as she had once deceived me.

The jury added a rider to their finding. "We wish to record that we consider Mrs. Markham's conduct in the matter irreproachable."

My counsel added a crowning insult.

"It was my duty to my unfortunate client to put certain questions to Mrs. Markham," he said; "but I hope these cannot be construed as any reflection upon her. I entirely agree with the jury's rider, and consider that the fact that my client so misunderstood her kindness is a further proof that he was not responsible for his actions, and should not suffer any punishment other than detention in a comfortable asylum, where his friends are prepared to place him. I earnestly urge that the sentence may take that form."

I tried to reach him, but the warders were too strong for me. When I escape, perhaps I shall kill him, too, but I shall not let private revenge interfere with my public duty. It is a painful duty, a very painful duty. She is *such* a pretty woman!

· · · · ·

THE LIVING PORTRAIT

TOD ROBBINS

I am not insane! You doctors who wag your pointed beards over me, you specialists who attempt to analyze my brain in all its separate cells, you nurses and keepers who buzz about me continually like summer flies, have you no pity for a man robbed of everything which can make life dear—a man unjustly accused of homicidal mania—a man forcibly deprived of the sovereign rights which accompany intelligence?

You have incarcerated me in this beehive of insanity because the scope of human imagination cannot embrace an unusual chain of events. Like Christ, I find myself abused because I am neither understood nor believed. Very well—but I shall snarl a bit.

May I ask, learned doctors, in what way your combined intelligences overshadow my single mind? You who follow in dead men's footsteps; you, the apprentices of a profession which it has been my lot to advance into a yet unexplored wilderness; you, pitiful practitioners of a knowledge handed down to you between the covers of countless books, dare to put your hands upon me and lead me to this dungeon!

Like Gulliver, I am at the mercy of Lilliputian minds!

But if I could once escape from here, if I could once break down the barrier that you have so carefully erected, what then, learned doctors?

There are elements in the sea and air as yet unknown to science. I have the key that unlocks the arsenal of the heavens. Did you think, when the Purple Veil lies ready to my hand, that I would strike with a poniard?

If so, you little guessed your man—if so, you did rightly by confining me in this place. It is written that one's acts cannot exceed one's intelligence.

And yet it is not with your stupidity that I quarrel—it is rather with the teaspoonful of knowledge that you have absorbed and which has made you incapable of understanding the slightest truth not written on a printed page. You smile—wagging your beards at me, you smile.

But will you smile at my translucent child, the Purple Veil? I doubt it very much, my genial friends.

But I must not wander. Even though the moon has pressed her soft, leprous face against my barred window, I must not wander.

And yet, what a strange power rests behind those haggard, sightless eyes! With them she beckons from us our calm, collected thoughts. Like a mother, she bends over us—a sad, shy mother who dares visit her children only at night.

She has stolen into the nursery to see us play. Now she is shaking her black, tangled locks over the world. They trail out behind her; and, afar off, through their moving blackness, tiny trembling disks of light appear.

She, our mother, has plundered the infinite. Like a mad queen, she steals to my window, her diadem of precious stones caught and dangling from the intertangled meshes of her hair.

"Play!" she commands with a wide, toothless smile. "Play!"

But I will not play—not tonight. Even *she* shall not dominate my mind. It is necessary that I first give to the world a clear, collected account of the strange chain of events which has drawn me hither—a narrative which shall prove to unborn generations that Gustave Ericson was a victim to the stupidity of his age rather than to the slow inroads of egomania.

After that, if she is still there and still smiling—well, perhaps—

I

Two Discoveries

I was not born to battle for existence. My father had amassed a considerable fortune before I came into the world. He was a large, obese man with round, protruding eyes that gave his florid face a look of perpetual astonishment.

He never understood me; and it tickled the ribs of my humor to set his slow mind revolving on the axis of a new idea. At these times, he would regard me with an air of amazement and pique—the air, in fact, of a hen that has inadvertently mothered a duck's egg, with brain-numbing results. Undoubtedly I was the cause of much mental worry to the poor old man.

It is not my purpose to bore you with a long dissertation on my boyhood. Suffice it to say that even at that time I had an instinctive love for chemistry. Soon I fitted up a room in the house as a miniature laboratory, and with a school friend, Paul Grey, experienced the various vicissitudes common to most youthful exponents of science.

What soul-stirring odors permeated the atmosphere of that house! What ear-jarring explosions rattled the window panes!

Daily the expression of rapt astonishment on my father's face deepened. I was at last breaking through the barrier of his mercantile calm; I was proving the fact that life is precious only because it is precarious.

Paul Grey, even in his teens, gave promise of someday making his mark in the world. He was my direct opposite in every physical and mental attribute.

Excessively blond, with pale blue eyes and the girlish trick of turning fiery red at any emotional crisis, he fluttered about our laboratory like a pigeon, swooping after each stray crumb of knowledge, while I, with my swarthy skin and unmanageable tangle of blue-black hair, followed as sedately as a crow.

And yet, although he was far quicker, he lacked the depth of insight that makes toward originality of thought. It was *I* who unearthed hidden knowledge in later years; it was *he* who put it to an immediate, practical use.

I was very attached to Paul—I am still attached to his memory, despite his colossal theft of my discovery. You smile incredulously, but it is a fact, I assure you.

One could not cherish a lasting hatred for such a sunny personality. Even a thief is forgiven, if he can amuse.

We grew up together like two brothers, united by the chain of a common interest. At school and college we were inseparable.

I shared the burden of his wild escapades; he dispelled the gloom of my rather melancholy temperament. He was sunshine; I, shadow.

We were as united as day and night, as moonshine and madness, as sorrow and joy. Then one day the old, old story—a woman came between us.

Only a month ago, Evelyn testified at my trial. As she stood in the witness box, I looked at her quite calmly. There was no feverish throbbing of the senses, no wild beating of the heart, no feeling of sadness or of joy.

On the contrary, this slender figure in black conjured up nothing but a kind of dull resentment. *What a tiny speck of dust,* I thought, *to slow down the wheel of Progress!*

And suddenly this inconsequential doll in her widow's weeds, this female straw whom I had loved, lost all semblance to humanity and became a meaningless automaton—an automaton created by my attorney to squeak out on the silent air one mechanical phrase:

"He is insane—he is insane—he is insane!"

Ah, no, waxen puppet, Gustave Ericson is not insane! Squeak on till the end of time that lying phrase and still it will find no echo of the truth.

Many years ago, perhaps, there were chords of moonlight in my brain which you could play upon, intertangled threads of wild desire which throbbed at your slightest touch—but now I am reason itself enthroned, silent and smiling, as impervious to that small, petty passion as is the mountain peak to the fretful, flickering lightning.

I do not attempt to justify my youthful infatuation. Evelyn Lawrence, as I saw her in the courtroom—her eyes red from weeping, her dark hair prematurely streaked with gray—makes that impossible.

But there was a time, not so many years ago, when she possessed a certain languid charm which one associates with a warm summer afternoon spent in the country. She was the kind of woman toward whom an overworked man naturally turns with thoughts of rest.

I remember distinctly how I chanced to meet her. It was two years after my graduation from college. Paul and I had been working steadily in the laboratory for upward of a month.

I was at that time on the point of discovering Zodium, the life-giving chemical that was afterward to revolutionize medicine. We were both worn out and plunged into a fit of depression. We had gone far, but still success trembled in the balance.

Suddenly Paul, with a muttered imprecation, flung himself on the leather couch in one corner. Spots of color flamed up in his cheeks, and he began to pluck at his lower lip—a sure sign that he was out of sorts with the world.

"What's the matter?" I asked, looking up from the test tube which I was heating ever an electric burner.

Paul's blue eyes wandered to the window.

"It's hell to be cooped up in here day after day!" he murmured. "I've grown to feel like a run-down machine. Let's chuck it and get out into the air."

"But there's our experiment," I expostulated. "We may find the secret any day now."

"That's what you've been saying for the last week!" he cried impatiently. "Let Zodium wait a while. My aunt's having some sort of an affair over the weekend. Let's go!"

"Who'll be there?"

"Oh, there'll be the Turners and a cousin of theirs—Evelyn Lawrence, I believe her name is. She's quite a beauty, Aunt Grace tells me."

I snorted contemptuously. Here we were, on the brink of one of the most noteworthy discoveries of the age, and Paul was yapping about house-parties and pretty girls!

As fond as I was of him, I was never quite reconciled to this frivolous strain in his nature—a strain that kept popping up at the most inopportune moments, interfering with hard, conscientious work toward the furthering of science. And yet it was necessary to humor him on these occasions—otherwise, he would sulk for days and be of no use in the laboratory.

"Well, if *you* go on a strike, I suppose the shop must close up!" I said regretfully. "But it seems a shame when—"

He cut me short with the gleeful shout of a released schoolboy:

"Now you're talking!" he cried. "Get your things together and we'll be off in two shakes! And, remember, not a word about chemistry until after Sunday."

The upshot of the affair was that I spent the weekend out of town and met Evelyn Lawrence. I can only explain the emotional crisis I passed through by the fact that I was in an exhausted mental condition, and that the girl's languid atmosphere soothed my tingling nerves like a sleeping draft.

Certainly love at first sight is a ridiculous hypothesis to be entertained for an instant by the scientific mind. And yet, on the evening of the second day— as we drifted lazily along on the smooth, moonlit waters of Lake Deerfoot in one of Miss Grey's canoes, seemingly as far distant from the noisy, frivolous world as the small, remote stars—I had all I could do to refrain from voicing an ardent protestation of an enduring passion.

What a fool! Even then, the moon exerted an undue influence over me.

On the following day I regained a measure of common sense. Here I was wasting the precious moments when I might be at work in my laboratory.

If I happened to be in love—well, even love must wait its turn on science. After I had completed my discovery, why, then it would be time enough to analyze my emotions toward the girl.

I pointed out to Paul that our holiday was over. He seemed very loath to leave the country.

Finally he said that he would follow me into town later in the day, but that no consideration could move him to travel on such a warm morning. I had to content myself with his promise, and, after saying my farewells to Evelyn and Miss Grey, caught the ten-thirty for town.

I have always prided myself on an ability to banish everything from my mind but the work at hand. Perfect concentration is the ladder by which man may ascend to unknown heights.

And yet, on returning home, I had great difficulty in fixing my attention on Zodium. For the first hour or so in the laboratory, Evelyn Lawrence's face hung like a brilliant, languid moon over my mental horizon, drawing my thoughts away from the hunt for unknown knowledge. I broke fully three test tubes and scalded my hand severely before I regained my usual mental equilibrium.

Paul, in spite of his promise, failed to put in an appearance during the afternoon. I did not see him for the entire week—in fact, not until after I had made the final, triumphant experiment that gave Zodium to the world.

By an acute chain of reasoning, I had succeeded in discovering the essential without him, and was actually holding a vial of the precious amber-colored liquid in my hand when he made a rather shamefaced appearance in the doorway of the laboratory.

At the moment, I was so flushed with success that I greeted him with no shade of reproach in my tone.

"Let me introduce you to Zodium, Paul!" I cried, leaping to my feet and advancing toward him. "At last the secret is ours!"

His face, which had worn a ruefully penitent expression, flushed on a sudden to deep red. He advanced a step and examined the contents of the vial that I held out for his inspection.

"You don't say!" he muttered. "So you got it, after all!" His eyes avoided mine and wandered to the window. "Well, now you've discovered it," he said almost belligerently, "of what practical use is it?"

"Of what practical use?" I cried. "Why, you talk like a grocer, Paul! How should I know as yet? But undoubtedly, it will be invaluable for medical purposes."

"Perhaps," he muttered. "That remains to be seen. But tell me how you happened to hit upon it."

When one has worked unremittingly to the successful conclusion of a problem—worked both day and night, as I had done—one often finds recompense for one's labor by explaining the solution to an enthusiastic, comprehending listener.

So it was in my case. It was a pleasure to unburden my mind to Paul. I even went so far as to repeat with equally good results my triumphant experiment.

"You see how near we were to the solution last week," I finished. "If you hadn't insisted on taking a holiday, it might have been *you* who discovered Zodium."

He laughed a trifle bitterly.

"You deserve all the credit, Gustave. It was your idea in the first place. But I made a discovery this week which puts Zodium in the shade."

"You did? Why, I didn't know you were working this week. What is it?"

I had an uncomfortable feeling that Paul had stolen a march on me.

"You wouldn't call it work, exactly," he answered with one of his vivid flushes. "My discovery is simply this: I am in love!"

In spite of myself, a feeling of relief permeated me. So it was just another one of his silly, sentimental affairs and no startling chemical discovery that might overshadow Zodium.

Paul, in spite of his brilliancy, was as susceptible to Cupid's darts as any schoolgirl. A lack of constancy alone had pulled him up short on the very brink of matrimony at least a score of times.

"Who's the lucky girl now?" I asked indulgently.

"Mrs. Paul Grey."

"Mrs. Paul Grey?" I repeated, aghast. "You don't mean to tell me that you're married?"

"Just that," he said simply.

"But after that affair with Laura LeRue, I thought—"

He cut me short impatiently.

"That was just moonshine and nonsense. This is an entirely different thing. Evelyn Lawrence is a girl any man would be proud of winning.

"We loved each other from the first day. What was the use of waiting? We were married this morning before a magistrate."

"Evelyn Lawrence!" I muttered. "You married *her,* Paul?"

Suddenly all the air seemed to have been pumped out of the room. It became difficult to breathe. He had been right—this discovery of his had completely overshadowed Zodium.

"To be sure, Evelyn Lawrence," he continued joyously. "You remember her, don't you?"

And then I could not refrain from smiling. Remember her? Good God, I should always do that—always! And this red-faced fool had dared to ask me, Gustave Ericson, if I—

But I must be quite calm, smiling, cheerful. He must never know that he had blundered unpardonably into the web of my attachment. While I had been working like a slave for science, he, the shirker, the woman-seeker, had slipped out and stolen my life's happiness!

Very well—but someday he should answer for that! Now it was necessary that no shadow of the truth should fall between us.

Rising, I grasped his hand.

"My heartiest congratulations, Paul!" I cried. "She is indeed a prize well worth winning!"

How much longer we talked, I do not know. I was like a man coming out of an opiate to the presence of feverish pain. And everything I said did not seem to come from myself, but rather from a talking-machine which had suddenly been placed in my breast, wound, and started; and everything he said fell on my eardrums like the relentless beating of tiny steel hammers. *Tip! tap! tip tap!* his words sounded, driving in painful thoughts which were like red-hot nails.

And all the time the vial of Zodium grinned at me from the table like a tiny, misshapen Judas.

II

The Portrait

There is no medicine in all nature's apothecary shop so potent, so soothing as the slow-falling sands of time. They cover up in due course the painful, bleeding wounds of yesterday; and when we attempt to retrace our steps into that bygone era, when we attempt to portray the agonies which once seemed so real to us, we stumble over the mounds of buried feeling like strangers in an unknown graveyard.

My infatuation for Evelyn was real enough at the time—so real indeed that it caused me unparalleled agony to think of her as another man's wife.

Even my sincere affection for Paul failed to lessen the weight of the blow. Realizing that I could no longer put my mind on science, I closed up the laboratory and left the city.

For several months I traveled aimlessly from place to place, driven on by a restless energy to be moving. Gradually, peace began to settle over my tormented mind.

And then, a year after Paul's marriage—just as I had begun to take a brighter view of life—I met the man who was unconsciously to play such an important part in future events.

At the time, I was living at a small hotel in one of those picturesque little towns to be found in Virginia. I was in the third week of my stay when a young man stepped up to where I was sitting on the veranda and accosted me.

"You have a most interesting face," he said without any preamble. "I would like to paint your portrait."

Naturally, I was rather taken aback by his bluntness. However, I had already learned never to take offense at an artist. One might as well grow angry at a hummingbird. It is a waste of energy.

Besides, there was a pleasing frankness in this young man's manner that was very attractive. He stood with his legs wide apart, cocking his head at me as though I were some strange specimen under a microscope.

"You flatter me!" I said with a half-smile. "But may I ask why you find my face of interest?"

Before he answered, he scrutinized me with a pair of very keen gray eyes. In spite of his immaculate flannels, pink cheeks and youthfully egotistical mustache, there was something of the wolf about this young man. He had the air of one sniffing at the heels of vanishing Truth.

"Before I tell you that," said he, "I wish you would visit my studio. I'm sure I could explain everything more easily there.

"An artist can only be natural when he is surrounded by the works of his art. Can I presume upon your good nature to the extent of enticing you up three flights of stairs?"

I rose to my feet willingly enough. The boredom which so often accompanies loneliness had weighed down my spirits of late. Perhaps the company of this ingenious young man would prove amusing.

"I must warn you beforehand that I know nothing about art!" I told him as we entered the hotel together.

"No matter," he rejoined lightly. "You, yourself—if you will pardon my frankness—are a work of art, a walking portrait of an advanced passion.

"There is a look in your eyes at times—a certain twist to your lips that— But, no matter, I will explain later."

As we mounted to his room, he told me that he was the famous portrait painter, Anthony Worthington, of New York, and that his doctor had ordered him to take a protracted rest in the country. He had already been away from town for nearly two months, and during that time had not done a single stroke of work.

"I'm fairly itching to get back at it," he continued. "And when I saw your face at breakfast this morning, I knew that the moment had come."

Anthony Worthington had secured the largest and brightest room in the hotel. It had two long French windows, through which the sunlight streamed, lighting every corner and illumining several dark portraits on the wall.

The whole place had absorbed the personality of its occupant. It was indisputably the abode of a painter.

"Is this some of your work?" I asked, stepping up to the wall and examining the portrait of a bull-necked individual with a jaw that jutted out like the prow of a battleship.

"Yes," he answered, offering me a cigarette and lighting one himself. "That's Bill Sands. I painted him a week before he was arrested for murder.

"You may remember the case. He killed his father and robbed him of a cheap watch. The most primitive type. But still we must have a beginning."

"Am I to understand that you are interested in painting criminal types?"

"Murderers!" he replied simply. "It's my life's work! We all have our hobbies, we artists. Some of us paint cows, sheep, geese—even pigs.

"But give me murderers every time. I've painted dozens of them in the last five years."

"But isn't it rather difficult to find sitters?" I asked.

"Not at all," he told me. "Any city is loaded with murderers. Walk a block and you'll meet ten.

"Most of them are of the primitive type like Bill, here; and, of course, nearly all of them are in the embryonic state. These remain out of jail merely because the peculiar twist in their characters has never been properly developed."

This poor young man is mentally deranged, I thought to myself. *What a shame it is that so many artists live on the borderland of reason!* Aloud I said:

"But I suppose, in time, they all succumb to their natural tendencies?"

"Not necessarily," he answered lightly. "On the contrary, very few attain a full mental growth. Perhaps the natural fear of the consequences holds them in check, or perhaps the psychological moment never enters their lives."

I began to feel a strange interest in this crack-brained artist's theory. He stated his opinion with such evident sincerity that I knew well enough that he was not joking.

Could there be any truth in such a bizarre belief? If so, it would cause timid folk like my father no end of worry—timid folk who had amassed large fortunes and whose progeny would be benefited by an early demise.

"And some of these embryonic murderers go through life never guessing the truth about themselves?" I suggested.

"Just so," said he. "It often takes war to wake them up. A great international conflict serves as a mammoth incubator for all the vices. It hatches out some strange chicks, my friend—some very strange chicks."

He paused for a moment, and I caught the glint of his sharp, gray eyes as he turned toward the window.

"A fair light," he murmured. "If you would oblige—"

"You want me to sit for you?" I asked, "*I* am, then, one of these embryonic murderers?"

I had spoken facetiously and was scarcely prepared for his answer. When he said:

"Out of your own mouth you have spoken it," I started involuntarily. "But not at all like Bill," he went on encouragingly. "You're of a very uncommon type. Just glance at that other portrait near the window."

To humor him, I did as he told me. I saw a strikingly handsome face, lean, dark, esthetic—a face with haunting eyes and drooping, crimson lips—a face which one felt instinctively to be quite soulless, quite malign.

Like an assassin's mask, time had carefully carved it out of ivory to conceal the grimaces of the soul. And yet, through the slanting eyelids, death looked out at the world; and behind those languid, crimson lips, one sensed the cruel white fangs.

"That," Anthony Worthington continued, "is Burgess Corell. He murdered his wife by mental suggestion. He forced her to commit suicide.

"The law could never touch him. That is the face of an advanced type of murderer, just as Bill's is the primitive type. Together they represent crime's ultimates."

I turned from the portrait with an involuntary shudder. The atmosphere of this mad artist had got on my nerves. Of course, what he had said about me was ridiculous.

And yet, there had been a time, a year ago now, when Paul had stood in my laboratory and told me that—

What nonsense! Of course I had been hurt and angry. What man would not? But I had long since reconciled myself to my loss. I could now view the affair with a philosophic calm. All my affection for Paul had returned.

"Do these murderers whom you paint confess their crimes to you?" I asked.

"Very often," my host answered genially. "It's embarrassing. Murderers are inclined to be too communicative, if anything.

"They're all great egotists at heart. Many a confession has been made because the guilty man thought the story too good to keep all to himself."

"To be the confidant of a murderer, I should think, would be a trifle dangerous. They might repent of their loquacity at leisure."

Anthony Worthington smiled pleasantly.

"You're right," he said. "It is dangerous. After a few unpleasant experiences, I always put wads of cotton in my ears and made sure that my models saw me do it. Now, if you'll be kind enough to sit in that chair by the window, I'll get to work."

"You think that my face really deserves your attention?" I asked as I seated myself.

"It stirs me!" he cried enthusiastically. "You have a remarkable expression. Turn your head a trifle to the right, please. The chin a little higher. Ah, that's it! Splendid! Splendid!"

He began to take aim at me with a piece of charcoal.

And I, in spite of my great sanity, once more experienced an involuntary tremor. At first, this young man's silly, pretense had amused me. I had looked on him as a crack-brained child and had humored him accordingly.

But the portrait of Burgess Corell had unaccountably affected me. For an instant, it had seemed that I was looking into a distorted mirror at my own face.

There was something about the tilt of the chin, something in the curve of the lips and the lifted eyebrows, which resembled the Gustave Ericson I met each morning in the shaving-mirror. It was just coincidence, of course, but then—

Anthony Worthington's voice broke in on my thoughts. He stood before his easel, making quick, definite strokes; and while he worked, he talked coherently.

"We all have two faces," he was saying. "Men go about in masks. It is the art of the portrait-painter to unmask humanity. He must see more than the surface values; he must get a glimpse of the soul, or he is merely a photographer.

"It is difficult in some cases; and especially difficult with you. Now, if you would kindly think of some especial enemy of yours—some person whom you hate with all your soul."

"I have no enemies," I answered coldly. "I hate no one."

"Have you seen the morning paper?" he asked hopefully. "No? Well, there's a most interesting murder on the first page, and a rather vivid description of the details. Allow me."

He rose, and, picking up a copy of the *Sentinel,* presented it to me.

"Read it carefully," he pleaded. "It's the first column to the right. All about the murder of an old woman in Roanoke."

I smiled in spite of myself.

"I have no interest in such things," I assured him. "Well, if you insist." I took the paper and glanced at it. The next moment I had all I could do to stifle a cry of astonishment.

My eyes had become riveted upon an article to the left where he had pointed—an article which bore the heading:

YOUNG SCIENTIST GIVES ZODIUM TO THE WORLD

I had great difficulty in holding the paper steady while I read the short paragraph.

> One of the most interesting discoveries of modern times was recently made by the young chemist and scientist, Paul Grey. And he has put his discovery to an eminently practical use. Zodium, we have been told, is likely to revolutionize medicine. Dr. Madden, an eminent physician and specialist, prophesies that this drug will add at least ten years to the longevity of the race. It acts as a powerful stimulant on diseased and worn-out organs, and is said to be a sure cure for hardening of the arteries.

For a moment, the room seemed to be revolving slowly about me. Allowing the newspaper to slip to the floor, I seized the arms of the chair. And then a great wave of blood swam up into my head, blurring my vision with a curtain of dancing purple.

So Paul had betrayed me! Not contented with robbing me of a wife, he had now robbed me of my discovery. Like a sneaking hound, he had waited till my back was turned before stretching out his plundering hands to my treasure.

And I had trusted him always! What a fool I had been! But now— Why, he would smart a bit. I would see to that. I would—

"Hold it, hold it!" Anthony Worthington cried out. He was working like a madman.

"The very expression I wanted! Hold it, man—for God's sake, hold it! Hold it; and I will paint a portrait of you which shall be life itself—as true as your own soul!"

III

"I Have Painted Your Soul"

Two weeks after I learned of Paul's treachery, Anthony Worthington wrote his name on the canvas and stepped back with a sigh of content. My portrait was finished.

"Come and look at yourself," he called he. "This is a sample of my very best work."

With no small amount of curiosity, I took my stand beside him and examined the painting. Up to this time I had purposely refrained from looking at it.

It is unfair to judge a man's work until it is the finished product of its creator. The satisfying results often rest in the very last touch of the master's hand.

For some time I looked at this painted likeness of myself with amazement. This could not be I! This face, distorted by passion, with pinched nostrils and glaring eyes, was not the face of Gustave Ericson—that calm, thoughtful face which had so often looked reassuringly at me from the mirror.

Like Medusa's head, this horrible apparition froze me into dumb immobility. The painted figure seemed to be crouched there, waiting but for the signal to spring forward to all its murderous length; and while thus waiting, the stored-up venom of the world was welling into cruel lines about the lips, glowing dully behind the starting eyeballs, writing its message to the world on the furrowed parchment of the forehead.

Shuddering, I turned away.

"This is a portrait painted by a madman," I said aloud.

Anthony Worthington smiled.

"It is you," he answered. "I have painted your soul."

For an instant hot anger overmastered me. It took all my self-command to hold in check a wild desire to pick up one of the pallet-knives and cut into shreds the painted lie.

What right had this crack-brained artist to so parody my emotions? I had been a fool to sit for him!

"It is a very fine piece of work," he continued, rubbing his hands together gleefully. "If you don't want it, I'll hang it in my studio at home."

I was silent for several moments. It would never do to let him have this portrait. He might show it to his friends; he might even put it on exhibition or sell it.

In my mind's eye I could see a crowd of the curious surrounding this abomination and commenting on the model who was so very different. Such a portrait could well nigh brand a man a felon. I had a shrinking shame that other eyes might see it.

No, that would never do. I would buy it and destroy it at my leisure.

Once more I looked long at the painting. It was necessary to humor the artist until I rescued it from his clutches.

After that? Well, after that I could destroy it in a thousand different ways.

"It improves on a second glance," I told him. "In fact, it isn't at all bad. You seem to have got the—er—"

"The hidden expression," he broke in impatiently. "This is your real face, my friend."

"To be sure," I said mildly, "to be sure. The hidden expression, that's what I meant. Now, I want this portrait, Mr. Worthington. The price?"

"In your case, nothing. It was a positive joy to paint you. I would like to do another one of you."

"I am leaving for home tomorrow," I told him hastily. "Perhaps some other time."

"That's a shame," said he. "However, as you say, perhaps some other time. When I return to the city, I intend painting my conception of the Spanish Inquisition. You will be invaluable as a model. May I call on you?"

"Certainly," I lied. "And my portrait?"

"I'll have it crated up and sent to your address."

We parted with this understanding; and on the following afternoon I boarded the train for home. Strange to say, I had a feeling of unbounded relief as the wheels began to revolve. It was as though I were escaping some imminent peril. Try as I would, I could not then account for this uncalled-for sensation.

On arriving home, I found my father greatly altered. During my absence, he had aged considerably.

His face, once as round and red as a harvest moon, had dwindled. Now it was as shriveled as a winter apple; and his large, protruding, brown eyes looked out of it with the hopeless expression of a sick animal.

Also his disposition had altered for the worse. He now evinced an impatience toward the petty little annoyances of everyday life which he would have blushed for at an earlier period.

He greeted me with an unpleasant allusion to my long absence that was galling in the extreme. It was all I could do to refrain from voicing my opinion of his churlishness.

"Well, now that you're home," he continued, "I hope you'll go into the office and be of some credit to me."

The mere thought of Gustave Ericson in an office made me smile. An eagle in a hencoop could not be more incongruous.

"My dear father," I said patiently enough, "do you not realize that I am a scientist? My time is invaluable to the progress of the world. No business is important enough to absorb my mentality."

Now this truthful answer should have silenced him. But it did not silence him. On the contrary, it seemed to infuriate him.

The poor old man was such a mental dullard that he could not appreciate the gifts of his son. No doubt my words sounded to him like hollow boasting.

"A scientist!" he sneered. "What have you ever discovered? All *you* do is to make vile stinks in your laboratory.

"Now, if you were like Paul Grey, and really did something, I'd put up with it. If you had discovered Zodium, which is of practical use, why, then—"

Suddenly he paused, and his eyes seemed to fairly pop out at me. He had the look of one who beholds an unaccountable transformation.

"Why, what's the matter, Gustave? Aren't you well?"

"Certainly, father. Do I look ill?"

"No, not now. A moment ago your face seemed to change. It must be my eyes."

He put his hand to his forehead with a weary gesture.

"I haven't been myself lately. What was I saying? Oh, yes! You must go into the office, Gustave. I'll not support you in idleness."

"Idleness!" I cried angrily. "Have you no conception of my life? I have worked very hard."

"Where are the results?" he asked in an aggravating tone.

I had opened my lips for a bitter reply when the tall figure of the butler appeared in the doorway, interrupting for a time the family quarrel.

"The express company just left a large box for you, Mr. Gustave," he said. "Where shall I put it, sir?"

Instantly the feeling of exhilaration which I had experienced since leaving Virginia vanished. It was as though an invisible weight had descended upon me.

I had a sensation of guilt—a sensation as though I were in immediate danger of being detected in some crime. If the butler had been a relentless policeman, and I a cowering felon, his words could not have caused me a greater shock.

Ridiculous as it now seems, beads of perspiration gathered on my forehead, and my knees began to tremble.

"You may put it in my laboratory, Tom," I said at length.

"Shall I take the crate off, sir?"

"No!" burst from me with such vehemence that my father and the butler both started involuntarily. "I'll open it myself!"

"Very well, sir," said Tom in a grieved tone. "I'll leave a hammer on the table."

"Why did you shout at Tom like that?" my father asked when the butler had gone. "That's no way to speak to servants, Gustave. I won't tolerate that kind of thing in *my* house."

"It won't happen again, father."

I turned on my heel and strode into the laboratory, leaving the old man pacing up and down the room with the pompous air of one who has come off best in a battle of words.

Tom had obeyed me with rather more than his customary alacrity. I found a tall, crated package leaning up against one of the walls. Undoubtedly it was the portrait.

Picking up a hammer, I began to tear the laths free. They gave readily enough, coming out with the sharp, rasping sound of nails torn from wood; and, in a moment more, I lowered the paper-swathed portrait to the floor and began to unwrap it. Soon the painted apparition of myself glared up at me with all its blood-curdling ferocity.

While I had been at work, my nerves had been steady enough; but now, as I met the fixed regard of the portrait, I noted something that at the time I thought a foolish fancy. The figure in the gold frame seemed to writhe from side to side, as if in a death agony, its thin, red lips drew back from long, white fangs; its breast rose and fell spasmodically; and its malignant, narrow-lidded eyes rolled wildly, as though seeking some loophole of escape.

And then a strange hallucination possessed me. For an instant it seemed that we had struggled together, this painted creature and I; that we had had a fierce combat in this very room; that at last I had thrown it on its back and was holding it there.

Sweat poured down my face and my knees were trembling from fatigue; yet an overmastering hatred burned my veins like molten lava. I would destroy it forever. That was my only hope, my only salvation.

I would bring the hammer down on its leering face again and again till nothing was left but an unrecognizable pulp. Now for a straight blow and a strong blow. I raised the hammer aloft.

Suddenly a human hand grasped my arm and a loud voice called out: "What are you doing, Gustave?"

Instantly the strange hallucination passed. I found myself on my feet, the hammer still gripped tightly in my hand.

My father stood near me, his face unnaturally white and his eyes staring. He had raised one arm on a level with his head, as though to protect himself from a blow.

"What do you say?" I muttered hoarsely. The hammer slipped from my hand to the floor.

He lowered his arm, and his face became suffused with blood. He seemed to be in a towering rage.

"You must be insane!" he shouted. "I'll have no madman in my house! Whether you like it or not, I tell you that that painting does resemble you.

"Just a moment ago, when you lifted the hammer to strike me, your face was exactly like that."

"*I* lifted the hammer to strike you, father?" I cried, dumfounded. "Why, I didn't know you were in the room!"

"You're lying or you're mad," he said. "I knew you had an abominable temper, but I didn't think—" He paused and shot a suspicious glance at the portrait.

"If I hadn't seen you in time, you'd have killed me, Gustave! I know it. I could see it in your face—it's in the face of your portrait now. Good God, what a son!"

He began sidling toward the door, his frightened eyes still fixed upon me.

"But I don't know what you're talking about!" I cried in desperation. "I was unpacking the portrait and didn't even know—"

He cut me short.

"It's no use lying," he sneered. "I came in here and found you on your knees, staring at that painting. Looking over your shoulder I said that I thought it was a very good likeness.

"At that you shouted out, 'You lie!' and, springing to your feet, attacked me with a hammer. I avoided your first blow, and then you came to your senses."

"A ridiculous story!" I shouted after him.

"Perhaps so," said he. "But if the facts were known, you'd get a term in prison. From now on we'll not live under the same roof. I think you'd better be off on your travels again tomorrow."

Once more he gave me a fearful look over his shoulder, and then, without another word, slammed the door in my face. Soon the sound of his shuffling footsteps died away.

IV

The Murder

Someone has said: "Truth is stranger than fiction." Bear this well in mind as you peruse the chronicle of the startling events which befell me and do not deafen your ears to these unparalleled experiences because they seem unbelievable. Once more I repeat: "I am sane, quite sane!" And as a proof of my sanity, I refer you triumphantly to Zodium and the Purple Veil. Which one of you, my readers, has given to the world such proofs of sound mentality as these?

On the night of our altercation, my father was stricken with a severe attack of paralysis. Perhaps the abnormal excitement under which he had been laboring brought it on prematurely; but, as I look back on the scene, as I weigh again on the scales of time his uncalled-for accusation, I exonerate myself from any shadow of blame. Thus all my life, I have been more sinned against than sinning.

It is terrifying to see a robust man stricken down in an instant—at one moment to see him strong, upright, master of his powers; at the next, a fallen tree-trunk, twisted, motionless, dumb.

An unseen ax has been at work for days, months, years—but we have noticed nothing till the fall. Who wields this ax so silently, so mysteriously?

Even now the shadowy woodsman may have signaled us out in the waiting forest; even now he may be chopping through the essence of our lives. Who, then, is safe?

My father, once a virile, boisterous man, had become an inanimate, voiceless lump of humanity—an odd, waxen dummy that lay motionless in its large, four-posted bed.

Only his eyes moved. In them had centered the spark of life. They followed the nurse, the doctor and myself about with feverish anxiety; and often, when my back was turned, I knew that they were still staring at me.

Although he had lost both the power of speech and the power of motion, in fact was as completely shut off from human intercourse as if he were already dead and buried, I knew by the expression in his eyes that he feared me and would continue to fear me up to the very end. If nothing else, fear dwelt behind those eyes.

How ridiculous, how laughably absurd! He should have been as immune from fear as a fallen tree is immune from the rising storm.

Suppose his ridiculous surmise *had* been correct; suppose I had once threatened him with physical violence, what then? Surely he was now quite safe from me. I could offer him nothing but a blessed relief.

A man of limited intelligence, he remained one to the very end.

I had a consultation with the family doctor shortly after my father's stroke. He offered no hopes of recovery, but seemed to think that his patient might retain this feeble spark of life for years. It was at that time I made the statement which was later to count so heavily against me at my trial. It was simply this: "It would be a work of kindness to put my father out of his misery."

Surely it was a very innocent and truthful remark. And yet, how sinister it has been made to appear when repeated triumphantly by the prosecuting attorney!

For a time my father's illness caused me to forget the portrait. I had a thousand and one things to attend to. It was necessary that his business interests should be looked after. I was plunged into a whirlpool of commercial affairs.

Exactly two weeks after my homecoming, I entered the laboratory for the second time. It was evening and the room was bathed in blackness. Lighting the electric lamp, I glanced about me.

Unconsciously my eyes sought the corner where my portrait had rested against the wall. It was no longer there.

An unaccountable tremor passed through me. I circled the room with my eyes apprehensively and at the next moment uttered an ejaculation of relief. Someone had hung the portrait above the fireplace.

Now it looked down at me with sneering, sardonic contempt—the look of a lifelong enemy who has suddenly obtained the upper hand. "I am here for all time," it seemed to be saying.

Instantly all my old hatred and repugnance for this painted abomination returned in full force. Seating myself opposite it, I repaid its baleful stare with all my mental strength, attempting to break its almost hypnotic influence.

And sitting thus, apparently in repose, but in reality tingling all over from an overmastering sensation of loathing and fear, I soon beheld a clarified vision of the truth. It was simply this:

Suddenly my painted likeness moved, its breast rose and fell, and its lips lengthened in a mocking smile. Then, nodding its head at me solemnly, re-provingly, it spoke.

Like dry, wind-swept leaves, its word came to me—leaves that halt for an instant, only to rustle on again about our feet.

"Gustave Ericson, why do you deny me?"

And then it seemed to me that hot, angry speech tore my lips apart, that challenging words leaped forth like an army going out in battle array.

"I know what you want," I cried aloud. "But I will not obey you! How dare you claim to be my soul?—you, with your murderous eyes and loathsome lips! I will do more than deny you—I will destroy you!"

"No man can destroy his own thoughts," the portrait murmured.

"You are not my thoughts," I answered. "You are but another's painted fancy of my thoughts."

Again the portrait smiled.

"Your father found me true. Do you not remember when you denied me first?"

An involuntary shudder passed through my frame.

"It was *you* then," I gasped, "who threatened him with a hammer?"

The portrait bowed and smiled. Placing one of its long, thin hands over its heart, it bowed and smiled.

"You or me, what can it matter?" it murmured politely. "In the eyes of the world, it will not matter."

"In the eyes of the world, it will not matter," I repeated dully. The portent of its words sounded a brazen alarm somewhere in my breast. God! how true that was. In the eyes of the world, it would not matter.

What it did, I must answer for. And if it could once escape from its golden prison, what might it not do?

I feared the look in its eyes, the crimson cruelty of its lips, the long, thin hands that seemed to vibrate with evil energy. I must destroy it now or never!

"You wish me to kill my father?" I said at length, glancing about furtively for some weapon to use against it.

"I *demand* that you kill your father," the portrait answered calmly. "We need his fortune to advance science. How can you hesitate?"

At that moment my wandering eyes encountered what they had been in search of—a bottle containing a powerful chemical that had gone into the making of Zodium. A few drops of this sprinkled on the canvas and I would be rid of my loathsome visitor for all time.

Rising, I took the bottle from the shelf and approached the portrait.

"You're right," I said in a reassuring tone; "it is evidently my duty. But there are the means to be considered.

"Now, this chemical is deadly and leaves no telltale traces. If I gave him a drop in his sleeping draft, he would never wake again."

The portrait's lips were once more contorted in an evil smile, and for an instant its eyes were covered with a gray film.

"Poison?" it muttered. "To be sure, *poison*. Let me see!"

By now I had reached the wall and stood directly beneath the portrait.

"Perhaps you are unfamiliar with this chemical," I murmured, uncorking the bottle deftly. "It is guaranteed to be efficacious—to remove all the stains from our lives. Here, take it in the face, you dog!"

The portrait made a protective movement with its thin, white hands. But it was too late. With the speed of lightning I had thrown the contents of the bottle straight into its leering eyes.

Now the fiery liquid was running down the canvas, burning and destroying everything in its path. I heard a choking cry, and then all was silence.

Picking up a large sponge from the laboratory table, I began to pass it up and down the canvas till every square inch of paint was saturated with the liquid. Then I seated myself with a feeling of relief and watched the grizzly apparition decompose and fade away before my eyes.

Soon the canvas offered nothing but a bare expanse of withered white. My portrait was no more.

And now a great drowsiness descended on me like a soft, languorous sea of mist. The mental struggle through which I had passed left me weary in both body and mind.

Closing my eyes, I was soon wafted away to the land of dreams—dreams, gigantic and ponderous, under which the subconscious mind toiled wearily along up mountain peaks and down deep declivities, on and on till the break of dawn.

And through these dreams, like the motif in music, as persistent and relentless as the voice of eternal alarm, rang these words in strange cadence: "What it does, I must answer for; what it does, I must answer for," till all the weird valleys of sleep took up the refrain and whispered it softly.

When I awoke, a sickly morning peered in at me through the trembling curtains. The room was still a ghostly battlefield for day and night.

In the corners, an army of shadows lurked, dark-browed and sinister, crawling ever back before the spearpoints of dawn. Suddenly the picture above my head was illumined, and I uttered a cry of horror.

Surely I could not have dreamed that I had destroyed the portrait! There was the empty bottle to prove that I had not dreamed. And yet the canvas no longer coffered a bare, seamed expanse.

No, there was my abominable painted likeness glaring down at me with an added venom in its eyes! And, while before the crouching figure had seemed several paces in the background, now it appeared closer, as if it had made a long stride forward while I slept.

Rubbing my eyes, I stared at it. But no stare of mine could wipe it out. If the acid had failed, was there anything in the world that *could* wipe it out?

And the portrait seemed to answer silently with its eyes: *No man can destroy his own thoughts.*

How long I sat confronting this incomprehensible apparition, I do not know. I was suddenly brought to myself by the sound of the door opening behind my back.

Starting, I turned and saw the butler's long, lugubrious face peering in at me.

"Well?" I asked sharply.

The man's watery eyes avoided mine. He licked his lips as though they were dry.

"I went for the doctor as you told me, sir," he said at last.

"You went for the doctor?" I cried at a loss. "When did *I* tell you to go for the doctor?"

Again Tom moistened his lips.

"Why, only two hours ago, sir! You must remember, sir, it was when I ran against you in the dark, just as you were coming out of the sick room."

"Nonsense! I haven't been near my father all night long."

"If you'll pardon me, sir," Tom continued more firmly, "I advise you to take a little rest. You're not yourself, sir. Your father's sudden death has—"

"My father's death!" I cried, aghast. "You don't mean to tell me that he's dead?"

"Yes, sir. It was as you thought—he was dead when I met you in the hall. Dr. Parkinson said it must have been his heart that failed him, at the last.

"Now brace up, sir! Don't give way! Just lean on my arm, sir. That's right; that's right."

My overstrung nerves had suddenly snapped at the butler's news. Trembling from head to foot, I burst out into uncontrolled sobs. So this was where my portrait had vanished to while I—slept.

I had thought the acid had destroyed it, while in reality it had only liberated it for a time to do a ghastly business. There had been a few drops of the chemical left in the bottle—enough to kill an old man; and when I had dozed off, *it* had used them.

See, the bottle was now bone-dry. God help me! What was I to do?

"Come into your own room and lie down, Mr. Gustave," Tom pleaded. "You need rest, sir."

I could no longer resist him. Indeed, I was so weak both in body and mind that I could not have found the strength to disobey a child.

What I needed was sleep—an ocean of tranquil, dreamless sleep. In the future lay a silent struggle between this painted demon and me, an heroic struggle for which I could expect no help from the world.

Before I quitted the room, I glanced over my shoulder at the painting. And as I did so, I saw its crimson lips curl up like a cat's, I saw it place its hand on its breast and bow ever so gracefully, like a famous actor responding to an encore. Bowing and smiling, it followed me with its eyes.

"Can I destroy it?" I murmured. "Will I ever be able to destroy it?"

V

The Purple Veil

Fortunately, my father's death called for no unpleasant investigations.

It was natural enough that a man well past the prime of life, suffering from paralysis and a weak heart, should flicker out without a moment's warning.

After the funeral I was plunged into a whirlwind of financial affairs that kept me thoroughly occupied. My father's estate proved to be a complex affair and one that took the family lawyer and myself many weeks to straighten out.

And yet, I was not able to forget my painted evil genius at this time. It would obtrude itself before my mental vision at the most inopportune moments, parting the calm, collected chain of thought with its ghostly hand, bowing and smiling at me in mockery from the picture frames which hung in the lawyer's office, and even interrupting me as I spoke solemnly of my affliction with some ribald jest at the expense of my poor, dead father—jests which my companions evidently considered as proceeding from my own lips, and which soon won for me an unenviable reputation.

And I was powerless to clear myself! Even then I realized that any accusation launched against the portrait would rebound and destroy me. The incredulity of a world given over to safety and sanity—a world marked out into squares of possibility like a chessboard—offers no mercy to a man such as I, a man lost in the labyrinth of unparalleled experience.

But do not think that I suffered meekly and in silence. No, on returning home from some scene in which I had been made to appear odious, I would steal into the laboratory, close the door softly, and take my stand before the portrait. Then, with a heart heavy with horror, I would upbraid it.

"You are a murderer!" I would say.

And my portrait would smirk at me with vivid lips, smirk and bow with its hand on its heart.

"I am a thought," it would murmur— "I am your crimson thought!"

"But why do you persecute me?"

"Do you not deny me?"

"And if I did not deny you?"

"Why, then we would be as one, united and peaceful—quite happy with one another. Do you not long for rest?"

And then, somewhere in my breast, the strident voice of eternal alarm would cry out, "Not yet—not yet!" And fear would ripple over me like an ice-crowned wave; and it would become difficult to face the portrait.

Shivering and drawing my dressing gown about me for warmth, I would steal out of the laboratory and up the creaking stairs to my room. God! how cold it was!

A month after I came into my inheritance, I once more took up my scientific studies. Under the eyes of the portrait, grimly and in silence, I experimented with various chemicals.

And such was my concentration that even its gorgon-like regard failed to shatter a theory that was springing up in my brain. Already I had visualized my translucent child, the Purple Veil.

You, who have experienced the poisonous gases on foreign battlefields can have but a minimized conception of the Purple Veil. Imagine, if you can, a thick, purplish smoke, shot here and there with tiny iridescent specks of flame like spangles in an eastern shawl—a thick, purplish smoke which coils about its victim fold on fold, smothering and burning till all life is transformed into blackened ashes.

Imagine this, and you may have some slight conception of the Purple Veil.

Hate is one of the great motive forces in the world. Often, like love, it inspires its devotees to unprecedented achievement.

It is a matter for speculation as to how many artistic masterpieces have been inspired by the transcending delirium of rage. And if this is true of Art, so also is it true of its calm but more deadly sisters, Science and Invention.

Hate drove me to the discovery of the Purple Veil—hate and fear. The leering, evil face of the portrait lashed me to Herculean mental efforts.

Perhaps, I thought, my salvation rests in such a discovery. This grimacing, painted thing has life—life hard to touch, indeed; but still life—and what has life can surely be smothered in the Purple Veil.

Thinking in this wise, I redoubled my efforts to reach the goal, slaving both day and night till my brain reeled and my nerves seemed like tightly drawn, throbbing wires. And while I toiled thus, my portrait looked down on me calmly, ironically, seemingly quite safe in its impregnable immortality. Often now it conversed with me.

"Why do you toil thus?"

"Because I hate deeply."

"And whom do you hate?"

"I hate the world. It has taken another to its breast in my place."

"And you would destroy the world?"

"Yes, I would destroy it! I would clothe it in the Purple Veil! Death shall hover over its cities and towns, over its valleys and mountaintops."

And then my portrait would smile as though well pleased; and it would moisten its crimson lips like one who is athirst. Ah, my cunning was more than a match for it!

How eagerly it swallowed the bait! Little did it guess for whom I was so carefully preparing the Purple Veil.

Once it said: "But is there no one among the multitudes, no especial enemy whom you have signaled out?"

At that, I nearly dropped the test tube I was holding. Had it guessed my secret? No, evidently not. It was smiling at me with a new, strange affection in its eyes—a loathsome affection that made my flesh crawl with unspeakable horror and dread.

For an instant I felt that I was stripped bare, that I could move neither hand nor foot, and that its eyes had multiplied into thousands of cold, slimy creatures which were crawling over me in a noisome wave—creatures which nestled against my body with a sickening sentimentality! It was possible to bear its hatred, but its love—

After a moment I answered:

"Yes, there *is* one. No doubt you have guessed. I would strike the false friend who robbed me of my discovery—that false friend whose treachery was responsible for your existence."

And then my portrait laughed a low laugh of satisfaction.

"We have become as brothers," it murmured, barely moving its lips. "No longer will we struggle with one another. We will enjoy a lifelong peace."

There came a day at last when my toil culminated in triumph—a day when the Purple Veil became a reality. A dozen tiny glass globes lay on the laboratory table, each one of which contained a thimbleful of crimson liquid—glass globes which, if broken, would exude a poisonous purple vapor spangled here and there with tiny iridescent sparks of living fire.

And my own self-protection had not been neglected. I had taken no risks. Upstairs, in my bedroom, there hung a suit of asbestos and a gas mask warranted to protect its wearer from the fatal fumes. Also, I had designed a covering of asbestos for the picture frame.

It was a melancholy afternoon in late autumn, an afternoon when Nature seems grieving over the sins of a prodigal youth. Through the laboratory window I could see the rainswept street glistening dully where the early electric illuminations touched it. Above the heads of passers-by, umbrellas would open their petals like parched buds welcoming the moisture.

And I thought with a grim smile: "What a commotion would be caused in this slow-moving stream of people if I dropped one of the little glass globes at their feet! How they would take to their heels if the Purple Veil were cast among them! Then this multitude of umbrellas, which are passing so sedately, would be caught up and blown away in an instant by a gale of fear."

"Why not do it?" the portrait murmured from its shadowed corner.

But I shook my head.

"You must not forget my personal enemy," I answered. "He comes first, so that others may follow."

"True," said the portrait, believing that I spoke of Paul. "Of course he must be the first and then—"

Suddenly it broke off and cautioned me to silence by a stealthy finger lifted to its lips. Someone was coming. I heard footsteps in the hall, the murmuring of voices; and then the door swung open, letting in a stream of golden light. I rose to my feet, my heart beating great waves of blood up into my head.

Paul stood on the threshold in the very center of this river of light—Paul, like a vision of the past, who had stolen from me both love and fame! Time had not even touched him in its passage. He looked not a day older than when I had seen him last.

"So you have come!" I cried.

He shaded his eyes with his hand and peered in.

"Is that you, Gustave?" he asked. "It's so dark in here that it's hard to make things out. I can see your face now, but—"

He broke off suddenly and uttered an ejaculation of astonishment.

"Why, what are you doing?" he cried, "Why are you standing on a chair before the fireplace?"

Instinctively my eyes followed his. A shaft of light from the street rested on the portrait's face; but everything else was in unstable, tottering shadow. One could see indistinctly the leather armchair beneath it; but that was all.

He had evidently taken Anthony Worthington's painted lie to be his friend whom it so brazenly caricatured. It was scarcely complimentary.

A month before, no doubt, I would have been unable to control my temper at this insult. But since then I had learned caution from close association with the portrait.

Now my answer was cooled by cunning before it left my lips. One had to be on guard against the stupid misapprehension of the world.

"This is a case of mistaken identity, Paul," I replied, touching the electric button at my elbow that illumined the room.

He evinced a ludicrous surprise when he realized his mistake. Wheeling about, he stammered:

"Why, I could have sworn that it was you! It seemed to move and smile!"

"Merely the play of light and shadow," I rejoined carelessly. "Surely to a scientific mind there can be nothing incomprehensible in natural phenomena? But what do you think of the portrait?"

"Not at all flattering," he muttered at length. "It portrays you in an ugly mood. But it's you, old man; it's undoubtedly you. I've seen you look just like that."

"When?" I asked curiously.

"Let me see." He paused for an instant and plucked at his lower lip with nervous fingers. "Why, the last time I saw you. You were put out because I had deserted the laboratory for a week to get married. I remember—"

"You didn't lose anything by that desertion," my portrait broke in ironically.

As was usual on such occasions, its words seemed to come from my own mouth. Paul thought that I had spoken to upbraid him for his theft of my discovery. His face flushed to a dark crimson.

"I came here to see you about that, Gustave," he began in a halting voice. "You don't know how I've suffered ever since. I wouldn't have done it if it hadn't been for Evelyn. All my money went in that Wall Street panic and I had to do something."

"Your money went?" I said kindly enough. "How was that?"

He ran his hand feverishly through his flaxen hair.

"It was my father's fault," he continued hastily. "He was always a gambler, you know. Someone gave him the wrong tip; he put everything he had on it and even borrowed Evelyn's little fortune.

"Then came the crash. Everything went—everything! We were all in debt up to our ears."

"That left—Zodium," I suggested.

"Yes, Zodium was our only chance. I tried to get hold of you; but your father didn't know where you were. From the first, I knew that there was a practical side to Zodium—a side worth millions if we could get the medical profession interested.

"Here was a great scheme lying idle, Evelyn and I at our wits' end, and you somewhere in the wilds. It *was* a temptation. I couldn't wait for you—I simply couldn't! You had shown me the formula; I went ahead and made Zodium and put it to a practical, money-getting use."

"You appeared in the eyes of the world as its discoverer," the portrait said coldly.

"That was necessary," Paul answered, evidently again laboring under the delusion that *I* had spoken. "I couldn't have sold it otherwise."

"But now," I cried joyfully, "you'll make full reparation; won't you, Paul?"

All my confidence in him had returned. As I spoke, I gazed challengingly at the portrait, which repaid my regard with an almost imperceptible curl of the lip. Evidently it was my friend's enemy as well as mine.

"Most certainly, Gustave," Paul rejoined solemnly. "I've come to offer full reparation. I have prospered in the last year. I am now able to pay you back every cent Zodium has made for me.

"And as for the fame, I will renounce that, too. I have already sent a letter to the *Scientific Monthly,* telling the whole truth about the matter and naming you as the discoverer."

I was overjoyed. All my old-time affection for Paul returned. His offense had not been so heinous as I had imagined. When one considered the temptation, one had to acknowledge that it would have taken a supernaturally moral man to have resisted. And besides, was he not making full reparation?

Grasping his hand, I told him that there was now nothing to forgive; I assured him of my friendship and spoke so warmly that I soon saw suspicious drops of moisture in his eyes.

And all the time, behind his back, my evil painted passion and mocked and moued, parodying our emotions with ugly grimaces that furrowed its face into wicked lines.

And on the table, within arm's reach, lay the little glass globes, each with a beating, crimson heart—the little glass globes in which lay waiting for any murderous hand, the Purple Veil.

VI

In the Laboratory

I spent that evening with Paul. He insisted that I return home with him; and I, nothing loath, accompanied him through the glistening streets.

As we sauntered along, side by side, two united shadows in a world of shadows, it seemed to me that nothing could ever again come between us.

A ten-minute walk brought us to his house. It was a large, pretentious-looking building—a building that reminded me of public libraries one finds in small Southern towns. It exuded an atmosphere of frigid learning not at all in keeping with its laughter-loving master.

At first I rather dreaded meeting Evelyn again. Perhaps she could still play upon my emotion—perhaps I had not yet outgrown my passion. And if this were so, would not my reborn affection for Paul be eaten away in an instant by that deadly chemical, jealousy?

But I might have spared myself all fears. That foolish sentiment had been buried somewhere in the past. As I greeted her, it was as though I were meeting her for the first time.

I saw a rather tall, anemic-looking girl with the dissatisfied expression of one who attempts to find happiness in material luxuries. What had become of that languid lily which had grown to such rare beauty in the fertile soil of my imagination?

I dined with Paul and his wife; and he and I talked of the past. We went over again our school and college days, while Evelyn struggled against boredom. At last our conversation flowed into the present.

"What are you working on now, Paul?" I asked.

"Nothing at present," he murmured, flushing slightly. "Evelyn has me nicely crucified on the cross of society. What with bridge, dances and receptions, I haven't been able to draw a free breath in months."

"But it's a very good thing for you to go about!" Evelyn broke in with a note of irritation in her voice. "You were almost a hermit when I married you."

Paul a hermit! I allowed myself a smile. My friend had never been *that*. On the contrary, his mixing propensities had interfered greatly with his scientific studies.

"And what are *you* doing now?" Paul asked eagerly. "Have you made another remarkable discovery?"

Before I answered him, my eyes wandered to a large oil landscape that hung on the opposite wall. To my horror, a familiar figure suddenly stepped out of a grove of trees in the background of this painting and warned me to silence with a ghostly finger lifted to its lips.

There was something immeasurably terrifying in thus being confronted by my relentless enemy. With a muffled exclamation of dismay, I stared at the canvas.

"Why, what is it?" Evelyn cried in alarm. "What do you see, Mr. Ericson?"

With a superhuman effort of will, I turned my head, glanced at her, and even smiled.

"Nothing," I murmured. "I was trying to discover if there were any human figures in that landscape. A shepherd, perhaps?"

"No," Evelyn answered wonderingly. "There are no figures."

"Quite so," I said lightly. "My eyes have been playing me tricks lately."

"But you haven't told me what you've been doing!" Paul broke in. "Have you come across anything as good as Zodium?"

Stiffening my will, forcing my eyes away from the tiny figure of fear in the painted meadow, I answered truthfully:

"Yes, I believe I *have* discovered something as good as Zodium."

Paul's cheeks were suddenly suffused with blood, his eyes shone brightly.

"I'd like to be let into the secret, old man," he muttered, "Perhaps I could be of some help. Of course, after what has happened, it seems—"

He broke off lamely with a muttered "damn" under his breath and a quick look at Evelyn. Evidently she knew nothing of what had formerly transpired.

And now the tiny figure in the painted meadow was waving its arms about as though possessed. "Stop! Stop!" it seemed to be screaming through its wide-open mouth.

But my determination to trust Paul was adamant. There was a look in his eyes that wrung my heart. For the once I would prove that I was stronger than my enemy—I would speak.

"My new discovery is called 'The Purple Veil,'" I began. "It is the most powerful, the most deadly chemical compound ever known to man. It is invaluable for military purposes. A shell containing the Purple Veil could destroy a city and the population of a city."

"If that is true," Paul cried with flashing eyes, "you can ask your own price for it! Any nation in command of such a secret would soon rule the world. I suppose you invented it with the idea of making it the most powerful weapon of modern warfare?"

Smiling slightly, I bent forward and murmured in his ear:

"I invented it to destroy a portrait which has become loathsome to me."

Evidently Paul considered this remark as an attempted joke. He laughed rather foolishly and immediately suggested showing me his laboratory that was situated in the garden at the rear of the house. Evelyn excused herself, saying that she had some domestic matters to attend to and would perhaps join us later.

Strange as it might once have seemed to me, I was glad to be rid of her. Tonight I wanted no one but Paul. We had so many things to talk over, he and I, that the presence of an unsympathetic listener seemed an irksome encumbrance.

With a sigh of relief, I followed my friend out of the house and down a winding garden path that led to a small cement building a score of yards away.

"Why didn't you have your laboratory in the house?" I asked idly.

"Because of Evelyn," he called back over his shoulder. "She didn't like the idea of having all those combustibles so near her."

What a blessed escape I have had! was my thought as I followed him up a flight of stone steps and waited while he swung back the heavy door of his laboratory.

The out-house consisted of a single large room lighted by electricity. The walls and ceiling were of stone; and in the center was a long metal table, on which were grouped several bottles of chemicals and the various appliances to be found in most laboratories. There was a musty odor about the place that called out for thorough airing and cleansing.

"You haven't been very busy here?" I suggested, pointing out several glass jars that were gray with dust.

"No," he answered with an almost inaudible sigh. "I have let my ambition go to the dogs. I've always needed you, Gustave, to keep me going."

He seated himself on the table.

"This is a wonderful workshop," he continued, glancing about him, "and yet it's of no use to me. No ideas stirring, Gustave."

"Why not help me with the Purple Veil?" I asked.

Paul leaped down and took a stride toward me with outstretched hands. "You mean that, Gustave?" he cried. "After all that's happened, you can still trust me? That's awfully decent of you, old man! I'd work my fingers to the bone; I'd—"

I have always had a dread of sentimental outbursts. Now I broke in on him abruptly.

"This is an excellent place to experiment with such a powerful chemical. Nothing can be hurt in this vault."

"When can we begin?" he cried excitedly. "I'd like to start tonight."

"Would you?" I asked. "Well, why not? I've got several vials of the Purple Veil in my laboratory now. It's barely a ten-minute walk. I'll step around and bring them over, if you say the word."

"That would be corking! I'm in just the mood for a little work. Shall I go with you?"

"No, don't do that," I answered. "You stay here and remove every inflammable object that may be about. I tell you, the Purple Veil is the nearest thing to hell's fire ever uncorked."

"Very well," he said with a laugh. "I'll see that everything's shipshape before you get back."

"Will I have to go out through the house?" I asked.

"No, there's a gate in the garden which opens on the street. Come this way."

Paul conducted me to a large iron gate set in the garden wall. At first he had some difficulty in unlocking it; but at last, with a shrill, complaining sound, the key turned in the lock and the gate swung slowly outward. I followed my friend through this aperture and into a side street.

"I'll leave the gate on the latch," Paul said as we parted. "You can come right in any time. You'll find me in the laboratory when you get back."

"Very well," I answered. "I won't be long."

Turning, I left him standing bareheaded under an arc light and hurried up the street. At the corner, I turned and looked back.

He was still standing where I had left him. To this day I can see him thus— one hand resting on the rusted bars of the gate; the other shading his eyes from the bright electric rays which streamed down on his flaxen hair. And to this day there is a great love in my heart for that slim, upright figure—a great love and a great sorrow.

VII

Conquered!

Now, as I near the end of my tale, once more horror holds my beating heart in the hollow of her hand. It is as if I were once again facing the terrors of the past. I am cold, bitterly cold—so cold that the pencil shakes between my trembling fingers.

And yet I must force myself to finish this chronicle. Truth has lain for months buried deep. Before she crumbles to dust, I must unearth her! Yes, although it is a ghastly business, I must unearth her!

After I had left Paul, I hurried home. Opening the door with my latch key, I mounted the stairs to my own room. Here I found everything as I had left it—the asbestos suit over the back of a chair, the gas mask hanging from a peg on the wall.

It was but the work of a moment to don this gray uniform; and then, resembling some tattered derelict that has slept all night on a dust heap, I began to descend the stairs to the laboratory. At every step I made a swishing sound as though I were clothed in paper.

I had not as yet put on the gas mask. I carried it in my hand as if it were a lantern. Now and then it swung against my thigh, causing me to start involuntarily.

The laboratory was plunged in blackness. Turning on the lights, I took a quick survey of the premises. *There* were the tiny globes in which glistened the Purple Veil; *there* was the picture frame cover of asbestos in which I intended placing the portrait at the last moment.

The portrait! I wheeled about and met its satanic regard. During the last few days it had grown ever more lifelike. Now one could fairly see the blood coursing behind the swarthy skin, the beastlike moisture on the crimson lips, the vibrating tension of the curling fingers.

There it crouched—malevolent as a spider—studying me with its unbearable eyes. Would I be able to destroy it? Would I *ever* be able to destroy it?

"Well," I said at last, "why do you stare at me thus?"

Then its thin, red lips curled in a sneer.

"You interest me," it murmured. "You are such a fool—such a weak fool!"

"I do not understand you," I answered coldly.

"You do not understand me?" it cried vehemently. "I thought we had become friends, you and I! Well, I will make my meaning clear. Is it wise to trust one who is untrustworthy—one who has proved himself untrustworthy?

"Did you not see me warning you from that picture in Paul's house? Surely you saw me; and yet you still persevered. Why have you given yourself into the hands of your enemy?"

Veiling the hatred in my eyes, I laughed aloud. Surely I was more than a match for it! It had called itself a *crimson thought* —well, even a crimson thought can be the toy of man. Now I would play a little game with it—a game of life or death.

"*I* do not trust Paul," I answered. "Have I not told you that I intend to kill him?"

"Then why did you speak to him of the Purple Veil?"

"Crude, stupid passion," I cried, "you are like some frenzied wild beast! You have no cunning, no subtlety. I spoke to Paul of the Purple Veil because I intend to choke him with it.

"He himself has opened the way. He has offered to help me in an experiment tonight—he has given me the use of his laboratory."

"So that he may rob you again," the portrait broke in.

"Perhaps. But in reality I shall rob him. I shall take his most precious possession—his life!

"There will be an unavoidable accident, you understand? His widow will have the consolation of knowing that her husband died in the service of science."

The portrait began to chuckle. The rasping sound of its merriment, the gray film that covered its eyes, and lastly, the greedy way it licked its lips, made my flesh crawl. And yet, it was necessary for me to go on building a dwelling of lies in which it might feel secure.

"That is the reason I came back and put on my asbestos suit," I continued. "Paul is now awaiting me in the laboratory. I shall take him one of these little glass globes and then we will experiment.

"How I wish I could be there!" the portrait murmured. "Are there any paintings in his laboratory? If so, I might manage it. I have access to all paintings."

"I'm sorry to say that there are not," I said regretfully. "However, I think it could be managed. I'll take you under my arm as a gift to him— you understand? But first you must put on this picture frame cover of asbestos. It will protect you from the Purple Veil."

The portrait gave me a look of loathsome affection.

"You are growing very fond of me," it whispered. "We are becoming as brothers, Let us hurry. I am anxious to see Paul enshrouded in the Purple Veil."

Still masking the hate in my eyes, I slipped the asbestos cover over its frame; next I went to the table and picked up one of the tiny glass globes. Then I returned to the portrait, which still regarded me with its loose-lipped smile.

Does it suspect anything? I wondered. *If I can only put on my gas mask before it suspects anything!*

At that instant, the portrait pointed out my path. It said anxiously:

"How can you carry me when you have that mask in your hand?"

"That is true!" I cried with a laugh. "I'll have to wear the mask then."

With fingers that shook, I slipped the contrivance over my head.

"You will appear ridiculous on the street," the portrait expostulated. "But take me down and let us hurry."

Suddenly its voice changed and it eyed me intently.

"What are you waiting for?" it cried. "Ah, traitor—traitor! You dare not!"

"I dare everything!" I cried exultantly and cast the tiny glass globe straight at its terror-stricken eyes.

What happened then was photographed on the film of my brain for all time. The blinding flash as the glass globe exploded, the thin stream of purplish vapor which coiled over the canvas like twisting snakes, the iridescent sparks of flame which whirled hither and thither in a mad dance—all these I had expected to see.

But the passing of the portrait! Ah, that was different—that was enough to turn a strong man's brain to quivering jelly!

At first the portrait remained motionless, its mouth agape in ludicrous astonishment. But when a stream of the Purple Veil coiled about its knees, it began to struggle.

With distended eyeballs and lolling tongue, with foaming lips and bursting lungs, it writhed back and forth in its efforts to escape. And as it fought for life, silently, vindictively, its venomous eyes were still fixed upon my face.

But soon there came a change. The Purple Veil squirmed upward till it reached the portrait's gaping mouth. For an instant I saw my enemy's breast rise and fall in a last convulsive movement.

At that superhuman effort, its lungs must have broken like wind-distened bags. At the next moment, the portrait toppled forward on its face.

Yet all was not over. It still held tenaciously to life. Like a wounded spider, it lay there, quivering slightly.

And now the tiny sparks of flame gathered on the fallen body like fireflies settling on a withered branch. Burning now green, now white, now green again, they fell on the portrait in a shower. In vain it writhed beneath their fiery weight.

Soon they had buried it; and the whole canvas was aflame. Then long fingers of fire reached upward till they touched the asbestos-covered frame, retiring sullenly and attempting an outlet on another side.

And I stood looking aghast at this living painting of hell. Long after my enemy had fallen, I saw the heap of red-hot ashes, under which it lay, stir slightly.

At that I turned on my heel, sick and dizzy, and dared not look again till the canvas was but blackened ashes. Then, at last, I realized that I was free.

Trembling with excitement, I then opened the window and let the cool night air cleanse the poisonous atmosphere. Next I removed the gas mask, and, sinking into the nearest chair, closed my eyes.

A great fatigue had overmastered me. As on a former occasion, I felt myself drifting out on the drowsy sea of dreams. Even Paul had become a secondary consideration.

Why should I not sleep? Had I not earned the right to sleep? I had at last conquered; and to the conqueror, what more blessed wreath than sleep?

VIII

Charged With Murder

I awoke with a start to a feeling of dread. Sitting up, I rubbed my eyes and looked about me. A pallid, ghostly light stole in through the open window; and the air was damp with the promise of dawn.

While I had slept a breeze had sprung up. Now the curtains in the alcove, like phantoms of bygone courtiers, seemed curtsying and bowing to one another.

Long habit turned my eyes to the portrait. With a feeling of unbounded joy, I saw that this time I had really succeeded. The entire surface of the canvas was charred a deep black.

What delight took possession of me then!—a delight which carried me to childish lengths. I rose and capered about the room, I shook my fist at it, I even laughed aloud.

Suddenly I was brought to myself by the far-away, brazen voice of the doorbell. Who could be ringing at this hour, I wondered. And as I turned this question over in my mind, I once again glanced at the charred canvas.

My God! Will I ever be able to forget what I saw then?

My eyes had fallen on the left-hand corner of the portrait—the side nearest the window. With an inarticulate cry of horror, I saw something stirring there.

It was yellow and small, and not unlike an oddly shaped autumn leaf; and it twitched spasmodically.

"It *must* be a leaf," I told myself firmly—"a leaf which has blown in through the open window and caught there."

Once more I looked, and hope deserted me. It was not a leaf—ah, no! It was a human hand—a human hand that felt its way with writhing fingers—a human hand which I knew only too well!

Ah, *there* was the arm, long and slender; and there was the body itself sidling into the canvas! Like a thief in the night, it stole forward with averted face.

Crouching, it crawled along till it reached its old spot; and then—ah, then it turned and I saw its eyes!

For an instant I stood there, motionless, dumb, staring into my enemy's face; and then, with a cry of terror, I fled to the door and threw it open. As I hesitated on the threshold, I heard the sound of footsteps in the hall.

"There he is now, sir," I heard Tom's voice say; and the next moment I was confronted by two strangers.

Any human manifestation was welcome indeed on such a night. Instantly I was calm and even smiling.

"You wish to see me, gentlemen?" I asked, wiping the cold perspiration from my forehead. "Won't you step into my laboratory?"

The presence of these strangers had given me confidence. Perhaps, after all, I had dreamed of the reappearance of my enemy. At any rate, it would be as well to get normal opinion on such a phenomenon.

"Now, gentlemen, will you kindly fix your attention on that canvas," I said. "Is there a figure in it, or is there not? My common sense tells me that there is not."

"Certainly, there's a figure there," said one of my guests brusquely. "It's a full-length portrait of you; and a very good likeness, I'd call it."

I turned to the other one in despair. "Do you also see it?" I cried.

But he cut me short with even more brusqueness than his companion.

"We've got a warrant for your arrest, Mr. Ericson," he said.

"My arrest! You are police officers, then? Under what charge?"

But before he answered me, I knew well enough what had happened while I had slept. I saw it all in a blinding flash.

Not I, but my portrait, had kept the rendezvous with Paul. As on a previous occasion, in my attempt to destroy my enemy I had only succeeded in loosing it on the world.

"You are charged with the murder of Paul Grey," one of the police officers said heavily.

It was as I had suspected then—Paul was dead! Poor old Paul, whom I had loved like a brother! And now I was charged with his death, *I* who would not have harmed a hair of his head!

"You're going a little bit too far in this!" I cried angrily. "You have no reason to accuse *me*. Are there not others about as capable of committing crimes as I—others who hated Paul while I loved him?

"Look at that face on the canvas! What does it tell you?"

I glanced full at the portrait as I spoke; and, to my joy, it was bowing and smiling—bowing and smiling with its hand on its heart.

"Look, look!" I cried in an agonized voice. "Can't you see it silently affirming my words? Where are you taking me? Stop! I demand justice! The real murderer hangs on the wall!"

But my captors were deaf to my words. They had handcuffed me and were leading me toward the door. On the threshold I cast a last glance over my shoulder.

My portrait was still bowing and smiling like a mechanical doll. And I knew then that it had conquered for all time.

And *I?* Why, I must suffer for it in silence and solitude. And because of its victory—like a famous actor who has played his role to the applause of the house—it would continue bowing and smiling, bowing and smiling, bowing and smiling.

IX

Find the Murderer!

I have but little more to add. You, who have followed my trial in the papers, will remember Evelyn's testimony—how, on the night of the murder, she visited her husband's laboratory at a late hour to find his charred remains on the stone floor and a crazed being, whom she falsely declared to be Gustave Ericson, crouched in one corner, mumbling to itself; how, when it saw her, this creature leaped to its feet and fled screaming; how she made her way back to the house and called in the police.

And also you will remember that, in spite of my brilliant speech accusing the portrait of the crime, the jury was swayed by the opinions of certain learned asses and brought in a verdict of homicidal mania; and that shortly after my trial, I was removed to this asylum for the criminal insane.

But have you ever thought of what a terrible punishment it is to be incarcerated among mental derelicts—to be exposed night after night to the caresses of our mother of madness, the moon? When she commands us to play, it is difficult to resist.

And have you ever longed, in your safety and sanity, to throw back your head and howl like wolves? We do strange, unaccountable things here—acts which we blush for when the sun again rules the world.

No, this is not a healthy spot. While I still possess all my mental powers un-dimmed, I have certain presentiments that make me anxious for the future.

It is on account of these presentiments that I have written this truthful chronicle, hoping that it will fall into the hands of some worthy person who will gather sufficient evidence to secure my release.

And yet, how few there are who can see the truth even when it is pointed out to them! For instance, we hear on all sides such phrases as these: "That painting has life," "this book will live." Yet, who of us actually believes that these statements are true?

When I tried to prove that Anthony Worthington's portrait of me had life, I was laughed at and labeled insane. And even my fellow sufferers mock me when I tell them that I have actually discovered that books may live.

We have a library in the asylum, with some splendid books. They whisper all night long. They tell their separate stories over and over again, each vying with the other, each attempting to drown out the other with its low, sibilant whisper.

I have sat in this library listening to them until sometimes my brain began to swim—there are so many of them, each is so convinced of its own immortality!

Please pardon this digression, which perhaps is not such a great digression after all. It may at least be of interest to the kind of man who will be my savior and friend—a man broad enough to acknowledge the still, small area of plowed soil in this wilderness we call the "world"—a man with humanity enough to acknowledge that there may be phenomena of which he is ignorant.

And when my unknown friend has read this chronicle and believed, let him go out and hunt my portrait down. I understand that my relatives have sold all my effects; therefore, the search may be difficult.

But to the strong in heart all things are possible. Somewhere in the city—perhaps in some art-dealer's—the real murderer of Paul Grey is lurking. Hunt down the assassin and deliver it to justice!

Now, give heed, my unknown friend. It is the portrait of a strikingly handsome young man—swarthy, with cruel, crimson lips and a mole on its right cheek. But if this description is not sufficient, it has other telltale characteristics.

The portrait to which I refer—that living portrait of an evil passion—like a great actor responding to an encore, is continually bowing and smiling, bowing and smiling, bowing and smiling.

And because of these calm, graceful salutations, it should not be difficult to recognize it among thousands.

• • • • •

An Offer of
Two for One

TALBOT MUNDY

Levy shrugged his great muscle-bound shoulders and straightened his bull neck with an air of finality—the air that some of his business acquaintances had learned to recognize as terminating a discussion.

"Bah!" he exclaimed. "You can't tell me! It's a lot of old women's talk, and that's all there to it!"

There were four other men sitting at the table with him in the rather dingy, cheap restaurant, but Levy seemed to be an unsatisfactory kind of man to argue with, for not one of them ventured to contradict him; his big, fat fist, that he held clenched on the table in front of him, was the physical token of the mental attitude they were likely to meet with if they did.

"See here!" he said. "Money talks, don't it? Here's my money." He drew a fat wad of yellow bills from his pocket and placed it on the table beside him.

"I'll bet you that!" he said. "Now, then—who's going to cover it? If anybody here thinks he can scare me stiff, let him put up his money and try!" Nobody answered him.

"I'll lay two to one!" he sneered; again nobody answered him, so he put the money back into his pocket with the air of a man who had proved his case conclusively.

"All the same," said the man who was sitting next to him, "there's something in it."

"Something, your grandmother!" answered Levy. "If you're so sure about it, why don't you bet? There are heaps of ways of killing a man; you can hit him with a blackjack, or shoot him; or if you want to be scientific, you can squirt the germs of typhoid into him with a syringe; or you can give him poison, or throw half a brick at him, or push him over the roof of a house.

"But kill him by suggestion—bah! You make me tired! Tell a man he's going to die, and then expect him to lie down and do it, eh? Huh! Try it on me and see what happens!"

"It has been done," said the man who had spoken before.

"You'll say you did it yourself next!" sneered Levy. "Go on—try it on me!"

"All the same," repeated the other quietly, "it has been done."

"You bet it has!" sneered Levy. "The fellow who did it must have picked his man mighty carefully—picked some poor devil with a weak heart and scared him till his heart lay down on him! I haven't got a weak heart; try me!" He threw out his great drum of a chest and thumped it.

"I'm sound all the way through, I am. They accepted me for a ten-thousand-dollar policy a week ago, so you bet I'm sound. Try it on me; I'm fair game!"

Nobody accepted the offer, and Levy rose with the air of contempt that he habitually assumed when he considered that he had had the better of an argument; and that is only another way of saying that he rose with his usual air; it was part of his stock in trade.

He tossed a ten-cent piece to the waiter, much as another man might throw a bone to a stray dog, and left the restaurant without a word of farewell to anybody, squaring his great ugly shoulders and pushing past the people in the doorway with brutal effrontery.

He pushed and elbowed his way through the midday crush, straight back to his stool behind the counter in the Nassau Street loan office. As junior partner in the firm of Harris, Hart & Levy, better known through their advertisement in the financial columns of the daily papers as the "Cosmopolitan Quick Loan Company," his was the strenuous share of the game.

It was his business to sit like Cerberus in the doorway, listening to the tales of necessity. It was he who passed up likely applicants, or turned down unlikely ones, and kicked truculent visitors unceremoniously down the stone steps that were placed so conveniently for the purpose outside.

A professional witness sat on either side of him, assistant brigands at twenty dollars a week, masquerading as clerks; their chief duty was to remember or forget exactly what happened to be expedient, and to lie glibly on the spur of the moment as the interests of the firm might dictate.

"There's been a man in here to see you, Mr. Levy," said one of them as Levy took his seat. "He wouldn't give his name, but I've seen him before. He's a lawyer, name of Evans, and I've got an idea he's acting for that feller Hopkins, that's two weeks behind in his payments."

"Big man?" asked Levy laconically, eying a nightstick that swung from a hook conveniently to his right hand.

"No. Quiet little runt, with a squeaky sort o' voice."

"Guess I'll fix him!" said Levy. "You finish getting out those final demand notes I told you about this morning—and you, Watts, write to Gettam and Ficks and tell them to attach Hopkins's goods at once. We may as well collect now as later—we've sucked him about dry."

At that minute a small, quiet-looking man entered the office door and asked whether Mr. Levy was back yet.

"That's me," said Levy. "You were here to see me half an hour ago, weren't you? What do you want?"

"My name is Evans," said the newcomer; "here is my card."

Levy squinted at the piece of pasteboard and tore it in halves insolently.

"We've got no use for lawyers in here," he answered. "We've no business to put your way and no time to waste talking."

The lawyer stared at him in amazement; he was accustomed to at least the outward forms of civility even in the presence of the enemy. Then his face grew a little harder, and his voice the least shade firmer, as he stated his business.

"I'm acting for Mr. Weldon Hopkins," he stated. "I understand that he borrowed a sum of money from your firm some time ago."

"If you mean Weldon Hopkins of 365 Welsbach Avenue, you're right; he did."

"May I see a copy of your agreement with him?"

"You may not!"

"But this is scandalous! The law—"

"See here," said Levy, "if you've come here to talk law, we've no time to listen to you! We've got lawyers of our own, and they give us advice when we ask for it!"

"My client tells me that he never saw a copy of the agreement, and certainly never had one in his possession. He says that you gave him a paper to sign, and that he signed it. I would like to see what he signed."

"Didn't we give him a copy?" asked Levy, turning to the clerk on his right.

"We certainly did!" said the clerk promptly. "I gave it to him myself in your presence, and he sat down on that chair and read it before he signed the original."

"There you are!" said Levy. "That satisfy you?"

"My client assures me that nothing of the kind took place," answered the lawyer.

"Then he'd better learn to tell the truth!" said Levy. "Anything else?"

"Yes," said the lawyer, "this: two hundred and forty per cent is not legal interest. That's what you appear to have charged my client, and unless you can come to terms with him right now, I warn you that I shall take the matter into court and give your ways of doing business the benefit of a little publicity."

"Go ahead!" said Levy. "Get busy! If you think you can squeeze a fee out of Hopkins, all right! You know your own business best. As long as we get what's coming to us, you're welcome to what's left. Good afternoon!"

It was evident that Mr. Levy was not in the least afraid of the law, and that threats left him unscathed. The lawyer left the office without wasting any more breath on argument, and he felt rather than saw Levy's offensive grin as he went through the doorway. It sent a tingle of indignation all up and down the small of his back.

But he realized it would be hopeless to try to resent it, for he recognized the type of man that Levy was—not an altogether uncommon one in his legal experience—the type that is secure in the knowledge of strength and that can only be crushed into subjection by the actual application of superior strength. A bluff would be a waste of breath.

He must either fight, and fight hard, or do the other thing, and as his client had no money left for fighting, it was the other thing that appeared to him wisest. Before the door of the elevator had clanged behind him, he had made up his mind to do nothing, which was exactly what Levy counted on.

The only thing in America that could scare Levy was Congress; and not even Congress could do it until a bill to abolish money-lenders had become law. The bill would have had to be very well drawn to scare him even then, and he would be likely to wait for the Supreme Court to declare the law constitutional before changing his tactics to any extent.

For state laws he cared nothing, save inasmuch as they cost him money to evade, and he cared still less for threats of physical violence. In any kind of personal encounter, he was well able to take care of himself.

Two rather seedy-looking customers strolled into the office that afternoon, one behind the other, and each with a hand in his hip pocket.

"I've come to have a talk with you, Levy," said one of them.

"Git!" ordered Levy. He recognized an old customer who had been bled dry and discarded.

"Not yet," the fellow answered, keeping his right hand in his hip-pocket and leaning his left elbow on the counter. The second man retained his point of vantage near the door. Levy laid his right hand surreptitiously on the nightstick, but thought better of it.

Instead, he made a grab for the fellow's throat with his left hand, and vaulted suddenly across the counter. Then he banged the two men's heads together, pushed them through the doorway, and kicked them both ignominiously down the stairs.

"Shoot me up, would they?" he muttered. "I'll teach 'em!" Then he returned to his seat by the more leisurely route, through the door at one end of the counter. He could not by any means be called a timid man.

Five o'clock was closing time. When the time came, he told the clerks to go, and turned himself to the strongroom, the door of which opened behind him. He always made it a point to go through the day's accumulation of contracts, file them, and lock them up himself before leaving the office, for he was nothing if not careful, and he trusted nobody.

As the clerks left the office, he stepped inside the strongroom in order to get to a shelf at the back of it.

One of the senior partners, on his way to the elevator, passed through the outer office, saw that the clerks had gone, noticed Levy's hat hanging on a peg, and supposing Levy had left the strongroom door open while he left the office for a minute—possibly to recall one of them—he shut it, locked it with the key that was hanging in the lock, and put the key in his pocket.

"Levy's growing careless all at once!" he muttered. "I'll get here early tomorrow and call him down over this." Then he hurried for his train.

Inside the strongroom Levy kicked at the steel door, and beat on it with his bare fists, and shouted until his voice gave out and his throat emitted nothing more than a hoarse croak. Then he sat down on the cement floor to consider.

He knew the time, thank goodness! and he had his watch with him; he could not see it in the pitch darkness, but he pulled it out and broke the glass cautiously, in order to be able to feel the time with his fingers—and as he thumbed it clumsily, he broke off the minute-hand.

He swore savagely at that, and then held the watch up to his ear to see whether it still ticked. It did. He still had the hour-hand.

It would be good company through the night. He did not dare put the watch back in his pocket again, now that the glass face was missing, so he laid it on the floor carefully, face upward.

He realized that there was practically no chance of his getting out before morning, when his partner reopened the safe. He would simply have to sit there and think—what he would say to his partner would not be half a bad thing to think about.

He wished, though, that he had something to drink in there; he remembered that he had felt thirsty already at four o'clock, but had postponed getting a drink until after he had closed the office. What with shouting himself hoarse, and getting the dust off the strongroom shelves into his throat, his thirst was becoming actually painful.

Still, he was a strong man; he prided himself on his strength of mind and body. He thought he could go without a drink for twelve hours or so without making a fuss.

Then he began to long for tobacco and some matches, and he searched his clothes carefully to see whether he had any. He found none, and on second thought he was glad of it; tobacco smoke would have soon made the atmosphere in that tiny place almost unbreathable.

That started another train of thought. In the black darkness, the size of the strongroom was unguessable; the walls being invisible, he had given no thought to them. Now he remembered suddenly how small the strongroom was.

He figured it out—six, by ten, by twelve, more or less—say seven hundred and twenty cubic feet. How many cubic feet a minute did a man breathe? He remembered reading about it somewhere, in a Sunday paper probably, but he could not for the life of him recall the details.

He knew, though, that the quantity had astonished him at the time. And how many times, he wondered, could a man breathe the same air over again before it became absolutely poisonous? Twice? Three times? Four times? He began to figure out his chances of surviving until the morning, assuming that it was four times.

The air began to feel stuffy already, and he got up to see whether it was fresher higher up; as he did so, he stepped on the watch and smashed it. For a moment that sent him into a panic, and he started beating the door again with both hands and shouting—almost screaming—until he realized the futility of it, and felt ashamed of himself, and sat down again.

He had no idea of the passage of time now; he only knew that the sense of stuffiness was gaining on him, and he judged by that that he must have been in there a long time. The air was beginning to taste beastly, and his ears and temples were throbbing; once, when a small boy, he had been nearly suffocated, and he recalled the sensation, and recognized it.

So his time had come, had it? It seemed a rotten way to die, didn't it? Well, he wasn't afraid at all events; he could die game; he would take it quietly. By the throbbing of his temples and the singing in his ears, he thought it must be almost a matter of minutes now.

How many minutes? he wondered. His brain was working very fast—too fast; he was rather ashamed of it; he despised a man who became panicky. He calmed himself by an effort, and made himself think slowly, casting his mind backward over the events of the day, until he came to lunchtime, and the conversation after lunch.

What rot those fellows had talked! How often he met men who talked that sort of rot, but were afraid to back their alleged opinions with good money!

Gee! But the air was getting vile. The singing in his ears had become the noise of a waterfall, and his head seemed to be swimming round in a Saturn-ring of streaky light. He wondered where the light came from.

Anyway it was unpleasant. Perhaps if he lay down, it would go away. He lay down full length on the cement floor, feeling drowsy and stupid, and presently all sensation ceased.

The senior partner was the first to arrive in the morning, as he had promised he would be. It was he who opened the strongroom door, he who staggered back half fainting at the sight of what was in there, and he who telephoned for the doctor.

"How long has that door been opened?" asked the doctor.

The senior partner looked at his watch. "About seven minutes," he answered.

"H-m-m!" said the doctor, sniffing. "The air seems to be quite fresh inside! Quite dead," he added, bending over Levy's prostrate form. "Been dead seven or eight hours at the very least."

"Poor fellow!" said the senior partner, "suffocated, I suppose?"

"No," said the doctor; "he can't have been. The air's quite fresh. Can you get the janitor?"

The janitor came.

"Is this strongroom ventilated?" the doctor asked him.

"Certainly it is," said the janitor. "That's no strongroom. It's nothing but a very small office with a safe-door fitted onto it. It's a sort of recess. There's a ventilator at the back—look, you can see it—that communicates with the main ventilating shaft of the building. Every room in this building is ventilated."

"What killed him then?" asked the senior partner, amazed.

"Couldn't say without an autopsy," answered the doctor.

"Looks to me though— Ever hear of auto-suggestion?"

"No," said the senior partner.

"Ah! Well, you wouldn't understand then," said the doctor. "No, you needn't trouble; I'll telephone the coroner. Good morning."

• • • • •

BEYOND THE VIOLET

J.U. GIESY

There were four of us in the lounge of the club. There was Carnick, the broker, a man who dealt with material values, stocks and bonds and such things. There was Abbington, the banker, whose interests in life were pretty much along the same line as those of his friend. Then there was Vance, M.D., B.S., and some other things, I believe, the neurologist, who, having served his time in a base hospital on the other side as a part of the Medical Corps, A.E.F., had come back and resumed the practice he had laid down at such time as the call of his citizen's duty sent him a volunteer, heart and soul, into the army life.

The fourth member of our group was myself, who dabbled somewhat with typewriter and pen.

Carnick and Abbington were reading: the former a current magazine, the latter an evening paper, and I was simply lounging back in a deep chair and smoking when Vance strolled up.

"Gentlemen," he said, smiling. We all knew him—a slender, dapper, almost effeminate sort of chap, unless one happened to catch his eyes, as cold and steady a blue as the chilled steel of a surgeon's knife.

Carnick glanced up. "Hello, Vance," he mumbled.

Abbington nodded.

I returned the doctor's smile.

He took up a paper and found himself a chair, respecting the mood of the others. And I continued to enjoy my cigar.

All at once Carnick cast his magazine aside. "Rot!" he snorted. "Bosh! What's got into people inside the last few months is more than I can understand! Two years ago you couldn't have got that sort of stuff into a standard magazine."

Vance lifted his eyes over the edge of his paper, and Carnick saw he had gained his attention. "I suppose you'd call it a sort of universal hysteria, wouldn't you, Vance? I believe that state is characterized by the belief on the part of the one afflicted that he sees and hears nonexistent things."

Vance's customary smile twitched at his lips. He glanced from the broker to the paper again. "I presume you refer to the prevalence of articles dealing with the possibility of a future life and its demonstration?" he suggested.

Carnick nodded. "Yes. They're getting to be an epidemic. Some publication runs one, and the others all follow like sheep. What I can't comprehend, however, is the effect the thing seems to have had not only on the popular mind, but on some of those we have been in the habit of considering the world's biggest men. They've fallen for it, and they've fallen for it strong."

Abbington laid down his paper. I sat holding my cigar in my hand. Carnick had pushed himself up in his chair and was regarding Vance with a sort of impersonal frown.

For a time the physician made no answer, and then: "He is a rather bold man, I fancy, Carnick, who undertakes to say what does or does not lie beyond the borderline."

Carnick took it with no evidence of any full understanding. "Borderline?" he repeated. "Just what do you mean by borderline?"

"The limit," said Vance slowly, "of the sensory perception of mankind, meaning thereby the individuals inhabiting a world bounded by a minimum and a maximum perceptive zone—violet for the sense of sight, or for hearing the most rapid vibratory rate which can be consciously denominated sound."

Abbington nodded. "That's a pretty comprehensive definition, too, I imagine," he said.

Carnick somewhat widened his eyes. "You think there *is* something— beyond?" he asked.

Vance smiled again. "It's presumable, isn't it, at least? We've proven the X-ray as regards light already. Man senses what lies within his limitations. Sticking to the sense of sight—presupposing that our eyes turned merely sidewise—we would be conscious of only length and breadth, and thickness, for us, would not exist."

Carnick grinned. "As it is, we have three dimensions; do you mean to insinuate that there may be a fourth?"

"I'm not a metaphysician," said Vance. "But a questioning of the possibility of a stage beyond mere corporeal existence is a blow at the very foundations of religion, is it not?"

"I never went in for religion," Carnick said quickly, and added: "Of course, I suppose I recognize some casual reason back of what we call life. But beyond that, I've never given the matter much thought."

"Exactly." Vance smiled again. I noted a slight contraction of the corners of his lids. "You recognize something, Carnick, and you don't know what it is. Thus far we've spoken of sensory perception, yet a man—some men—may perceive something without exactly sensing its absolute nature. It comes down then to a question of what life is. A moment ago I spoke of a vibratory rate, and it is not too far a cry to assume that life, like all other force, is in itself a ratio of vibration. If that is correct, then life is a harmony in the midst of a universal scale, and man may perceive certain things beyond the scope of his senses, in very much the same way that the string of a violin may be set into vibration by the sounding of a sympathetic chord.

"I think that may be the explanation for the universal racial belief in the possibility of a future life—a sort of sympathetic perception of a truth. Take the violin again, for instance, and tune it without lifting the bridge. What then would happen if, after the tuning were finished, the bridge were raised?"

Carnick frowned again. "I suppose," he said after a moment, "that the result would be to raise the pitch."

"Precisely." Vance nodded. "For the rest you must accept my statement that certain things may at times have the same effect on the human brain and nerves."

Abbington sat forward. "Raising the pitch, you mean?"

"Yes."

"So that—one can see—beyond the violet?"

"Why, yes—that's a very good way to put it," said Vance.

Carnick eyed the physician in a shrewd way he had at times and brought the matter to an issue: "See here, do you know of any concrete example?"

Vance met him directly. "Coming to a showdown, eh, Carnick? Well, as a matter of fact, I do know of one such instance. It was the most interesting demonstration of what I think we may best call sensory hyperesthesia I have ever encountered."

"He could see—beyond?"

"Yes. At least I am convinced that is the explanation. Something happened to his optic nerves or center, which actually raised his visual perceptibility an octave, if we may still employ a musical parallel, with the result that his sight was shifted up on the scale."

Carnick puffed out his lips. He glanced at Abbington and me, and then leaned back in his chair. "All right, doctor," he said, "tell the story, but spare me your technical terms. If I get you, this chap saw things that, in so far as those around him were concerned, weren't there."

"He saw things 'beyond the violet,' as Abbington puts it," Vance returned. "As a matter of fact, violet was the only mundane color as we know it, of which he retained any perception. In his scheme of things after I came to know him, violet was his minimum rate of vibration, and in so much corresponded to our red."

He tossed his paper aside, produced and lighted a cigar. "You've all heard of shell shock cases, or read of them," he resumed. "And I'll merely say that the condition, in so far as we men who observed them were able to determine, was with all respect to Carnick's restriction on my use of medical parlance, a hyperesthesia or excessive irritability of the brain and nerves. The victims of the complaint were subject to various mental and physical aberrations, with certain forms of hallucination—though mainly of a subjective nature, meaning thereby that their imaginary ills and experiences were largely if not wholly centered about themselves—their immediate condition and future welfare, that is.

"As you know, I was connected during my medical service on the other side with a convalescent base. That's how Edward Stinson came to us. The history that came with him indicated very clearly that, in the opinion of those who had observed him, he was mentally deranged. I do not mean violent—there had been no manifestations of that nature at any time, but there was something about him decidedly strange. And in addition, he was blind."

"Hold on," Carnick interrupted.

Vance shook his head and smiled. "Blind in the ordinary sense, I mean. I'm not mussing up my facts, my friend. The man had to be cared for like any other blind man. You want to remember that, Carnick. He couldn't see a thing that went on around him, because violet was the minimum of his sight perception, and the last link that bound him to the color scheme of the everyday world.

"He had been an infantry Looie with the Twelfth Field. You know that outfit did some very heavy work, and, well—Stinson didn't know exactly what happened to him after he was advancing under fire with his men, and had a sudden sensation of going up in the air, until he woke up in an evacuation hospital back of the line and an entirely different world. He told me the whole thing himself. The trouble seemed to be with his eyes, or the mechanism of his sight.

"At first he told me he thought he had surely died, except that he could not harmonize that idea with the fact that he was able to hear all that went on around him distinctly, to sense ordinary odors, to taste the food that was given to him, and was exquisitely sensitive to any ministering touch.

"But so far as his sight was concerned, Edward Stinson came back to a world of ghosts."

"Good God!" Abbington exclaimed a bit thickly; "do you mean he saw—things like that?"

"Exactly." Vance inclined his head.

"He had a slight wound when he was picked up—a shell gutter across one thigh, which was debrided and promptly healed, and save for that he didn't show a scratch. They diagnosed his case as 'shell shock' partly because of his subsequent condition and partly because they learned that he had been bowled over by a shell burst during the attack by the Twelfth on an enemy position in which he had taken part.

"They sent him to a base and kept him there till his leg healed, and waited for his other symptoms to clear up. But they didn't. There weren't any, as a matter of fact, except the one I've mentioned, and that stuck. They transferred him to us, with an addendum to the diagnosis to the effect that he was suffering from visual hallucinations, which was natural enough, even though it undershot the truth."

"What was the truth?" Carnick asked all of a sudden.

Vance looked him in the eye. "I think I've pretty clearly indicated by my remark that Stinson woke up in a world of ghosts," he said slowly. "It depends on how one looks at it, of course."

"You mean—he saw—"

"The living dead," said Vance. "He described it to me as I've said. It was rather weird. He likened his condition to that of a man viewing the movements of a number of mute actors through the medium of a violet-tinted glass. He was normal in every way except for that one thing in so far as his conversation went—as shown by every known test we applied. He was a man of more than average education. He could understand, after a time, the effect he was having on everybody else. He had hard work holding himself together right at the first; in getting along in the borderland existence which had suddenly become his.

"You see, it was hard for him to realize what had happened—that he was still corporeally alive in so far as his creature needs were involved, and yet perfectly capable of perceiving the stage of existence those of his fellow men who had died. It was a sort of No Man's Land in which he found himself—a place peopled with souls which had been violently torn out of their bodies, or had slipped out of them after a due course of dissolution. He saw men die—actually saw something leave their bodies. Day after day and night after night, he saw that thing happen in the wards. He saw the life, if you wish to call it that, steal forth from them and pass him. What is it the Orientals say—that they hear their souls bidding their bodies farewell? Well—Stinson saw that happen, and after a time he came to realize that it was only the bodies of those men that had died, and that the men themselves were still alive—that they had simply shaken off the body, which was no longer essential to their continued life.

"That, however, was later, when he had gained a better appreciation of his condition. The first time he saw it happen, it upset him, and he called the nurse on duty and told her that something was coming out of another man's body. That man died, and the nurse was terribly impressed. She was on edge. There were times when the corps in the hospitals were overworked as a matter of course. She reported the matter and the result was that Stinson was pretty closely watched. That's how the visual hallucinations got tacked onto his diagnosis, before he came to us.

"I've told you he was intelligent, however, and by the time I first saw him, he had accepted his condition, and it had made a most remarkable change in the man himself. You see, he had come by then, regardless of the opinion of others, or the questions they had asked him after they got an inkling of what they believed he thought he was seeing, to consider the whole thing as a visual demonstration—an irrefutable proof of a definite existence on the other side of the grave. The thing had lifted him out of the depression one would have naturally expected, into a state of something like a spiritual exaltation. He was a man with his feet on the earth and his head in the skies—wholly convinced of the truth of what he was seeing."

"So is the man with hallucinations—the victim of a monomania," said Carnick. "They're absolutely convinced of the truth of their convictions—dead sure they're right."

Vance's eyes twinkled.

"Meaning that you want proof," he said.

Carnick chuckled. "Well, yes. I'm from Missouri. Outside the fact of your observation, which I'm not doubting, and the man's own say-so, which I'm willing to admit as genuine in so far as his own belief, where does it get you, any more than the statement of these writers in the magazines that so and so received a message from someone who has passed on through a medium or one of these automatic writers who claim to set down what simply flows off their pencil or pen?"

Abbington nodded. "Carnick's right," he seconded his friend. "Listing Stinson's alleged ability as a very interesting matter from your viewpoint, doctor, how are you going to nail it down?"

I looked at Vance to see how he was taking their questions.

He was smiling again. "I think the proof lies in the fact that Stinson fell in love before he came to us," he returned.

"Fell in love?" Canuck started. "With a ghost—a soul—a spirit?"

Vance shook his head. "Not at first. Lieutenant Stinson fell in love with the sound of a voice, the touch of a hand, a pair of violet eyes—or let us say their color. Hold on—" as the broker would have interrupted, "I've been laying for you, Carnick. I've held out this part of my story for the last. Now let us review briefly Stinson's case. He could hear, feel, taste, touch, smell anything in normal fashion. He could see violet as the one remaining elementary color in the everyday scale—and Allison Towne, United States Army nurse, had violet eyes. More than that, she was on duty at the base to which Stinson was sent first."

Abbington dragged his chair a little closer. The movement seemed to say he intended missing no word. Carnick pursed out his lips again.

Vance went on: "Stinson was under her charge. Day after day he saw those spots of violet bending above him—came to associate the voice behind them with the woman whose eyes he knew they were because he asked her if that was their color—came to associate their presence with her touch—the fragrance of her feminine presence. And remember that those twin pools of living light were the binding links which, in those days, when he was trying to adjust himself to the change that had come upon him, seemed to hold the man to earth. She talked with him at times, told him her name and some other trivial details, sympathized with him, and he confided to her a great deal about himself and the experience he was undergoing, after the first edge of the thing had worn off. Particularly was that true after his so-called hallucinations had become general knowledge.

"Then came the influenza epidemic—the second big outbreak—and the girl was taken sick. One night, lying in his bed, Stinson saw her pass.

"The next morning he asked about her, and learned that she had died, and the hour of her death. The information merely confirmed his fears, because he had felt that the form he had seen drifting wraithlike past him was her spiritual entity, suddenly freed from her body—and now, although he had never been able to see more than the color of her eyes while she was physically living, he knew absolutely—had a full and vivid perception of how she appeared, and described her to the nurse he had questioned with a clearness that moved the woman to tears.

"That settled the thing for Stinson. He missed the girl immensely; but, as he said to me, he came out of the experience with the settled knowledge that no matter what might have happened to her body, Allison Towne was as much as ever alive, and that he loved her—so that you see, Carnick, in the end, the boy was literally in love with a shade, as you suggested. It was rather odd."

"Odd, yes," Carnick assented. "But what does it prove?"

"Nothing," Vance said. "It merely lays the foundation for what followed, brings out the point that Stinson never saw the girl while she was physically alive, and gained his entire picture of her only after the change which we de-nominate death, but which he came to feel assured was merely a change and nothing worse. But wait.

"I told you I watched his case for weeks. We got to be pretty good friends in those days. I think I convinced him of my interest, and we used to take short walks about the grounds in the evenings. He liked to get out then, because of the peculiar violet quality in the twilight. He was always seeking for something of a violet color, with very much the same avidity that the average child will seize on anything that is red. During the time he was in our institution, I made several attempts to tune him down, as it were, but with no success. In the end he was sent home unimproved, and I lost track of him completely until the other day, when he walked into my office with his vision normally restored."

"Normally—he could see things the same as before?" asked Carnick.

"Even as you and I," said Vance, and smiled.

"What happened?" Abbington asked.

"Heaven only knows," Vance said, "though, of course, we may assume that whatever process lifted his vision to a temporarily higher scale of perceptiv-ity, and maintained it there through a period of months, was by some means removed."

"Something let down the bridge," Carnick suggested, harking back to the doctor's first comparison anent the violin.

Vance nodded. "Yes. Stinson told me what happened, of course. When he left us, they put him aboard a transport and brought him across. The trip was uneventful until the steamer docked. He was slated for a hospital on this side and was loaded with some of the others into an ambulance because of his condition, though he was a 'sitting' case.

"Something went wrong after they started for the hospital, and the ambu-lance motor caught fire. Quick work got the passengers out—and just about that time the machine blew up.

"Stinson wasn't hurt a bit, but all the same, he fainted, or lost conscious-ness at the instant of the explosion. When he came to, he was in a hospital bed again, and a nurse was bending over his bed. He looked up into Allison Towne's face—or that's what he thought at first. One can imagine that he was pretty well shaken both by the face into which he was looking and the fact that he had regained his normal sight.

"He tried to speak. 'You—you! Miss Towne!'

"For a moment, he says, he couldn't for the life of him determine whether he had finally died and the girl was really Allison herself, or was alive and had dreamed everything that went before that moment. But he hadn't been injured, and although his brain was whirling, he came up quickly. He hitched himself up on an elbow and kept staring into the face of the nurse. And he found it wide-eyed, rather startled, as it might be by his sudden recognition.

"'You are Miss Towne, aren't you?' he asked, because the girl beside him was as like to the spirit, soul, wraith or whatever you like the call it, of Allison Towne as two peas from the same pod.

"She nodded. 'Yes, I am Miss Towne,' she said, 'But how do you know? I don't think I've ever seen you.'

"Stinson let himself back on the pillow. You must remember that Allison Towne had told him a bit about herself.

"'You were born in Paterson?' he said in a sudden flash of comprehension.

"She assented.

"'You had a sister? Her name was Allison?' said Stinson.

"She nodded again.

"Then Stinson knew the truth. 'You're very much like her in appearance, aren't you?' he said.

"'Why, yes,' The girl had grown a trifle pale. 'Allison and I looked a great deal alike, except that I'm a bit younger. But—'

"'Wait,' Stinson interrupted. 'I know what you're going to say, Miss Towne, because—I knew your sister. She was very good to me. She told me about you. Your name is Arline. I've—Miss Towne, I've been through a most remarkable experience, and I've come back out of it to find—you.'

"Then he told her exactly what had occurred. 'That's why it startled me so,' he said at the last, 'when I looked up just now and saw your face. It is like hers—like the face of the woman I never really saw, until after, as men say, she had died. It—it was as though I had suddenly waked up and found that I had been caught in the toils of some nightmare, and you had wakened me again to life. For a moment it baffled me, and then I remembered she had told me she had a sister, who was also a nurse.'

"'I know,' said the girl. 'Allison wrote me about you. She—she believed you saw what you said. She said she wouldn't be afraid of death if it came to her after talking to you, because—she felt sure that what had happened to you was proof of—a future life. I—I think she loved you, Lieutenant Stinson. I—I think that's why you saw her after she had passed. I think she let you see her true self.'"

Vance smiled again as he came to the end of his story. "There, Carnick," he said, "is your proof. Stinson recognized the younger girl by her likeness to the sister he had known, but had never been able to see in her physical life."

Carnick sat frowning. "I don't know," he said at last.

"None of us knows—really." Once more Vance smiled.

"That wasn't the end of it, was it?" Abbington asked.

Vance laughed. "Hardly. You see, Stinson had been living for months in a world of ghosts. The explosion of the ambulance did something to undo the work of the shell burst, of course. And the first thing he saw when he came back to the world he had formerly known was Arline Towne's face. The other day, when he came to my office, he brought me—this."

He reached into an inner pocket and produced an envelope of heavy texture, handing it to the banker.

Abbington thrust his fingers inside it and drew out a—wedding invitation. He read it: "Arline Towne—to—Lieutenant Edward Stinson," and gave it back.

Vance took it. "Render unto Caesar those things that are Caesar's," he said.

"Meaning?" Abbington grumbled.

"Meaning" said Vance, " that man, as man, lives within the limitations of his sensory perceptions, and that Arline Towne is a charming girl. I had luncheon with her and Stinson the other day."

· · · · ·

THE ELIXIR OF LIFE

C. LANGTON CLARKE

"Look at it how you will, it is a most unaccountable disappearance. There is absolutely no clue. His accounts are in perfect shape—Jim Allerlee was always a most methodical person. Happy home—Mrs. Allerlee is one of the most charming women I know. An income more than enough to supply his wants. No entanglements—of that I am positive—and here Jim goes and disappears as if the earth had swallowed him. It beats me."

With these words, Allan Mortimer dropped the end of his cigar into a convenient ashtray, hoisted his long figure out of the depths of an easy chair and, with a glance at the clock, prepared to bid his host good night.

"You are giving yourself a lot of trouble over it."

"I am determined to get to the bottom of it," was Allan's reply. "Jim was always a good friend of mine, and besides, my bump of inquisitiveness has always been abnormal. Well, I must not keep you up any longer, or I shall be *persona non grata* with Mrs. Atkinson. Good night."

"Good night, and good luck in your quest," answered the other. "Let me know if you hear anything."

The two men passed out of the library into the dimly lit hall.

"I suppose," suggested Atkinson, as he helped his guest into his overcoat, "that Allerlee was never mixed up with any secret society—Nihilists, you know—or anything of that sort?"

"Hardly," laughed Allan. "Jim was not at all the kind of man for daggers or bombs."

The other echoed the laugh.

"Talking of bombs," he said, "there is a bomb, or what Mary looks upon as a bomb, in this house, and I wish you would take it away. You remember that can of powder you lent me to fill some shells? I have got it stowed away in a cupboard, and every time my wife goes there to get anything, she expects to be blown up. Wait a minute till I get it."

Atkinson ran upstairs, and in a few minutes returned, bearing a good-sized tea canister, half filled with gunpowder.

"Not too much trouble, I hope?" he remarked as he wrapped it up.

"Not at all," Allan replied conventionally.

He detested carrying parcels, especially on cold nights, but was too good-natured to refuse. He shook hands with his host, tucked the parcel under his arm, and, with his hands thrust into the pockets of his ulster, set forth for a half-mile walk to his quarters.

The hour was late and, with the exception of an occasional solitary police-man, not a soul seemed to be abroad. The absolute silence of the streets began to have a depressing effect on his spirits, and it was with a feeling of positive relief that, on turning a corner, he descried a hundred yards ahead of him the figure of a small man, walking in the same direction.

He quickened his pace, and had almost reached the stranger's side when he saw him slip and fall heavily on the sidewalk.

"I hope you are not hurt," Mortimer said, bending over the prostrate figure, which made no attempt to rise.

"Thank you," replied a low, musical voice, "I am rather badly shaken, and I fear that I have wrenched my ankle."

The stranger raised himself to a sitting posture and looked up. Allan gave an involuntary start as he gazed on the most remarkable face he had ever beheld.

It was the face of a man of about sixty years, of an extraordinary waxen pallor, covered with a close network of tiny wrinkles and framed in long locks of yellowish-white hair.

But what struck Allan most was the wonderful brilliance of the eyes; a bril-liance which flatly contradicted the impression of age conveyed by the other features, and betrayed a surprising degree of vitality.

"Might I beg your assistance?" the stranger went on, extending a small, gloved hand; and Allan, with a confused apology for his remissness, helped him to his feet.

The little man took one step, and would have fallen had not the other caught him by the elbow.

"An awkward predicament," he said with an embarrassed laugh. "I am only a few hundred yards from my house, but I do not see how I am going to reach it."

He looked up and down the street in a helpless sort of way, and Allan's heart went out to him in sympathy.

"If you would care to avail yourself of my arm," he said, "I shall be very glad to help you. Do you think you can manage to walk with my assistance?"

The stranger was profuse in his thanks, but declined the offer, alleging that he could not think of taking anyone out of his way at so late an hour. Allan was insistent, however, and the other finally allowed himself to be persuaded.

Their progress was slow, and when they turned up a side street, indifferently lighted, it became slower still. The injured man walked with difficulty, and was evidently suffering severe pain, and Allan was not sorry when he stopped at a gate in a low picket fence which enclosed a large lot.

"This is where I live," the stranger said, pointing to a low brick cottage which stood some distance back from the street and was dimly visible through the gloom. "An out-of-the-way place for a doctor, is it not? By the way, I forgot to introduce myself.

"I am Dr. Armitage. I am a physician, but I do not practice, and so this place suits me well enough. I prefer solitude. Crying babies and family pianos are not conducive to scientific research."

He pushed open the gate and Allan carefully assisted him along the slippery boardwalk and supported him while he inserted his latchkey.

"I am going to trespass a little further on your kindness," Dr. Armitage said as he crossed the threshold. "I am going to ask you to see me as far as my room. The man who attends to my wants has left for a day or two to visit his father, who is dying; otherwise, I would not trouble you. Once in my room, I shall require no assistance. I am doctor enough to attend to my own slight injuries."

He spoke with so much assurance of receiving the help asked that Allan, who had experienced a sudden depression of spirits, could not in common humanity refuse. There was something about the gloomy house and its odd-looking tenant which affected him strangely, and he could not repress a shiver.

"Cold?" queried the doctor anxiously. "I did wrong to bring you out of the way. It is comfortably warm in my room, but perhaps it is the darkness which affects you. We will soon remedy that."

He opened the inner door and touched a button on the wall. Instantly a blaze of light burst forth.

"Extravagant, is it not, to waste so much light on so small a house? But I am like you. I abominate cold and darkness. This is my sanctum."

He pushed aside a heavy curtain and, still leaning heavily on Allan's arm, entered a room which to the latter appeared the strangest he had ever seen.

It was a large apartment, running the full depth of the house, lit by a deep bay at the front and a window at the side.

The front half was furnished with sybaritic luxury. The floor was covered with a carpet into which the foot sank as into a bed of moss; valuable paintings hung on the walls, the furniture was costly and in excellent taste, and several massive bookcases contained rows of handsomely bound volumes.

The rear portion of the room formed a striking contrast.

The floor was without covering of any description, and the only articles of furniture were a long pine table and a rickety kitchen chair. The table was loaded with bottles, test tubes and scientific apparatus.

Flush with the wall at the end of the room were two wide, shallow iron doors, secured by a combination lock.

"An odd room, certainly," said Dr. Armitage, answering Allan's unspoken criticism, "but then I am an odd sort of man; a combination of extreme indolence and extraordinary energy. The fits alternate so rapidly that a room adapted to both was a positive necessity.

"At one minute I am extended in one of these exceedingly comfortable chairs, reading a novel; the next—my coat is off and I am hard at work among those bottles and retorts. But come—I cannot let you go without partaking of my hospitality. I have some whisky here which connoisseurs tell me is a dream."

He pointed to a table on which stood a cut-glass decanter, a siphon and two tall glasses.

"You were expecting a visitor?" Allan hazarded.

The other shot a sharp glance at him. "A friend of mine disappointed me," he said. "I grew tired of waiting for him, and was taking a turn in the fresh air to work off my annoyance when I met with the accident which procured me the pleasure of your acquaintance.

"And now kindly assist me to that chair. Thank you. And wheel up that one for yourself. No, not that, the one with the high back. You will find it ever so much more comfortable."

Allan complied, and his host, having compounded a couple of long drinks, took a copious draft from his glass.

"Confess now," he said, laughing and looking shrewdly into his guest's face. "A suspicion flashed across your mind that the whisky might be hocused."

Allan warmly repudiated any such notion; but the flush which mounted to his forehead belied his words. Partly to hide his confusion and partly to back up his denial, he drank some of his highball, and found that it fully deserved the encomiums bestowed upon it.

"I hope you find that chair comfortable," the doctor remarked.

"Very much so," Allan replied. "One of the most comfortable I ever sat in."

"It is an invention of my own," the other went on. "I amuse myself by inventing things sometimes, and that chair is one of my successes. I am thinking of taking out a patent for it.

"You will observe that the arms are continued down to meet that footrest at the bottom, and that by pressing the knees against them, it is possible to obtain a complete relaxation of the other muscles. Then again, by a simple mechanical contrivance, it can be adjusted to any angle. Allow me to show you."

The little man rose with some difficulty and hobbled to Allan's side.

"Let us suppose," he continued, "that you are tired of that position and wish to assume a more horizontal attitude. I have simply to touch this button, and—"

There was a faint click, and from the footrest a hinged steel shutter leaped, hissing like a snake, and, darting up a cunningly concealed groove in the arms, fastened itself about Allan's neck and pinned him to the back of the chair.

So sudden was the shock that for several seconds Mortimer could do nothing but stare, open mouthed, at his little host, who had taken a step backward and was regarding him with an evil smile.

Then, with a mighty heave, he tried to liberate himself from his narrow prison.

Once—twice—thrice he exerted all the power of arms, legs, and shoulders, but in vain. Had he been screwed down in his coffin, he could not have more thoroughly realized his own helplessness.

The doctor laughed; a low, vibrant laugh that made the flesh crawl.

"Believe me," he said, "you are tiring yourself unnecessarily. Hercules himself could not get out of that chair."

"Release me at once," Allan cried, his face purple with rage and exertion. "What is the meaning of this folly?"

The little doctor walked deliberately to a bureau, every vestige of lameness having vanished, opened a drawer, took out a cigar, lit it, and after inhaling several puffs with every appearance of relish, seated himself opposite his victim.

"I would offer you one as a sedative," he said, flicking off the ash, "but you might find it inconvenient, seeing that your hands are imprisoned. Just one word of advice: Don't call out. In the first place, it would necessitate my gagging you, which would deprive me of the pleasure of your conversation, and in the second place, no one would pay the slightest attention to a cry, even if it were heard. I have given out that my man is subject to fits, and it would simply he attributed to one of his outbursts."

A sickening sense of his helplessness overcame Allan.

"What is the meaning of this?" he asked faintly. "What are you going to do with me?"

"I am going to let you into a secret," was the reply. "The most remarkable scientific discovery of the day. I will not exact any pledge that you will not betray my confidence, because—well, because you will be the tenth man to learn it, and not one of the other nine has so far spoken of it. To use a conventional phrase, their lips have been sealed."

The significance of the smile which accompanied these words was unmistakable.

"You mean that you are going to murder me?"

"That is a very brutal way of putting it. Let us rather say that you will become a martyr to science."

"I should be glad if you would explain." Allan did his best to speak coolly, but his voice trembled.

"I am about to do so."

The doctor rose, stepped over to the mantel shelf, and, sliding back a panel, exposed the door of a small steel safe. This he unlocked, and from it took a morocco-bound album and a tiny glass vial half filled with a liquid of pale amber color in which strange lights seemed to play.

"Let us examine this little book first," he said. "It is customary, I believe, in certain circles, to entertain guests by allowing them to look over the family album."

He laughed at the conceit.

"This," he added, "is more interesting than most. Possibly you may recognize some acquaintance."

He turned the leaves slowly, and Allan shuddered as he looked.

Every photograph represented the fatal chair, with an occupant apparently dead or plunged in a deep slumber. The faces which appeared above the steel shutter were all different and wore an expression of peace.

As the last page was turned, Allan uttered a loud exclamation.

"Ah!" said the doctor. "You recognize my last subject, I see. A Mr. Allerlee,

I believe. I understand that his disappearance created a good deal of comment. Well—so much for my little portrait gallery. A foolish and perhaps a dangerous fad, but I confess to a weakness for interesting souvenirs."

He replaced the album in the safe, and, picking up the vial, reseated himself, listening with a pleasant smile as Allan poured out a flood of invective, threat and remonstrance.

"A waste of breath and energy," he said at last. "If only my subjects were less intractable, my results might be better. Now listen to me for a few minutes, and you will, I am sure, find what I have to say interesting.

"Some years ago, in the course of a series of scientific experiments, I was fortunate enough to establish the existence of a form of ether which, for lack of a better term, I will call Vitic Force. This exists to a greater or lesser degree in every form of animal life; the human, however, differentiating in several essentials from that in the brute creation. Into the latter form, we need not enter.

"To be brief, I discovered that every human being has from birth a varying amount of this vitic force, and that the greater the original quantity, which decreases at a fixed rate, the longer the term of the natural life. So much for the unpractical side of my discovery."

"To a scientist," Allan interrupted, "all this may be very interesting, but I fail to see how it can affect me."

"A moment's patience and you shall learn. Having arrived at this point in my researches, the next step was naturally to try to reduce this force to a substance which might be handled and applied to the renewal of exhausted vitality. In this, also, I was successful beyond my hopes.

"I discovered a drug which, injected hypodermically into the system, holds the vitic ether in suspense, and, immediately after the death of the subject, permits its distillation by means of a combination of extreme heat and powerful electric currents.

"In this little bottle"—he held up the vial—"are three hundred years of life, calculating on the basis that every drop means five years. It does not rejuvenate, but it checks decay and instills vitality. My only regret is that I did not discover the secret thirty years ago. As it is, however, I have before me a longer, if not more useful, life than others, provided that no accident befalls me."

"I pray to God that you may get run over on the first street corner," interjected Allan bitterly.

"Thank you," replied the other with a genial smile. "Under the circumstances, your sentiments are naturally antagonistic. I suppose it would be useless to ask you any questions about your ancestors—as to longevity, I mean? The information would be extremely useful, and would assist me materially in my calculations."

"Quite useless," Allan replied shortly. "And now, if this is not some ghastly practical joke, go on with your devil's work and do not torture me further. Why not have drugged my drink, as you suggested, and saved me from this hell of anticipation? Do you delight in cruelty for its own sake?"

Dr. Armitage lifted a deprecating hand.

"You do me wrong," he said. "My nature is rather kindly than otherwise. And you must forgive me that my pleasure as a scientist in imparting a valuable secret, which can never be revealed by the one who learns it, has perhaps obscured my natural impulses.

"As to drugging your whisky, I may tell you that I have tried that plan, and found it a complete failure. The presence of any other drug in the system counteracts the effects of that which I inject. It was in consequence of two successive failures and a most regrettable sacrifice of human life needlessly that I invented that chair.

"To relieve your apprehensions as far as possible, I may mention that your death will be absolutely painless. You will simply fall asleep like a child, and—never waken."

There was a long silence. The little doctor, his legs crossed and his elbows resting on the arms of his chair, sat playing tunes with one thin white hand on the fingertips of the other, and regarding his victim much after the fashion of a butcher estimating the mutton capacities of a fat sheep.

Allan hardly looked at him. His thoughts were busy with past scenes and incidents of the life he was about to leave.

He realized that he was absolutely in the power of the fiend before him, and that the end was only a matter of a few hours at most. He remembered reading an account of an execution in the paper that very morning and speculating on the feelings of the doomed man.

Then he fell to wondering what his friends would say about his disappearance, and what theories would be advanced. He had listened to many in the case of Allerlee, and some of them had been decidedly uncharitable.

Thank God he had no wife! There was a girl who would perhaps feel sorry. He hoped so, at any rate.

The swift train of thought was broken by Dr. Armitage taking out his watch.

"I can spare you half an hour," the doctor said. "In the meanwhile, let me ask you whether you have anyone dependent on you. One of my subjects had a wife and two children. They are now in receipt of a small annuity, which I send them regularly—anonymously of course. I am sorry that I cannot offer to communicate any last wishes or farewell messages, but so far as pecuniary assistance is concerned—"

"Blast you!" interrupted Allan. "If I knew that every relative I have in the world would starve within a week, they should not be beholden to you for one copper."

"How selfish is resentment!" was the response. "But I will not press my offer. Let us talk about something else."

"I will tell you this," Allan continued fiercely. "Your iniquities will surely be discovered, and your devil's brew will not save you from the gallows. You may kill me, and dispose of my body, but something will be left which will afford a clue to my disappearance."

The doctor laughed.

"You are wrong," he said—"altogether wrong. Nothing will be left—not a hair—nothing but a little insignificant pile of ash which one might almost lift between the finger and thumb. And that reminds me. I have explained my discovery, but I have not shown you the apparatus by which I attain my results. It will serve to wile away the half hour remaining."

He slipped the vial into his pocket, and, going over to the iron doors in the wall, unlocked and threw them open, revealing an intricate entanglement of wires and an array of silvered knobs.

"This," explained Dr. Armitage in the tone of a lecturer, "is a form of electric furnace, with the addition of strong alternating currents altogether independent of those which generate the heat. Beneath these porcelain bars which sustain the subject is an ingenious condenser which concentrates and distills the vitic ether. As you are not a scientist, a technical explanation would, I fear, be thrown away on you, but, speaking generally, I may say that this invention of mine is the most powerful dissolvent that exists. Nothing, not even metal, can resist it."

"I don't believe it," Allan said shortly. "Some clue will be left to hang you."

Dr. Armitage looked genuinely annoyed.

"How skeptical is the unscientific mind!" he replied. "It will believe nothing that the eyes have not seen. However, in this case, a practical illustration is easily given. You shall see for yourself."

His eyes wandered about the room as though seeking some suitable object for his experiment, and finally rested on the parcel which Allan had deposited on a table.

"What is that?" he asked, indicating the package with his finger.

Only for a fraction of a second did Allan hesitate in his reply, but in that infinitesimally brief space of time, a thousand hopes and fears alternately occupied his mind.

Predominant even over his desperate anxiety to escape was a wild desire for vengeance, and now his villainous host was himself offering a chance for the former and a certainty of the latter.

Therefore it was with a steady voice that Mortimer answered:

"It is a canister of tea that I am—or rather intended—taking home to my wife."

"Really?" said the doctor. "So you are a domestic character. Upon my word, I should not have suspected it. I am sorry that I am compelled to deprive Mrs. Mortimer not only of her husband, but of her tea as well. I could not, however, find a more suitable subject for my experiment."

He picked up the parcel and, having stripped off the wrapping, glanced at the label on the cannister.

"'Albuera Tea,'" he read aloud. "'A strong and palatable blend.' An excellent brand, no doubt, but I am not much in favor of tea as a beverage. Under other circumstances, I should have been happy to give you a little lecture on its deleterious properties, but it would, I fear, be wasted. However, there will not be much left of this to injure anyone when I get through with it."

"No," Allan muttered to himself, "nor of you, nor of me, nor your precious invention."

"Perhaps you would like me to wheel your chair a little closer," suggested the doctor, pausing halfway back to his furnace. "No trouble, I assure you."

"No, thank you," Allan replied. "I can see very well from where I am."

Every nerve of his body was tingling, but he managed to control his voice, and the doctor, suspecting nothing, went on about his preparations.

"Now," the doctor said at last, "we are all ready for the experiment. You see, I place this tin on the bars and close the doors and lock them, so. All I have to do now is to press this concealed button and set the powerful forces inside at work. In five minutes I will open the doors again, and you will see—nothing."

"Press the button, then, in God's name, and get it over!" Allan cried, tortured beyond endurance by the other's deliberation.

"Ta-ta-ta," Dr. Armitage answered, shaking his head. "The unscientific mind again."

He raised his hand to the wall, and Allan turned away his face.

There was a blinding flash of flame and a roar like a hundred pieces of artillery fired simultaneously. As in a dream, Allan felt the chair in which he sat caught up by an invisible hand and hurled violently against the opposite wall.

Then darkness came over him and he knew no more.

Three weeks later, he opened his eyes to find himself lying on a hospital cot, a mass of bandages, and his friend Atkinson seated beside him,

"What has happened?" he asked faintly.

"Steady, old man," replied the other soothingly. "You mustn't talk."

"Tell me," Allan insisted. "I must know. Dr. Armitage—? Was he killed?"

Atkinson shook his head.

"No," he said. "They dug you both out of the ruins at almost the same time, just before the fire reached you. He was, if anything, more badly hurt than you, but he made a marvelous recovery. The doctors say they never saw anything like it. His vitality was extraordinary. He left the hospital a week ago."

"And he was not arrested?"

"Arrested? No, why should he be? He explained that he was showing you an experiment when the compound unfortunately exploded."

Weak as he was, Allan ground his teeth with rage.

"And the chair—the horrible death trap in which I was fastened. Did that awaken no suspicion?"

"You were fastened in no chair," the other replied. "You have been having sick dreams, old man. There was a rafter across your chest, pinning you down, but that was all."

Allan groaned.

"The thing must have been torn apart by the explosion," he said, "but they must find it. It will hang that villain. Tell them to search the ruins."

"Hush," said Atkinson. "You must not excite yourself. The explosion set fire to the debris of the cottage and everything was consumed."

"Then tell them to arrest Dr. Armitage at once," the sick man cried excitedly. "He is a ghoul—a vampire! He carries the lives of nine men in his pocket, and God knows how many he has killed.

"He murdered Allerlee. He confessed it to me. There are pictures of the dead men in a little safe in the mantel shelf. I know where they are; let me get up. I will get up—do you hear?"

He made a desperate effort to rise, and fell back unconscious.

When Allan had recovered sufficiently to be able to tell a coherent story, a diligent search for the doctor was instituted, but in vain.

Dr. Armitage had vanished utterly.

·····

THE MYSTERY OF THE
SHRIVELED HAND

SAX ROHMER

We were back in Cairo again, and the conversation drifted into many channels. All sorts of topics were discussed, from racing to the latest feminine fashions, from ballroom dances to the mysteries of the Great Pyramid.

"What became of Adderley?" Jennings suddenly asked.

Several men in the party had been cronies during the time we were stationed in Cairo, and at Jennings's words, a sort of hush seemed to fall on those who had known Adderley. I cannot say whether Jennings noticed this, but it was perfectly evident to me that Dr. Matheson, the big-hearted, boyish American, had perceived it, for he glanced swiftly across in my direction in an oddly significant way.

"I don't know," replied Burton, who was an irrigation man. "He was rather an unsavory sort of character in some ways, but I heard that he came to a sticky end."

"You mean Sidney Adderley, the man who was so indecently rich?" someone interjected. "Had a place out at Gezireh, and was always talking about his father's millions?"

"That's the fellow," said Jennings. "There was some scandal, I know, but it was after my time here. Was there really anything in that story, or was it suggested by Adderley's unpleasant reputation?"

"Well," replied Burton, "it's really a sort of fairy tale, unless Marriott"—he glanced across in my direction—"can confirm it. But there was a story current during the latter part of Adderley's stay in Cairo to the effect that he had made the acquaintance of the wife, or some member of the household, of an old gentleman out Tanta way—a sort of Moslem saint, or *welee*."

"I can settle any doubts upon the point," said I.

I immediately became a focus of general curiosity.

"I met Adderley," I began, "here in this very hotel, one evening in the winter of 1917. He had been drinking rather heavily—a fact which he was quite unable to disguise. He was never, by any means, a real friend of mine. In fact, I doubt if he had a true friend in the world. However, I could see that he was lonely, and as I chanced to be at a loose end, I accepted an invitation to go over to what he termed his 'little place' at Gezireh."

"I even thought the place was something of a myth," declared Jennings.

"It proved to be a veritable palace," I replied. "The man privately—or secretly, to be more exact—kept up a sort of pagan state. He had any number of servants—he became a millionaire after the death of his father, as you will remember. Given more congenial company, I must confess that I might have spent a most enjoyable evening there.

"Adderley insisted upon priming me with champagne. After a while, I may as well admit, I lost something of my former reserve and began to feel that I was having a fairly good time. By the way, my host was now quite drunk. He got into that objectionable and dangerous mood which some of you will recall, and I could see by the light in his eyes that there was mischief brewing, although at the time I did not know its nature.

"I should explain that we were amusing ourselves in a room which was nearly as large as the lounge of this hotel, and furnished in a somewhat similar style. There were carved pillars and stained glass domes, a little fountain and other peculiarities of an Eastern household.

"Presently, Adderley gave an order to one of his servants and glanced at me with that sort of mocking, daredevil look in his eyes which I loathed— which everybody loathed who ever met the man. Of course, I had no idea what all this portended, but I was shortly to learn.

"While he was still looking at me, but stealing sidelong glances at a doorway before which was draped a most wonderful curtain of what one might call flamingo color, the curtain was suddenly pulled aside, and a girl came in.

"You must remember, that at the time of which I am speaking, the scandal respecting the Sheik of Tanta had not yet come to light. I could not guess, therefore, who the girl might be; but of her striking beauty there could be no doubt whatever. She was dressed in magnificent robes, and she literally glittered with jewels. She even wore jewels upon the toes of her little bare feet; but the first thing that struck me at the moment of her appearance was that her presence there was contrary to her wishes and inclinations. I have never seen a similar expression in any woman's eyes. She looked at Adderley as if she would gladly have slain him.

"Seeing this look, his mocking smile—in which there was something of triumph, of the joy of possession—turned to a scowl of positive brutality. He sprang to his feet—or lurched to his feet, rather—clenched his fists in a way that set me bristling, and advanced toward the girl. Although the width of the room divided them, she recoiled, and the significance of her expression and gesture was unmistakable. Adderley paused.

"'So you have made up your mind to dance, after all?' he shouted.

"The look in the girl's dark eyes was pitiful, and she turned to me with a glance of dumb entreaty.

"'No, no!' she cried. 'No, no! Why do you bring me here?'

"'Dance!' roared Adderley. 'Dance! That's what I want you to do.'

"Rebellion leaped again to the wonderful eyes, and she started back with a perfectly splendid gesture of defiance. At that, my brutal and drunken host lunged in her direction. I was on my feet now, but before I could act, the girl said something that checked him, sobered him, pulled him up short, as if he had encountered a stone wall.

"'Ah, God!' she cried. She was speaking, of course, in Arabic. 'His hand! His hand! Look! *His hand!*'

"To me, her words were meaningless, but, following the direction of her agonized glance, I saw that she was watching what seemed to me to be the shadow of someone moving behind the flame-like curtain. It produced an effect not unlike that of a huge, outstretched hand, the fingers crooked, claw fashion.

"'Marriott, Marriott!' whispered Adderley, grasping me by the shoulder and pointing with a quivering finger toward this indistinct shadow upon the curtain. 'Do you see it—do you see it?' he said huskily.

"'It is his hand—it is his hand!'

"Of the pair, I think the man was the more frightened; but the girl, uttering a frightful shriek, ran out of the room as if pursued by a demon. As she did so, whoever had been moving behind the curtain evidently withdrew. The shadow disappeared, and Adderley, still staring as if hypnotized at the spot where it had been, continued to hold my shoulder as in a vise. Then, sinking down upon a heap of cushions beside me, he loudly and shakily ordered more champagne.

"Utterly mystified by the incident, I finally left him in a state of stupor and returned to my quarters, wondering whether I had dreamed half of the episode or the whole of it, whether he really owned that wonderful palace at Gezireh or had borrowed it to impress me."

II

I ceased speaking. My story was received in stony silence.

"And this is all you know?" said Burton at last.

"Absolutely all. I left Egypt soon afterward."

"Yes, I remember. It was while you were away that the scandal arose about the Sheik of Tanta. Extraordinary story, Marriott! I should like to know what it all meant, and what the end of it was."

At this point, Dr. Matheson broke his long silence.

"Although I am afraid I cannot enlighten you respecting the end of the story," he said quietly, "perhaps I can carry it a step further."

"Really, doctor? What do you know about the matter?"

"I became connected with it accidentally," replied the American. "As you know, I was doing some work near Cairo at the time. One evening, presumably about the period of which Marriott is speaking, I was returning from the hospital at Gezireh, at which I sometimes acted as anesthetist, to my quarters in Cairo. I was just drifting along leisurely by the edge of the gardens, admiring the beauty of the night and the deceitful peace of the Nile.

"The hour was fairly late and not a soul was about. Nothing disturbed the silence except those vague sounds of the river which are so characteristic of the country. Presently, as I rambled on, with my thoughts wandering back to the dim ages, I literally fell over a man who lay in my path.

"I was naturally startled, but I carried an electric pocket torch, and by its light I discovered that the person over whom I had stumbled was a dignified-looking Arab, somewhat past middle age. His clothes, which were of good quality, were covered with dirt and blood, and he bore all the appearance of having recently been engaged in a very tough struggle. His face was notable for its possession of a jet-black mustache and a snow-white beard. He had swooned from loss of blood."

"Why, was he wounded?" exclaimed Jennings.

"His hand had been nearly severed from the wrist."

"Merciful Heavens!"

"Realizing the impossibility of carrying him so far as the hospital, I extemporized a rough tourniquet and left him under a tree by the path until I could obtain assistance. Later, at the hospital, following a consultation, we found it necessary to amputate."

"I suppose he objected fiercely, being a Moslem?"

"He was past objecting to anything; and if I sacrificed his chance of heaven, at least I gave him a chance of earth. He was under my care for some time, but I doubt if he was properly grateful. He had an iron constitution, however, and I finally allowed him to depart. One queer stipulation he had made—that the severed hand should be given to him when he left the hospital; and this bargain I faithfully carried out."

"Most extraordinary!" I said. "Did you ever learn the identity of the old gentleman?"

"He was very reticent, but I made a number of inquiries, and finally learned—with absolute certainty, I think—that he was the Sheik Abdulla Something-or-Other, an Arab of some repute in the neighborhood, and rather a big man in the religious world. Indeed, he was a minor prophet of some sort, and was known locally as the White Sheik."

"Did you learn how he came by his injury, doctor?"

Matheson smiled in his quiet fashion and selected a fresh cigar with great deliberation.

"I suppose it is scarcely a case of betraying a professional secret," he said; "but while my patient was recovering from the effects of the anesthetic, he unconsciously gave me several clues to the nature of the episode. Putting two and two together, I gathered that someone, although the name of this person never once passed the sheik's lips, had abducted his favorite wife. The sheik had traced the abductor, and presumably the girl, to some house which I gathered to be in the neighborhood of Gezireh. In an attempt to force an entrance—doubtless with the amiable purpose of slaying them both—he had been detected by the prime object of his hatred. In hurriedly descending from a window, he had been attacked with some weapon, possibly a sword, and had only made good his escape in the condition in which I found him. How far he had gone after being wounded, I cannot say, but I do not think the house can have been at any great distance from the spot where I found him."

"Comment is really superfluous," remarked Burton. "He was looking for Adderley."

"I agree," said Jennings.

"And," I added, "it was evidently after this episode that I had the privilege of visiting that interesting establishment!"

III

Fully six months elapsed, and on returning from Egypt I had forgotten all about Adderley, till one evening, strolling aimlessly along St. James's Street and wondering how I was going to kill time—for London can be infinitely more lonely than any desert—I saw a thick-set figure approaching along the other side of the street. The swing of the shoulders, the aggressive turn of the head, were vaguely familiar. While I was searching my memory and endeavoring to obtain a view of the man's face, he stared across in my direction.

Adderley!

He looked even more debauched than I remembered him. In Egypt he had had a sun-tanned skin, but now he looked unhealthily pallid and blotchy. He raised his hand.

"Marriott!" he cried, and ran across to greet me.

His boisterous manner and coarse geniality had made him popular with a certain set in former days, but I had never been deceived by it. Most people found Adderley out sooner or later, but I had detected the man's true nature from the very beginning. His eyes alone were danger signals for any amateur psychologist.

However, I returned his greeting civilly enough.

"Bless my soul, you are looking as fit as a fiddle!" he cried. "Where have you been, and what have you been doing since I saw you last?"

"Nothing much," I replied.

"Come along to my place," he suggested. "We'll have a cup of tea—or a whisky and soda, if you prefer it."

Probably I should have refused, but even as he spoke, I was mentally translated to the lounge of Shepheard's Hotel, and, prompted by a very human curiosity, I determined to accept his invitation. I wondered if Fate had thrown an opportunity in my way of learning the end of the peculiar story which I had heard in Cairo.

I accompanied Adderley to his chambers, which were within a stone's throw of the spot where I had met him. That his gift for making himself unpopular with all and sundry, high and low, had not deserted him was illustrated by the attitude of the liftman as we entered the hall of the chambers. He was barely civil to Adderley, and even regarded me with evident disfavor.

We were admitted by Adderley's man, whom I had not seen before, but who was some kind of foreigner—I think a Portuguese.

I had never felt at ease in his company, and now, as I sat, staring wonderingly at the strange and costly ornaments with which the room was overladen,

I bethought me of the object of my visit. How I should have brought the conversation back to our Cairo days I know not, but a suitable opening was presently offered by Adderley himself.

"Do you ever see any of the old gang?" he inquired.

"I was in Cairo about six months ago," I replied, "and I met some of them again."

"What? Had they drifted back to Egypt after all?"

"Two or three of them were taking what Dr. Matheson described as a busman's holiday."

At mention of Dr. Matheson's name, Adderley visibly started.

"So you know Matheson!" he murmured. "I didn't know you had ever met him."

Plainly to hide his confusion, he drew my attention to a rather fine silver bowl of early Persian ware. He was displaying its peculiar virtues, and showing a certain acquaintance with his subject, when he was interrupted. A door opened suddenly and a girl came in. Adderley put down the bowl and turned rapidly as I rose from my seat.

It was the lady of Gezireh!

I recognized her at once, although she wore a very up-to-date gown. While it did not suit her dark beauty so well as the native dress which she had worn at Cairo, yet it could not conceal the fact that, in a barbaric way, she was a very handsome woman.

"Oh!" she said, speaking in Arabic. "Why did you not tell me there was someone here?"

Adderley's reply—also spoken in Arabic—was characteristically brutal.

"Get out, you fool!" he said.

I turned to go, for I was conscious of an intense desire to attack my host.

"Don't go, Marriott, don't go!" he cried. "I am sorry for this—I am damned sorry, I—"

He paused and looked at me in a queer sort of appealing way. The girl, her big eyes widely open, retreated again to the door with curious, lithe steps, characteristically Oriental. The door regained, she paused for a moment and extended one small hand in Adderley's direction.

"I hate you!" she said slowly. "I hate you!"

She went out, quietly closing the door behind her. Adderley turned to me with an embarrassed laugh.

"I know you think I'm a brute and an outsider," he said, "and perhaps I am. Everybody says I am, so I suppose there must be something in it; but if ever man paid for his mistakes, I have paid for mine, Marriott. Good God, I haven't a friend in the world!"

"You probably don't deserve one," I retorted.

"I know I don't, and that's the tragedy of it," he replied. "You may not believe it, Marriott—I don't expect anybody to believe me—but for more than a year I have been walking on the edge of hell. Do you know where I have been since I saw you last?"

I shook my head in answer.

"I have been halfway around the world, Marriott. Trying to find peace."

"You don't know where to look for it," I said.

"If only you knew!" he whispered. "If only you knew!"

He sank down upon a settee, ruffling his hair with his hands and looking the picture of haggard misery.

"Hold on a bit, Marriott," he implored, seeing that I was still set upon departure. "Don't go yet. There is something I want to ask you—something very important."

He crossed to a sideboard and mixed himself a stiff whisky and soda. He asked me in to join him, but I refused.

"Won't you sit down again?"

I shook my head.

"You came to my place at Gezireh, once," he began abruptly. "I was drunk—I admit it; but something happened. Do you remember?"

I nodded.

"This is what I want to ask you—did you, or did you not, see—that *shadow?*"

I stared him hard in the face.

"I remember the episode to which you refer," I replied. "I certainly saw a shadow."

"But what sort of shadow?"

"To me, it seemed an indefinite, shapeless thing, as if caused by someone moving behind the curtain."

"It didn't look to you like—like the shadow of a *hand?*"

"It might have been, but I could not be positive."

Adderley groaned.

"Marriott," he said, "money is a curse. It has been a curse to me."

I was suffering the man's society only because of the intense curiosity which now possessed me on learning that the lady of Gezireh was still in Adderley's company. Whether my repugnance for his society would have permitted me to remain any longer, I cannot say; but as if Fate had deliberately planned that I should be a witness of the concluding phases of this secret drama, we were now interrupted a second time, and again in a dramatic fashion.

Adderley's nondescript valet came in with some letters. He also brought in a rather large brown-paper parcel, sealed and fastened with great care.

"Surely that is from Egypt!" muttered Adderley as the man went out.

Taking up the parcel, he seemed to become oblivious of my presence, and his face grew even more haggard as he studied the writing upon the wrapper. With unsteady fingers, he untied it. I lingered, watching curiously. Presently, out from the wrappings he took a very beautiful casket of ebony and ivory, cunningly carved and standing upon four claw-like legs.

"What the devil does this mean?" he muttered.

He opened the box, which was lined with sandalwood. Instantly he started back with a great cry, recoiling from the casket as if it had contained an adder.

My former sentiments forgotten, I stepped forward and peered into the interior. Then I, in turn, recoiled.

In the box lay a shriveled brown hand, neatly severed at the wrist. Upon one finger was a talismanic silver ring, having seven studs, such as one often sees upon the hands of desert Arabs.

Adderley sank down again upon the settee.

"My God!" he whispered. "His hand! His hand! He has sent me his hand!"

He began laughing. I could see that the man was practically hysterical because of his mysterious fears.

"Stop that!" I said sharply. "Pull yourself together, Adderley! What the deuce is the matter with you?"

"Take it away!" he moaned. "Take it away, Marriott! Take the accursed thing away!"

"I admit it is an unpleasant gift to send to anybody," I said; "but probably you know more about it than I do."

"Take it away," he repeated. "Take it away, for God's sake! Take it away, Marriott!"

He was quite beyond reason.

"Very well," I said, and wrapped the casket in the brown paper in which it had come. "But what do you want me to do with it?"

"Throw it into the river," he answered. "Burn it—do anything you like with it—but take it out of my sight!"

As I descended to the street, the liftman regarded me in a curious and rather significant way. Just as I was about to step out into the hall, he apparently decided that I was a fit person to converse with.

"Excuse me, sir," he said, "but are you a friend of Mr. Adderley's?"

"Why do you ask?"

"Well, sir, I hope you will excuse me, but at times I have thought the gentleman was just a little bit queer, like."

"You mean insane?" I asked sharply.

"Well, sir, I don't know, but he is always asking me if I can see shadows and things in the lift. Sometimes, when he comes in late of a night, he absolutely gives me the cold shivers, he does!"

I lingered, the box under my arm, reluctant to obtain confidences from a servant, but at the same time keenly interested.

"Then there's a lady friend of his who is always coming here," the man continued. "*She's* haunted by shadows, too." He paused, watching me narrowly. "There's nothing better in this world than a clear conscience, sir!" he concluded.

IV

Having returned to my room at the hotel, I sat down to the mysterious parcel, surveying it with much disfavor. That it contained the hand of the White Sheik—the hand which had been amputated by Dr. Matheson—I could not doubt. Its appearance in that dramatic fashion confirmed Matheson's idea that the Arab's injury had been received at the hands of Adderley. What did all this portend, unless that the White Sheik was dead? And if he were dead, why was Adderley more afraid of him dead than living?

I thought of the haunting shadow. I thought of the night at Gezireh. I thought of Dr. Matheson's words when he told us of his discovery of the sheik lying in the path that night beside the Nile.

I felt strangely disinclined to touch the relic, and it was only after some moments' hesitation that I undid the wrappings and raised the lid of the casket. Dusk was very near, and I had not yet lighted the lamps. At first, therefore, I doubted the evidence of my senses; but having lighted up and peered long and anxiously into the sandalwood lining of the casket, I could doubt no longer.

The casket was empty!

It was like a conjuring trick. That the hand had been in the box when I had taken it up from Adderley's table; I could have sworn before any jury. When and by whom it had been removed was a puzzle beyond my powers of unraveling.

Vaguely wondering if Adderley had played me a gruesome practical joke, I put the box on a sideboard and contemplated the telephone doubtfully for a moment. It was in my mind to ring him up. Finally, taking all things into consideration, I determined that I would have nothing more to do with the man's unsavory and mysterious affairs.

It was in vain, however, that I endeavored to dismiss the matter from my mind. Throughout the evening, which I spent at a theater with some friends, I found myself constantly thinking of Adderley and the ivory casket, of the Sheik of Tanta, and of the mystery of that shriveled, yellow hand.

I had been back at my room about half an hour, I suppose, and it was long past midnight when I was startled by a ringing of my telephone bell. I took up the receiver.

"Marriott, Marriott!" came a choking cry.

"Yes—who is speaking?"

"It is I, Adderley. For God's sake, come over to my place at once!"

His words were scarcely intelligible. Undoubtedly, he was in the grip of intense emotion.

"What do you mean? What is the matter?"

"It is here, Marriott—it is here! It is knocking on the door—knocking!"

"You have been drinking," I said sternly. "Where is your man?"

"The cur has bolted. He bolted the moment he heard that damned knocking. I am all alone—I have no one else to appeal to." There came a choking sound. "My God, Marriott, it is getting in! I can see the shadow on the blind!"

Convinced that Adderley's secret fears had driven him mad, I nevertheless felt called upon to comply with his urgent call, and without a moment's delay, I hurried to St. James's Street. The liftman was not on duty, the lower hall was in darkness, but I raced up the stairs and found, to my astonishment, that Adderley's door was wide open.

"Adderley!" I cried. "Adderley!"

There was no reply, and without further ceremony I entered and searched the chambers. They were empty.

Deeply mystified, I was about to go out of the place again when there came a ring at the doorbell. I walked to the door and found that a policeman was standing upon the landing.

"Good evening, sir," he said, and then paused, staring at me curiously.

"Good evening, constable," I replied.

"You are not the gentleman who ran out a while ago," he said, a note of suspicion coming into his voice.

I handed him my card and explained what had occurred.

"It must have been Mr. Adderley I saw," muttered the constable.

"You saw—when?"

"Just before you arrived, sir. He came racing out into St. James's Street and dashed off like a madman."

"In which direction was he going?"

"Toward Pall Mall."

The neighborhood was practically deserted at that hour; but from the guard on duty before St. James's Palace, we obtained our first evidence of Adderley's movements. He had raced by some five minutes before, frantically looking back over his shoulder, and behaving like a man flying for his life. No one else had seen him. No one else ever did see him alive.

At two o'clock there was no news, but I had informed Scotland Yard and official inquiries had been set afoot.

Nothing further came to light that night, but all readers of the daily press will remember, that on the following day, Adderley's body was taken out of the pond in St. James's Park. Death was due to drowning, but his throat was greatly discolored, as if it had been clutched in a fierce grip. It was I who identified the body.

As many people will know, the mystery of Adderley's death, in spite of the closest inquiries, has not been properly cleared up to this day. The identity of the lady who visited him at his chambers was never discovered. She completely disappeared.

The ebony and ivory casket lies on my table at this present moment, visible evidence of an invisible menace from which Adderley fled around the world.

Doubtless the full truth will never be known now. A significant discovery, however, was made some days after the recovery of Adderley's body. From the bottom of the pond in St. James's Park, a patient Scotland Yard official brought up the talismanic silver ring, with its seven mystical studs.

· · · · ·

FEAR

DAMON RUNYON

"I don't like to hit you, John," said the chief, fondling a piece of thick, solid rubber tire and glancing down at the man who cowered at his feet. "I don't like to hit you at all. You come in like a good fellow and it will be all right."

"I ain't got nothin' to come in wit', chief," whined the man. "I'm tellin' you true. I wasn't there. I couldn't 'a' been there. I hadn't got in town."

The chief, a huge fellow who seemed about ready to burst out of his gold-bedecked uniform, reached down and picked the man up by the collar, as easily as a terrier lifts a rubber ball. He tried to stand him on his feet, but the man was as limp as a wet string, so the chief held him dangling in the air at arm's length.

"I gave you a chance, John," he said, his voice almost soothing.

He raised his free arm and snapped it sharply in the air. The piece of tire swished forward like a buggy whip and struck the man in the face with a brisk slap.

The chief released his grasp and the man dropped to the floor and rolled over and over like a shot rabbit. It was not a hard blow; it was a blow struck with the knowledge of long experience.

The man was "out."

The chief sat down at his desk and glared at the silent form. A firm believer in the efficacy of physical punishment to break a man's nerve, he took a savage delight in such scenes as this. And yet they afforded him a problem that he had puzzled over many times.

"Why should a man be afraid of a little beating?" he had often remarked. "The average criminal has a good deal of courage; there is no doubt about that. They are certainly not afraid of death, because they face it in a hundred different forms every time they undertake a crime.

"It requires nerve to break into a house. You don't know what minute your life will be snuffed out without any warning. It takes nerve to kill a man. I couldn't do it deliberately, but the average criminal is prepared to take life the instant he is interfered with.

"They don't fear imprisonment. That is shown by the fact that as soon as they complete a sentence, many of them immediately jeopardize their liberty by fresh crime. They've got nerve, all right; they'll stand up and fight against certain death when they are cornered without a tremor.

"Then why is it that the toughest, most hardened criminal, cannot take

159

a little physical punishment? I've seen men who had reputations from coast to coast as man-killers and daring crooks break down the moment they get a slap in the face. And ten minutes before, or ten minutes afterward, they would go out and kill an innocent person with no more thought of it than eating their dinner.

"They're not afraid of death in here. They know we won't go so far as to kill them. They know—or they ought to know—that if they took their beating and kept their mouths shut, we couldn't, in nine cases out of ten, convict them.

"In here, alone with me, or anyone else, they lose their nerve at once. In a house at midnight, alone with any man, they would fight like rats if they knew they were going to be killed.

"If one of them had the nerve to jump me the moment I closed the door of my office, they might get away with it. Certainly it is worth a chance, but none of them ever takes it. Why, they even confess when they are absolutely innocent, which is a good thing for us, of course. It gives us a reputation for efficiency without any work,

"But why do they do it? If I had nerve enough to commit a crime, I'd have nerve enough to keep my head closed. You could beat the life out of me, but I wouldn't confess, unless I knew you had a cinch on me."

The chief was a brave man, too; physically, at least. He had won promotion through personal daring. He had jeopardized his life a score of times in the performance of his duty. He had utter contempt for a coward, and it was with a feeling of contempt that he watched the silent figure on the floor.

He was becoming a trifle angry, for the prisoner was unusually obdurate. For full five minutes the chief sat looking at the heap on the floor. Then the man stirred, opened his eyes, and countered the glare of the officer. He shivered slightly, and the chief grinned.

"Now, John," he said, his voice a little harder than before, " I don't want to hurt you, but you've got to come in. That's all."

He rose and dealt the man a vicious kick.

"Get up!" he ordered roughly. The man rose to his feet, shaking in every fiber. The chief seized his wrist and commenced turning it around in his powerful hand.

"Oh, don't, chief!" whined the man, his voice rising. "Please don't, chief!"

Slowly the chief twisted the wrist, and the man's face grew purple. His voice arose to a scream.

"Oh, please don't, chief!" he shrieked.

He tried to fall to the floor, but the chief held him upright. Suddenly the officer's left hand shot out, and there was a sharp smack as it came in contact with the man's jaw. Again the man dropped to the floor, unconscious, and the chief sat down.

He was now thoroughly enraged. He waited a few minutes, and as the man on the floor lay quite still, he reached for a glass of water. Then he caught a slight flicker of the man's eyelid.

"Faking it, eh?" growled the chief, jumping to his feet.

A torrent of oaths spat from his lips. He leaped at the man, and both feet landed square on the fellow's upturned face. The blood spurted from mouth and nose. The chief seized the limp form in both hands and commenced pounding it up and down on the floor, kicking at it when it rebounded. The man screamed in agony.

"I'll come in, chief!" he yelled dismally. "Oh, please don't; please, please stop!"

The chief beat him against the floor a few times more and then tossed him into a chair, where the man crouched, bleeding and shivering and gulping.

Breathing somewhat heavily, the chief sat down again and touched a bell. A uniformed sergeant appeared at the door.

"Send in a stenographer," said the chief. "John's decided to make a confession."

The warden of the state penitentiary was an earnest man and an honest man. He made a long trip to see the chief.

"I tell you, Sullivan, Kinzie must have had wings to get here in time to turn that trick. I didn't spring him till the day before the murder. You know it's hardly probable, even if it is possible, for a man to make that trip under forty-eight hours."

"Well, he says he did; you can't go back of that," replied the chief grouchily.

"Was he drunk?" asked the warden.

"Well, he'd been drinking a little," said the chief. "He wasn't drunk when he came through."

"There's something strange about it," remarked the warden. "If he says he did, I guess he did; but—"

The warden took his departure, not so much puzzled as annoyed, because the warden had talked with many prisoners who had been through the chief's "sweating" process, and had dropped a good many pounds in weight at it, too. The warden had his suspicions, but it wouldn't do to express them.

In the meantime, the newspapers were paying much attention to John Kinzie, ex-convict, who had confessed to the murder of a prominent citizen, shot down in cold blood because he resisted a hold-up.

"Huh!" remarked big "Red" Simmons, after he had laboriously read an account of the confession. "If it was raining money, that guy Kinzie'd be under a shed somewhere. He's the unluckiest stiff I ever see."

"Small" Gordon wrinkled his fox-terrier nose into an appreciative grin.

"He fell for the third degree fine," continued Simmons.

"How you s'pose they come to light on him?" asked Gordon.

"How? Why, the chief gets his little list of guys released from the big skookum every day, don't he?" said Simmons. "Kinzie happened to be the only one sprung just before this job, and so the chief tells his elbows to fetch in Kinzie the moment he lands in town."

"Too bad you had to croak that guy," said Gordon.

"Too bad for Kinzie," answered Simmons briefly.

The pair were sitting in a "noodle joint," eating noodles and chop suey and watching the crowd around them. There was a steady buzz of voices and the shrill cries of the Chinese waiters, calling into the kitchen.

Simmons, a giant fellow, with a strong, massive face and fierce eyes, rolled a cigarette with calm fingers, and Gordon, little and rat-eyed, ate in business-like fashion.

"Wot'll they do to Kinzie?" asked Gordon between mouthfuls.

"Oh, they'll only swing him up a little," replied Simmons sarcastically. Gordon shivered.

"They can't prove he did it," he suggested.

"And he can't prove he didn't," said Simmons.

"I used to see him once in a while when I was doing my speck up yonder," said Gordon thoughtfully. "He worked in the quarry."

"He's a cheap dip," remarked Simmons with scorn. "Anybody that knows him, knows he couldn't have croaked that guy. It isn't his line, and, besides, he ain't got the nerve. But it ain't our funeral."

Gordon finished his chop suey.

"Let's go," he said, rising.

They walked out into the brilliantly lighted street and were sauntering slowly along when Gordon nervously clutched at the arm of his companion.

"Nix! Nix!" said Simmons between his teeth. "I saw him. Wot's the matter with you, anyhow?"

The chief of police, in civilian clothing, passed them with a number of women and a couple of children. The chief was carrying a big suitcase in either hand, and the women bore grips and bundles.

"Going to the depot," remarked Simmons after the party passed. "That woman in black is the big guy's wife. Saw her at headquarters once when I was in explaining."

The two turned into a saloon rather notorious for the class to which it catered and ordered drinks. As they were standing at the bar, a flashily dressed individual approached them. He was known as "Boston" Carey, and was a pickpocket of some renown among his kind, but an object of some contempt to Simmons and Kinzie, who dealt in more hazardous enterprises.

"Just in time," said Simmons. Carey ordered beer.

"See they picked up John Kinzie for that hill job," he remarked casually. Simmons merely nodded.

"I used to know him in the East," continued the garrulous Carey, not noticing Simmons's frown. "He was going back there and be decent, I heard; but I guess his foot slipped."

Still Simmons and Gordon remained silent.

"He's got a wife and kid here," said Carey.

"What?" demanded Simmons and Gordon together.

"A wife and kid," repeated Carey, pleased at having roused some interest.

"They came on here to meet him. Kinzie made a little money peddling these horsehair bridles while he was up yonder, and they were all going back together."

"Where are they now?" demanded Simmons.

"Oh, somewhere round town," said Carey carelessly. "I guess it's all off with Kinzie, ain't it? Wot'd the stiff want to give up for, anyway?"

Simmons finished his liquor and nodded to Gordon.

"See you later," he said to Carey, and Gordon followed him out into the street.

"Jemmy," said Simmons, linking arms with his little partner, "if we was like these guys you read about, we'd go to the chief and tell him the low-down on this business."

Gordon looked alarmed. He knew his big partner as a capricious fellow, whose humors took strange turns. Sober, Gordon himself was the most cautious man in the world; but a couple of drinks of whisky made him vainglorious, and as reckless as Simmons was at all times. Just now Gordon was sober.

"Let's don't," he said.

Simmons laughed so loudly that passers-by turned to look at the pair.

"Don't get scared," he said reassuringly. "But if we was story-book crooks, we'd do something grand and noble for Kinzie and his wife and kid."

"Wot could we do, anyhow?" asked Gordon.

"Well, we could go see the chief," said Simmons.

"He went out of town," said Gordon, relieved.

"No, I have a hunch he was just seeing his women folks off," replied Simmons.

"Let's don't go, just the same," protested Gordon. "Wot's the use of getting nutty at this stage of the game? We've got our tickets and a blowstake, and let's make it. They're raising such a fuss about this business, they'd swing a guy in a minute if they thought they had it on him right."

Simmons and Gordon had decided on the City of Mexico as their next stopping place. Red looked at his under-sized partner in amused fashion, and changed the subject.

Along toward midnight, frequent libations had put them both in a very amiable mood. Gordon, the cautious, reverted to the proposal which Simmons had forgotten.

"Let's do go see the chief, Red," he suggested finally. "We've got an hour and a half yet to make a little call—and I owe him one."

Without reply, Simmons turned and led the way up a side street.

The chief, in a huddle of bed clothing, awoke to the grip of a strong hand clutching the neck of his pajamas.

"Wha—what!" he gurgled sleepily, opening his eyes.

"Keep still!" commanded Simmons, taking an extra twist. "Keep still, you big stiff!"

He slapped the chief soundly with his open hand, and the officer was thoroughly awake.

A single electric light was burning in the room, and he recognized Simmons. Gordon stood behind his big partner with an ominous looking revolver in his hand.

"What the—" growled the chief.

"Shut up!" said Simmons, slapping him again. "And get up," he added, hauling the big man out of the covers as a boy jerks a ground-squirrel from its hole.

As the chief was stood upon his feet, he thought for a brief second of making an outcry. Then, as he glanced at Red's face, heavy with rage and liquor, and at the weasel-like Gordon, who danced lightly back and forth with the gun leveled at the chief's breast and grinning wickedly, he thought better of it.

The chief knew both Simmons and Gordon. He knew them as desperate crooks. He knew that human life was one of the things they held very cheaply, indeed. And yet, they were the very type he held in contempt because he knew their weak points.

"What's the matter with you fellows?" he asked quietly.

"We come to tell you Kinzie didn't do that hill job," said Red.

"I know it," replied the chief. "But that's no skin off you, is it? I don't doubt you guys know something about it, but I didn't have nothing on you."

"Remember the time you dumped me for the Carson robbery that I didn't do?" demanded Simmons. "Beat me up a little too, if you recollect."

"Now, Red—" began the chief in a conciliatory tone.

Red slapped him so viciously that the big man almost fell over.

"And the time you settled me for the Heenan job?" squeaked Gordon, leering spitefully. "You hit me in the nose, you big cheese!"

"We're going away, chief," said Simmons. "We're going away for good, but we thought we'd pay you a final call just to tell you that you've got the wrong man in Kinzie. Oh, I know what you're thinking about. You think you'll have us before morning, but you won't. You won't be able. Every phone and bell wire in your joint is cut off."

He was lashing himself into a rage, and the chief trembled; but it was from the chill of the room.

Then as he looked upon the faces of these two men, the first uneasy feeling, the first sense of danger he had ever realized, came over him. He strove to analyze it, but the nearest he could come to analysis was a recollection of the way he had once felt when he was a small boy, and had been locked in a closet by a school teacher to await, at the hands of the principal, the only whipping he had ever received.

These men were displaying something entirely foreign to all his years of criminal observation. He did not fear them personally, but the new and unknown element in their composition disturbed him.

The chief did not fear death. He did not believe the men intended killing him. In fact, he felt certain they did not.

What was it, then, that he feared?

He did not know it, but in his eyes was the same expression that had been in the eyes of the man on the floor of his office that morning.

Simmons and Gordon had become very silent. Simmons, looming large under the dim light, appeared to grow larger as the chief watched him, while the ratlike Gordon grew smaller by contrast. Simmons's face seemed abnormally big, and every lineament spelled brute force.

Simmons suddenly began moving toward the chief, his great hands working like claws and his lips parted in a vast snarl. No word was spoken. The chief stood transfixed, unable to utter a sound. He felt himself wondering what the big man intended doing.

A great fear stirred within him. He wasn't afraid of Simmons; that was certain. He was simply afraid because he did not know what the man meant to do. Something seemed to suddenly give way inside the chief's breast as Simmons moved toward him; expression dropped from his face like a mask, and he backed up, laughing hideously.

Simmons stopped. Gordon peered around his leg like a little dog.

"Let's get out of here!" yelled the small man, with a backward leap. "Look at that face!"

Squealing in terror, he fled, and Simmons lumbered after him, while behind them they heard the horrible chattering laugh of the chief.

In a café in Mexico City, Red Simmons and Small Gordon sat at a table piled high with American newspapers. They had been reading for some time.

"See where Danny Coogan got it all for that Cleburne job?" remarked Simmons with interest.

"He's a stiff, anyhow," said Gordon.

"Here you are!" announced Red after another silence, broken only by the rattling of the papers. He read:

> John Kinzie, who once confessed to the murder of John Moore, a prominent citizen, and afterward repudiated the confession, claiming it was obtained under duress, was today acquitted by a jury in the criminal court after a short trial. The inability of former Chief of Police Sullivan to testify is declared by the district attorney to be the principal reason why he could not produce evidence sufficient to convict Kinzie, but the prisoner proved a complete alibi through the testimony of Warden Pierce of the state penitentiary.

"Yes, but listen here!" said Gordon so excitedly that Simmons gave him a warning look:

> Former Chief of Police Simmons, whose unfortunate and very mysterious case has roused great sympathy, was last night removed to the state insane

asylum at Corbin. The physicians declare his reason has gone forever.

"*Hi, hombre!*" interrupted Simmons, motioning at a passing waiter. "A couple more o' the same!"

. . . . .

Monsieur de Guise

PERLEY POORE SHEEHAN

That anyone should live in the center of Cedar Swamp was in itself so singular as to set all sorts of queer ideas to running through my head.

A more sinister morass I had never seen. It was as beautiful and deadly as one of its own red moccasins, as treacherous and fascinating.

It was a tangle of cypress and cedar almost thirty miles square, most of it under water—a maze of jungle-covered islands and black bayous. There were alligators and panthers, bear and wild pig. There were groans and grunts and queer cries at night, and silence, dead silence, by day.

That was Cedar Swamp as I knew it after a week of solitary hunting there. I no longer missed the sun. My eyes had become used to the perpetual twilight. My nerves no longer bothered me when I stepped into opaque water, or watched a section of gliding snake. But the silence was getting to be more than I could bear. It was too uncanny.

And now, just after I had noticed it, and wondered at it for the hundredth time, I heard a voice. It was low and clear—that of a woman who sings alto. There were four or five notes like the fragment of a strange song. And then, before I had recovered from the shock of it, there was silence again.

I was up to my knees in water at the time, wading a narrow branch between two islands. I must have stood there for a full minute, waiting for the voice to resume, but the silence closed in on me deeper than ever. With a little shiver creeping over one part of my body after another, I stole ashore.

The island was one of the highest I had yet encountered. I had not taken a dozen steps up through the dank growth of its shelving shore before I found a deeply worn path. This, I could see, ran down to the waterfront in one direction, where I caught a glimpse of a boathouse masked by trees. I turned and followed the path in the other direction, up a gentle slope.

As I advanced, the jungle around me thinned out and became almost park-like. There were open stretches of meadow and clumps of trees, suggesting the landscape garden. But I was so intent on discovering the owner of the voice that the wonder of this did not at first impress me. I had, moreover, an eerie, uneasy sensation of being watched.

I walked slowly. I carried my gun with affected carelessness. I looked around me as though I were a mere tourist dropped in to see the sights.

I had thus covered, perhaps, a quarter of a mile when the path turned into an avenue of cabbage palmetto, at the further end of which I saw a house. It was large and white, with a pillared porch, such as they used to build before the war. It was shaded by a magnificent grove of live-oak trees. There were beds of geranium and roses in front, and clusters of crepe-myrtle and flowering oleander on a well-clipped lawn.

It all gave an impression of infinite care, of painstaking upkeep, of neatness and wealth, yet there was not a soul in sight. Not a servant was there. No dog barked. I saw no horses, no chickens, no pigeons, nor sheep; no familiar animate emblem whatever of the prosperous farm.

I stood in the presence of this silent and lonely magnificence with a feeling that was not exactly fear, but rather stupefaction. For a moment I was persuaded that I had emerged from the great swamp into some unknown plantation of its littoral. But a moment was enough to convince me that this could not be. I was, without the slightest doubt, almost at the exact center of the morass. I was too familiar with its circumference and general contour to be wrong as to that. For a dozen miles at least, in every direction, Cedar Swamp surrounded this island of mystery with its own mysterious forests and bayous.

Once again, I was acutely aware of being stared at. Almost at the same instant, a man's voice addressed me from behind my back.

"Monsieur," it asked, "why do you hesitate?"

I might as well confess it right away—I believe in ghosts. I have seen too many things in my life that were not to be explained by the commonly accepted laws of nature. I have lived too much among the half-civilized and learned too much of their odd wisdom to recognize any hard and fast definition of what is real and what is not.

From the moment I heard that bit of song in the swamp, I felt that I was passing from the commonplace into the weird. My succeeding impressions had confirmed this feeling. And now, when I heard the voice behind me —"Monsieur, why do you hesitate?"—I was not sure that it was the voice of a human being at all. I turned slowly, my mind telling me that I should see no one.

It was with a distinct feeling of relief, therefore, that I saw a small, pale, well-dressed old man smiling at me as though he had read my secret thoughts. His face was cleanly shaven and bloodless. His head, partly covered by a black velvet skullcap, was extremely large. His snow-white hair was silky and long. His eyes, which were deeply sunken, were large and dark. His appearance, as well as the question which he had just put to me, suggested the foreigner. He was not alone un-American; he appeared to be of another century as well.

I said something about intruding. He made a brusque gesture, almost of impatience, and, telling me to follow him, started for the house.

It was as though I was an expected guest. Only the absence of servants maintained that feeling of the bizarre, which never left me. The interior of the house was in keeping with its outward, appearance—sumptuous and immaculate. My host led me to the door of a vast chamber on the first floor, motioned me to enter, and, standing at the door, said:

"Monsieur, luncheon will be served when you reappear. Pray, make yourself at home."

Then he left me.

Two details of this room impressed me —the superlative richness of the toilet articles, all of which were engraved with a coat-of-arms, and the portrait of a woman, by Largillière. All women were beautiful to Largillière, but in the present instance he had surpassed himself. The gentle, aristocratic face, with its tender, lustrous eyes, was the most alluring thing I had ever seen. At the bottom of the massive frame was the inscription: *Anne-Marie, Duchesse de Guise. Anno 1733.*

I was still marveling at the miracle which had brought such an apparition to the heart of an American swamp when I heard a light step in the hallway, and I knew that my host was awaiting me.

The luncheon, which was served cold in a splendid dining room, had been laid for two. I wondered at this, for still no servant appeared, and surely I could not have been expected. And my host added to my mystification rather than lessened it when he said: "Monsieur, I offer you the place usually reserved for my wife."

Apart from this simple statement, the meal was completed in silence. Now and then, I thought I surprised him, nodding gravely as though someone else were present. I suspected him several times of speaking in an undertone. But, my mind was so preoccupied with the inexplicable happenings of the preceding hour that I was not in a condition to attack fresh mysteries now.

He scarcely touched his food. Indeed, his presence there seemed to be more in the nature of an act of courtesy than for the purpose of taking nourishment. As soon as I had finished, he at once arose and invited me to follow him.

Across the hall was a music room, with high French windows opening on the porch. He paused at one of these windows now and plucked the flower from a potted heliotrope. The perfume of it seemed to stimulate him strangely. He at once became more animated. A slight trace of color mounted to his waxen cheeks. Turning to me abruptly, he remarked:

"I mentioned just now my wife. Perhaps you noticed her portrait?"

As he spoke, a faint breath of the heliotrope came to me, and with it, by one of those odd associations of ideas, the portrait by Largillière. I saw again the gentle face and the lustrous eyes, but the date—1733. Surely this was not the portrait he referred to.

But he had seen the perplexity in my face, and he broke out in French: *"Oui, oui, c'est moi, Monsieur de Guise."* And then, in English: "It was the portrait of my wife you saw, *madame la duchesse par monsieur Largillière.*"

"But then, *madame,* your wife," I stammered, "is dead."

He was still smelling the heliotrope. He looked up at me with his somber eyes for a moment as though he had failed to grasp my meaning. Then he said:

"No, no. There is no such thing as death—only life. For, what is life?—the smile, the perfume, the voice. Ah, the voice! Will you hear her sing?"

For a brief instant my head turned giddily. The world I had always known, the world of tragedies, of sorrows, of physical joys and pains, the world of life and death, in short, was whirling away from beneath my feet. And I began to recall certain old stories I had heard about the visible servants of the invisible, the earthly agents of the unearthly. Such things have been known to exist.

M. de Guise was walking up and down the room, murmuring to himself in French. I could catch an occasional word of endearment. Once I saw him distinctly press the heliotrope to his lips. He had forgotten my presence, apparently. He was in the company of someone whom he alone could see. And then he seated himself at the piano.

I had a presentiment of what was coming. I dropped into a chair and closed my eyes. Again the heliotrope perfumed the air around me. I saw the smooth brow, the sympathetic eyes, the magic smile of the Duchesse de Guise, and then a voice—that voice I had heard in the swamp—began to sing, so soft, so sweet that a little spasm twitched at my throat and a chill crept down my back. It was a love song, such as they sang centuries ago. I know little French, but it told of love in life and death—*"Moi, je t'ai, vive et morte, incessament aimée."*

And when I opened my eyes again, all that I saw was the shriveled black figure of Monsieur de Guise, his silvered head thrown back with the air of one who has seen a vision.

Subconsciously, I had heard something else while listening to the song. It was the swift, muffled throb of an approaching motor boat. M. de Guise had heard it, too, for now he left the piano and approached the window. Presently, I could see a dozen Negroes approaching along the avenue of palms. They seemed strangely silent for their race.

"These are my people," said my host. "Once a week I send them to the village. They will carry you away."

The afternoon was far advanced when I bade M. de Guise farewell. As I looked back for the last time, the sunset was rapidly dissolving the great white house and its gardens in a golden haze. His figure on the porch was all that linked it to the world of man.

Late that night, I was landed at a corner of Cedar Swamp adjacent to my home. My black boatman, who had spoken never a word, immediately backed his barge away into the darkness, leaving me there alone. And, although I have since made several efforts to repeat my visit to M. de Guise, I have never been successful. Once, indeed, I found again what I believed to be his island, but it was covered entirely with a dense, forbidding jungle. Which will doubtless discredit this story, as it has caused even me to reflect.

But grant that the story is true, and that M. de Guise was merely mad. Why, then, in a certain event, which I need not mention, may God send me madness, too!

· · · · ·

THE SHIP OF SILENT MEN

PHILIP M. FISHER, JR.

I

The Electric Storm

The steamship *Lanoa*, Carden Line of San Francisco, with nine thousand tons of raw sugar in her holds and a deckload of bananas and pines, was two days out from Honolulu when the electric storm broke upon us. We were still in the warm belt and would not expect bad weather or cold for at least another forty-eight hours. That was the rule—and even when this nature's rule was transgressed, the weather was only moderate, the temperature simply low enough to suggest the possibility of donning one's light coat. Neither heat nor cold came in extreme.

Yet suddenly, on this second day out, at about ten-twenty in the morning and without barometric warning, a blanketing chill dropped over the ship, enveloped us with searching aggressiveness and literally froze our tropic-acclimated selves, body and soul.

Every man on board piled into his coast underwear and wartime sweater and socks—but it did no good. Every man's nose and cheeks were hard-looking and purple gray—every man's breath exhaled in a cloud of fog. And we three passengers, half-hid in coats and rugs, were yet forced to the engine room for comfort.

This was the first symptom of the strange meteorological condition that was to harry us for the next two days. And it was, in the annals of marine history, unlogged, unprecedented.

The next indication of extraordinary weather conditions was the sudden failure of the radio. This started perhaps an hour after the falling of the mercury. The apparatus worked intermittently—one moment normally registering the Press Association news, the next moment, tune it as the operator would, he could send, or receive, nothing. The transmitter hashed its spark—the receivers were absolutely dead.

Then, without warning, the code would come singing in the puzzled man's ears once more—as though nothing at all had occurred; as though—

171

paradoxically—the wires had been cut, held apart for some minutes, then put in contact again. Then the whole thing would be repeated again—and again. This went on for the next two days—along with that deathly chill—went on until there came, as a climax, that final beautiful yet awe-inspiring occurrence which brought us to that thing which will I fear for all time haunt my dreams, the thing that is the seaman's nightmare, of all seas the seaman's ghost.

The electric lights worked badly, too, dimming unaccountably at times, then flaring up until one expected momentarily that the filament would go to pieces. The engine crew and the firemen did not like it at all—especially with the triple expansion Corliss turning over her usual eighty-seven and the generator turbine steady as a clock.

They were a superstitious lot, too—Belgians and Swedes and Welsh—and I found myself colder yet as I listened to the yarns they told. At sea, with the illimitable waste about one, and the loneliness of it all, stories of the strange and unexplainable always thrill more than they do on land. And when they are told when the actual conditions then existent are strange and unexplainable too, and the nearest land is a mere speck seven hundred miles back, the thrill changes into something more like spine-prickling uneasiness. The crew were that way—and, I confess, so were the passengers three.

The cold became more penetrating. The bridge officer—wool-wrapped—paced stumblingly. The radio had lapses an hour long—the wireless operator was frantic. The shadows below decks became as of the dead alive and the black gang forgot its tales and cursed softly.

Then came darkness, and with it a doubled phosphorescence in our wake. The air was permeated with that weird sea feel, hardly to be called an odor, or ozone. And at about seven bells of the first watch, just before midnight, the steel rigging was alive with bluish flickering—electric streamlets, running, pausing, dancing, now quiescent and dying dim—now pulsingly alive, now peacefully aglow—now madly, enthusiastically, and at times almost malevolently rampant.

The deck watch shivered a bit from more than the cold—the below-decks crew, about to come on watch and up for a breath of air, stared thoughtfully and stowed back their half-filled pipes, and felt their way down to the comfort of their still steady engines.

Eight bells, and midnight came. The chill reached the marrow of our bones. The electricity on the rigging silently threatened. The shadows blacked and grayed with a hundred shifting, shapeless things that stared and kept one's chin on one's shoulder in breathless moments when the lights went nearly out.

On my way to my cabin, I stopped at the wireless room.

"Still out," growled the operator—"since four bells, not a snitch or a buzz. Two hours—"

He adjusted and readjusted his head-gear.

"But what *is* the matter?" I whispered, half to myself.

"How the hell do I know?" the man snapped.

I shrugged my shoulders and went on.

Grahame and Stevenot, the two passengers, grinned weakly as the globes in our room slowly came to life.

"Queer combination," grunted Grahame as he crawled into the double lower berth, and I followed.

"Humph!" came from Stevenot, above our heads. "Turn out that foot-light."

I crawled out again.

"What's the use?" muttered Grahame, then: "Damn peculiar—cursed if it ain't!"

"Shut up," said Stevenot. "Shut up—and go to sleep."

"An' the stars," Grahame doggedly continued. "I'd swear I saw the masthead knock one off an' it ran down the forestay there, an'—"

"Drowned itself in the sea," shouted Stevenot. "Go to sleep."

The next morning, things were the same. And the crew was getting itchy—and silent. One of the wipers, when I went below for warmth, whispered to me that he'd seen something in the starboard alley that beckoned to him. He'd thrown a monkey wrench at it, and then climbed around the steering engine and felt his way for'ard along the port alley. And when he'd gone below again, there was his wrench in its regular place in the rack under the revolution indicator. What did I think of that?

Then came the first breath of real trouble.

At three in the afternoon, one of the men came below and told us that the wireless had worked for a few minutes, and the operator had picked up an S.O.S. The gang eyed each other silently.

I climbed top side.

Grahame and Stevenot were in the radio office. The mate was there, too. The operator was penciling on his tablet—a bit white in the face.

"God!" muttered the mate. "If the damn thing will only hold out—hold out—"

He peered at the operator's pencil point as the letters slowly, spasmodically, jerked out.

Grahame pressed my arm, and pointed.

I read the message so far written.

"S.O.S.—S.O.S."—the letters were scrawled—"S.O.S.—" Then a word, evidently the name of the ship in distress—*Karnak*. Then again: "S.O.S., Lat. 52—19—" Then there was a break—then the same thing repeated.

"Must have been sending that for an hour," Grahame whispered. "Been several breaks, you know—each time got's far as the latitude the poor devil's in. But no longitude—an' how can they tell where to go? The mate says the old man'll order the ship about if he can tell where to head her, but he'll be cursed if he'll play hide and seek on the forty-second parallel with the bit of frozen mystery we're in now. If they can only get the longitude, they'll be fixed, but so far—"

He stopped abruptly. The pencil had begun to move. Every man of us grew tense. The operator's corded hand was white despite the blue chill of his office.

Again the same message.

"S.O.S.—S.O.S.—S.O.S.—*Karnak*—Lat. 52—19—" Here the operator hunched suddenly, and a wild oath escaped his tight lips. His hand jerked. "Long.," he wrote—and a sigh came from the mate—from all of us—"152—37—"

The mate, jaw set, elbowed out. He had the pleading vessel's location at last.

Stevenot grinned.

"Gee!" he said thickly. "I'm glad we picked it all up at last. Got on my nerves."

Grahame pulled his mustache.

"Blame queer, I'd say," he murmured.

The wireless operator still hunched, one hand on his tuning lever, the other repeating on paper the same call for aid.

"Let's get out in the air," said Stevenot.

II
S.O.S.

The helmsman already had wheel orders for an approximate course, and the ship's head was swinging. The three of us, lone passengers, had been given access to all parts of the *Lanoa,* so stayed now on the bridge—still wrapped, even though the sun was blindingly on high, in all our sweaters and robes.

The skipper, pulling violently on the Manila man-killer he chewed, and quite oblivious to the fact that it was unlit, waved his arms and clapped his mittened hands before and behind him as he paced. In the wheelhouse, the steersman showed a pale and thoughtful countenance.

The mate was bending over a chart, and the second was wildly turning the pages of his Bowditch. For several minutes, they figured—then checked their work. Then the mate brought out the chart and the figures to the skipper, who nodded with a glance about the awning, at the sun; the mate nodded to the second and the latter stood beside the wheelsman and gave the exact course which would bring the *Lanoa* to the ship that, out of all this mysterious and unprecedented weather, on a smooth sea and beneath a bright sun, cried so persistently for help.

The *Lanoa* straightened out on the northerly course that should bring her to the *Karnak*—and a half-dozen revolutions were added to the turn of the screw.

Again that night did the blue flame flicker ghostily in the rigging. Still did the shadows below decks rise and fall as spasmodically, as slowly, as terribly in their awful hesitation as the breath of a dying man. Still was the wireless a practically useless thing and our ship cut off from all the world in all this sea of mystery. Still the chill of the cold crept into our hearts, and chilled our very souls.

Once, just after nine o'clock, out of the crystal starred blackness of the night, came the same cry for help from the *Karnak*. "S.O.S.," it called—"*Karnak*—Lat. 52—19—Long. 152—17—" then repeated the same.

But when our operator sent our word that rescue was coming—there came again no answer except the same repeated plea.

The mate and skipper, when they heard this, stared at each other. Then the mate shook his head. And Stevenot evidently voiced the officer's thought—for he started and turned and stared again when Stevenot said:

"And here a whole day has passed and they send the same latitude and the same longitude. Even with engine's broken down, I should think they'd drift a good many minutes just in the Japan current. Yet here—the same—"

And that's where the mate seized the skipper's arm and abruptly dragged him from the radio office.

Grahame grunted.

"Blamed peculiar," he muttered.

And Stevenot, without a word, led us out to the open deck. The stars were a comfort—one had but to stand on tiptoe and he might pluck the brightest out, one by one. But that weirdly running blue flame on ratlines and stays and cargo booms—we didn't like.

Yet we stayed on deck—and smoked a bit—and said nothing—only thought and stared—and wondered what was yet to come—and shivered in the cold.

Then, suddenly—deep away in the sparkling blue-black bowl that capped the oily sea—appeared a moving glow. It grew in size; it flashed across the zenith in northerly flight. It changed in color from ghostly white to yellow flame. It changed in form from nebulous shapelessness to clear-cut crystal.

Even though its flight was over us, and away, toward the north, it grew to a vastness that colored all the sea—and gleamed on the faces and eyes of my two companions as they stared.

A great humming filled the air—changed slowly to an ear-straining hissing sound—then to a vast, droning roar as it fell away toward the line where the starry heavens, dimmed to almost nothingness now, met the sea.

Then even as the shape itself rushed beyond our sight, there came a blinding flash of yellow light—and as we stiffly leaned against the rail, a thunderlike detonation that rattled everything on board the ship and all but threw us off our feet.

Stevenot seized my arm, and clung there like a frightened child. Grahame, mouth open, pointed tensely northward.

"The *Karnak*," he cried hoarsely. "The *Karnak*—it fell—it fell—toward the *Karnak*."

Then, suddenly, rang a cry from the bridge—and the mate came running down the gangway to the maindeck.

"The cold—" he cried, "the cold—" and sped by us into the radio room.

Stevenot's grasp relaxed.

"By Heaven!" he gasped, tearing off his blanket—"it's warm as—as toast"—

ending with most innocuous comparison.

"And the blue flame—gone—" I cried as my senses returned. "Gone—"

"And the lights—" gasped Stevenot.

I peeled my coat, for the cold, even as the great electric mass seemed to burst, was lifted from us, and the gentle warmth of the semi-tropic sea dropped in its place. And the air smelled clean again. And the dancing electricity on the rigging had vanished—the lights glowed steady white—and even as we stood in wonder, the motor of the radio turned up its crescendo hum, and the regulated yet intermittent crashing of the spark told us that once again the wireless was in commission.

In that flash, things were back to normal—and we breathed. The strangeness was gone—the tenseness was gone—and we breathed.

Then, even as our pulse became regular, our breathing even, the mate came out of the radio office.

"All right again," he said stiffly. "And the machine is working all right. But—well," he nodded toward the office—"he can't seem to connect."

Stevenot jumped.

"That meteor—or electric bolt—whatever it was"—he jerked out—"toward the north—toward the *Karnak*—"

The mate nodded silently. There was a solemn pause.

Then the officer muttered.

"And the instruments are O.K., too. But the *Karnak*—"

"No answer?" cried Stevenot.

The mate shook his head: "Not a jot," he said briefly, and with a tenseness I well remember, a tenseness that brought to me a reminiscence of the chill which had gripped us for the past two days. And then he left and climbed up the ladder to the bridge deck.

I called after him.

"But you're not going to—"

He turned.

"We're going on to—to find the *Karnak*," he said.

My heart jolted once—and I felt a great relief. We were going to help—if help were yet of any avail. I wondered if it would be.

And Grahame, as he felt in the dark for the single sheet beneath which we now tried to sleep, gave vent to his feelings, too.

"Peculiar," he muttered. "Blamed peculiar, I'd say."

III

The Silence of the Ship

So on we steamed.

Our wireless continued to stay in proper order—but we could get no word from the *Karnak*. For all we knew, she had vanished from the surface of the seas—and Heaven knew what manner, and Heaven knew where.

And when we spoke with other ships, none had received her call. Nor were there other vessels now nearer to the location the *Karnak* had given to render her, did she yet need it, a quicker assistance than would be ours. So ours was the job—we must speed on. So, on we steamed.

The sea was smooth—conditions were normal. Peace and tranquillity were over all, even as had been that blanketing chill before and the fearsome uneasiness it laid upon us. And as the sun beamed down upon us with all its old genial warmth, and the blue sea sparkled so happily about, we nearly forgot that we were hundreds of miles off our course—nearly forgot the strange, the sad errand that might yet be ours.

The nights, too, were calm and full of gentle comfort. Slightly cooler, of course, for we were northing, and the Japan current had but little warming effect as yet. Yet the rigging was untouched by even a hint of dancing blue—the electric globes pulsed steadily under the dynamos humming below decks—the radio operators were at peace with the world.

Yet still no news of the *Karnak*—no answer from the stricken ship.

Then came the mate—next morning.

"We ought to sight her around eleven o'clock," he said quietly.

He accepted my cigar—then added:

"Yes—we ought to."

Stevenot—we three passengers were as one, ever together, and had been companions in travel and adventure since long before the War—we and one other, the dear fellow who had been number four—Stevenot, ever quick to sense a thing out of order, asked:

"Then you do not expect—"

The mate, match rising under his palm as he held it to his cigar, shook his head vehemently.

"I didn't say that—no! I simply said we *ought* to sight her about eleven. Maybe we will—maybe not. But I know where we are—and the point where she said she was. Ought to—that's all."

This was at eight-thirty.

And yet not ten minutes had passed before the bridge lookout sighted a smudge of smoke to the northward.

We wirelessed at once—and received no answer. And we knew that all steamers must carry wireless—yet here, a steamer, and no answer to our call. Perhaps its apparatus was out of order—perhaps not. We conjectured as to possibilities—could it be the *Karnak*—this early?

Gradually we drew upon it—and finally the ship's hull came up. With glasses we made her out to be a vessel of perhaps seventy-five hundred tons, high-pooped and high-bowed, with bridge deck midships and two black funnels. And that to a "T" was the *Ship's Register* description of the *Karnak*—the vessel that had called for help. We had sighted her some three hours before expected.

And she had way on her, too, heading as near as we could make out, southeast.

We wirelessed again—no answer.

So, knowing they could see us as plainly as we them, we broke out the International Code pennant and ran up a line of flags.

The mate and skipper, glasses glued to their eyes, cursed softly. The *Karnak* did not answer our visual signal.

Visions of mutiny aboard arose before me. I pictured a crew of grim fellows doing away with their officers, determined to making one rich haul, and then a quick getaway. Here they signaled for help in order to get some vessel to come to them—faked trouble—and when the rescuer came close enough, with some wartime gun mounted behind falling bulwarks, hold it up and practice a bit of modern piracy

The *Karnak* continued silent. We headed in to cross her close astern—and made ready the little signal gun on the observation deck above the bridge.

The gun boomed—if the *Karnak* had for some inexplicable cause not seen us, this would speedily wake her up.

We waited tensely—for hours it seemed. The *Karnak* did not answer.

She did not answer wireless. She did not answer our flag hoist. She did not answer the roar of our signal gun.

The mate and skipper stared. The wheelsman's eyes popped.

"What in hell's the matter?" growled the old man. "Look at the dodgin' she's doing."

We stared at the vessel, now not a quarter mile away.

"Steers most peculiar I ever saw," muttered Grahame. "Zigzaggin' for subs—looks like."

We shot the gun again.

With glasses—without glasses—we could see movement—the crew on board—working on the decks.

Yet the *Karnak* did not answer.

The captain cursed—broke out the United States ensign—ordered the second mate to take the wheel.

"Get her close, and stick by her," he ordered.

Then he took the megaphone.

"Ahoy there, *Karnak!*" he roared across the fifty-fathom stretch of blue that now separated us. He roared again. Visible members of the crew did not even look up. An officer pacing the bridge above did not alter his step, nor move a hand. The skipper bellowed once more—still, the *Karnak* did not answer.

"By gosh!" cried the captain, "I'm going aboard to wake 'em up. Get out the motor launch," he ordered. "Six men and rifles! Run up the rags for her to heave to; and load that damn pea shooter with a bit of solid iron. I'll stand for no monkey business. The sea's goin' to the dogs these days, anyhow!"

Grahame and Stevenot and I, ever one when adventure was in the air, looked at each other with the same question in our eyes. Then, as one, we nodded. I, as usual, was the spokesman.

I turned to the skipper, who had just come out of his cabin buckling a forty-five automatic about his bulgy waist.

"Captain—" I started.

"Yes, yes, yes!" he cried explosively, "get your guns and come along. My cursed crew are seein' yellow as it is—don't know a bowline from a binnacle! Jump!"

We jumped. There were times during the next few days when I dearly wished we had not. But we did—and I don't regret it now. Yet in my dreams—

Stevenot remarked casually—he was generally casual when real concrete danger was at hand, or when we thought it was at hand:

"Old man seems a bit excited—wot?"

"Blamed peculiar, I'd say," muttered Grahame.

I said nothing, though in my heart I felt both to be right.

The *Lanoa* had slowed down a bit so we might get off safely. The *Karnak* was forging ahead. We climbed into the fast motor launch which was ready to be swung out. The new signal was up—the *Karnak* still held her erratic course—still was silent.

"Yellow looking gang," said the skipper quietly to me as I sat on the thwart beside him. "And wearing sweaters and heavy rags, too. Ain't cold today, is it?"

I shook my head. It was not cold now—it was warm.

I stared across at a couple of the *Karnak's* crew, muffled in sweaters, wiping her starboard rail. Their appearance, even from the distance, was decidedly peculiar. Faces and hands were pasty yellow—sickly yellow—of a yellow that was ghastly and sickening to see.

A sudden thought came to me.

"Disease?" I whispered to the old man. "Yellow fever—or some—"

"Don't get that at sea, man," the captain replied. "And they ain't too sick to work, are they?"

They certainly were not. Yet as I watched the two, it seemed that they worked strangely, mechanically, spasmodically—as if each move were not that of a smoothly regulated and continuous thought, but prompted each by a single jerky impulse.

We dropped to the smooth running water to the squeal of seldom used blocks—the after falls were released, the motor started, then—I remember the delightful thrill of being cut off from the great ship—we released the forward falls and cut across to the silent *Karnak*.

A small grapnel was brought along so that we might get a line over the rail and board her. But as we rounded the stern and came up on the *Karnak's* lee, what should we find there but the two dangling blocks from a pair of davits on the high deck midships!

The skipper growled something under his breath.

Stevenot whispered to me:

"Why should a boat have left that ship? And the rest of the crew left her lines adangling? That's not seamanship."

We ran alongside.

The skipper, with jaw set, seized the after falls himself and bent the painter about its four parts. Then, with a growl: "You four aft stand by the launch—

and your guns. Rest of you—come on—" He climbed hand over hand up the standing part of the fall, swung himself over the davit head, and slid to the *Karnak's* deck—crouched, gun in hand.

Stevenot, crowding ahead of the mate, was at his side in a moment—and watchful, too—and ready.

The mate followed with three rifles slung over his shoulder; and he hauled up the rope ladder and hooked it over the rail. Up this I clambered, and the others followed.

IV

Aboard the Karnak

Even as I drew my gun and stood leaning expectantly forward beside the rest, an officer came aft along the deck. Every one of us was instantly stiffly tense— wondering and ready.

The man's face was of the same awful yellow as those of the two seamen on the starboard side. I wondered too, at this officer, pacing so smartly toward us, that he should be so unshaven—and so thickly muffled in clothes. And then—this all happened in ten seconds, you must know—the man, eyes straight ahead, passed by us without a look or a word. Passed as though we, strangers on board his ship, were not even there.

I gasped—the man's cap had the device "Second Mate" upon it, and on board ship a second mate is supposed to be all eyes. Yet the man had not even noticed us. A sigh breathed from my companions.

The skipper sprang into life.

"Mate!" he cried after the man. "Just a moment!"

The officer did not turn a fraction of an inch, or falter a second in his quick, jerky step. Then he wheeled to the left and entered an open passage.

The old man gasped again—hunched forward with automatic raised.

Grahame, coming to my side—on tiptoe—nodded toward the passage into which the man had disappeared.

"Notice his shoes?" he whispered.

I shook my head.

"One black—one tan." Grahame's voice trembled a bit with excitement. "And he wore a sweater under his coat. And he didn't take a rap of notice of us, either. Blamed peculiar, I'd say."

The skipper shook himself savagely. Then turned to us.

"Keep together and follow me. Don't shoot unless I give the order." He leaned against the davit a moment and called down to those in the motor launch. "Keep the engine turning," he cried, "and be ready to cast off." Then to us: "Come on!" And he started forward. "We'll make a round of the decks first."

The captain led. On his left stepped the eager mate—but warily, gun in hand. At his right Stevenot had pushed in—ever quick-scented when on a trail, despite the apprehension he so often voiced. Grahame and I held the flanks, and behind us were four of the crew—tiptoeing softly and quick-eyed.

The other two members of the gang were the two oilers who stayed with the boat. Our party thus was nine, all armed, all mystified, all a bit scared deep within our secret selves—but all eager and all ready.

We stepped as though over a mined field.

We watched for a sudden descent upon us of a piratical, knife slinging crew of mutinied cut-throats. We expected every moment for some silent yellow-skinned something to spring upon her backs out of the silent nothingness about us and claw, and rip, and rend, and tear.

The silence continued. We peered into passageways and cabin ports—and saw nothing—heard nothing. My skin began to prickle slightly. The four men behind us stepped upon our heels. The old man cursed softly as he peered about.

Grahame spoke—startling us.

"A man aloft, polishing the flute," he said briefly.

We looked up at the forward funnel.

A seaman in dungarees, with one leg hooked over the rungs of the iron ladder that ran up to the lip of the funnel, was industriously scrubbing the great brass whistle. In his left hand he held a glass bottle, of polish I suppose, and his body was twisted to the left as he reached with his right hand about the big tube of the thing.

Suddenly he lost his balance, grabbed at the rungs—and the glass bottle crashed on the deck below. He righted himself carefully—and went right on polishing.

He acted strangely, it seemed to me. Made peculiar motions.

Grahame spoke again:

"Why, he's mad! Look—he makes the same motion with his left hand as though he still had that bottle of polish in it. Shakes it up—and pours it on his rag—*and nothing there!*"

We stared.

The captain, after a pause, shouted. His voice seemed a trifle high to me.

"Aloft there! You at the flute!"

The man continued to shake and polish—he made no sign of hearing or answer.

After a moment, the skipper cursed again.

"Crazy—or deaf!"

Stevenot shook his head.

"But they ought to *see* us, even if they can't hear—or if they are mad."

The captain and mate both grunted.

"Come on," jerked the old man then.

We followed him to the bridge—where from our ship we had seen an officer pacing. That officer was still there, still pacing.

The skipper went up to him—met him as he wheeled at the starboard end of the bridge and stood directly in his path—holding out his right hand, gun in left behind his back.

We held our breaths—I know not why.

The yellow-faced officer jerky-stepped, head turned slightly toward the bows and eyes there too, without the slightest pause or notice of the captain's presence, ignored the proffered hand. And before the skipper could sidestep, the man walked straight into him, knocked him down by sheer mechanical momentum, staggered a bit, then continued on his way to the port end of the bridge.

As they collided, the skipper's gun went off with a bang—from nervousness, or accident, or in what he thought was self-defense, I know not. But it startled us all—the captain himself, too. And Stevenot whispered:

"Now we get it—ready!"

But naught followed that ringing shot.

The captain leaped to his feet—pale and shaky.

"Walked right over me," he sputtered, "'s if I wasn't there—into me—knocked me down—what in hell's a matter—" He shivered a bit—the officer had wheeled at the bridge end and was jerkily pacing back, face turned toward the bows, now on his left, eyes cast ahead as well. "By Heaven!" the captain swore, "I'll show him—"

And he seized the officer by his right hand and neck—and instantly, with a startled cry, jerked his hands away and rubbed them on his trousers.

"What's the matter?" cried the mate.

"Cold!" muttered the skipper, rubbing his hands still on his trouser legs, and staring at the retreating figure. "Cold—his hand—his neck—cold as ice."

"Cold!" cried Stevenot.

And he ran forward and touched the officer's hand—and dropped it with a cry.

"It is—cold—as ice!" he whispered tensely.

The officer himself took no notice of either the skipper's touch or Stevenot's. He swayed lightly as each touched him, but kept on pacing.

Stevenot and the captain stared at each other.

"Let him alone," the skipper then ordered huskily. "Try the wheelhouse."

He glanced again at the pacing officer, and shivered slightly once more.

As we entered, the man at the wheel was spinning her for a left rudder.

"What's he doin' that for?" demanded the captain. "What's his course?"

A clipped paper hung near the binnacle. On it was the course—172°.

I leaned over the binnacle—the man at the wheel took no notice of me. The lubber's line of the compass showed that the ship was swinging toward 215°. The course should have been, according to the navigator's slip hanging in sight, a few degrees east of south. And yet here was the man at the wheel holding the *Karnak* almost southwest—43° off her course.

I showed the skipper. Even as I did so, the wheelsman spun the gear for a right rudder and straightened her out on 215°.

For some minutes we watched.

Then the mate burst out:

"He's crazy—he's holding her against yawing when she's not yawing an inch! And he let's her go when she swings clear off. Look at him spin her there—he's off, I tell you. Here—"

He seized the man's hand and started to tear it from the spokes—then snatched his own hand away and looked at us with sudden consternation in his eyes.

V
Something Wrong!

The skipper and Stevenot and he exchanged glances.

"Cold—as ice—that man—cold!" muttered the mate. Stevenot nodded.

"Like the officer outside," he said.

Grahame leaned forward and touched the wheelsman's hand.

"Ugh!" he exclaimed. "Blamed peculiar, I'd say. Let's see somethin' else."

At that moment came a rush of feet outside—and loud cries.

"Good!" cried the skipper, relief in his voice. "Now they're coming. Wait till I give—"

Then he stopped. It was not an attacking party. It was the four men we'd left in the launch.

"We heard a shot," one of the oilers started. "We thought—" Then he stared at the wheelsman, yellow-faced, besweatered. Then to the old man: "If you say, sir, we'll—we'll go back."

The captain tapped his teeth thoughtfully. Then nodded. Then turned to the four men with rifles.

"You too—if you wish."

Without a word the whole eight of them, huddled closely, left the house. Outside the door they stepped slowly at first, on tip-toe, and with chins upon their shoulders. Then, as a flock of sheep, they broke and ran—and in a moment slid out of sight overside.

The skipper, watching, grunted. Stevenot, with a wry smile, muttered something I did not get.

"Let's get on," Grahame suggested.

It seemed that we all were open to suggestion—the captain started for the door and had one foot over the raised sill when he stopped and backed in again, one hand up for silence.

The same officer we had seen when we first climbed aboard stepped high over the sill and entered. He went straight for the chart table on the starboard and opened a case and took out a sextant. This he wiped perfunctorily—then left, as oblivious to our presence as though we had not been there.

The captain's eyes followed him.

"A sight?" he questioned us all. "Is he going to take a sight at this hour in the morning—at sea? What time is it?"

I looked at my watch.

"Almost ten-thirty, captain," I said.

"Why in hell at ten-thirty?" he complained. "Didn't he get his morning shot at eight—it's clear enough! Your watch right?"

I nodded—and Grahame and the mate, examining theirs, confirmed the accuracy of mine.

"Ten-thirty," they said as one.

The captain wheeled to the chart table. On it was pinned a Mercator chart. A series of courses was drawn from a point in Alaska to San Francisco Bay, and several lightly penciled marks showed where the navigator had marked each day's progress. And between the marks were the dates for each run. We huddled about the table—for the captain had stared at the chart as though half hypnotized.

After a minute or more, the old man pointed pudgily at the last run marked.

"What's the date today?" he asked.

"August 24," the mate replied.

"Humph!" grunted the captain. "Look at the last date put down there."

With wonder we looked.

The date for the last run made was that of three days before—August 21.

Stevenot bent close. Then straightened and his eye shifted about to each of us. He shook his head.

"I don't quite get all this," he said quietly. "The last date there is August 21, and if you'll look closely, you'll see it's been repeated, almost over the first date, twice. As if it had been gone over to make it clearer, though Heaven knows it's never done.

"And there"—he put his finger where the last criss-cross marked the end of the August 21 run—"that's been crossed twice again, too. It's just as if—"

He hesitated. Then shrugged his shoulders.

"As if what?" snapped the captain, his eye piercing Stevenot's.

"Well," said Stevenot, "I don't know exactly, myself. But these men are all—all—oh, but that's utter nonsense. Let's see more first."

The old man glared.

"But I want to know just what you mean," he demanded.

Stevenot stared.

"I'm not quite sure myself," he answered stiffly. "I can't quite—"

He stopped short.

"Back!" he cried curtly. "Back!" And he spread his arms wide and pushed us from the table.

The officer, yellow-faced, sweater clad, and with the odd-colored shoes upon his feet, returned with the sextant. He held it carefully in his hand, adjusted the reading glass and held it beneath the electric globe so that the light shown upon the vernier. He examined this closely—pulled a sheet of coordinate paper from a pigeonhole on the bulkhead, and set down the sextant reading—the altitude of the sun above the horizon.

The mate leaned forward and read it. Then bent down and picked up a similar piece of paper which lay on the floor near the littered waste basket. He looked at the figures on this and grunted. I peered over his shoulder. The first figures on it were those of the same sextant altitude as the officer had just put down. Identical.

The man had sat down in the chair before the desk, and was now working out his latitude from a form he had taken from another pigeonhole.

The mate leaned across and picked up the instrument—adjusted the focus of the eyepiece—and then drew a long, sharp whistle.

"What's a matter!" snapped the skipper.

"Read the thing," said the mate. "Then see what this fellow's put down."

The captain read—then seized the paper from the mate's hand. He stared at the reading set down there, then at the one the officer had just jotted down— then again glued his eye to the glass over the vernier of the sextant. Then he said under his breath.

"Well, I'll be damned!"

The mate nodded.

"So will I," he said quietly.

"What—" I started.

The captain turned quickly—he always did when I started to question. I don't know why.

"The man just put down a reading that's several full degrees off what the sextant here indicates. Look for yourself." He thrust the sextant at me, and I, having tried the thing on the Lanoa's bridge before, read, and saw for myself. The captain ran on:

"And that other paper, that old one—it must be yesterday's or 'twould have been swept out—the same handwriting has put down the same reading there—the same identical reading to a quarter of a minute. And yet the sextant reads—you saw yourself."

I nodded dumbly. Vague thoughts began to run through my mind. Theories. And conjectures. And I began at last to associate more and more the strange meteorological conditions of the past few days, the coldness and all, with this ship and the strange men who ran her—or, second thought prompted this, who appeared to run her—who went through all the motions, but—

And there I had to stop. As I stopped, I felt a sudden thrill crawl from my toes to my head and creep chillily over my skin—for I thought I glimpsed what the captain had tried to get Stevenot to say. And to tell the truth, I liked it not. No man would. It was just a bit too gruesome. And too uncannily close.

I watched, with the others, that yellow and overwarmly clad man at the table as he plied his pencil.

The mate, eyes alternately on the paper he held and that on which the man was working, followed every figure with an intentness that was almost hypnotic. I began to watch too—and started before I had got halfway down— the figures were identical—even one error that was made on each and crossed out and the figuring redone.

And then a thing happened that was small in itself, but so fearsome in all that it might indicate that I cannot help but set it down with all the rest I saw and heard and felt on board that awful ship.

As the officer wrote—his pencil point suddenly snapped, and flew against the bulkhead. But he, apparently unaware that what he now figured with made not a mark or jot, continued to work on. The thrill I'd felt before came now again—and left me cold.

And when the man reached for his log book, and opened up at a mark ready placed, and began to put down, with a pencil that made no mark, figures identical with those we now could see had been already retraced twice before, my confidence in what I had believed possible and impossible gave way.

This was too much. I shivered, and seized Stevenot's arm. He started violently, and I noticed that his forehead showed damp in the yellow glow of the bulb.

"Let's get out on deck," I suggested.

Stevenot nodded.

We left.

And as one, the rest followed—the captain, the mate and Grahame—into the open, beneath the warming sun, where we could breathe.

"The same figures—same mistakes," ejaculated Grahame, "the same. Darned peculiar, I'd say."

The mate nodded.

"And the wrong reading at that," he added.

"Humph!" grunted the skipper as he stared, back into the wheelhouse at the steersman who again was spinning for rudder to counteract a yawing that was not there.

"And it's so warm here, yet they—sweaters and all—" started Stevenot. Then he shuddered a bit.

Then looked at his hand, and rubbed it on his sleeve. When he glanced up, I caught his eye. He reddened slightly. It was the hand with which he had seized that of the silent, yellow, heavily-clad officer who even yet was pacing the bridge—the officer who had so callously, so coldly, so mechanically, walked into, knocked down and stepped upon our own captain—the officer who, like these others of the *Karnak's* crew, was so uncanny in appearance, so icy to the touch.

There was a long silence. Instinctively the captain and the mate drew together and slightly apart from us. And as instinctively too, or is it from the gravitation of mutual interest, Grahame and Stevenot and I had grouped, too.

Apart from the officers, Stevenot spoke:

"I've my notions of this," he said. "But I'd like to see more—first."

Grahame nodded and looked at me. I met his questioning eye.

Stevenot went on, whispering.

"Something's dead wrong—with ship and crew," he declared. "And the old man has sense. It's scary—and he's scared himself, though Lord knows he's been to sea long enough to know that it's never done with mystery, and probably never will be.

"But he's got sense—and a nose for finance. And he'll dope it out as salvage—the situation, I mean. He's scared—but not scared of money. And if he can get this ship to port, it'll mean—" Stevenot broke off abruptly. Then,

with a vague glance inside, where the officer still vainly penciled, he muttered:.
"I wonder what the cargo is—from Alaska."

He started for the door.

The captain wheeled.

"Hey! Where you going?" His voice a bit high-pitched. He was not as calm
as a captain should be.

Stevenot's chin went up a moment. Then with a slight smile he answered.

"To get the log-book."

"Oh," answered the skipper, and fell back to talking to his mate again.

VI

With a Cargo of Ore

Stevenot was in the house for some minutes. I glanced after him, naturally,
and saw him reach for the log and take it from under the officer's hands. Then
he pulled open a little drawer under the pigeon-holes, puttered in it. Then
another—and from this he drew something I could not make out.

Then he bent over the officer and gingerly picked up the latter's right
hand. A full minute thus—then he took up the book, and came out rubbing
his hands as before, alternately, on his trousers.

His face was very sober now.

Yet he opened the book at once and fingered for the first page of the *Karnak's* trip. There, as our own officers listened, he read the date the vessel had
cleared, various other routine remarks, then:

"'With a cargo of ore,'" he said, and stopped.

The captain's eyes and the mate's met for a second.

"Ore," repeated Stevenot—with a glance at Grahame and me.

The old man coughed slightly.

"She's salvage," he jerked out. "We'll take her in to port—salvage."

Stevenot eyed him.

"But the crew's still running her," he said with a slight upward intonation
in his voice—and a nod at the wheelsman.

The captain shook his head.

"Dead men can't run a ship," he grunted, watching Stevenot's face.

"Dead men!" cried Stevenot.

"You said it," grunted the skipper again. "An' it's salvage. We'll put a gang
on board an' take her in. These—things—now on ship—they'll have to be—
I'll—"

Stevenot held him with his eye.

"Dead men?" he questioned again. "And you'll—"

The skipper flushed up.

"Well, maybe they are—maybe not. But we'll fix 'em up some way. And
I'll get a gang aboard, and take her in."

The mate nodded with him.

"I've seen enough to be satisfied," said the skipper, as he led us to the davits below which was the launch. "The ship's out of gear—and the crew's—it ain't worth a cent. It's salvage. I'll send a gang—"

He stopped short, and his breath wheezed.

"By the Lord!" cried the mate, "the launch is gone!"

It was indeed. On a ship that was as near a tomb as a ship might be, and with a crew of men who might as well be dead, we five were marooned. My heart gave a great jolt as two seamen with mops and buckets stepped mechanically up the gangway from the after-waist of the ship and started to swab about the decks.

They, too, were yellow, and muffled up in sweaters though the sun was hot above them, gleaming hot. They, too, looked cold and lifeless. Yet they, too, went at once to work—and swabbed, and squeezed, and wiped. I shuddered—how like men from the grave they looked! Did the captain really think—

We ran across decks to the starboard side. The launch was just coming under the *Lanoa's* lee. A moment more, even as we frantically waved, the launch was hove up, and we saw the crew move in a body up decks to the bridge.

They disappeared in chart house and cabins—and a few moments more come out again.

Then the *Lanoa's* propeller churned white under the stern, and slowly, she drew away.

What had happened? Had our own officers, those left on board, deserted us? A chill ran through me as I glanced back at the yellow, frigid-looking seamen at their labors twenty feet away. Then hot anger as the *Lanoa* still forged ahead.

The captain with a curse, ran to the wheelhouse, and immediately afterward the *Karnak's* whistle gave four feeble toots.

This was answered by four mocking blasts from the *Lanoa's* deep bass; and on the *Lanoa* steamed.

We were dumfounded. The skipper was white. The mate was biting his lower lip. But Stevenot grinned with gusto, and cried:

"With a ship of dead men—this is sport!"

"Sport, hell!" snapped the skipper, apparently ignoring Stevenot's insinuation regarding the *Karnak's* crew. "Wait'll you're with this gang a week. Ugh! What will we do now?"

"You're the boss," hinted Stevenot.

The captain flushed.

"Why not use the wireless, and get help?" Grahame suggested.

The office was at the after end of the bridge deck— I imagine so that the varying currents used might not interfere with the compass. The captain threw open the door with an oath—and stared once more.

Over his shoulder I could see the operator sitting at his instrument—yellow, and muffled as from cold. Silent he was—and, but for his right hand, motionless. But the hand upon the key was moving—and, from what knowledge I had gleaned while serving in our wartime navy, I caught one familiar grouping of sound among all the rest.

Three shorts, three longs, three shorts—three dots, three dashes, three dots—S.O.S. of the International Code. Then came more I could not make out—then breaking in again: S.O.S.—S.O.S.

Thus the key clicked on—and on—and on—as we watched in frozen silence.

The captain gasped.

"The machine isn't working! It's not working! But he—he—"

"You're right—it's useless—dead!" affirmed Stevenot in a whisper.

And he was right. The spark of the old-fashioned apparatus was not working. The machine was quite dead. And yet, the operator, apparently quite oblivious to the fact that it was vain labor, was steadily tapping his key, still sending out his call for help.

"Machine's dead, I tell you," cried the skipper. "Machine's dead—and by Heaven, so's the man." He peered wildly about him, then backed away. "And here we're stuck," he cursed soulfully. "And my ship—gone. And these dead—"

"Nonsense!" muttered Stevenot. "Dead? And yet working the ship?"

The skipper turned on him.

"What did you say?" he demanded. "It's salvage, I tell you!"

The mate seized him by the shoulder.

"Come on, cap," he exclaimed bruskly, but with a certain quaver in his voice.

"We're all a bit nervous now. Let's run through below decks and see what we can see. We're stuck—let's make the most of it."

The captain frowned a moment at Stevenot. Then turned and stared at the *Lanoa*, now fast dropping in the swells about us. Then, with a short grunt, he started for the gangway leading to the after-waist.

We followed, closely bunched.

And of what we saw below decks, and forward later in the fo'c's'le, a book might well be written. Suffice it here to say that the crew was at its regular routine. The firemen—the *Karnak* burned oil—were watching by the boilers—yellow and cold, they too.

In the engine room, the second assistant engineer was on watch, and his wipers and oilers were about their tasks, caring for the ponderously moving iron and steel that was their charge—all yellow, and chilled, and silent, too.

And none took notice of us.

Yet, to watch them, the mechanical manner in which each moved about; the strange errors they made; how they would wipe where no wiping was needed; how they would oil where the oil already overflowed; how they would pick up bits of stuff where no stuff was, and carry them over to the waste can and there deposit them—nothing—solemnly, with painstaking care—that would make the book.

VII

Bound for Seattle

Keeping close together, we climbed the slippery ladders to the open air again and went forward. In the fo'c's'le were three seamen lying in their tiered bunks, shoes off, arms flung about their heads—apparently asleep, or resting—yellow, cold-looking, as were all.

And on a bench before the door of his tiny quarters sat the bosun, pipe—long since dead—in hand, staring before him at the fo'c's'le's high-silled entrance. And he, too, was yellow and hard-skinned, and muffled up in woolen stuffs.

We retreated to the bridge-deck, and held a conference.

And we decided to stick by the ship. The captain himself was vehement for it. It meant money—good money to him. And we were even more enthusiastic—wholesouledly so. This was adventure—and adventure was our life.

It was Stevenot who showed us the way.

"All that is needed," he declared, "is for us to take turn about at the wheel. The captain here can dope out a course to Seattle, say, and we can follow it. If these—*men*—continue to fire ship and tend the engines, that's enough. We'll steer and get the *Karnak* in."

And so it was decided.

We wondered how we could relieve the man now at the wheel—but that turned out to be easy enough. We simply took his hands off the thing and led him to one of the cabins, and laid him on the bunk, and locked the door upon him.

I drew first watch—and was glad it came in daylight.

Grahame drew the next. Then Stevenot. Then the mate. Then the skipper.

We decided at first on two-hour shifts—thus each man had two on, and eight off. No one on the bridge.

But the skipper objected to this. He was in command now, he said, and he demanded a bridge lookout, as well as a man at the wheel. I had my own opinion why, and Stevenot's eyes showed that he had one, too. So we had to shift things so as to have two go on at a time, and changed over thuswise: We kept the order of watches as we had drawn, but when each of us first went on, he was to take the wheel two hours, then the bridge for another two, while the next man in order took the wheel. This made four hours on and only six off—but the man at the wheel would always be fairly fresh, and six hours rest a couple times out of each twenty-four would not be bad.

Then we chose cabins.

The skipper and mate naturally fell together—and commenced a great cleaning up.

And the rest of us found one, on the port side, that would take in three—it was the engineer officers' cabin, but we carried the chief and the first assistant to one of the others, laid them out and locked them in as we had the steersman.

Then we went below and washed mightily. Then invaded the galley, where the cooks puttered mechanically, and took up enough of tinned stuff and fruit and bread to withstand a siege.

At noon we started our routine—I on the bridge for only two hours, Grahame at the wheel.

I believe the captain and mate sat in their cabin most of the time. Stevenot went exploring about ship.

Then Grahame took the deck, and Stevenot the wheel.

Then Stevenot the deck, and the mate the wheel.

Then the mate had the deck, and the old man steered.

And so on it went.

We had no difficulty with the men of the *Karnak's* crew when dutifully, and wrapped in their warmest togs, and yellow and cold and tight-skinned, they came to relieve the watch. We simply treated them as we had the others—steered them to a cabin and locked them in. The below decks force, of course, we did not touch—as long as they made steam and did not blow up the boilers, we worried not. We simply wanted no interference with our steering.

The *Lanoa* slowly sank out of sight.

Night came down, and a great loneliness seized us. At eight I came on again, the skipper on deck.

Five men we were—on a great ship. Five men—and some forty others who were men and yet not men, alive and yet—I hesitate to say—not alive. I felt as the blackness grew that my nerves were getting a bit on edge, too—like those of the captain. And I wondered what had happened to these men—and what might happen to us during the long days I knew must drift past before we sighted solid land.

Those hours of blackness passed slowly indeed. Ofttimes I fancied I heard footsteps about me, and would startle violently and swing about. But naught occurred.

However, I felt continually atingle, as though every nerve fiber of me were vibrating with involuntary fear. This grew and grew until finally I found myself in a sudden chill, and 'twas all I could do to stand there at the wheel, or hold the lubber's line to the degree we steered. Now and again the bulky shadow of the old man crossed the glass before me, yet strange to say, the captain's presence gave me but little confidence.

He certainly had not inspired any during the day—even though at first he had so boldly led the way. Bold enough—yet when, just where he tramped so loudly now, and puffed so strenuously at the cigar he'd taken from the box in the cabin of the *Karnak's* captain—who, by the way, we'd found there lying on his bunk, evidently off watch, and locked in as per usual—when, I say, in so peculiar a manner he had been trod upon by the icy mate and then felt that terrible iciness itself, that boldness had been sapped away.

Then Grahame relieved me at the wheel—and I took the deck while the captain sought the seclusion that his cabin granted. I felt better with Grahame at the wheel—and occasionally stepped in for a chat.

Grahame could not account for the appearance and actions of the *Karnak's* crew. I hinted of my theory—and he listened, but did not commit himself.

I reminded him that the captain swore they were all dead men. He asked if I thought the captain had ever read the "Ancient Mariner"—and grinned. Ask Stevenot, he said—he'd a theory that was near right. Meanwhile go back to your job and step lively too. I went out on the bridge again—and listened to the lap of black waters alongside, and the dash of spray ahead against the bows.

Then I was relieved and went to our cabin.

And there, an hour later, I was suddenly awakened by someone trying to crawl into my bunk—I had a double lower. It was quite dark, but I figured it was one of my mates just off watch.

"Tired?" I muttered.

There was no answer.

And a second later, a chill touch sent my nerves flying and my hair aprickle. With a wild yell, I dashed out of the cabin. I heard Grahame, who had evidently taken the upper as I slept, give a cry too—and a moment later the light flashed upon the second assistant engineer, whom we had entirely forgotten, and who must have just come off watch to get a bit of rest and sleep. As if those—*men*—needed sleep!

There he lay on the lower berth—yellow, and icy cold—he'd crawled in with *me!*

Picture if you can the whiteness of my face, the condition of my nerves, the crawling of my flesh, when Grahame and I carried that awful thing to the cabin where we'd locked the others.

VIII

The Second Day

And picture again my consternation when, at six o'clock I went to relieve the captain at the wheel, I could find neither the captain nor the mate anywhere about.

I aroused the others.

We made search.

And on the starboard side another lifeboat was gone. Sometime in the night the captain and mate had deserted us—somewhere even now, they floated on the blackness of the heaving sea, preferring it to the terror and mystery and the yellow, icy, mechanical human *things* aboard the *Karnak.*

We held a conference—low-voiced. We changed the method of our watch—just a man at the wheel—four hours on, four off. Our navigators were gone, but we knew the general course—anywhere east would bring us to land, and with slight knowledge of the sextant, and care in lookout, we could pilot the *Karnak* to some harbor along the coast.

Little did we know then that the *Karnak* was destined never again to see the land. Had we known that, we might have deserted her and that crew of strange and silent men even as had the old man and his first. And when we did see, did understand—the shock on our nerves of what *might* have been was a fiber-shattering thing.

I, for one, believe its effect on me will never wear off. Even when now it comes upon me, that recollection, my whole body goes atremble and a coldness seizes me even as chill as that which, for those first two days of electric storm and extraordinary cold, held the *Lanoa,* and the *Karnak.*

During the day naught occurred but the now usual actions of the strange men yet about the decks.

Yet here we did note a curious thing. The man who had been polishing the whistle when first we came aboard repeated every action of the day before. He lost his balance, his hands jerked as though the bottle had fallen, he regained his equilibrium and commenced again to use the bottle when he had none in his hands.

Every motion was almost identical with that he'd made the day before. His every move a repetition—a duplicate—of what, the day before, we had seen him do.

Another thing: The second mate had not been locked up with the rest. Around nine-thirty he took another shot at the sun. Then he came down to the chart table and read the vernier. Then, exactly as he'd done the day before, and I suppose for three days before that, he set down the same sextant altitude of the sun—absolutely wrong, absolutely *not* that which the sextant showed—but the same identical figures that he'd set down before. And when he figured, he made the same error as he had before. He, too, was repeating himself—every move, every act.

To test him, I drew the paper from beneath the pencil—the skipper had sharpened it when he'd worked out our course—and the yellow-faced man kept penciling on the tabletop. He did not know the paper was not there—or knowing, heeded the omission not one whit.

Then he drew out the log-book which we had replaced—and over the old entries, at the page marked, he penciled the same figures again.

As I stared, I wondered just what he was—what had happened to him—what he *was now.*

And then, queerly enough, I wondered what Stevenot had done to him, or discovered about him, when the day before he had gone into the wheel-house to get the log-book and ascertain the *Karnak's* cargo. Why had he looked so doubly serious when he came out?

By noon that day we had made 192.7 miles—as near as I could figure from the Negus log trailing aft and the revolution indicator in the engine room. We had yet many days of slow steaming ahead—provided our strange crew held out. I recalled my old war-navy school work—and practical navigation.

And already our engine room counter had dropped ten revolutions a minute.

We tried to find out why—but knowing little of the *Karnak's* machinery, our investigations came to naught. We shivered a bit, too, watching the yellow, staring-eyed men perform at their tasks.

We shivered more during the next night.

IX

The Third Day

Grahame, awakening me next morning to relieve Stevenot at the wheel, mentioned it to me.

"I felt a queer tingling all last night," he complained. "My back—whole spine. Oh, it wasn't fear—although I don't like the situation at all, I admit. It was something different. I rolled over, too, in my sleep—and awoke to find my whole side atingle, as though it were asleep."

I started.

"That's exactly what I felt," I said.

We mentioned it to Stevenot.

He nodded.

"Me, too," he answered. "As if that part of me were asleep."

"It's blamed peculiar," muttered Grahame.

Stevenot nodded quietly.

"Maybe it is—maybe it isn't," he said thoughtfully.

Then I took the wheel.

The lights were acting poorly now, too—as they had on the *Lanoa* during those two eerie days.

And as I tried to keep the compass steady, the dim thought worked up within me that perhaps the captain and mate had not been such great fools when they had deserted the *Karnak*.

This thought took hold of me, somehow, up there in the loneliness of the wheelhouse. The sea sparkled so happily about, the sun was so whitely bright outside—yet this ship—this crew! Why had I awakened the night before, even before that icy engineer had started to crawl into his old bunk by my side, and been so singularly alarmed by the persistent tingling that was upon me?

And by what strange coincidence, then, than the preying of a subconscious fear, had each of us three felt the same sensation? And then, too, the sudden little chills that, nervelike, shot now and again through me. Surely I was not that deeply frightened.

I held my hand out. It was as steady as the chronometers in their soft racks beneath the chart table's hinged top. I was not afraid. Mystified, yes—but not afraid.

Then why that curious and softly alarming sensation—as of part of me asleep. And why those chilling waves that swept my body—when the night was warm, and I a well man.

I wondered if I were quite well.

When I went off watch, I searched among the captain's effects and found a clinical thermometer.

And then I was thoroughly frightened—my temperature, even though I now felt quite warm, was some *eight degrees below normal.* In sudden anxiety, I ran out up to Grahame, now at the wheel.

His temperature had dropped, too—to 94°, and 98.5°is normal.

In palpitating fear, I sought Stevenot, who as usual, fearless, curious, was prowling around below.

He nodded when I told him—but was almost precipitous in putting the thermometer under his tongue. And his temperature was even lower than mine—88°!

"Good God!" he cried softly, and stared at me.

"Well?" I queried.

He stared steadily at the yellow, thick-clad man puttering about the deck. And when he saw the fellow stoop and make all the motions of picking up something that was not there, and carry it to the rail and toss it lightly overboard, he started, and his eyes found mine.

"They—they are very cold—very cold—themselves!" he muttered half to himself. "And now—"

"I don't like it," I burst out.

He stared at me.

"And do you know," he said, "that this ship rides at least two feet lower in the water than when we boarded her?"

"What?" I exclaimed.

"I've been around her more than you two," he nodded quietly. "And been investigating. And she's loaded with ore—ore won't float, you know."

"Let's tell Grahame," I whispered.

We all whispered—the silence of all these men about seemed to literally force us to.

Grahame took it calmly enough.

"We haven't been using the pumps," he said, exhaling smoke from one of the *Karnak's* cigars.

Stevenot's answer chilled me.

"They've been working full power ever since we've been aboard. I've been looking around, you know."

"What'll we do?" I queried. "Take to a boat?"

"It might be well to provision another lifeboat," Stevenot replied quietly. "The pumps are still working—there's plenty of time. And every mile we stay with the *Karnak*— Also, we can't tell—these fellows—these cold—they may yet—" He shrugged his shoulders.

Grahame nodded, then stooped and furtively picked up his cigar. He'd bitten it through.

In half an hour, No. 3 lifeboat, next to the swinging falls where had hung the whaleboat the captain and mate had taken, was ready for sea. And we were overjoyed at finding beneath her canvas cover a small portable motor. We clamped this on the stern—it made us feel nearer home. Of provisions we put in enough to last a dozen men a month.

I felt foolish as I worked at this. Then the sudden appearance of one of the yellow crew doubled my efforts.

That night the tingling was decidedly pronounced—all over me now, not simply on the side that was beneath. And alternately I was swept by great surging waves of chill and heat.

The sweat broke out on me—cold sweat. I felt sudden nausea. And then a black juggernaut of fear almost paralyzed me. I struggled against it—and, almost fainting, cried aloud to Grahame above me.

At once he answered.

"Let's get out," he cried—and his voice was weak—his words sharp, spasmodic.

We seized clothes and tumbled out on the deck. And there we met Stevenot—deserted from the wheel.

"The lights are out," he cried. "And the ship—the ship."

And then I noted for the first time that every bit of metal on the *Karnak* was faintly aglow—not with the blue electric flame that had danced on the *Lanoa's* rigging before the great electric bolt had fallen—but half-luminous with quiet, almost menacing, phosphorescence.

Again a way of icy chill clutched at me—and then, with terrifying coincidence, in the moony radiance of all about me, there passed as silently as a ghost, a staring-eyed member of the crew.

As one, we madly dashed for the lifeboat, and five minutes later, our motor chugging hopefully, we were floating a hundred yards away from the weirdly glowing *Karnak,* that followed us with slowly turning wheel.

We had deserted the *Karnak,* too.

And perhaps a half hour later, Stevenot, who sat in the bow facing aft, pointed and cried: "The *Karnak*—the *Karnak!*"

We turned—and even as we turned, the great vessel, glowing as though impregnated in every part with eerie moonlight, looming like a vast ghost of the sea, dropped with all her crew, and as silently as her crew had labored, beneath the surface of the sea.

And to tell the truth, a sigh of vast relief breathed from us all.

We were free—we were safe, in a small, open boat on the great northern sea. But the *Karnak*—we were not with her.

And three days later, yet some hundreds of miles from land, we were picked up by one of the salmon ships bound with her thousands of cases for San Francisco Bay. We were safe! But the *Karnak* and her fearsome crew were at the bottom of the sea—hid deep away—even as they well should be—and as are many others of ocean's mysteries aud ocean's tragedies, too—even as they well should be—and safe.

X
Why?

That first night out, under the stars that now watched with such twinkling comfort upon us, Stevenot gave us his explanation of the thing. I myself like puzzles solved, and all puzzles, it must be remembered, do have their solutions.

Stevenot's solution may be the right one, may not be. Yet it does, in my estimation, untwist every thread of the *Karnak's* strange tangle. And I, for one, even out there on the deep, with the strange ship and, crew perhaps yet plunging deeper into the abysmal black beneath us, heard and was satisfied. So, with the account of the mystery itself, I offer my companion's explanation here.

"Why, you ask?" questioned Stevenot from the bows. "Why was it so—and how—and what? Simple enough, I think.

"I'd call it coincidence—and one that never yet has been brought to man's attention—and that man live. It may have happened before—ships disappear, you know—but none lived to tell the tale.

"We saw the thing start on the *Lanoa*—only the *Lanoa* was loaded with sugar, not with ore. We were chilled by the same cold as was the *Karnak*. The blue flowing electricity was as rampant on our rigging as it must have been upon the *Karnak's*. Our wireless was off and on, even as was that of the unfortunate ship just gone to its destined end.

"But we were farther from the influence of the great electric masses of the north. We were far to the south of that place whence the *Karnak* pleaded for help. And we were loaded with raw sugar; we did not have a steel hull packed with metallic ore—ore that attracted electricity, ore that was imbued with electric action itself, ore that perhaps was slightly radioactive, as are many of the mineral products of the countries of the north.

"What happened, you ask? Again I say, 'tis simple—again; coincidence.

"The electric storm descended, and with it, or as a consequence, the cold. With us, it was a matter of temporary inconvenience. With the *Karnak,* the stuff took permanent and relentless hold. We were a simple ship laden with vegetable produce—the *Karnak* was a huge electromagnet. The electricity literally soaked into her—we shed it as a duck sheds water—she soaked it up as a sponge.

"I believe her master realized this—and so called for help while his radio would allow. He himself felt the tingling and the same evil chills as did we—and realized what their portent was. He knew with what his holds were full—and how the electricity would work upon the iron plates of the hull itself, and rot, and rot, and rot, until the seams would open up, the bottom of the ship fall out beneath them all, and the *Karnak,* plummetlike, would drop from the ken of man as we just have seen it do.

"The *Karnak's* captain knew this all, I say, and called for men to help. But others felt it, too, perhaps; and thus did one boatload desert before there came that final electric blast—which on the *Lanoa,* we saw and heard—which fell upon the *Karnak,* and overwhelmed it and all the crew—and sapped the life out of every man. Sapped it out, sucked it out, with terrible, unthinking, relentless malevolence—and in its place put part of its own self, its own electric mass, its own electric energizing power."

Stevenot paused a moment, his hands folded about his knees—huddled beneath the blanket he'd thrown about his shoulders.

"The *Karnak* called for help—until the bolt came and killed the wireless—and even then, the radio operator stuck on the job. Why? You wonder why these men, yellow and icy, and yet wrapped in the thick woolens they donned when the chill fell upon them all, why they continued, though dead men in every sense of the word, to go about their routine tasks?

"Simply because the electricity about them and in them, impregnating every cell of their flesh and bone and blood, had crystallized, in the last day of its vast intensity, the brain fibers regulating every act they had performed—crystallized their brains—even, to put it crudely, as sound waves are crystallized on a phonographic record.

"At the same time, every nerve, every cell, though the real soul, the real man, was dead, was yet alive with electricity. *Rigor mortis*, under such stimulus, could not set in. And so, under the electric impulse—perhaps, too, forced on by the slight radioactivity of the thousands of tons of ore in the holds—the crystallized routine thought continued to impel—continued to operate the messages along the nerves—the muscles reacted to the electric impulse—the body performed all its functions—mechanically, automatically, regularly.

"Thus, when we landed, the mate did not see us, or hear us call. His action was simply a *motographic*, if I may use the word, reproduction, of his *thought action of the day before.* He turned in at the passage without noticing us, because he had done the same the day before. And were we there the day before?

"You see now?

"It was the same with the man polishing up the whistle—losing his balance, dropping the bottle. It was the same with the officer on the bridge—knocking the captain down—the wonder that he regained his balance and paced on.

"It was the same with the man at the wheel—who steered to avoid a yawing that affected the ship the last day when he really was alive, when his brain was actually recording thought and being crystallized by the surging electricity in him, and the cold about. So, too, with the mate taking observations—he set down what he had read when last he had read the vernier *alive* and *thinking.*

"It was watching him that gave me my first real clue. And surreptitiously, knowing it was a test for death, I pricked his hand with a pin I found in a drawer by the chart table—no blood came forth—the man was not alive, then—but dead, *dead.* Yet I didn't want to scare the captain out yet.

"So in dressing—they still clothed themselves to withstand cold. And some, groping, found odd clothing—even as did the second mate with his shoes.

"And thus with every man on board—even him who crawled, dead and icy cold, into the berth with you. All, from the captain who lay sleeping, exhausted from his watching, I suppose—down to the humblest of the crew, from fire-room to fo'c's'le—all were dead men, but put in jerky action by the energizing power of the electricity in which they had been drenched.

"And the great bolt, when it came, attracted by the metallic cargo the *Karnak* held, overwhelmed them all, struck out what real life was yet left, finally crystallized their thought action; and set them into machinelike motion—made of live men, dead—automatons.

"Then we arrived—you know the rest."

Stevenot paused again, and even in the darkness I felt his eyes on mine. Grahame at my side, the tiller of the chugging little boat under his arm, coughed slightly. I gazed deep into the unfathomable mystery of the myriad of twinkling stars above—worlds and suns, like ours, all; and with our troubles, our mysteries, our joys, too.

"You see now—you understand?" Stevenot's voice drifted quietly to us again.

Grahame's answer came with mine—softly, too, for the influence of the days before, and of this night, was on him too.

"Yes," we answered as one, "I do understand."

And, in all faith, I believe Stevenot had hit upon the truth.

It was simple after all—as most mysteries are. Simple—and yet how awful during that time the thing was mystery.

I have many times since awakened in the night in cold sweat, dreaming that that icy engineer was crawling between my sheets as I lay asleep. I have many times since felt the icy tingling run through me—an actual physical reminiscence, I do believe, of those electric chills we felt aboard the *Karnak*, chills which would have made us in time, too, even as were those unfortunate members of the *Karnak's* crew—yellow, icy, machinelike, as had been the *Karnak's* second mate, the officer on the bridge, the man at the wheel and all the rest. And, too, walking alone in the lonely shadow of a moonlit road—I still start with sudden fright—seeing in the shadow's rise and fall the movement of those men, the dead-alive.

I have often wondered, too, if those dead-alive—deep beneath the sea—went on, and on, and on—I hope not. And I believe not.

Fate, Nature, is too kind to allow such tragedy. And the good old sea, too, has given them burial, and will give them peace. Nature, in the end, is kind. And the *Karnak*, and those silent men, are finally at rest—at peace!

· · · · ·

ABOUT THE AUTHORS

ABRAHAM MERRITT (1884–1943) was a renowned craftsman of eerie, haunting fantasy tales that have found eager and appreciative audiences in every generation since their initial publication. Merritt was associate editor, and later editor, of William Randolph Hearst's *American Weekly* from 1912 until his death, a job that consumed much of his time and limited his fantasy works to just a handful of novels and shorter tales. "The People of the Pit" was one of his first published stories.

FRANCIS STEVENS (Gertrude Barrows Bennett, 1884–1939?) sold a short science fiction story to *The Argosy* in 1904 and then abandoned professional writing until 1917, when she used that skill to provide for her family after the death of her husband. Although her output was relatively small, the originality of her work was outstanding, and she has been credited with creating the first "dark fantasy" and "alternate universe" stories, both of which blossomed into hugely popular genres long after her death.

EDGAR RICE BURROUGHS (1875–1950) is, of course, best known for his novels of Tarzan of the Apes and John Carter of Mars, plus numerous other adventure fiction series. Like Walt Disney, Burroughs was a pioneer of marketing his literary characters, which made Tarzan not only a movie star and a household name, but a dominating presence on the radio and in countless magazines, comic books, toys, dolls, games, cereals, candies, lunch boxes and virtually every medium of the 1930s and beyond. The excerpt featured here is from his non-series novel, *A Man Without a Soul* (1913), later published in book form as *The Monster Men.*

JOHN BLUNT (no biographical information available) was credited with a total of ten stories in *The All Story* and *The Argosy* between 1911 and 1917. The name may have been a pseudonym.

GEORGE ALLAN ENGLAND (1877–1936) was once, with H.G. Wells and Edgar Rice Burroughs, acknowledged as a master of the "scientific romance," the genre that later became known as "science fiction." He is remembered today almost solely for the *Darkness and Dawn* trilogy, depicting life after a holocaust destroys civilization. His 1914 science fiction novel, *The Empire In the Air,* is available from Black Dog Books.

ACHMED ABDULLAH (Nadir Khan Romanoffski, 1881–1945) published numerous works with Middle and Far Eastern themes. Perhaps his best-known work is his 1924 novelization of the early fantasy film, *Thief of Baghdad*, starring Douglas Fairbanks. He also wrote under the pseudonyms A.A. Nadir and John Hamilton.

OWEN OLIVER (Sir Joshua Albert Flynn, 1863–1933) was a British economist and adviser to Lord Kitchener, and was knighted in 1919. He was also a prolific writer of short stories in the first decades of the twentieth century. A number of his early efforts were highly imaginative fantasies and weird fiction, including "Out of the Deep" (1904), a variation on *The War of the Worlds* in which mankind is threatened by mechanical war machines created and operated by denizens of earth's oceans. Oliver eventually abandoned fantasy for what Everett F. Bleiler aptly describes as "shopgirl romances," which he turned out by the hundreds. He also wrote a number of sentimental Christmas stories that were published in the December issues of various British and American magazines for decades.

TOD ROBBINS (Clarence Aaron Robbins, 1888–1949) specialized in weird fiction throughout his lengthy writing career. His 1917 novel, *The Terrible Three*, which first appeared in Munsey's *All Story*, was filmed as *The Unholy Three* in 1925 and again in 1930, both versions starring Lon Chaney. His short story, "The Bibulous Baby" (1919), about a man who ages backwards from old man to infant, may have inspired F. Scott Fitzgerald's very similar "The Curious Case of Benjamin Button" (1922), filmed in 2008 with Brad Pitt in the title role. Robbins is primarily remembered for a single story, "Spurs" (1923), adapted by director Tod Browning as the legendary horror film, *Freaks!* (1932).

TALBOT MUNDY (William Lancaster Gribbon, 1879–1940) is famous for his numerous tales of British soldiers fighting for Queen and country in exotic locales from India to South Africa and beyond. During the late 1930s, Mundy scripted the famous *Jack Armstrong, All American Boy* radio show. Black Dog Books is publishing The Talbot Mundy Library, a multi-volume series collecting his early works.

J.U. GIESY (1877–1948) was a prolific contributor to the fantasy genre, primarily remembered for his Jason Croft trilogy (1918–1921) and more than thirty lengthy tales featuring occult detective Semi-Dual, which were written in collaboration with Junius B. Smith.

C[HARLES] LANGTON CLARKE (1857–1936) was a Canadian engineer, editor and author. He published more than forty stories in various Munsey publications (*The Argosy*, *The Cavalier* and *The Scrap Book*), and at least one science fiction tale in the British *Royal Magazine*.

SAX ROHMER (Arthur Sarsfield Ward, 1883–1959) is synonymous with the insidious Dr. Fu Manchu, "the Yellow Peril incarnate in one man," whom he created in 1913 and whose adventures he eventually chronicled in thirteen novels and four shorter tales. Rohmer also produced scores of other works, primarily mysteries of the Middle and Far East, and wrote on the occult.

DAMON RUNYON (1880–1946), a newspaper reporter and veteran sports writer, captured the public's imagination with his slangy tales of shady Broadway characters Nathan Detroit, Skye Masterson and many others, published throughout the 1930s and '40s. Those works became the basis of the hit Broadway musical, *Guys and Dolls,* brought to the silver screen in 1956, starring Frank Sinatra, Marlon Brando and Jean Simmons.

PERLEY POORE SHEEHAN (1875–1943) was a versatile craftsman of both mainstream and fantasy fiction, as well as an early Hollywood screenwriter. Fantasy fandom remembers Sheehan for his lost-race novel, *The Abyss of Wonders (The Argosy,* 1915). *The Red Road to Shamballah,* an adventure novel with fantastic elements, is available from Black Dog Books.

PHILIP M. FISHER, JR. (1891–1973), a newspaperman and executive, authored a number of fantastic tales, most of which were published in *Munsey's Magazine, All Story Weekly* and *The Argosy* between 1917 and 1924. He continued to write until at least 1951.

Order these and other titles from our website.

Visit www.blackdogbooks.net for more information,
or write to info@blackdogbooks.net.

LESTER DENT

Before Lester Dent began to chronicle the exploits of
Doc Savage, he produced scores of novels, shorter fiction and
articles spanning the range of pulp fiction genres—tales of two-
fisted action, mysteries, aviation adventures, war stories,
romances and westerns. Unavailable for decades these
works have been collected and are now available
for the first time in book form!

The Lester Dent Library from Black Dog Books

Dead Men's Bones (vol. 1) 619-81

High-octane adventure! Ride the blazing skies in this collection of eight thrilling tales,
collecting all of Lester Dent's published air-adventure stories. With many of these works
appearing in print for the first time in decades, this book is sure to be an instant collector's
item. If you enjoy The Man of Bronze, you'll love these two-fisted sky adventures!

The Skull Squadron (vol. 2) 619-80

Blazing action and adventure. Duck! as the sound of the Vickers machine guns echo
again, while Spads and Fokkers tumble through the skies in these eleven thrilling tales
of mystery and adventure set against the backdrop of World War I. For the first time
in book form, this volume collects all of Dent's published air-war stories from rare
aviation pulps *War Birds, War Aces, Flying Aces, Sky Birds* and *Lone Eagle.* An instant
collector's item!

Hell's Hoofprints (vol. 3) 619-58

Draw, pilgrim! Hit the owl-hoot trail with this collection of eighteen wild west tales. With
an introduction by historian Will Murray, this book of previously uncollected material
is a welcome addition for all collectors of the writings of Lester Dent.

Order these and other titles through our website:

www.blackdogbooks.net